Mr. Darcy's Promise

By Jeanna Ellsworth

Check out other books by Hey Lady Publications:
https://www.heyladypublications.com
Follow Jeanna Ellsworth on Twitter: @ellsworthjeanna
Like me on Facebook:
https://www.facebook.com/pages/Jeanna-
Ellsworth/156635624486987

Acknowledgements

Thank you so much for all those who cheered me on in this process. There were plenty of nay-sayers, but there were many more yay-sayers. A special thanks to my daughters Paige, Madison, and Avery, who giggled with me at the funny parts, cried with me at the sad parts, and swooned with me when the moment was just right. A mother could not ever express the love I have for you. You are my inspiration.

I owe an especially large thank you to my sister, KaraLynne Mackrory, whose book, Falling for Mr. Darcy, inspired my love of the man. Who knew an addiction could be contagious? Her patience with my first attempts to write was much appreciated. She fights my mom for the award of biggest fan, thanks Patsy Putnam.

Thank you to my editor, Camie Schaefer, whose vision for the book seemed to match mine in almost every way. She took a diamond in the rough and polished it until it shined.

Dedication

There is nothing I want more than to dedicate this book to my daughters. May you find your own Mr. Darcy and be cherished and loved as deeply as you deserve.

Table of Contents

Chapter 1

Georgiana struggled again with her once strongly-held conviction that she was doing the right thing in surprising her brother at Netherfield. She looked across the carriage at Mrs. Annesley, who was quietly reading her book. Georgiana was never one to deceive anyone, and certainly not the companion who had been so kind to her. Her brother had taken meticulous care in hiring Mrs. Annesley, because of the disastrous previous companion, Mrs. Younge. She knew her brother blamed himself for the significant role Mrs. Younge had played in Georgiana's near elopement with George Wickham just a few months ago.

Georgiana willed herself not to think of that awful incident at Ramsgate. It had been meant to be a relaxing holiday at the shore, and she had been manipulated into believing that she was in love with George Wickham, all because he wanted her dowry. Just remembering the hateful words that Wickham spat at her once he learned he would not get any of her dowry made her shudder. Once again, Georgiana thanked God that her brother had surprised them at Ramsgate and that she had shown the forethought to disclose their plan to elope— ending it before it happened. She remembered the fierce look in her brother's eyes when she told him about Wickham. She did not want to see that look again. Georgiana took a deep breath to calm herself. She hoped she was doing the right thing in surprising him. She took out the letter she received from him a few days ago and reread the lines that had led her to make this decision.

My dearest Georgiana,

Things are going well for Mr. Bingley at Netherfield. He seems to be handling the responsibilities of running his own estate remarkably well. Country life seems to be quite acceptable to him. I too have enjoyed the hunting and grounds at Netherfield. I have met several amiable people here in Meryton, one of whom is uniquely lively. I find Miss Elizabeth Bennet's wit engaging and a welcome relief to the exhausting flattery of Miss Bingley. I have had many occasions to appreciate her willful opinions, some of which have been aimed directly at me, and they seem to be shed as quickly as breath itself. Her mind is so intelligent and charming, that I must admit that I cannot help but listen as she speaks. I have never met a lady with such decided opinions . . .

Georgiana folded the letter. He had gone on to ask about her studies and wrote wishes to see her soon, but it was the part about Miss Bennet that had intrigued her and made her deceive Mrs. Annesley in this way. He had never written of a lady before and he certainly had never expressed his admiration for one before. She tucked the letter away and regained her courage. *Yes, this is the right thing to do. My brother is in love and I must see it for myself.* The carriage turned off the main road and she could see a large stone building ahead of them. She would see soon enough what her brother thought of her arriving at Netherfield unannounced.

The house was not as grand as Pemberley, but seemed large and pleasant. As they neared, Georgiana looked up at the beautiful ivy climbing up the sides of the doorway and around the corners of the building. On closer examination, she could tell that the ivy had recently been trimmed back. Perhaps it was encroaching where it was not wanted, just like she was doing now to William. Georgiana blinked back tears and tried to rally her courage again. She had come to see the lady who had taken hold of her brother's heart. They exited the carriage and knocked on the door. Georgiana took one more breath to calm herself.

As they were escorted inside by the servant, she looked around the vestibule. In doing so she caught sight of a young lady with brown curly hair standing in the doorway a few doors down. The lady smiled briefly when their eyes met, and Georgiana was somewhat shocked that the lady would even acknowledge Georgiana at all since they did not know each other. Georgiana heard her own name announced down the hall to her right, followed by jubilant exclamations from Mr. Bingley, followed by her brother's deeper, more concerned voice. Both voices were rapidly approaching.

Mr. Darcy took long strides out the study door and saw that it really was his sister, Georgiana. Why was she here? Her face showed concern when she saw him and she smiled slightly but somewhat nervously. When he had first heard Georgiana announced by the servant he was quite concerned. Upon seeing her appear healthy, although apprehensive, he relaxed a little.

"Georgiana? Has something happened? Why are you at Netherfield?" Before he could finish the last sentence Georgiana ran to him and threw her arms around his neck. He embraced her tenderly and kissed the top of her head, but he could tell she had started to cry. "There now, Georgie, I am just surprised to see you." He continued whispering comforting things in her ear, tucking stray curls behind her ear. It took several minutes of these ministrations before she improved. When the tears seemed to have subsided, he took her shoulders and pulled her away to get a good look at her. "It is so good to see you! I have missed you so much, but what has brought you to Netherfield?"

"Were you not expecting us, sir?" Mrs. Annesley asked. "Georgiana told me you had summoned her!"

Mr. Darcy looked at the embarrassment on Georgiana's face and the shock on Mrs. Annesley's face. He then noticed Elizabeth standing in the doorway watching the exchange. This was not the time or place to talk to Georgiana about her ruse. He was just so grateful to see her. "It is no concern! I will take my sister any day, any time! Come my sweet, there is someone I want you to meet." He took Georgiana's hand and led her towards Miss Elizabeth.

Elizabeth had watched the warm welcome between brother and sister and did not know what to make of it. Mr. Darcy was so animated and caring to his sister. He had kissed her and embraced her so tenderly. This was not the prideful "Master of Pemberley" that had been introduced at the Meryton Assembly and had snubbed her for a dancing partner. And it certainly wasn't the same aloof man who judged all those around him. She was quite baffled. She realized they were heading her way. *Surely he does not mean to introduce her to me? Mr. Darcy can hardly think well of me!* But just a quick moment later, Mr. Darcy had stopped right in front of Elizabeth.

"Miss Elizabeth Bennet, allow me to introduce you to my dear sister, Miss Georgiana Darcy. Georgiana, I would like to introduce you to Miss Elizabeth Bennet."

Elizabeth watched an enormous smile grace Georgiana's face and she saw a little something else in her eyes . . . mischief? She could not tell. She was so taken back by the warm welcome and change in Mr. Darcy's manner and the hint of something else in Georgiana's eyes that she almost forgot to curtsy. "It is a great pleasure, Miss Darcy."

"No, the pleasure is all mine. Brother, do you think we could order tea for all of us? The road was long and tiring." As she had addressed her brother, she noticed that his eyes were fixed on Miss Elizabeth. He had a small grin on his face that lightened the creases by his eyes. She would have to watch closely to judge his feelings further, but at the moment it appeared she was right. Her brother loved Miss Elizabeth Bennet.

Bingley spoke up from behind them. "Miss Darcy, I will ring for tea. Please, make yourself welcome in the drawing room." He motioned to the room where Elizabeth still stood in the doorway. "I just have a few things to do to get ready for the hunting party, but I will be back shortly." Bingley then motioned for all to follow Elizabeth into the drawing room.

Darcy eyed Georgiana suspiciously. He watched her as she struggled to decide on where to sit. It wasn't until Miss Elizabeth took her seat that Georgiana found one, which happened to be right next to Miss Elizabeth. It seemed a little odd to Darcy that his overly shy sister would chose a seat so close to someone to whom she had just been introduced, but he dismissed the concern immediately. He looked at Elizabeth who had already started up a conversation with Georgiana, asking about her travels, the weather, and even what musical composition Georgiana was practicing. He was in awe that they seemed to get along so well. He found he was content just watching them and thought to himself that he had never seen Georgiana so open and assertive.

Why is Mr. Darcy staring at me like that? Elizabeth felt quite uncomfortable under his scrutiny and with his strange looks. She decided she had enough and said, "Miss Darcy, I am so glad to have met you. I look forward to seeing more of you, but for the moment I must take my leave of you to attend to my sister." She stood and left the room, giving Mr. Darcy her own strange look as she passed him. She thought she heard a chuckle from him which only added to her confusion as she left the room. Why was Mr. Darcy so altered with his sister? *Could I have been mistaken in his character?* Her confusion worsened as she exited the room.

"Well, Georgiana! Now that we are alone, do you mind telling me why you felt the need to come to Netherfield and surprise me?" Mr. Darcy asked. Georgiana's mood shifted back to the embarrassed and anxious state she was in when she first came. Mr. Darcy listened as she made excuses about how her studies were going well but she needed a rest; and then she said the air in London was too poor for her health. She had started on another excuse when Mr. Darcy interrupted her.

"Come now, I am not cross with you! I just think you should have written with the news that you were coming. I would have let you come at any time, but what if something happened on the road and I had no knowledge of your travels? If you had left two days ago, you would have been caught in a terrible rainstorm!" Mr. Darcy knew just how long ago it had been because that was when Elizabeth's sister Jane had arrived and taken ill while dining with Bingley's sisters. The next day he was graced with the most beautiful sight, a rosy-cheeked Elizabeth. She had walked the three miles to Netherfield to look after her ill sister. Her eyes had been so bright from the exercise that he wanted to kiss her right then! Of course, he did not. But it was the first time he had ever experienced such an overwhelming impulse, and it had taken him by surprise.

"I am sorry, William. I missed you. Thank you for not being angry with me." She paused and then continued. "Why is Miss Bennet here at Netherfield?"

Mr. Darcy brought his mind back to the present. "Miss Bennet caught a fever and cold two days ago, but she is recovering well."

Georgiana was even more confused. "But she did not look ill a moment ago."

"Forgive me, allow me to clarify. Miss Elizabeth Bennet is here to care for her eldest sister, Miss Jane Bennet. It is she who is ill."

That made more sense to Georgiana. It pleased her that Miss Elizabeth was staying here, for that meant she would have more opportunities to observe her brother in Miss Elizabeth's presence. Just then Mr. Bingley returned to claim Darcy for the hunting party. He was followed by Miss Bingley and Mrs. Hurst, both of whom welcomed her profusely, already fussing over how grown up she was and how bright and cheerful she looked. Georgiana shyly greeted them and looked to William. She knew from experience that as soon as William left, Miss Bingley would let up, but until then she had to endure the constant compliments that always were said just loud enough for William to hear.

*****

Georgiana watched William all through dinner. His eyes drifted quite often in Miss Elizabeth's direction, where he would hold back a smile and then look away. He wasn't directly addressing Elizabeth in any way, but Georgiana imagined it was because Miss Bingley was diverting his attention in a very persistent manner. Every time her brother would look at Elizabeth, Miss Bingley would ask him another question, solicit his opinion on the latest news from London, or compliment him on his fine use of the silverware. To her it seemed that Miss Bingley was showing extra care in engaging her brother's attention. It was frustrating because it was evident to Georgiana that William wanted to be talking with Miss Elizabeth!

Elizabeth too had noticed how Miss Bingley was trying so hard to monopolize Mr. Darcy's attentions, though Mr. Darcy was barely civil in his responses. The kind, gentle man she saw welcome his sister in the vestibule had been replaced with the haughty Master of Pemberley that she knew all too well, and to be truthful, was more comfortable in seeing. She didn't know what to think of the lovely exchange she witnessed earlier with his sister. Perhaps she had misjudged him to some extent. Although, she thought, listening to him reply tersely to another of Miss Bingley's ridiculous questions, perhaps not.

Miss Bingley put some ridiculous question to him and Mr. Darcy, trying to discourage the constant flattery and ridiculous conversation from Miss Bingley, gave a small sigh as he started to answer. Elizabeth couldn't help herself and giggled. The scene in front of her was too funny! Mr. Darcy then looked straight at her with a surprised look. It was a look he would have given if she had belched instead of giggled. She stifled her laugh and pressed her hand to her mouth. Then she met his gaze head-on and raised her eyebrow, defying him to judge her further. *There!* she thought. *You shall not be confused by my character, Mr. Darcy!*

Georgiana decided that she had better do something or William might lose his temper with Miss Bingley right in front of Miss Elizabeth. It wasn't like her to be so forward, but she needed to see William interact more with Miss Elizabeth. "Miss Elizabeth, how is your sister faring? Is she any better?"

"I am afraid not," Elizabeth said, immediately sobering at the question. "The fever is just as high as this morning but she is at least receiving good rest, and we all know how rest heals the body." Elizabeth looked to Mr. Bingley who seemed to perk up with Georgiana's question. Deep concern was written all over his face.

"Do you think we should call for the apothecary again tomorrow?" Mr. Bingley asked. "I feel terrible that she is so ill."

Elizabeth was pleased he was so attentive to Jane. Especially since Jane and she had just had a conversation about Mr. Bingley's attachment to her sister. He may not be Jane's Mr. Bingley yet, but the concern on his face showed that he cared a great deal. "No, Mr. Bingley, I am sure she will feel better soon. Then we can both return to Longbourn and we will not have to trespass on your kind hospitality any longer." She stole a glance at Mr. Darcy even though she willed herself not to. She knew he was the member of the household that was the most uncomfortable with their stay at Netherfield, and knew he would be pleased to see them leave sooner rather than later. What she saw on Mr. Darcy's face only confused her. She expected relief to be evident in hearing they would be leaving soon, but relief was not how she would describe the expression as. *Have I read his character wrongly?* She could not deny that she felt some mortification at the thought. She diverted her eyes in an attempt to mask her confusion.

Mr. Bingley suggested they forgo the separation of sexes after dinner to spend the evening enjoying each other's company. All parties agreed and Elizabeth took the opportunity to check on Jane. When she returned, Miss Bingley was playing something lively on the pianoforte. As she entered the room, Mr. Darcy stood and walked in her direction. His strides were long and determined but his arms were stiffly at his sides. Why was he coming directly over to her? He appeared to be determined to address her right in front of everyone!

Mr. Darcy hadn't meant to be anxiously awaiting her return, but when he saw her, he knew he wanted nothing more than to hold her in his arms. Since he couldn't do that, and he knew it, the inner turmoil within himself pushed him to ask her to dance instead. "Miss Bennet, will you do me the honor of dancing a jig with me?" His hand was stretched forth and his head bowed slightly.

Elizabeth was shocked into momentary silence. All she could think of was how he had scorned her at the Meryton Assembly and how he had said she was merely "tolerable" and "not handsome enough to tempt" him. Remembering this comment, she saucily raised her eyebrows and said, "It is tempting, Mr. Darcy . . ." She was at loss on how exactly to finish the perfectly impertinent refusal, when he took her hand and led her to the center of the room. *How could he presume that was an affirmative answer? How could I have let him think so?* Her cheeks flushed. She certainly had not wanted to demonstrate any special attention to Mr. Darcy. She could already hear her mother's shrill celebration of his income. She almost refused, but then caught a glimpse of Georgiana's sweet smile. She could not embarrass him in front of his sister.

Once they began to dance, Miss Bingley's tempo seemed to quicken and she played with energized fervor, leaving Elizabeth quite short of breath. Her heart was pounding and her hands were on fire every time the movements brought their hands back together. Soon Bingley asked Georgiana to dance which made the dance less of an intimate performance and Elizabeth relaxed a little. She laughed at Georgiana's shyness to dance, but Bingley was too kind and encouraging. Could there be some feeling on Mr. Bingley's part for

Mr. Darcy's Promise

Georgiana? Surely his attentions to Jane were genuine; she would not believe anything else. Elizabeth continued to watch the two dance, if for nothing else but to avoid Mr. Darcy's penetrating gaze.

Oh, how lovely! Elizabeth's cheeks were bright pink once again! Darcy couldn't quite decide if her eyes or cheeks were brighter. He longed to kiss those cheeks and feel their warmth on his lips. This was something he knew he could not do and he decided he had better keep his thoughts to himself. He was pleased to see her relax and laugh merrily as Bingley and Georgiana danced. All too soon the music ended and Miss Bingley stated her fingers were tired and asked Georgiana to play. Mr. Darcy took Elizabeth's hand and escorted her to her seat and took the seat next to her. *Why did I do that?* He knew he could not show a preference for Miss Elizabeth! He struggled with the rudeness of leaving and sitting elsewhere after he had already sat down. If he wasn't careful, his impulses would take over and he would give encouragement when the reality of developing a relationship was absurd! He had enough experience with eligible ladies throwing themselves at him that he did not wish another one, even if her eyes were fine and her mind engaging. He stood up again and claimed need of refreshment. On impulse, he asked if others needed something to drink and looked at Elizabeth. But it wasn't Elizabeth that answered.

"Oh yes, thank you, Mr. Darcy! My fingers got such exercise with that tune!" Miss Bingley said dramatically.

Mr. Darcy turned to Miss Bingley and said, "Of course, Miss Bingley, tea or wine?"

"Wine, please." Miss Bingley then sat in Darcy's vacated spot next to Elizabeth solely to prevent him from sitting in it again.

Elizabeth was quite amused at Miss Bingley and smiled to herself. *Surely she knows I want nothing to do with Mr. Darcy!*

*****

The next few days were spent between strange looks from Mr. Darcy, smiles of mischief from Miss Darcy, and frowns of frustration from Miss Bingley. Elizabeth was greatly relieved when Jane was finally feeling well enough to come down. The last few days without her had been wild! First Mr. Darcy greeted his sister with such tenderness she could scarcely believe it was him, and much more strangely, he asked her to dance a jig. A jig, of all things! He seemed much more relaxed with Georgiana around and she scarcely knew what to think of him!

It was Sunday morning and Jane and Elizabeth were hours away from returning to Longbourn. All Elizabeth had to do was patiently wait for church services to finish and then Mr. Bingley would have his carriage return them home. Church seemed to be taking especially long this morning! Elizabeth realized she had heard very little of what the clergyman said because of the reflection she was doing on Mr. Darcy. Why was he so changed towards her? She again wondered if she misjudged him. It hadn't been all that unpleasant dancing with him either. *What am I doing? Why would I enjoy a dance with a man who has always held me in such contempt?* She did not know what to think of it.

The clergyman did not have Mr. Darcy's attention either. More than anything, Mr. Darcy was overcome with the realization that Elizabeth was leaving Netherfield and he would not see her every day. Oh, the torture this thought brought! Her charming smiles, the merriness of her laughter, the way she crossed her ankles, the looks of impertinence, the soft full lips as she spoke his name . . . No, this would not do! He must marry and marry well! Marriage? Who said anything about marriage? He had simply been admiring her intelligence.

If Mr. Darcy was being honest with himself, which he was not, he would have said there was no other woman like her. No other woman stirred feelings of admiration and sparked sensations of curiosity to know more, like Miss Elizabeth did. But Mr. Darcy was not being honest with himself. Instead he was thinking of their one dance together and that relaxed smile on her lips and how much he wanted to kiss them. He thought about how well she got along with Georgiana and how quickly Georgiana had opened up to her. He was thinking about how nice it would be for Georgiana to have Elizabeth's influence in her life, and in a moment of honesty, in his life.

"William, the song is over, you can sit down now," Georgiana whispered, pulling on his hand.

He quickly sat down and whispered his thanks. Look what Elizabeth was doing to him! *Focus, man!*

After the closing prayer, Georgiana leaned over and continued, "I think I would like to call on Miss Elizabeth tomorrow. Would that be acceptable?"

A small smile spread across his face, but only briefly, as he realized he would not be calling on Elizabeth with Georgiana. For the life of him he couldn't think of a single excuse to do so! He then thought of Georgiana in the presence of the other Bennets and frowned. Elizabeth's youngest sisters alone would be the worst influence possible! And Mrs. Bennet was something else! How could anyone live with such a shrill voice calling out orders, opinions, and innuendos so quickly that people were dizzy just listening for five minutes! He looked at Georgiana, ready to tell her exactly what he thought when he saw the expectant look in her hopeful eyes and it undid him. Why was he always a sucker for fine eyes?

"Georgiana, if you would like to, you certainly may, but not alone. See if Miss Bingley or Mrs. Annesley will go with you."

Georgiana frowned. If her plan was going to work, he needed to accompany her! "I was hoping to have you . . ."

Then he heard her. That voice, and it was certainly as loud and obnoxious as ever.

"Mr. Bingley! Oh Mr. Bingley! Thank you so much for the care you gave to my dear Jane! She is looking so much better then when I saw her last, does she not?" asked Mrs. Bennet.

"Of course, I have never seen her more beautiful!" Mr. Bingley replied.

"And the church lighting near the altar is so becoming of her complexion!" Mrs. Bennet then proceeded to lead Mr. Bingley by the arm as if to place him closer to the very altar she spoke of.

Elizabeth was caught between amusement and shame at her mother's behavior, but then her feelings quickly turned to concern for Jane, who was now the object of much scrutiny by the people passing them down the aisle. Only their mother would push her matchmaking skills in the middle of church! She looked at Mr. Darcy and saw his disapproval written all over his face. Yes, he was quite displeased.

Promises to return the Bennet daughters as soon as possible were made and Mr. Darcy quickly escorted Georgiana out.

That! That was precisely why he could not align himself with any Bennet, much less Elizabeth! Her family was so ridiculous he would be laughed at wherever they went! Master of Pemberley laughed at? He could not bear it. He would no longer think on her fine eyes or the oft-raised eyebrow. He would no longer seek out her company, no longer look at her, nor let his mind drift to those chocolate curls. No, he decided. He simply would no longer desire her. No sooner had he decided this then he found his very own hand reaching for Elizabeth's to assist her into the carriage. The surge of sensation running from his hand up his arm was so strong he dropped it as soon as possible, opening and closing his hand trying to dispel the sensation. He could still feel the heat and tingling that merely touching her caused.

Elizabeth noticed the quickly dropped hand as well. So the old Mr. Darcy was back in fine form, so prideful and conceited that he could not properly hand a lady into a carriage. Of course all these people were watching and she curtailed the temptation to say something smart when she bit her lip. Only a few more minutes with him and then she should never see him again! But she knew that wasn't true, especially if Jane and Bingley got married. She would be thrown in his path over and over again! This realization did not help her mood any.

Georgiana saw Elizabeth bite her lip and turned to Miss Bingley and asked, "Miss Bingley, could I persuade you to pay a call to Miss Bennet and Miss Elizabeth tomorrow with me? I have heard such lovely things about Longbourn's gardens and I know you would feel it appropriate to check in on Miss Bennet's health."

Mr. Bingley piped up and said, "What a marvelous idea!"

Seeing the rudeness of a refusal right in front of the Bennet sisters, Miss Bingley said, "Of course, Georgiana, it would be my pleasure!"

Both Mr. Darcy and Miss Bingley noticed the broad grin that splayed across Georgiana's features. Elizabeth, however, had been looking out the window to avoid seeing what she knew would be further displeasure on Mr. Darcy's face.

*****

The next morning's weather was somewhat dreary and Elizabeth was ready and looking forward to going out walking when Mr. Bennet called her into his study.

"My dear sweet Lizzy, how I have missed you. Did you give Netherfield a good once over?" Mr. Bennet was a father first before anything else, and he had noticed the quiet mood his Elizabeth had been in since returning from Netherfield. He suspected she was contemplating some great issue and he wanted to let her know he was available to talk. Since it was hardly natural for him to express his concern openly, he preferred to make light of it.

"No, Papa, I am afraid I did not, but I did try! Some in the Netherfield party may have wished to part with my company sooner, but I could not leave Jane." She looked at her hands then.

Mr. Bennet loved hearing his favorite daughter call him "Papa," for it always warmed his heart. It was what he called his own late father. Only his Lizzy used it on him and only to her advantage. His teasing usually curtailed quickly when Lizzy used this endearment. He suspected that the "some" of Netherfield party was Mr. Darcy. He didn't know much about the man, but had heard on more than one occasion how he scorned Elizabeth at the Meryton assembly. The fact that she hinted at his wishes for her to leave only made him suspicious that Mr. Darcy was the real reason for the quiet mood. Could his Elizabeth have developed feelings for Mr. Darcy? He could not imagine that such a fancy would go far, and regretted again the entail that had so reduced his daughter's dowries. But, Mr. Bennet reasoned, he could be wrong. So once again, humor was far easier than asking her feelings for the man outright.

"Well, I hope the old Mr. Darcy was not too hard on you. Knowing you, your impertinence only made him curious about you. After all, not all women speak to gentlemen the way you do, my dear, and I am guessing Mr. Darcy appreciates your opinions as opposed to silly conversations about dresses and bonnets. Do not worry; Mr. Darcy is sure to be an intelligent man who likes intelligent conversation. And I have no doubt you gave him that!"

Elizabeth looked up at her father. Was he teasing her about Mr. Darcy? Sudden memories engulfed her of the warmth of his hands as they danced and that warm welcome she witnessed with his sister, and that smile . . . the smile that changed his features into something quite handsome. She had been shocked with her father teasing her, but more shocked that she was examining his handsome smile in her mind. Where were these foreign feelings coming from? She colored slightly and became further embarrassed when she saw the grin on her father's face. *It will not do to have two parents scheming to be matchmakers!* "Perhaps I best be off on my walk, Papa," she said abruptly while she curtsied and hurriedly exited the room. But she had not exited soon enough to avoid hearing her father chuckle and mumble something about his dear Lizzy's heart.

It was this departing experience that sent her mind into turmoil. What did it matter that Mr. Darcy had a side of him that can be charming and pleasant? She certainly did not care! She rehearsed in her mind all the looks of disdain and haughty pride that she was more used to seeing and that provided much-needed comfort. She thought about everything he had said and done that was proof that he only looked down on her. It felt less foreign to think of Mr. Darcy as he had always been, and not someone she could admire. She tried to convince herself of this thought but it only frustrated her. Why would she blush when her father asked about him? By the time she returned from her walk she had worked herself up into quite a frenzy and was not looking forward to Georgiana's visit, let alone Caroline Bingley's!

Lydia came down the stairs at that time and grabbed Elizabeth by the shoulders, "Lizzy! You should not have gone out walking! Kitty and I are going to walk to Meryton to see all the officers that are sure to be in town! Oh, please come! Those red coats make any man so handsome!"

"I am sorry Lydia, but I am expecting guests this morning." She shrugged her shoulders free and went to get a scone for breakfast. She could tolerate her younger sisters most days with good spirit and affection, but not in the mood she was currently experiencing. She heard her youngest sisters shout their goodbyes as they left for Meryton. *For a moment,* Elizabeth thought, *the silence of any Darcy is preferable to the silliness of my sisters.*

*****

"Miss Darcy and Miss Bingley," Mrs. Hill announced. Elizabeth and Jane stood and welcomed their guests into the sitting room.

Jane coughed delicately into her handkerchief. "Welcome Miss Darcy, Miss Bingley." Jane said.

Georgiana took her seat, "Please call me Georgiana, after spending three days with the two of you I feel like we are almost sisters! I would not know though, as I have no sisters, only one brother." Georgiana was nervous and knew she was not being the most refined guest. She was perhaps even being a little awkward.

Elizabeth smiled at her, "Well Georgiana, then you shall call me Elizabeth. And although having sisters can be wonderful, quarrels over whose bonnet looks best on whom can get tiring and I cannot always recommend it!"

Georgiana felt herself relax and laughed. "Someday I hope to have a sister, and until then I shall tell you every day how lucky you are to have them. I imagine sisters are closer than friends."

Tea was brought in and they all discussed the weather and Elizabeth asked Georgiana if she had mastered the section she had been struggling with on the concerto she was practicing. Miss Bingley commented with faux concern on how Jane's cough had not improved. It was during this lull in conversation that giggles and laughter could be heard from the front door.

"I am sorry, that will be my two youngest sisters. They walked to Meryton this morning." Elizabeth knew this would be the first of many apologies she would make to Georgiana regarding her family; she seemed to be doing that a great deal with the Darcys of late. They all turned their heads as the door opened. Lydia came walking in holding tightly to the arm of a tall, lean, and handsome officer while Kitty did the same with a shorter but still-handsome officer. Giggles and squeals of laughter echoed throughout the house. Georgiana,

Jeanna Ellsworth   15

most peculiarly, started making a ridiculous amount of noise with her tea cup.

When Elizabeth looked towards her, she was surprised to see Georgiana pale as a ghost; the tea cup rattling against the saucer in her shaking hands. Georgiana placed the distracting tea cup down and Elizabeth turned her attention back to her sisters and the officers, but she continued to wonder whatever could be the matter with Georgiana.

Lydia saw that they were not alone and put her hand up to her mouth to stifle the latest giggle. "Oh! These must be the callers you were going to have this morning! This fine officer is Mr. Wickham, and Kitty there is on the arm of Mr. Denny. Are they not so handsome in their red coats? They offered to walk us home!"

"Of course," Elizabeth said, still concerned about Georgiana, "Allow me to introduce you to Miss Darcy of Pemberley, and Miss Bingley of Netherfield Park—"

With a bow and a tip of the hat Wickham interrupted, smiling, "I believe I am quite acquainted with Miss Darcy. We are long family friends, are we not? And how are you, Miss Georgiana? You look mighty fine this morning!"

Georgiana stood and said, "Elizabeth, Miss Bennet, it was a pleasure to see you both again. It appears that it is now time to take our leave. Good day, Mr. Wickham." Georgiana could not move quickly enough out the door but she made it before her tears came. She didn't even realize she left her gloves and pelisse at the door. All she cared about was getting away from Wickham. Why was he here in Meryton? And how could he speak to her as if nothing had happened between them? All her memories of his charm and deceit flooded over her and she broke down in sobs. She climbed into the carriage and hoped that Miss Bingley would soon follow.

An astonished Miss Bingley collected their things and entered the carriage. Although glad to be gone so quickly, she soon came across a tearful and sobbing Georgiana who became quite inconsolable on the way back to Netherfield. By the time of their arrival, Georgiana was in near hysterics. Miss Bingley had no idea what to make of her behavior and so decided to get Mr. Darcy. She exited the carriage alone.

Mr. Darcy and Mr. Bingley were just dismounting their horses when they noticed Miss Bingley step out of the carriage. They were back so soon? *Odd,* Darcy thought, *where was Georgiana?* Then Mr. Darcy heard the sobs. *Georgiana!* He ran all the way to the carriage and climbed in with one fluid movement. Her face was wet and pink, her eyes swollen and red. "Whatever is the matter, Georgie? Did something happen at the Bennet's?" He knew he should not have let her go; those Bennets were insufferable! Well, his mind amended, all but the two eldest daughters.

The thought was stricken by his next realization. He had only seen her like this one other time— Ramsgate! "Please tell me, dear Georgie; it pains me to see you like this again." Suddenly she was in worse hysterics and mumbling something incoherently. She stumbled out of the carriage in such a hurry that her pelisse caught on the handle and was pulled from her shoulders. She stripped her arms free of the confining garment and ran inside blindly.

Mr. Darcy exited the carriage and turned infuriated, to Miss Bingley. "What happened?" His voice was low and full of suppressed fury. "I have not seen her like this since . . . well, for several months. And that . . ." pointing after Georgiana, "is not how she left here this morning!"

Feeling the full baritone wrath of Mr. Darcy upon her, Miss Bingley was quick to come to her own defense. "Mr. Darcy, I can have no idea. We were having tea when the younger Bennets came in with some officers who had escorted them home. No sooner had Georgiana been introduced that she exited the room! I confess she was very nearly rude! I am sure I do not know what to think!"

"Do you mean to tell me that she is like that because of Miss Bennet's sisters? How dare they! Bring me back my horse! I will get to the bottom of this."

Mr. Bingley had never seen his friend quite so irate. He reached for Darcy's arm and tried to calm him. He reminded Darcy that Georgiana needed him now and it was not right to head to

Longbourn so angry. "You do not even know what happened. You could say things that could leave lasting damage . . ."

Mr. Darcy looked angrily at Bingley and said, "I do not care about you and Miss Bennet right now, Bingley. Can you not see their family is beneath you? Look what they have done to Georgiana in the space of half an hour!" Bingley continued to calm him and remind him of the necessity of caring for Georgiana. Slowly, ever so slowly, Darcy conceded. He then ran the few steps into the house to check on Georgiana.

Darcy didn't linger to see the smile on Miss Bingley's face or hear her say, "Thank goodness we will never have to call on them again!"

Mr. Bingley shot a quick look at his sister. "Caroline!" he said sharply, who returned his gaze with a puzzled look.

She had never seen her brother look so stern, and certainly not with the flash of anger that she now saw. Was his attachment to Miss Bennet more than she had realized? "What? What did I say?"

*****

Mr. Wickham bowed over Elizabeth's hand but his eyes never left hers. "It is a pleasure, Miss Elizabeth."

Elizabeth could feel his gaze burrow deep into her and suddenly she felt embarrassed and flattered at the same time. She peered into his gorgeous blue eyes until Jane's cough reminded her to look elsewhere. Fresh tea was ordered and the guests were seated. Lydia was all giggles and laughter, but Wickham seemed to handle the attentions well. Elizabeth caught him looking at her numerous times with the most charming smile, his eyes bright and cheerful. Much different from when Mr. Darcy regarded her with disdain!

"Mr. Wickham, how long will the militia be in Meryton?" Jane asked.

"I am not certain, madam. We came just a few weeks ago and we usually stay encamped in one area for three to four months. Or so I am told. I have just joined myself."

"And how to do you find the people and town?" Elizabeth asked.

"I find the town grand, but not so grand that one would miss the beauties it holds," he said, looking directly at Elizabeth.

Lydia took his arm then and giggled, "Oh Mr. Wickham, you are too charming! Lizzy, did you know Mr. Denny is a favorite with Colonel Forster?"

Elizabeth turned her attention to the other officer, "Is that so, Mr. Denny?"

Mr. Wickham spoke up and said, "Yes, his charms have even affected Forster's wife! I for one, see no need to flirt with married ladies when there are so many pleasant unmarried ladies to be acquainted with." He gave Elizabeth a dazzling smile.

Elizabeth blushed to find herself under his piercing gaze, again feeling oddly flattered. How could she find a man she barely knew to be so devilishly handsome and charming? He continued to humor and stare with admiration at Elizabeth, all the while with his hands on Lydia's arm which was still neatly tucked into his. Could Wickham find her attractive?

The officers took their leave and bowed again over the hands of the ladies. Wickham again kept his eyes on Elizabeth as he bowed over her hand and whispered, "Miss Elizabeth, I look forward to seeing you soon. The time apart is sure to be pleasurable only to the extent that now I have memories of you to keep me from being lonely."

Trying to find her voice again she said, "Thank you, but I advise you hurry back to camp, Mr. Wickham. You seem to be in danger of needing to be warned that the weather looks like rain." Weather was always a safe topic and wit was a far easier defense than any other. She had learned a few things from her father.

"Why, I think you are right, Miss Elizabeth. Perhaps we shall meet again on a clearer day." He and Denny turned and left, leaving Elizabeth with a pounding heart and a very strange look coming from Jane.

She did not need Jane's interrogation on the charming Wickham, for she did not know what to think of it herself! "Not now," she mouthed to Jane.

*****

Darcy knocked again at Georgiana's door for the third time. She was calmer, he could tell, but still sniffling. "Please do not turn me away again, Georgie, I want to know what happened to make you so distraught!" He calmed his voice and took the deep timbre out once again and spoke as calmly as possible. "Was it something Miss Elizabeth said or did?" He dearly hoped not, but he knew the spirited nature of Elizabeth and feared for his timid sister. He leaned against the door and wondered if it was right in introducing Georgiana and Miss Elizabeth. Miss Elizabeth was so full of life and vigor it could almost be considered contagious! But was she too much for his shy sister? He had felt her influence in his own heart. He hadn't had this much joy in his heart for years. Not since his mother's passing, in fact. But he also had never known this much confusion, torn between what his heart wanted and what he knew of duty! He was contemplating Elizabeth and the joy she brought into his heart every time she smiled, or laughed, or gave him one of her impertinent looks, when the door flung open and he found himself confronted with a red-faced Georgiana.

"How could you say such a thing?" she bellowed.

What had he said? "Georgie!" He entered the room and embraced her and barely got a chance to kiss her forehead when she pushed him away. Hurt and confused, he again wondered what he had said to convince her to finally open the door.

"Elizabeth is the most wonderful person I have ever met! And you think so too! Do not you try to deny it; I see the way you look at her!"

Darcy was keenly aware that Miss Bingley could be very near and listening. He closed her door behind them before turning sternly to Georgiana. He lowered his voice and said, "You must not say such things, you forget yourself." Her tears started again and he reached for her, "I am sorry, dearest, I am just trying to understand what happened. Will you not tell me?" He wanted to divert the accusation that he had feelings for Elizabeth, because that was not a conversation he wished to have with himself— let alone one with his young sister!

Mr. Darcy's Promise

"You like her, do you not?"

Sighing, Darcy appeased her, "Yes, I like her . . ."

"Very much?"

"Georgie, what is this about? I think Eliz . . . Miss Elizabeth Bennet is a fine lady." *With beautiful eyes,* he thought, *one who has bewitched me beyond words!*

Her eyes lit up and a small smile came to the corners of her mouth, "And does a fine lady deserve a fine gentleman?"

Getting a little suspicious, he warily said, "Yes, I am sure someday she will meet a fine man." The thought of her married to someone else troubled him deeply. "But as for my feelings for her . . . wait . . . you . . . tell me again why you came to surprise me at Netherfield?"

It all came out in a rush. How after she got his letter talking of Elizabeth she knew she had to come. She told of how he had never written to her about a lady before and how she so badly wanted to meet this intelligent lady who teased her brother and was lively and full of wit. She hurried said all this, then said how she was sure that he was in love, and how she wanted to meet her future sister.

His countenance dropped as she spoke but he couldn't let her go on like this. "Georgiana, I must stop you there. There is no possible way that I could ask for Miss Elizabeth Bennet's hand in marriage. I have a duty to you and our family to marry well. Miss Elizabeth just is not right for me, for us! She may be a very charming young lady who has most definitely impressed me but I cannot marry her. You saw her mother at church! By gads! Could you imagine introducing my mother-in-law to the *ton?*"

"But if you love her . . ."

"No. Just no. And we are not having this discussion." He turned on his heel and left the room but Georgiana's words kept ringing in his ears, "*But if you love her . . .*" He needed to think and grabbed his riding gear and hat. He heard Bingley calling out for him as he opened the door.

"Do not worry, Bingley, I am not going to Longbourn!" His heart was beating far faster than it should for not have even gotten on the horse yet. Could he offer marriage? She had no fortune but that was hardly a concern. He reached the stable and saddled his own horse. There was no use waiting on a groom to do it when he had been raised in this knowledge. Yes, those problems— of horses and finances and managing Pemberley— he could manage very well on his own.

He tightened the last loop and with one fluid movement was up on Calypso, stroking her mane and giving her a gentle kick. Yes, his horse knew him too well, a gentle kick and off she went! He groaned as he felt the horse respond to each well placed foot and pull. If only the heart was like this horse! Tell it to go one way, and off it goes. Tell it to stop, and just for emphasis, he reigned in Calypso and came to a complete stop . . . it stops. "See? It is not so hard is it?" "*But if you love her . . .*" He groaned loudly.

"Go Calypso! Run!" He gave her a hard kick. She took off fast and hard. He took her up the hills and down even into the small stream getting his pants wet above his boots. Yes, if only the heart could be turned like this horse. The wind feeling cool on the wet legs seemed to calm him some. He had felt completely in control of his heart and body just one month before! He knew what he wanted in life and how to get it. It was simple: hard work and fortitude. Except now he didn't know what he wanted. No, that wasn't true, he wanted her. Just her. If he was truthful with himself, he didn't care for the ton or society when she was at stake.

But it wouldn't work! This was not as simple as riding Calypso or appointing a new parson. Offering marriage was much more complicated than that. But he could think of nothing else. He could smell her fragrant toilette water as she danced with him, smiling and laughing. She had enjoyed it, hadn't she? He could almost taste the scent now. He wondered if his imagination had gone wild. *No, this would not do.* He could not let his heart nor imagination run free without reins. Seeing he was in a field of lavender he now understood why his imagination was so keen. Lavender. That was what she smelled like. Fresh linen and lavender.

Out of pure need to control something, anything, he pulled hard to the right, firmly prodded Calypso on the left and pulled hard to the left. First one way, then the other. He sped up, and then halted.

He kicked Calypso again and took off hard and fast. He then leapt over a fence, and then landed hard, leaning far too forward to control the horse. "Whoa, Calypso. That fence almost did us in, almost." He righted himself and slowed the horse. Fences were not hard to jump; he had done it many times. Most fences were there to keep sheep and goats in check, but not him. He could jump just about any fence. "*But if you love her . . .*" Now there was a fence he feared he could not jump.

Sighing, he leaned forward and thanked Calypso. She liked these hard rides just as much as he did. He got off the horse and led her to a stream, the same stream that had cooled his legs. He was sweaty and hot now. Yes, he could marry Elizabeth, but would his love be enough? Could he look past her relations: the relatives in Cheapside, the silliness of Mrs. Bennet, the ridiculous younger sisters? He realized that all his previous objections to her family and lack of connections seemed somewhat ridiculous now that he had considered his true feelings for her. She was a gracious and lively woman, and he could not ask for anything more than that. Her relations would be over one hundred miles from Pemberley. It would be difficult, but that was merely another obstacle on his course. He might be willing to jump that fence, if only because, and he said it out loud this time, "I love her."

Mr. Darcy's Promise

Chapter 2

Elizabeth had effectively dodged Jane since yesterday afternoon. Every time Lydia would mention how handsome the officers were, Jane looked at Lizzy with arched eyebrows. Elizabeth even grabbed her book on two occasions when Jane came over to talk to her. Avoiding any discussion would and should help her nerves. She was certainly flattered, but Mr. Wickham was so bold! Sighing, she took her book in hand. No more looks from smiling sisters or fathers. No more shrill comments from her mother about how she would have liked to marry an officer in a red coat. No more gigging silly sisters who gave little to no thought of their actions. Yes, a walk was just what she needed.

She wandered down the road towards Meryton and just before she approached Lucas Lodge, she stopped and sat down on a fallen log. She didn't actually want to talk to her friend Charlotte, but it was a fairly quiet road and she would be able to read alone. It was so quiet and peaceful, and with no one around she delved into her book. She felt the late afternoon sun warming her and she closed her eyes to feel it on her face. *This is more like it.* No one around to give strange looks that only confused her. No more smiles in varying degrees of charm. No more uncontrolled embarrassment and flattery. She took off her bonnet to allow more sun to shine on her face.

"Ahh, now there is a sight for sore eyes."

Elizabeth startled and stood upright and her book fell to the ground. "Mr. Wickham! Why, what are you doing here?" Elizabeth cried.

"Enjoying the sights." He looked at her with the same smile that had made the color rise to her cheeks before.

So much for wishing piercing looks, smiles, and embarrassment away. She was suddenly self-conscious that her bonnet was off. She quickly put it back on, her fingers shaking all the while. Feeling the awkwardness of being alone with a man, she said, "I should be getting home."

He said, "I was going that way anyway and there was something I wish to discuss with you." He offered his arm to her and smiled another one of his smiles.

Curiosity and, yes, succumbing to a little of the flattery, allowed her to take his offered arm as they walked to Longbourn.

"I was surprised to see Miss Darcy yesterday. Has she been in town long?" he probed.

"No, she came and surprised her brother who is visiting his friend at Netherfield, an estate on the north side of Meryton."

So Fitzwilliam Darcy of Pemberley was in Meryton, right here in Meryton? Wickham thought. *So why has he let Georgiana be intimate friends with these lowly country daughters of a gentleman? Darcy would not let her "mingle" with him last spring! There was something curious about this relationship with the Bennets.*

"So tell me, how is she? Is her brother in good health?"

"Well, she left yesterday so hurriedly that we did not get a chance to get to ask after her health, but when I was at Netherfield the day before, both were well." Elizabeth heard a horse ahead and tried to pull her arm out of his, but he reached for it and held it close. They walked in silence for a few minutes.

"So Mr. Darcy is in good health, that is good. Are you fond of Mr. Darcy?" He was definitely curious, as she colored deeper than he'd ever seen her and he had made it his mission to see those pinks run scarlet. *Yes, there was something curious about the Bennets.*

She then let out a laugh and raised her eyebrow at him quizzically. *Why should he pry into my feelings like that? I scarcely know him!* But no sooner had she thought it, she was answering his question! "Ha! Now there is one area I am quite decided upon! He must be the proudest man I have ever met!" She didn't know why she was being so open with him, but she continued. "You know, the first time I heard him speak, he said I was not handsome enough to tempt him."

"No!" and then he leaned in and whispered, "Now I know he must not only be proud but blind too, as you are the handsomest lady I have ever seen!"

She heard what was probably a rabbit in the brush to the left. She had not been fishing for a compliment and changed the subject quickly. "He is devoted to his sister, though." She spoke softly this time.

He lifted his chin and decided he would have to investigate the question of Darcy a little more. Wickham tried his luck again. His curiosity was piqued, especially since Elizabeth had blushed a moment ago when asked about Mr. Darcy. "So does Mr. Darcy have a lady's affections yet?" he inquired.

Her heart fluttered and thought about how he danced with no one but Miss Bingley and Mrs. Hurst at the Meryton Assembly and how he didn't seem to enjoy himself then. She thought about how his eyes smiled when he danced with her at Netherfield. *But that was when no one was watching! He can have no feelings for you!* The longer she took to contemplate Mr. Darcy's different manner during the Meryton Assembly, versus the dance she had with him, the worse she got confused.

It was only at the sound of Wickham's step that she realized she had not answered him. "I am afraid there is one particular lady who has her eyes set on him, but he does not seem to care to notice her in that way. In fact he seems to avoid her even though she is his best friend's sister." Feeling the shame of talking so rudely about Mr. Darcy to someone she barely knew, she said, "I am terribly sorry Mr. Wickham, I should not be talking so of someone when they are not here to defend themselves. I must be off." She dropped his arm and nearly ran to the direction of Longbourn. She got around the bend and realized that she had left her book by Charlotte's house on the road. She didn't want to run into Wickham again so she waited half an hour to head back for it. All the while she thought about the nice Mr. Wickham and the proud Mr. Darcy. Why had she been so forward with her opinions? She usually held those sort of unkind opinions close until she understood them better and even then she knew better than to gossip to someone else about it! Perhaps she felt even worse for saying such unkind things because she was not as convinced of Mr. Darcy's prideful nature as she sounded.

*****

Darcy could not believe his eyes. What was Wickham doing here on the arm of Miss Elizabeth? He had recognized her light pleasing figure immediately before him and he led Calypso off the road and into the brush. They were walking his way when he soon recognized Wickham's confident strut. Why was he here? And how did he know Elizabeth? How can it be? The last he knew, Wickham was still chasing women in brothels and recklessly gambling any money he found.

As they approached, he heard his name spoken. "Are you fond of Mr. Darcy?" was the question . . . *Hmmm, yes, what does Elizabeth think of me . . . what? Proud?* A certain degree of pride was appropriate for the Master of Pemberley! He listened closer. Oh, no, she had heard him at the assembly say that awful comment about not being handsome! He had regretted it the moment it had left his lips, but he never imagined that it would have made its way to her ears. He listened closer as Wickham said something he could not make out and it made her blush. No! First Georgiana and now his Elizabeth? He reminded himself that she was not *his* Elizabeth, and from the sounds of it she wanted nothing to do with him. He sat down on the moist ground. They were out of earshot anyway. *My valet will not appreciate the grass stains on my breeches.* He sat there contemplating for quite a while what this meant. How could she not like him? Hadn't she enjoyed the time at Netherfield? Hadn't she smiled at him while dancing with him? And those looks! The half-smiles with one eyebrow arched in that teasing manner. Surely she has some feelings for him! So much for offering for her! How could she not at least admire him? He was wealthy, and many young ladies had commented to him about how they thought him handsome. He knew he was well-read, as was she, and they had shared a few conversations about books at Netherfield. She seemed to challenge his every thought, which was such a refreshing tone as most ladies just agreed with him and offered little intelligence to the conversation. He stood up. *Surely she must care a little about me.*

Finally he got up and took his horse and walked it towards Meryton. His mood was low indeed. He must find a way to warn Elizabeth about Wickham! He led Calypso on and almost mounted her when he saw a book in the grass. It was titled *Evelina*. *Is this not the same book Elizabeth was reading at Netherfield and tapping her foot so temptingly in the library?* He picked it up and paged through it. Yes, he was sure it was hers. It had the same water stain on the front leather. He remembered it well because as he was "trying" not to look at her in that library and "trying" not to be seduced by the gentle tapping of those tiny slippered feet, and "trying" not to watch her lips move with the words of the book . . . he focused hard on the book. Yes, it was hers. He knew it was at best a flimsy excuse to pay a call at Longbourn, but perhaps he could return it to her. He told Calypso, "Looks as if we will get to see her today afterall."

He had hardly turned his horse around when he caught sight of her coming around the bend humming a bouncy tune. He knew that tune. It was the same one they danced to! Could she be thinking of him and their dance together?

He spoke then, obviously startling her as she looked up in alarm, "Miss Elizabeth, if I am not mistaken, this is your book. I was walking and found it, you must have . . ."

She closed the distance between them. "Oh! Yes, I dropped it when I ran into an acquaintance. Thank you." She reached her hand out for it.

He hesitated, keeping the book near his person. "Perhaps I might walk you to your destination? The sun is getting close to setting and I would hate for you to walk alone in the dark." *Please, please say yes!*

"Oh, no, I just came back for my book." She held her arm out again, but when he didn't give it to her she raised her eyebrow and said, "Mr. Darcy, what do I have to do for you to give me my book?"

His breath caught as he smiled and thought of a few good ideas, but none of them involved her keeping her reputation intact.

She looked at him in as stern a way as possible and then bit her lip. *Why isn't he giving me my book?* She dropped her arm and said,

"Very well, if you insist, you may walk me back to Longbourn. But I insist you give me my book by the time we get there."

"Agreed." He let out his breath. She was teasing him. That was a good sign. He must warn her about Wickham! "There is something I would like to talk to you about."

Oh no, not another man asking probing questions that I do not want to answer! She looked saucily at him and laughed. "This sounds a serious matter!"

Although he loved to hear her laugh, he was not in a laughing mood. "I will get right to the point, a Mr. Wickham . . . he is in town?"

"Yes, he is an officer stationed here; he mentioned that he knew Georgiana and yourself."

He blurted out, "He is not to be trusted. You must avoid his attentions at all costs!"

"Mr. Darcy, it is not for you to decide who I am to be acquainted with. Is there a reason you have taken a dislike to him?"

He stopped walking and in doing so, so did she. She looked at him in that taunting look that said "defy me." Could he reveal Georgiana's near elopement with Wickham at Ramsgate? How much should she know? Would Georgiana appreciate him telling her new friend about her falling for such a mercenary man? All that man had wanted was her thirty-thousand pounds! He had not cared for Georgiana at all! Then he remembered Georgiana in her distress yesterday and how much it reminded him of that near-elopement. He still did not know the cause because Georgiana was still keeping to her room. "I must ask you a question first. Yesterday Georgiana came home from Longbourn prematurely and very tearful. Do you know what happened?"

Elizabeth had been so taken back by Wickham's presence that she hadn't had time to think about how suddenly Georgiana had left. "It was rather odd now what you mention it. I thought she was just being shy with strangers. No sooner had Lydia and Kitty came home that she left! I hardly had time to introduce her to . . ."

"So it was your sisters after all! I should have known." He started walking quickly again, torn between poor Georgiana and his dear Elizabeth. He hadn't taken but a few steps when suddenly he realized Elizabeth had not started walking also and he turned around to face her. She had her hands on her hips and her jaw was set. He knew that look. She had it in a more subtle form after every snide comment Miss Bingley made about the Bennet relations. Remembering "Oh your uncle is in trade, that must be nice," then that look. "Oh they live in Cheapside; at least they are in London," then that look. He was going to get it for sure. He reminded himself that her family's poor manners meant little to him now that he knew of his feelings for her. It was a new conviction, just days old, but he needed to be better about accepting her family for who they were. He recommitted himself to look past her poor relations and lack of connections. "Miss Elizabeth, I am sorry I interrupted you. Forgive me for what I said, I have just been so worried . . . wait, who did you introduce Georgiana to?"

"Mr. Darcy, you are unbelievable! You mock me and my family, are mortified by any public interaction with them, nearly throw me into the carriage to avoid any other humiliating occurrences, and you think you can just apologize? I think not! Now give me my book, NOW!" She reached for her book and snatched it away but in doing so her bookmark fell out. It was a white crocheted bookmark that Jane had made for her two years ago. She reached down for it at the same time Mr. Darcy did, but he was quicker.

"Your bookmark, Miss Elizabeth. But please, do not take my thoughtlessness as any sign that you should not head my warnings about *Wickham*." The way he said that bastard's name was more like a curse. He recalled himself and stiffened. "Pardon me, Miss Bennet. I truly apologize for any offense I may have caused you."

She was taken aback by this level of disdain from even Mr. Darcy. Was there really some reason to be careful around Mr. Wickham besides Darcy's pride? What had he said? "He is not to be trusted. You must avoid his attentions at all costs." She had had quite enough of Mr. Darcy! Who was he to determine that Wickham was not worthy of her attention? All her previous confusion abated as she gazed at him. In spite of any kind attention he had given to his sister,

Mr. Darcy remained as prideful as ever. Especially when it came to his so-called social inferiors, she thought. She was biting her lip, but even that couldn't hold back her next remark. "Well, perhaps Mr. Bingley should not invite the officers to the Netherfield Ball he promised next Tuesday! Then I would not have to choose between a man that has a selfish disdain for others and a man who is charming and handsome." She snatched her bookmark and marched towards Longbourn.

The look of scorn on Elizabeth's face was grave indeed. Selfish disdain? Charming and handsome? It didn't take him long to figure out which man was who. *She hates me.*

*****

I must do something! But what? Elizabeth will not listen and I have already tried to warn her. Remembering her words, "It is not for you to decide who I am to be acquainted with," he knew she was right. He had tried to warn her but it was not his place to do so. *Perhaps I could warn Mr. Bennet.* But not in person— a letter would have to suffice. But could he trust Mr. Bennet to keep the story of Georgiana in confidence? It was a story that, if widely known, could ruin Georgiana. Darcy did not know Mr. Bennet well, and although he looked like a sensible man, he was still married to Mrs. Bennet. An anonymous letter would be best. He sat down on his writing table and started writing out the most painful memory of coming upon Georgiana and Mr. Wickham a mere day before their planned elopement. As he wrote, the pain became fresh all over again. It hurt to think he had procured the services of Mrs. Younge without truly looking into her references. It pained him that he had been so impressed with outward manners that he did not recognize the special needs of Georgiana at the time. It pained him that Wickham, who was one of his closest friends growing up, could be so inherently bad. Even his own father had been deceived by the charming ways of Wickham. There were several times since his father died that he felt that each experience with Wickham would be the last, but he was always wrong. He doubted that this time was any different. Somehow he felt that Wickham was up to something. At least this letter would help protect Elizabeth. He continued writing until he was spent. He couldn't quite figure out how to close the letter. He had decided to make it anonymous, but how should he sign it? He decided that "a concerned observer" would suffice. He sealed it without his usual crest and sent it by way of express.

He then pondered all that had happened in the last two days. Miss Bingley said that the Bennet sisters came home with officers. Wickham was an officer now stationed here in Meryton. Both Miss Bingley and Elizabeth mentioned an introduction of some sort. The level of distress Georgiana had was great indeed. It suddenly hit him. Wickham must have been one of the officers at Longbourn! That would surely explain Miss Bingley's description of how quickly and "nearly rude" Georgiana had left. Yes, poor Georgie ran into that blasted Wickham! He now understood why Georgiana was so distraught. Wickham! How could one man bring such turmoil in his life? And now he was influencing Elizabeth! Charming and handsome indeed!

No matter the degree of anger he felt for Wickham, he could not stop the heartbreak he felt upon hearing how Elizabeth thought him prideful and how he had a "selfish disdain" for others. Selfish disdain? He had never had the ease that Bingley or his cousin Colonel Richard Fitzwilliam had in meeting new people. He never seemed to smoothly grasp the importance of a conversation when he was not familiar with the other party. He wasn't witty and rarely even teased his own sister! Yet he was drawn to these types of people. Richard, Bingley, Elizabeth, and if he was being honest, at one time, even Wickham. They all seemed to have the social ease to talk freely and without restraint. It seemed to him that their confidence was far greater than his own. But how could she interpret his lack of confidence and social shyness as pride? It didn't make any sense to Mr. Darcy. No easy answers came to him, no matter how long he thought on it. One thing was for certain, Elizabeth didn't know him well enough; she needed more time to get to know him. Perhaps the better explanation for her interpreting his behavior as prideful was that he didn't know her well enough to feel comfortable and be relaxed. It was so much better at Netherfield. He felt more comfortable in a small setting and especially with Georgiana there. Perhaps a small setting was the answer to this problem. If he was going to show Elizabeth that he was indeed pleasant he would have to have more interactions with her. Now that he had admitted his feelings for her, thanks to Calypso, he wouldn't avoid her anymore. Fighting the feelings that were stirring in him was the only reason he didn't seek her out as often as he would have liked at Netherfield.

*****

Mr. Bennet didn't usually get letters by way of express. It came late in the evening and he went to his study. No identifying marks or crests were on it which made him all the more curious. Who could be sending something of an urgent manner at this time of evening? He opened it and read:

Dear Mr. Bennet,

It has come to my attention that a certain officer named George Wickham is stationed in Meryton. I have a long standing relationship with the man and I feel I must warn you on behalf of your daughters. It pains me to reveal an incident that occurred in spring this year, and I must impress upon you my strong desire for your continued secrecy on the matter.

I had employed an older lady to be a companion for my fifteen year old sister. It was not long before the two took a holiday to the beach at Ramsgate. Mr. Wickham schemed with this companion to encourage private meetings and unchaperoned walks, which led to my sister feeling very much in love. Mr. Wickham then enlisted the companion's help in convincing my sister to elope, all the while promising the companion a handsome share of the thirty-thousand pound dowry given upon said marriage. I happened to surprise her the day before the proposed elopement and she confided in me. If I had been just one day later he would have succeeded! Mr. Wickham had only mercenary motives as he left her heartbroken as soon as I made it clear that he would not get a farthing. He is not to be trusted! I cannot emphasize this enough!

I recognize that this may be difficult to hear, but I am under the impression that he has been calling on your daughters. I pray you will be prudent in your decisions on this matter.

From a concerned observer

Mr. Bennet folded the letter back up. He placed it carefully on his desk and wondered about this man Wickham. If Wickham truly was mercenary then there was no harm to his daughters as they had little dowry and all of Meryton knew that! The masculine handwriting never mentioned any other motives or dangers besides financial ones. He had heard his Lydia mention Mr. Wickham, but only about how charming and handsome he was. Perhaps he had better look into Mr. Wickham and meet him himself. He picked up his book and relaxed back into his chair. *Perhaps another day.*

*****

"Well, Denny! I think Meryton has many prospects that will be quite the source of, shall we say, entertainment? I can think of a few muslin skirts around here I would like to be raised," and then as an afterthought as he saw the barmaid was near enough to hear, "in dance, that is." Mr. Wickham smirked and brought the whiskey back up to his lips. He knew he was well into his cups but his heart was light. Mr. Darcy of Pemberley, here in Meryton!

Mr. Denny said, "To the young, beautiful ladies of Meryton!" He raised his glass and heard the crack of glass against glass as they toasted. Denny wasn't raised the son of a steward of a wealthy land owner like Wickham, nor did he go to Cambridge like Wickham but he had seen his fair share of "society." He had been raised in a shady inn along the road to London since he was six years old. Although born to a gentleman, his mother was widowed early on and none of his "gentlemen" relatives took them in. His mother was forced to work as a barmaid just to have food on the table. And growing up with a mother as a barmaid meant he'd been drinking whiskey almost since he could remember. This was why he could keep his head about him during high stakes card games like this. Not with Wickham, however, for that man could keep his wits about him when he drank.

Growing up, Denny had seen gentlemen come in their fine clothes on their way to London and stop at the inn and "accidentally" brush up against his mother or outwardly grope her as she served them. He saw her place coins in her breasts and sneak out to the alley where soon enough, so did the said gentleman. No, he did not have any respect for those who called themselves gentlemen. He chose the militia so eventually he could give them their marching orders! So far his six months had been time well served. It seemed the red coat was quite useful with the ladies and he'd met many friends that seemed to have the same taste for women that he had.

"Denny, I feel my luck is changing!" Wickham looked at his cards in his hands and the last few coins he had in front of him. *Well, maybe not at this game tonight, but it is changing.*

Denny was a little nervous as he looked at his own hand; it was good, but not a sure bet. He had already bet quite a bit hoping for that ace or jack to come along. His winnings were substantial and Wickham already owed him six months' salary! If he didn't know where Wickham was day and night, he would certainly be demanding payment. Wickham must have a pretty good hand to feel his luck was changing. "Luck? Who needs luck? It just takes knowing your enemy's weakness to make your own luck!"

Wickham smiled mischievously. "Too true, too true. To knowing your enemy's weakness!" He raised his glass and clanked it with Denny's before he drained it in one swallow. He called for another round of drinks.

"And who gonna pay for it mist'a, you already owe me for them last two weeks!" the barmaid said.

"I am feeling quite lucky tonight, Velda! Now off you go!" Wickham said.

He had asked around town about Mr. Darcy and his friend. It seemed his friend, Mr. Bingley, was amiable and well liked, but not Mr. Darcy. Surprise, surprise! The man didn't have a charming bone in his body. But for Darcy to submit himself for such a long time in a small country town was unusual indeed. With further investigation it seemed that his friend Bingley was quite smitten with the eldest Miss Bennet. And the young Miss Darcy was calling on both Miss Elizabeth and the eldest Miss Bennet which left only Miss Elizabeth. Was Mr. Darcy enamored with Miss Elizabeth Bennet? He smiled again. Yes, she was quite beautiful and amiable. Surely she wouldn't fall for a man like Darcy unless . . . yes . . . she must be mercenary. Rumors that Bingley was having a ball at Netherfield were spreading and he and the other officers were invited. It seemed they needed a few more gentlemen. Perhaps the ball would be the answer to this conundrum. He looked up to Denny who had just drawn his card and his lip twitched. *Oh no, looks like I have lost this round again,* Wickham thought. That twitch was a poorly disguised smile that Wickham noticed on Denny every time he got the card he wanted. But losing one card game wasn't going to spoil his mood tonight. Darcy might very well be in love and that was going to be his ticket to the easy life. *Finally!*

Finally, Denny thought! *A jack!* The whiskey came and Velda left. Denny then said, "Are you going to draw or fold?" It was already one o'clock and he knew soon they would be asked to leave.

"Me? Give up? I think not! Not until I get what should have been mine long ago. There was a time, Denny, when I had my sights on a lady with a dowry so large that I would have never wanted for a thing. That plan was spoiled by our dear Mr. Darcy. Like I said though, I believe my luck is changing. I have had an idea that will pay you double what I owe you if you are interested. Double or nothing?" Wickham put down his poor hand of cards and saw Denny look at them and smile.

"Well, sir," said Denny, reaching for his winnings at the same time flashing his better hand of cards in Wickham's direction, "double or nothing is my kind of game. From that smirk on your face it seems there is a handsome lady involved?"

"Indeed, indeed." *More importantly, Mr. Darcy would finally get what was his due. And it seemed money wasn't the only weakness of this particular enemy.* No, losing that hand was worth getting Denny's help, and he would need it this time.

*****

"A Mr. Wickham and Mr. Denny," said Mrs. Hill, the housekeeper. Elizabeth's heart started to race. She looked to Jane whose expression had already flashed surprise in Elizabeth's direction. Last night Jane had finally got Elizabeth to talk about Mr. Wickham's obvious regard for her.

Remembering the conversation was troubling. Jane had been so sweet as she said she saw nothing but "charm and good taste" in Wickham. "He is most handsome!" Jane had said.

"Yes, I did not know someone could have such blue eyes! When he looked at me it was like he could see right through me!" Elizabeth had colored slightly just remembering the piercing gaze when he bowed over her hand. "But he is so bold! One wonders if he is truly charming or if he has learned the art of flattery and does not mean all he says!"

"Lizzy, I saw nothing odd about someone who speaks his mind in such a charming manner. If it was not true that would be one thing, but we all know you are handsome."

Elizabeth loved her sister Jane more than anyone in her family, but she was always so positive and trusting that it sometimes became a fault rather than a virtue. That was one of the reasons she followed Jane to Netherfield in the first place. Of course, Jane was ill and needed help, but there was an element of concern since it looked like her favorite sister was in serious danger of losing her heart. Jane had only good things to say about Mr. Bingley, and although Elizabeth could tell he was very lively and amiable, she wanted to see for herself how he interacted in his home. How did he treat his sisters without the formality of a social setting? How did he treat the servants? And more importantly how did he act when Mr. Darcy wasn't around? Elizabeth feared that Mr. Darcy had a great deal of influence on Bingley in all matters of importance, large and small. Most of these fears had been put to rest at Netherfield while Jane was sick. Bingley was truly a good man who cared for Jane. His attention to both their needs had been extensive and greatly appreciated.

Elizabeth sighed, "Oh Jane, do you ever question the motives of someone without assuming the motives are all good? I admit I am flattered by his obvious regard, but we hardly know each other and yet he continues in that way!" She then told Jane about meeting him while reading her book and how he had asked about Mr. Darcy. "I could not help wondering why he was so curious. If he was a close family friend like he claims to be, why does he not ask Mr. Darcy himself?"

Jane looked thoughtful, "Maybe Mr. Wickham and Darcy have not been close lately. People grow apart all the time, Lizzy. Or maybe distance has been the problem; Pemberley is a long way away."

"I got the impression that he was looking for more than to be reacquainted with him. It was like he was hiding some secret from me! I would love to see how they react when face to face with each other. That will tell me a lot about them both. Imagine, boring Mr. Darcy and charming Mr. Wickham in the same room!"

"Oh Lizzy, if you accuse me of seeing the good in others, I must accuse you of seeing the drama and faults of others! You judge so quickly. And I must say you are positively decided on your opinion of Mr. Darcy. It makes me wonder if you truly feel such distaste for him as you say you do. After all, he has been most polite and accommodating to you. For example, when Miss Bingley talked about all those things that make a lady accomplished . . . Mr. Darcy spoke up and said a lady needed to be well-read as well. Lizzy, he knows you are an avid reader and you were reading a book at that very time!"

"Jane, this is the longest speech you have made in a year!" Elizabeth teased, trying to direct the conversation away from Mr. Darcy. After meeting him on the road to Meryton, Elizabeth had felt terrible that she had been so rude to Mr. Darcy. He really had been different since Georgiana came and seeing that side of him was somewhat confusing. Not only because she was trying to understand him, as well as her possible misjudgment of him, but also because she seemed to be emotionally invested to a certain extent. She was embarrassed that both her father and Jane had made suggestions that Elizabeth had feelings for the man.

"Nevertheless, Mr. Wickham's attentions must be difficult for you. It is the first person to show you preference since Mr. Goulding's nephew."

Elizabeth flashed Jane a teasing smile. "At least with him I knew I was simply a piece of meat for sale!" The two of them laughed for quite a while.

"Well, I for one, am very much looking forward to the Netherfield Ball and getting to dance with Mr. Bingley again," Jane said wistfully.

"I too would love to dance at the ball with Mr. Dar . . . I mean Mr. Wickham!" Elizabeth could not believe she almost said Mr. Darcy! Oh, how embarrassing! Nothing could be further from the truth! Right? She did not mean to say she wanted to dance with Mr. Darcy, did she? All this talk of the gentleman left her quite decided on the matter. *I want to dance with* Mr. Wickham!

Jane gave her a small knowing smile and patted her hand. "I know you do. And I am sure you will get your chance. Mr. Bingley said the officers were invited."

Her mother's shrill voice returned Elizabeth's thoughts to the present as now the two officers were standing in front of them, waiting to be seated.

Mrs. Bennet could be heard calling up the stairs to Lydia and Kitty, "Hurry, hurry! They are here!" She could hear Lydia's voice grumble something about company. "It is the officers!"

Rustlings of skirts and some other commotion could be heard as Kitty and Lydia hit walls, most likely from pushing and pulling each other while they ran down the stairs, each obviously trying to reach the sitting room before the other. Lydia reached the bottom of the stairs first and smoothed her skirts before lifting her head up to the two gentlemen who had watched the whole commotion with delight. "Mr. Wickham, Mr. Denny, it is a pleasure to see you again!" Lydia said as she gave her best smile.

Wickham spoke up first and formally addressed the whole room, his eyes resting briefly on Elizabeth, "We had such an enjoyable time a few days ago; surely you do not think we could stay away from such beautiful ladies!"

Mrs. Bennet ushered them in and then saw Mr. Bennet in the door of his study quietly observing the chaos.

Mr. Bennet had heard Mr. Wickham being announced and thought he had better make his presence known and finally meet the gentleman. The two officers had not yet noticed his presence so he cleared his throat and they turned around. "And who might these men be? It seems my book is less diverting than it was a moment ago." He raised the book in his hands which still had a finger in it holding his place.

"Oh Mr. Bennet, you try my nerves! This is Mr. Wickham and Mr. Denny, they are the *officers*!" Mrs. Bennet said.

The way she said "officers" was meant to imply something important but Mr. Bennet didn't seem to understand. All he knew was that this was the so-called mercenary man spoken of in the anonymous letter.

"I can see that from the uniform," Mr. Bennet said dryly, then turned to the officers, "It appears you know my daughters. Perhaps you would like some tea? I am feeling a little parched myself." Mr. Bennet then walked into the sitting room and found his favorite chair which offered great light from the window for reading. It also offered the best spot to observe the visitors who had now found their own chairs. He noticed that Denny sat nearest to Kitty, across from Elizabeth, who was on the chaise next to Mr. Bennet's chair. Then Lydia led Wickham to the chaise opposite of Elizabeth, and sat much too closely to Mr. Wickham for Mr. Bennet's taste.

Lydia started engaging Mr. Wickham in conversation; some silly remarks about a bonnet she just purchased. "Would you like to see the bonnet?" Lydia asked jumping up and nearly skipping to the front entrance.

Elizabeth was looking at Lydia with a frown on her face. *I am sure Mr. Wickham does not want to see your new bonnet, Lydia!* Elizabeth saw Lydia look out the front window.

"La! It is Mr. Bingley and Mr. Darcy! Oh, and we were sure to have a fun afternoon!" Lydia marched back to the sitting room and hastily plopped herself back down by Wickham.

Jane looked to Elizabeth with both concern and amusement showing in her eyes. *Mr. Darcy and Mr. Wickham in the same room? This will be interesting!* Elizabeth glanced at Wickham and saw him straighten his posture a little. He shifted his feet slightly and looked at Elizabeth and smiled. It was the subtlest change, but she still noticed it and wondered to its import.

"Oh, Jane!" Mrs. Bennet cried, "It is *Mr. Bingley!*" She then turned towards her eldest daughter and motioned for her to sit up straighter, and then Mrs. Bennet gave Jane a knowing grin. The rest of the conversation was halted knowing that more visitors would be formally announced any moment. Elizabeth was so curious she couldn't find anything to say. Mrs. Bennet was scheming on how to replace Jane where Elizabeth was in order to encourage Mr. Bingley to sit with Jane. Lydia was rolling her eyes, thinking how her visit was ruined by the boring Mr. Darcy. Mr. Wickham was smiling at Elizabeth. Kitty was too embarrassed to speak because Denny was looking right at her. Jane was smoothing her skirt and crossing her ankles. Mr. Bennet had opened his book but was closely observing all of the above with not just a little bit of interest, especially the attentions Wickham was showing to Elizabeth.

Hill announced the arrival of the second set of gentlemen in the space of five minutes with slight frustration. "Mr. Bingley and Mr. Darcy."

The gentlemen entered with pleasant smiles on their faces and bowed to the Bennets, who had all stood to greet their visitors. Looks were exchanged all over the room. Elizabeth's gaze traveled from Mr. Wickham to Mr. Darcy. Mr. Bingley was searching for Jane, and beamed when he saw her. Wickham was amused as he looked at Mr. Darcy who had obviously not noticed him in the room yet, for Mr. Darcy's eyes were on Elizabeth and Elizabeth alone. Mr. Bennet watched Elizabeth wring her hands in her nervous way and he assumed it was only because Mr. Darcy was so keenly looking upon her.

Mr. Darcy could not believe how beautiful Elizabeth was with the afternoon sun behind her almost making her glow. Her cheeks had a gentle rose color to them that matched the pale pink gown she wore. The gown had two pleats in the center of the bodice that accentuated her slim but feminine figure. He could not believe that he had ever said she was "not handsome enough to tempt me." Her eyes were so bright and mischievous today. He assumed she looked away from him because of his intense evaluation of her presence. He looked away and reminded himself that if he was going to win Elizabeth's admiration and change her view of him he would have to be charming. He could do that. He could be charming. *What should I say?* He then turned to Mrs. Bennet who spoke in hushed tones and motioned with her hands for Elizabeth to go tell Hill that they would need tea for their visitors.

Darcy watched Elizabeth look confusedly at the servant's call bell. She opened her mouth to say something . . . *Yes, what impertinent remark will we have come out from your delicious lips? Something like, "why can we not just ring for tea?"* Then Elizabeth closed her mouth and obediently headed for the kitchen through the dining room. Darcy's eyes followed her until she nearly collided with the servant bringing the tea out of the kitchen. It seemed the servants must have anticipated the group's need for the tea. He flinched as Mrs. Bennet's shrill voice demanded that Jane go sit by her father on the chaise.

"He may need something, my dear."

Ahh, the matchmaking skills of Mrs. Bennet are clearly at work. Darcy also reminded himself that if he was going to make up for the accusation that he had made about Elizabeth's sisters causing Georgiana's distress, he would have to handle Mrs. Bennet better than the past. His love and admiration of Elizabeth meant accepting her family, no matter how uncouth they were. Mrs. Bennet offered the two gentleman seats with purposeful motions for Bingley to sit next to Jane who had done as her mother had told her. Elizabeth returned quickly, followed by the servant with the tea.

I hope I did not miss Mr. Darcy recognizing Mr. Wickham, Elizabeth thought as she entered the room again. *No, it does not appear so since Mr. Darcy is still looking at me. Whatever could he mean with that smile?*

Darcy then bowed to her deeply and spoke, "Miss Elizabeth, you look well this afternoon." *Was that charming enough? Should I say something else?* He had been the first to speak since Mrs. Bennet had offered them a seat and he felt uncomfortable. He watched as Elizabeth nodded her thanks and took the chair closest to the chaise which left him the only empty chair between Mrs. Bennet and Elizabeth. *Perfect. I am close enough to engage her in conversation and show her a little more of who I am.*

Elizabeth studied Mr. Darcy's countenance closely. It seemed she was about to witness a very interesting exchange. She looked quickly to Mr. Wickham who was sitting slightly taller than he normally did, but otherwise seemed to have a pleasant demeanor and did not appear all that nervous.

Mr. Darcy pulled his eyes away from Elizabeth and for the first time noticed that there were other visitors in the room. He had been so taken by Elizabeth's presence he didn't even acknowledge anyone else. He heard Lydia giggle and his eyes veered to that direction. That was when he saw him. *Wickham!* He was looking right back at him with the smallest smile on those lying, but according to Elizabeth, "charming," lips, and then Wickham leaned forward and made an ever so small seated bow. It would have been more like a tip of the hat if Wickham was wearing a hat. Darcy was slightly more prepared than Georgiana had been to see him, but it didn't make the experience any more pleasant.

Elizabeth saw it then, the change in Mr. Darcy. He no longer wore that small smile. His shoulders lifted to their full stature and seemed to grow wider at the same time. His eyes narrowed slightly and his lips turned inward into a straight line. So tight were his lips that they seemed to grow white with tension. She waited as the atmosphere in the room seemed to drop a few degrees even in spite of the sun pouring though the west-facing windows. And then, suddenly, it all changed. Darcy smiled broadly and chuckled. *Mr. Darcy laughing? Whatever could this mean?*

A confused Elizabeth then said, "Mr. Darcy I believe you know Mr. Wickham . . ." Elizabeth waited for a response before she finished, and then turned to the officers and continued, "Mr. Wickham, this is Mr. Bingley," and turning to Bingley, "and that gentleman next to Kitty is Mr. Denny. We had just seated them when your arrival was announced." She glanced back at Mr. Darcy to gauge his demeanor, but it wasn't all that necessary as he was still chuckling slightly.

Mr. Darcy thought to himself, *charming, remember to be charming.* "Ah yes, I have known George since we were young enough to wrestle." He turned to Wickham and spoke to him directly, "I have not seen you though since . . ."

"Mr. Darcy and I went to Cambridge together," Wickham said quickly. He sent a knowing smirk to Darcy in return.

"Too true, although you were a year behind me, and if I recall, you never finished. Was the life of a scholar too difficult?" He couldn't help himself. Wickham was a disgrace and Darcy couldn't stand even looking at him, let alone watch him smile politely. He could remember many times where college life was quite fitting for

Wickham, specifically the social scene and the womanizing. Yes, that part of Cambridge had suited him well. Wickham never seemed to study but seemed to get the grades he needed. Although Darcy could never prove he was cheating, it seemed highly probable at the time and even more so now.

Wickham saw this for what it was. Mr. Darcy was once again trying to put him in his place. *Is this how this is going to play out? Right here in front of your dear Miss Elizabeth? Very well, I am game.* "Cambridge was the most incredible experience of my life, but I did find that it did not suit me like I expected. I should have liked to go into the church and take that living your father so generously gifted in his will, but we both know why that did not happen."

How dare he mention my father's will so publicly! Mr. Darcy looked briefly away from Wickham and gauged the faces of the rest of the room. Mrs. Bennet looked confused. Mr. Bennet was sitting up and leaning forward, his expression quite amused at the spectacle in front of him. Lydia was bored and seemed to be looking to change the subject. Jane was looking at her hands, embarrassed. Bingley was astonished but was close-lipped, and Darcy didn't dare look at Elizabeth. "Yes, George, we do know of my father's wishes. It is a great pity, then, that you declined the living and decided to go practice law . . . but that did not work out either, did it?" He turned to the confused Mrs. Bennet to clarify some things, "Mr. Wickham was the son of my dear late father's steward. His good looks and charm worked his way into my father's heart and will." Then turning back to Wickham, he broadened his grin and chose his words carefully. "I always thought you turned down the parish because you did not like taking orders . . . but from the look of the uniform, it seems you have reconsidered taking orders."

Elizabeth could not believe what she was hearing! Mr. Darcy and Mr. Wickham were having a verbal duel right there in her sitting room! She looked to Mr. Wickham to see how he reacted to such a blow. He had shifted his weight slightly. Then he glanced at Elizabeth briefly before turning his eyes back to Darcy and said, "I rather think I would have enjoyed making sermons and helping those less fortunate than myself. Many do not seem to have the ability to speak kindly with those less fortunate." He lifted his chin slightly as he said that last bit. The glare aimed at Mr. Darcy sent a chill down Elizabeth's spine. Elizabeth looked back to Mr. Darcy. Although the words themselves were revealing enough, it was the manner in which they had unleashed them that made Elizabeth shudder. It was as if they had said "on guard!" and were fencing at this very moment, with smiles on their faces all the while!

"Many people ask for help when they have the means, ability and talent to help themselves to be self-sufficient. Financial generosity is not the only form of generosity, Mr. Wickham," Mr. Darcy fired out in what he knew was a less than charming manner. *I am losing myself in front of all these people! It is time for this to end.* "Bingley, I believe I have monopolized the conversation, and I have kept you from your purpose in calling."

Mr. Bingley sat up straighter and looked much relieved. The air in the parlor was lighter, or at least he knew it would be once he made his announcement. He reached into his coat and brought out a folded paper and said, "It is official. Netherfield Ball is to be held in four days and you all are invited!" He grinned as he could tell it truly did lift the spirit of the room.

Squeals and giggles could be heard from the two youngest Bennets. But it was not what took Elizabeth's attention, for she was watching Jane's reaction. There was a gentle smile as she and Bingley's eyes were locked on each other. It was so sweet! *They love each other so much!* The room had erupted in cries of excitement and exclamations of how greatly they would anticipate such an event.

Darcy interrupted her thoughts. "Miss Elizabeth? Will you do me the honor of dancing the first set with me? I would be honored if you would." He tried to smile as charmingly as possible.

Before staying at Netherfield, Elizabeth had been fearful that Darcy did not approve of Jane and Bingley. There was never anything said or done but he seemed to frown whenever Bingley showed any particular attention to Jane. It was like he was scrutinizing Jane and tallying marks on the side of either "worthy" or "unworthy." During her stay at Netherfield, she became more confident that Darcy didn't have as great an influence over Bingley as she once thought. Mostly because Bingley was so openly concerned about Jane, and how else should Darcy react to genuine concerns over someone's health? She did know, however, that Bingley still listened to Darcy's opinions and often before offering his own he would defer to Darcy's. If Darcy still had an influence on Bingley and subsequently, her sister's very happiness, there was little else to do but consent to dance with Mr. Darcy. She took a deep breath and thought for the first time how grateful she was that her sisters were giggling so loud that her mother didn't hear Mr. Darcy's request. *That is all I need, my matchmaking mother getting an inkling in her mind that Darcy had feelings for me. I can hear her now. "Ten thousand a year!" No, he thinks me far beneath him. After all, it is only one dance with him.*

"Miss Bennet?" Darcy addressed her more formally this time, concern reaching the corner of his eyes.

"I am sorry; I was lost in thought. I accept." Elizabeth let out her breath and noticed so did Mr. Darcy. She then quickly looked away to avoid acknowledging the broad grin on his face that she couldn't quite understand. *How strange a request! It is just a dance!*

Conversations waxed and waned, and the two officers began to take their leave. Elizabeth stood to properly say her farewell. Mr. Wickham made his way towards Elizabeth, glancing quickly to Mr. Darcy, who remained seated. He bowed deeply, once again keeping his eyes on Elizabeth. "Miss Elizabeth, would you do me the honor of dancing the first set with me at the ball?"

She colored slightly and said, "I am sorry. It seems that one has already been taken."

Wickham flashed a look at Darcy who had a small grin on his face that was obviously poorly hidden. "I see. Well, perhaps I shall have to stand in line as it seems your company is in high demand. But who could not be enamored with your beauty?" He didn't dare look directly back at Mr. Darcy, but Wickham could see out of the corner of his eye Darcy's lips tighten and his shoulders square a little. *So Darcy has asked her for the first dance already? Yes, my plan will work out to my liking quite nicely.* The officers then left, both in very lively moods for rather different reasons.

Mr. Darcy was in a poor mood and no longer wished to be "charming." Elizabeth had very nearly ignored him throughout the rest of the visit. He didn't know what to think of it. He kept trying to engage her in conversation but he could come up with little else besides the weather to ask about. He tried to ask about the book she was reading, but she gave brief answers and seemed to turn her attentions elsewhere. It was in this mood that he decided it was time to pull Bingley away from Jane and take their leave. "Bingley, you promised to show me the northeast fence that needed mending. Perhaps now is a good time before the sun sets." He saw Bingley's countenance drop, but he agreed it was time as well.

They took their leave and as soon as they had exited Longbourn, Bingley let out a hearty laugh and said, "Darcy, pray do tell me what happened in there!"

"Whatever do you mean?" Darcy inquired.

"I mean you and Mr. Wickham! That, my dear friend, was the closest thing to a cock fight I have ever witnessed!" Bingley's face was smiling so broadly that Darcy suspected his cheeks must hurt.

Darcy bowed his head and mumbled, "I was trying to be charming." Darcy pressed on but Bingley caught up and slapped him on the back.

Bingley laughed so loudly that the ladies at Longbourn were sure to have heard. "Charming? You had best keep the cock fighting to a minimum if you expect to be charming, my dear friend."

Chapter 3

The Bennets spent the next four days in varying degrees of anticipation for the Netherfield Ball. Lydia and Kitty, with Jane and Elizabeth as their companions, made numerous trips to Meryton to buy the necessary gloves, ribbons, and flowers. Fancy hairstyles were practiced and decided upon, but minds were changed repeatedly. Mrs. Bennet was perhaps the most undone, as she couldn't stop talking about how "this was surely going to be the night that Bingley asks for Jane's hand in marriage!"

After they were all squeezed into one carriage, Elizabeth finally began to feel some trepidation for the night ahead of them. In a short while she would be at Netherfield again, and so far, all she had to look forward to was her dance with Mr. Darcy! Why hadn't Wickham asked for a different dance when she told him the first was taken? She struggled with how she felt about each man. Wickham was too bold and from what she heard four days ago, Wickham seemed to have some serious faults. He had gained Darcy's father's favor, even offered a living in his will, yet he was an officer instead. He never finished Cambridge, and seemed to have shifted from wanting the living, to a preference for law, and now seemed to prefer a parson's lifestyle of servitude. Somehow his natural charm and flattery did not seem to fit well with that sort of existence. She had a sense that Wickham led a very daring and "free" life, especially with the ladies. His lines were too smoothly delivered; in fact, they felt almost practiced. It was along these lines that she convinced herself that she would be not be hurt if Wickham never asked her to dance a set with him.

Mr. Darcy, on the other hand, was an enigma she could not puzzle out. In frustration, she had attempted to stop trying to read his character. But as they neared Netherfield, her thoughts were most definitely drawn to him. She thought of his soft smile he had given her numerous times; this was always brought on slowly, starting at his lips and finally reaching the corners of his eyes. He was, she had to admit, handsome when his eyes smiled. She thought of his sweet sister and how Georgiana had praised him: "I could not ask for a better or more considerate brother. He anticipates my every need." Or when speaking of Pemberley, "All the servants are so devoted because he is so fair and generous. We almost never have servants leave because they know they could not have a more caring master." Yes, she could see Darcy being generous and devoted. He seemed to be, if nothing else, a deeply devoted brother. With Georgiana, he seemed to have an intensity about him that made him complex. Perhaps, Elizabeth conceded, even passionate. She thought about the passion he expressed in their conversations about books they had at Netherfield. Yes, she decided, perhaps Mr. Darcy wasn't as proud as she once thought. At the very least, it seemed he was more complex than haughty and spiteful. And it was only natural, wasn't it, that he should be more comfortable in front of some more than others? His disdain was evident for Mr. Wickham, though! She laughed out loud in the carriage at the memory of the verbal duel a few days ago. Her attentions were brought back to her family when she caught her father's watchful gaze.

Mr. Bennet noted the laugh curiously, but remained silent. The carriage had pulled to a stop and the groomsman opened the door to hand out the ladies. Lydia, of course, scrambled to get out first, and nearly knocked Kitty down in the process. Before Elizabeth left the carriage, Mr. Bennet reached for her arm to slow her progress. Unlike her sisters, he thought, she seemed to demonstrate a strange uneasiness about the ball. When all the others had exited, he turned to Elizabeth and said, "Now dear, do not fret over the evening. There will be many gentleman and officers ready to take a twirl with you."

Elizabeth sighed inwardly. She could take her father's teasing but not this strange sensitivity. In an attempt to lighten not only her own mood, but her father's as well, she teasingly said, "Now, Papa, I plan on having the night of my life. In fact, I would venture to say it will surely be life-changing!"

He smiled. "Is that so? Well, do not let me detain you from your fateful evening, my dear. I would hardly want to make you miss your dance with Mr. Darcy!" Mr. Bennet watched Elizabeth's reaction and sure enough, she blushed. There was surely some attraction towards the man.

Elizabeth looked shocked and confused. How did her father know about the first dance? "How . . ."

"Fathers have good eyes and ears, my dear Lizzy. It may seem— and granted it is sometimes true— that I never listen to those around me, but I notice a lot more than I let on. This has served me well in dealing with your mother's nerves. Now go, enjoy the evening." He leaned forward and kissed her on the forehead.

She exited the carriage and then turned back to her father. "In that case, Papa, I anticipate a highly entertaining evening for you, as Mr. Wickham and Mr. Darcy will both be in the same room again, and we know how the last meeting went!" She laughed brightly at him then.

*****

Darcy had been watching for the Bennet's carriage and he was not disappointed, as it was one of the first to arrive. He motioned to Bingley, who was greeting his guests, that the carriage was here. Bingley had asked him to keep an eye out for Miss Bennet. As it served Darcy's own purpose as well, he didn't object to performing such a task. It had been four days since he saw Elizabeth, and he was anxious to be in her presence again. He watched as all the Bennets besides Elizabeth and Mr. Bennet filed out of the carriage. He feared she was ill and not coming, but continued to watch with hopeful anticipation that she would indeed step out into the night. Bingley joined him now as the other Bennets made their way to the door. *Where was she?* He took a step forward, hoping to get a closer look, when she finally made her way to the door. He first saw her pale silvery purple gown when she stepped out of the carriage. Her neckline was rounded but modest, and had a fringe of darker lace at the center that matched the lace around the bodice. She wore white flowers in her beautifully braided hair that was wrapped into the most charming bun that had a single silver or white ribbon weaved into it. She turned back to the carriage and said something to her father who was exiting the carriage behind her. He found himself entranced by the short ringlets at the nape of her neck but when she turned around, he was mesmerized by her smile. Her chocolate curls were styled in ringlets that framed her face nicely and he could hear her vibrant laugh even through all the commotion of the Bennets.

Elizabeth caught up to her family and was witness to a very endearing look from Bingley to Jane which made Jane blush most becomingly. Elizabeth thought Jane looked more beautiful tonight than ever, and laughed softly as she realized Bingley was mimicking her own thoughts aloud. *It is more evident than ever that Jane will have a love match.* She smiled at the thought and wondering idly if she would ever get married. Were there two such Bingleys in England?

"Miss Elizabeth," Darcy said interrupting her thoughts, "I have never been as moved as I am right now."

Elizabeth assumed he had been watching the exchange between Bingley and Jane as well, and did not see his dark brooding eyes on her. "Yes," she said, touched by the attention to his friend's romance. "They do seem to be the picture of the perfect attachment."

Mr. Darcy was almost relieved that she seemed to not catch the essence of his comment. He attempted to calm his heart, which was beating louder in his ears than the musicians in the next room warming up. He tried again to compliment Elizabeth. "Yes, Bingley and your sister do seem to enjoy each other's company, but I find the whole night seems to have a somewhat magical feel to it. May I say how nice you look?" His hand reflexively reached up for those ringlets on the side of her face and brushed one away from her eye.

Elizabeth, startled by the touch, finally turned towards him and saw the look on his face. He was not looking at her, she thought, but rather through her . . . as if he was deep in thought. When his hand brushed the lock of hair away from her face, she felt quite conscious of how a gesture could be construed. "Mr. Darcy, might I remind you that that kind of gesture . . ."

He lowered his hand quickly and then clasped both tightly behind his back. "I am sorry, the hair was in your eye, I . . . I . . . I have no excuse, please forgive me." He looked sheepishly around and luckily it appeared no one had noticed. *Why do those eyes bewitch me so? This is not starting off well.* "It will not happen again, Miss Elizabeth, I promise."

He then turned into the ballroom, without even noticing the teasing quizzical look Mr. Bennet gave to Elizabeth. Darcy also didn't see Elizabeth shrug her shoulders and arch her eyebrow back at her father before entering the ballroom as well. *Papa, I will not be intimidated or teased tonight.*

Mr. Bennet just chuckled. No matter how hard Mr. Darcy and Elizabeth tried to be discreet, it was impossible for a father to miss their obvious attraction and flirtation. He assumed they had their reasons for not being open with their feelings. Perhaps Darcy could not bring himself to propose to a girl of so little fortune. His eyebrows drew together. He could not see Darcy being the sort of man to take advantage of a girl, and he knew Elizabeth had enough sense to avoid any kind of secret courtship. Whatever their attachment, he knew, he could assure himself that it would resolve itself in time.

Soon enough the musicians were ready and Darcy knew he had to face Elizabeth again. He chastised himself firmly in their time apart to keep his thoughts and especially his hands to himself. This next half hour would be trying in this new commitment as their persons would be not only near each other, but their hands would be touched and even held at times out of the necessity of the dance. He allowed himself one more glance at her fine figure before he addressed her. "Miss Elizabeth, I believe this is the dance you promised me." He extended his hand out to her.

She turned around and looked at the offered hand, before she arched an eyebrow saucily at him and teased, "So it is, but can I trust you and your hands, Mr. Darcy?" She had been longing for the opportunity to tease him about that awkward moment near the front door a few moments ago. But when she saw him flush deep red, she paused. Upon seeing his discomfort, somehow *she* was the one who most wanted to apologize. "Come now, Mr. Darcy, I was only teasing. And I believe if we do not hurry we will miss the beginning of our dance."

He took her offered hand, but couldn't think of a thing to say. Everything that came to mind was ridiculous and would only embarrass him further. Instead he gave her a weak smile and led her to her place. He continued in his embarrassment until the dance started and Elizabeth stepped forward with the rest of the ladies, curtsied, tilted her head down and to the left, then glanced up back at Darcy and gave him one of her moving smiles. He relaxed a little and stepped forward with the rest of the gentlemen, bowing more deeply than the others. He then smiled at Elizabeth. The men stepped back into place and the dance began.

Although the gentle pace of the music was calming to Elizabeth, it was not enough to slow her speeding heart as she looked at Mr. Darcy's graceful form. His posture was erect and he carried himself with smooth, easy movements. She noticed that every time they came together and their hands met, he would look her directly in the eye and his own would grow darker. The dance continued in this way for quite some time. Elizabeth was so moved by each encounter and look that she could hardly count on her feet to make the appropriate movements. The dance was one where both hands came together briefly for a spell and for that brief moment she was face to face with Mr. Darcy right before they turned. She would color each time the dance came to this particular movement. *Why does he not say something instead of look at me in that way?* She found her own thoughts were veering towards avenues that she had never gone before. *What would it be like to be held in those arms?* She blinked quickly and tried to chase these foreign feelings away. *This was Mr. Darcy! He would never . . .* Mr. Darcy interrupted those thoughts when he spoke for the first time during the dance.

"I believe our time is almost at an end," he said.

She found herself relieved to be speaking and able to avoid those intruding thoughts. "I believe so, Mr. Darcy."

"May I say how I have enjoyed our dance?"

"You may, but one must not bear false witness." She smiled easily back at him.

"And what makes you think I have not enjoyed myself?"

"Why, there has been no conversation of any sort. Not one word!"

He looked thoughtful. *I felt as though our bodies spoke volumes!* "But sometimes, surely, silence is golden. Somehow I feel idle talk of the weather would not have made the dance more enjoyable." They then came together one last time with both hands touching and he was overcome with her beauty. He inhaled cautiously. *Yes, I was right. She smells of fresh linen and lavender.* What a perfect way to end such a perfect dance. Right before he turned, however, he caught a strange movement behind Elizabeth and recognized the form immediately. Wickham was standing off to the side grinning widely at Darcy. Wickham's eyebrows rose slightly and his grin grew deeper when their eyes met. Darcy frowned. *What is Wickham planning? He is up to something, I know it!* Darcy suddenly was reminded that Georgiana was here in the same room as Wickham and he was struck with fear. Where was she? His eyes danced around the room and caught sight of her with Miss Bingley by the refreshment table, both looking at him dance with Miss Elizabeth. Georgiana had an amused smile on her face, while Miss Bingley was glaring heatedly at them.

Elizabeth saw Darcy's countenance change. Had her teasing finally ruined something for herself? "Are you ill, Mr. Darcy?"

Darcy looked back at Elizabeth. "No, forgive me. I was distracted. I do have a special request to ask of you, however."

"Well, you must do it quickly, as the dance is almost over."

"As you wish. Would it be acceptable for Georgiana to keep close proximity to you when you are not otherwise engaged? She is not yet out, and I think she would greatly benefit from some looking after. I, of course, will dance with her, as will Bingley . . ." The song ended, and the couples bowed and curtsied to each other. He offered her his arm, which she accepted and he began to lead her to Georgiana. He then continued, "But I fear that I do not approve of her dancing with any others in the room at this time."

Elizabeth pondered this request. "I have no objections to that; Georgiana is a very pleasant young lady. But surely she is growing up and you must consider letting her . . ."

"No," he said icily, thinking of Wickham. He then softened his tone. "I simply feel she is not ready." It was all he had time to say before they had arrived at the side of Georgiana and Miss Bingley.

Mr. Darcy greeted them politely and then asked Miss Bingley for the next dance, causing her to absolutely beam with pleasure. Before he escorted Miss Bingley to the dance floor, he leaned near Georgiana's ear to whisper something quietly.

Georgiana gave a slight nod before she spoke to Elizabeth. "Miss Elizabeth, would you care for some refreshment? Although I was not dancing, I feel like I have been sucking on a rock!" Elizabeth laughed at the image of the proper Miss Darcy actually sucking on a rock. She consented and both went for some lemonade.

The next few hours of the night were spent pleasantly for Elizabeth. She never was without a partner and would always ask her partners to return her to Georgiana. Georgiana must have gotten strict orders to stay where she was because she did not venture far from the refreshment table. Elizabeth noted that she was excruciatingly shy in this formal ball setting and would only briefly greet those she was introduced to. To Elizabeth, Georgiana seemed to be quite anxious the whole night. Charlotte Lucas was one person whose company Georgiana seemed to enjoy. They were together often, for unlike Elizabeth, Charlotte was not often asked to dance. Darcy spent a great deal of time with Georgiana, and therefore Elizabeth, throughout the night, except for the dances he danced with Miss Bingley and Mrs. Hurst. When it came time for the supper set, Elizabeth could see Mr. Goulding's nephew hailing her from across the room. She had just inwardly groaned when Darcy came up behind her.

"Miss Bennet, would you do me the honor of dancing this set with me?"

Darcy's smile once again reached his eyes, making them especially attractive. Relieved that she didn't have to dance with Mr. Goulding's nephew and his two left feet, she smiled and consented.

Darcy had never felt such relief. He was determined to engage her in conversation during this second dance, as the first dance had been nearly torturous with the silences and shared gazes. The thoughts that consequentially drifted into his mind were far from appropriate for a ballroom. Her beauty and grace had left him spell bound in that first dance. She had smiled back at him the whole time, and he had been moved with gratitude for the chance to have her all to himself for that brief time. He had spent the first dance contemplating how it would feel to hold her small frame in his arms, but stopped himself near the end of the dance when he finally spoke to clear his thoughts. He would not do the same for this dance. He knew he was in love with her, but his feelings came from more than her beauty or fine figure. It was every bit of her charm and wit. His favorite memories of Netherfield were her convictions that she expressed intelligently and with great passion. Darcy also knew if he could keep her in conversation during this second dance, he could contain his more diverting thoughts about her lips, her chocolate curls, her tiny waist, or her fine brown eyes . . . *Stop it, man! Remember, conversation!*

He offered his arm to Elizabeth before leaning into Georgiana and smiling. "You are next!"

This dance contained more laughter then smiles this time as they engaged each other in topics most diverting. Darcy was pleased to find he felt he was more relaxed than he had been before. Her laughter was music to his ears. *Perhaps*, he thought, *I was at least a little charming?*

They turned together towards where they had left Georgiana but they could not find her. A sudden bout of anxiety overcame Darcy and he very nearly panicked. He scanned the whole room. *Where could she be?* He scanned the room for the other person he had been keeping his eye on, Wickham. He was with Lydia and Mr. Denny.

Seeing his anxiously darting eyes, Elizabeth said, "I am sure Georgiana is freshening up for the dinner meal. What could happen to her at a ball?"

He pushed his anxiety down and focused on Elizabeth, "You are quite right, Miss Elizabeth. Would you like me to get you your food?" She nodded and he escorted her into the dining area and pulled out her chair. He was still full of trepidation, but when he returned with the food, he found Georgiana sitting next to Elizabeth with her own plate. "Georgie, where had you gone? We were worried about you!"

Elizabeth laughed softly. "I have to say 'we' had nothing to do with it. I suspect your brother thinks there is some fierce creature here at the ball that is waiting to devour you." She caught a glimpse of Mr. Darcy's frown out of the corner of her eye. Perhaps she had better not say her next teasing comment. *What did I say?* She turned to Georgiana who had the beginnings of tears in her eyes that she was blinking away quickly to control. *Oh dear, my tongue has done it again.* Although what it had done, precisely, Elizabeth was not sure. She reached for Georgiana's hand and held it tightly. Elizabeth might not know why Georgiana needed comforting, but she could at least hold her hand. They all ate in silence for a spell.

Jane and Bingley were only two seats away to the left, while Mrs. Bennet and Mrs. Long were across the table to the right. Mrs. Bennet's voice was as shrill and loud as ever. At first her topics were mercifully benign, but then Mrs. Long asked about Jane and Mr. Bingley. Elizabeth winced. *Not now, Mother! Bingley will hear you!*

"Oh, it is very nearly settled!" her high voice screeched. "I see nothing but wedding bells and trousseau shopping in the near-future! I would not be surprised if he asked her this very night! What a fine man for my Jane to catch! Mr. Bingley has five thousand a year, you know!"

She went on in this vein for nearly ten minutes. Elizabeth was embarrassed and pulled her eyes off her plate to see if Jane and Bingley had heard. Jane's complexion was a deep red and she was no longer eating. Mr. Bingley was looking at Mr. Darcy with concern. So it seems that her mother's voice was overheard by poor Mr. Bingley— and Mr. Darcy as well! *Now look what you have done, Mother! Mr. Darcy will influence Bingley to leave, and your "nearly settled" engagement will never happen!* She too was no longer hungry and raised her head ready to look straight on at anyone who dared meet her gaze. Luckily, the only one even looking at her was Mr. Wickham. He was standing a few feet away behind where Sir Lucas and Charlotte had just seated themselves. Once he caught her gaze, Mr. Wickham bowed slightly in acknowledgement. He smiled briefly before he turned and left. She had been having such a good time that she hadn't thought much about Wickham before now. She wondered if he would still ask her to dance. There were usually only a few sets after the meal and she knew she would have to accommodate Mr. Goulding's nephew for one of them. *So be it. I had already decided that I would not be hurt if Wickham did not ask me.*

Elizabeth was all too eager to resume dancing. Sure enough, Mr. Goulding's nephew found her out immediately after the meal. She graciously consented but inwardly groaned. During the dance, though, he stumbled a few times but fortunately seemed to have improved from the Meryton Assembly. There he had hardly known which way to turn and his rhythm had been atrocious! Once again, as the dance ended, she asked to be escorted back to Georgiana.

"Well, at least that is over with," she said once he left her. She smiled ruefully at Georgiana.

Georgiana let out a small laugh. "Who was that? He seems to have just learned to dance, and not well at that!"

It was the first laugh Elizabeth had heard from Georgiana all night and she was grateful that whatever had bothered her at dinner was somehow better. Elizabeth looked to her with amusement. If making a mockery of the dance with Mr. Gouding's nephew was what made Georgiana laugh, so be it! But Georgiana's laughter was suddenly halted and Elizabeth noticed Georgiana's hands had begun to shake. Whatever could be the problem? *I have only seen her that way one other time— when she last visited Longbourn.* She followed her gaze to discover what was the problem, and only saw Mr. Wickham advancing with a charming smile on his face.

He addressed Georgiana directly. "You look like a fine young lady tonight, Miss Darcy! Why, I would have never recognized you so all grown up in such a beautiful ball gown! It is very flattering!"

Elizabeth had continued to observe Georgiana's strange behavior, and suddenly things started falling into place. Wickham. Georgiana leaving Longbourn as soon as he arrived . . . Mr. Darcy asking her to stay close to Georgiana . . . Her anxious state all night . . . Mr. Darcy's warnings . . . *Georgiana was afraid of Mr. Wickham! Whatever for?*

When Georgiana didn't answer, Wickham continued. "Surely you could reserve the last dance of the evening for me, Miss Georgiana?"

Georgiana's face was stricken with fear! She looked to Elizabeth with eyes that seemed to plead for help. Elizabeth turned back to Wickham and at the same time took Georgiana's arm firmly in her own. "Mr. Wickham, I believe you owe me a dance. Since the first was taken, the last will suffice." She squared her shoulders and lifted her chin towards him. She felt a small squeeze on her arm from Georgiana. It gave her confidence that she had read the situation correctly. "I will risk Miss Darcy's displeasure in stealing her dance. In fact, I believe I will be quite offended if I cannot dance with the most charming man in the room." His grin got wider and he bowed slightly to them both.

"Miss Elizabeth, your preference is well taken. I believe it would be I who would be offended if we did not have the chance to dance a set before the night is over. I shall come back at the appropriate hour." He gave Georgiana and Elizabeth one more bow as he turned and left. Wickham was more pleased than ever. *That could not have gone better if I had planned it! She is playing right into my hands!* He then left to go find Denny to update him on the plans. *I just hope that this hurts the venerable Mr. Darcy as much I think it will.* He scanned the room until he found Darcy. Sure enough, Darcy had witnessed the whole thing and wore a furious look on his face. Wickham walked away grinning, but only to find a secluded corner in which he could observe Darcy's determined stride over to Georgiana and Elizabeth. *He is fretting now, but just wait until later!*

Mr. Darcy reached Georgiana just as the tears began to fill her eyes. *How dare Wickham address her in any way!* "Georgie, what did he say?" he forcefully whispered, careful to speak so no one but the three of them could hear. Elizabeth reached for Darcy's arm to calm him. He looked down, shocked at the touch of her hand on his arm. The warmth of her fingers as well as the tenderness of the gesture was very distracting. He had to consciously turn his thoughts back to Georgiana. He took the gesture from Elizabeth as a warning that perhaps he should be more sensitive. He lightened his voice and said, "Perhaps you would like some fresh air?" He looked at Elizabeth quizzically. Elizabeth gave him a subtle nod of approval and removed her hand. The absence of her hand on his arm was noticeable. Although it was a new sensation, it seemed to have belonged there. Her feminine little hand sparked a heated sensation that ran from his arm all the way up to his shoulder.

Georgiana nodded quickly, trying bravely to control her treacherous tears, and took his offered arm.

Elizabeth watched as the two left the room and went to the balcony. She felt that it was not her place to interfere, and from the look on Darcy's face when she had touched his arm, Darcy was not wanting Elizabeth's company. She rubbed her hand absently, trying to dispel the tingling in her hand. *Poor Georgiana! What did Wickham do to cause such distress!*

She suspected the two of them most likely would be a while, so Elizabeth made the social rounds in the room, avoiding the corner where Wickham was. She greeted and talked to several friends and listened carefully to the praise of Bingley for throwing such a grand ball. She was pleased to hear Jane wasn't mentioned too often in association with Bingley. Perhaps her mother's comments would not have a lasting effect on Jane, after all.

Thinking of Jane, she made her way in her direction. Jane had been quietly sitting speaking with the young Mackrory daughter who Elizabeth couldn't seem to remember the name of. It was something like Caroline, she thought. Nevertheless, when Elizabeth advanced to where Jane sat, Miss Mackrory said her goodbyes and left Jane and Elizabeth to themselves. Elizabeth looked around to ensure they were secluded.

"Jane, is everything well?" Elizabeth asked quietly. She was worried about Jane and Bingley, in part because they seemed inseparable before that careless display from their mother, but he now seemed occupied with other guests.

"Lizzy, you must not fret over me. We all know how Momma is."

"Yes, but that does not make the mortification any easier to bear. Where is Mr. Bingley?" Elizabeth saw the color drain from Jane's cheeks. When Jane looked at her hands and smoothed her skirt, yet still didn't answer, Elizabeth asked, "Has something happened?"

Jane swallowed. "I fear he may be rethinking his attentions to me after hearing Momma go on so long. He must think me only mercenary after Momma spoke so about his money and connections!"

Noticing she didn't answer her question, she asked again, "Where is Bingley now?"

"I do not know. At the beginning of dinner he asked me to dance the set after the meal, but he never came. He said he had to speak with Mr. Darcy briefly, and then he never came to collect me! Oh, Elizabeth, must we talk about this now? I fear I may lose control if you persist! Please, let us talk of other things."

Elizabeth face burned hot and her lips tightened. She remembered Mr. Darcy saying Jane and Bingley had looked happy at the beginning of the ball, but now it seemed his true opinions had surfaced. It was hard enough for two young people to fall in love when so many marriages were arranged for mere convenience; but to have people's ignorance, or worse, malice, disrupt this match was worse! First Momma unknowingly threw her premature opinions out for all of Meryton to hear, and now it seemed Mr. Darcy was knowingly trying to separate them! If she didn't know Mr. Darcy was with Georgiana right now she would suspect he would be avidly expressing his disproval of the match to Bingley directly.

She could only surmise that Darcy had most definitely already expressed himself effectively to Mr. Bingley. She could imagine him voicing exactly how her family was beneath them. He would be detailing again and again all the disadvantages of such a match. Of course, he would do it with no thought to Bingley's happiness. If only Bingley's feelings and decisions were not so easily influenced by Darcy! Then she was angered further. It was really Darcy's arrogance that was to blame! She knew that if there was anything in her power to help Jane she would do it, but what was there to do? "Jane, everything will work out. His feelings are as strong as ever, and I am sure he has every intention of continuing the friendship." If only Elizabeth could be certain her words would remain true! If only Darcy would stop interfering!

Elizabeth was asked once again to dance and although she could make her feet follow the movement of the steps, her mind was otherwise engaged. She tried to participate in the light conversation with the officer she was dancing with, but her heart wasn't in it. It kept feeling frustration with Mr. Darcy. One moment he was thoughtful and kind, other times he was proud and arrogant. Yet again other times still, as with Jane and Bingley, he was interfering and selfish. *I cannot believe I was letting myself imagine being in his arms!* The officer she was dancing with asked her a simple question which she answered easily without changing the course of her deeper thoughts. Her thoughts drifted to poor Georgiana. *What made Georgiana so afraid of Wickham?* She hoped Darcy was being kind to her. Somehow, though, she knew he was being a caring, devoted brother, regardless of Darcy's obvious anger with Wickham. She wondered if she would get a chance to ask Georgiana about Wickham before the night was over, but realized it wouldn't be possible because there was only one dance left, and that was Wickham's. The dance ended and this time she did not seek Georgiana out because she knew Wickham would be finding her soon. Instead, she saw Charlotte and made her way over there.

Charlotte was smiling curiously at her. "I have been meaning to ask all night about Mr. Darcy, but his sister was always with you! Why is he so solicitous to you, Elizabeth?"

Elizabeth groaned. She did not want to talk any more about Mr. Darcy. Her thoughts had gone in so many directions regarding that man that she was nearly dizzy! "I most definitely would not say he has been solicitous to me more than any other in the ballroom," she said dryly.

"Oh, come now, Lizzy, Charlotte said reproachfully. "He danced with you twice and ate the dinner meal with you! I would venture to say he has paid a most special attention to you. Are you two secretly courting?"

"Charlotte! How can you say such a thing? Of course not. I would never break with propriety like that! Now I must ask you to drop the conversation immediately or we shall lose a very close friendship." Elizabeth looked sternly at Charlotte.

Charlotte closed her mouth and gave her a knowing look. "Very well, I shall have to wait and see, I suppose."

Wickham was advancing towards them. It was time for the last dance. Elizabeth didn't know if she was anticipating it or dreading it. He gave one of his charming smiles and she felt his piercing gaze burrow into her somewhat invasively. *Anticipation, definitely anticipation,* she thought.

He collected her and offered his arm then bowed charmingly to Charlotte. Elizabeth saw Charlotte blush slightly from the kind attentions of Mr. Wickham. The dance was faster paced than most of the other dances, and she found it difficult to hold a conversation easily. Wickham was being his charming self and she soon relaxed a little. Further down the line she could see Georgiana dancing again with her brother. Elizabeth kept glancing in their direction even though they were several couples away from them. She found Mr. Darcy's eyes met hers every once in a while. She wondered if everything was better or if Georgiana was still upset. She certainly didn't look relaxed. The dance called for a set of two couples to exchange partners temporarily and she always took this opportunity to glance in Darcy's direction. *He does not look happy.* She kept wondering why Georgiana was so afraid of Wickham. Admittedly he was bold, but seemed kind and didn't strike her as violent in any way. The dance had not been going long when they returned to their original partners, and she decided to try her luck in attempting to get answers to this question directly from Mr. Wickham. "It appears that Georgiana and you have not seen each other for a while."

Wickham pondered this statement from Elizabeth. *This is exactly the kind of excuse I need!* "We saw each other briefly a few months back, in the spring," he said.

Elizabeth was quiet for a moment before she asked her next question. "Did you part on good terms?"

The dance separated and they switched partners once again before he could respond, which, luckily, gave him ample time to carefully choose his words. When partners were returned he said, "Not exactly, but this is not a conversation to have on the ballroom floor." He saw Elizabeth look curious and he chose his next words carefully, "I have been looking for a female mind to help me make sense of it. I am the first to admit that I do not have a keen understanding of the complex mind of a lady. Perhaps you could help me with the situation out on the balcony after the dance?"

Elizabeth eyebrows furrowed. She knew she wanted to know what was wrong with Georgiana but she couldn't go somewhere with a gentleman and have a private conversation. There were certain rules of behavior and for good reason too!

Wickham grew anxious at the hesitant look on her face. *If she does not come out to the balcony, my plan will not work!* He tried to reassure her. "The balcony has plenty of people around. I do not think it would be improper to take a moment for some fresh air. The ballroom is just so hot and I know I, for one, will need a moment after this quick number."

She looked to the balcony and it did seem that there were at least a few people out there. It was true, it was hardly improper to get fresh air! And she did want to know what was wrong with Georgiana. Wickham was smiling at Elizabeth charmingly. His blue eyes were kind, and from what she could tell, trustworthy. "I believe I would like to step outside as well." He smiled back at her.

The dance was only halfway through when Elizabeth noticed people were already departing for home. Bingley had not danced the last set, and was saying farewells to those departing. He seemed happy, and turned to look in Jane's direction. She was near the end of the row dancing with Mr. Goulding's nephew's two left feet. This made her laugh; Jane was so kind that she probably didn't even notice his terrible rhythm or misplaced steps. Although she was smiling at Mr. Goulding's nephew, Elizabeth could tell in a moment that Jane's eyes were sad. Her sister kept glancing in Bingley's direction. *If only there was something I could do to help her— I would do it in an instant!* Her thoughts were interrupted by Wickham.

"You seem very distracted. I usually do not have to contend with others for my partner's attentions. I hope you are not rethinking getting some fresh air; the air is getting stuffier and hotter the longer we dance."

She turned her attentions back to Mr. Wickham, "You are correct, I have been distracted. I was just thinking about Jane. No, I would still like to step outside. Fresh air is exactly what I need." As soon as she had said it, she knew fresh air would help clear her mind. Walking outside usually cleared her mind of her troubles. After all, she had her reasons why she was labeled a "great walker" by Miss Bingley. She took a deep breath of the thick air and casually brushed back the ringlets on the side of her face. She was suddenly reminded of Mr. Darcy doing the same thing. He must have done it without thinking because she couldn't imagine him breaking propriety with such a gesture. She smiled at the memory because he had "promised" it would not happen again. What a strange thing to promise! Of course it wouldn't happen again; it shouldn't have happened in the first place! Once again the partners switched and Elizabeth was surprised when she realized that it was the last time they would do so. She glanced over to Mr. Darcy one more time and saw that he was looking sternly in her direction. *Why do you look at me so, Mr. Darcy? I am not doing anything wrong!* The song ended and each party bowed and curtsied to their partner. Wickham offered her his arm and they headed away from Mr. Darcy to the balcony.

Wickham felt elated as the events of the next few minutes played out in his head. He scanned the room and made eye contact with Denny. He gave him a knowing look and smiled when Denny nodded understanding. He then looked around the room for Mr. Bennet and saw him with Mr. and Mrs. Long. His smile grew deeper and he nearly laughed out loud. He looked at his pocketwatch. *Perfect,* he thought.

As soon as they stepped out into the night air she felt lighter. She had not noticed how hot it had gotten in the ballroom. The night had grown quite dark as it seemed some storm clouds had moved in and it was threatening rain. No wonder it felt so much hotter in the ballroom with this storm on the verge of arriving. She took a deep breath of the early autumn air. She could hear the whistling angry wind in the trees drowning out the conversation of those around them, which was further testament that a storm was on its way. She watched as one couple turned to go inside. The potted flowers showed their age, for it was near the end of the season and their blooms were beginning to droop.

Wickham let her have a moment to breathe the fresh country air while he checked his pocketwatch again. *Five more minutes.* He could hear the musicians had stopped playing and he knew he only had a few more minutes to accomplish his task. He stepped closer to Elizabeth and said, "I believe you wanted to help me with my problem with Miss Georgiana?"

Elizabeth turned back to Wickham. "Yes. But if you feel Georgiana would not want me to know, then perhaps we should not discuss it and go back inside."

"No, no, she would probably appreciate a friend knowing the truth. At least then she would have someone to confide in."

"She is a darling girl and I can see how troubled she is."

He sighed almost dramatically, "We were in love you know . . ." He paused to let that sink in. He gauged her reaction. Her eyebrows raised and she put her hand to her mouth. She let out a small gasp. He continued, "We were going to get married."

"Married? But she is but . . ."

"Fifteen, I know. By gads, how I know!" He put on his best pained expression and looked forlornly at Elizabeth. Then he set the bait. "Proud Mr. Darcy did not approve."

"What do you mean he did not approve?" She was thinking of how he didn't approve of Jane and Bingley; but Georgiana was a girl of fifteen years old. She looked searchingly at Wickham. "Was there some reason he gave?"

Wickham checked his pocketwatch briefly. Three minutes. He had to speed things along. He stepped even closer to Elizabeth and reached for her hand. "It was because of my social status. I was not part of the ton, and, of course, I had little money. I could have supported her though. Our love would have been enough. It did not matter to Darcy that we were in love beyond words. When he refused his consent, I very nearly cried every night for months. I never thought I would recover from the heartbreak. You have met her; she is amazing and everything a man would want in a wife, or at least I thought that until a week ago . . ." He let his voice trail off. He could tell from her curious expression that he had her attention.

"What happened a week ago?"

He took Elizabeth's other hand and stepped even closer. "I met you."

Elizabeth flushed red and felt the heat in her cheeks. She felt very conscious of his proximity to her. His face was mere inches from hers and his gaze was burrowing deeply into hers. She glanced away and tried to remove her hands from his but he held them close. She looked around the balcony and realized that all the others had left and she was alone with Mr. Wickham holding her hands! She never appreciated his boldness and never done so less than at this moment! She looked defiantly back at him and firmly said, "I never sought your good opinion, Mr. Wickham. Now if you would please release me, I must go to my family." She once again tried to remove her hands, but his grip only tightened further.

"Do not push me away, Miss Elizabeth. I thought what I felt for Miss Georgiana was love . . . I thought she was what I wanted in a wife . . . then I met you . . . I thought that perhaps you and I could . . ."

"You thought wrong, Mr. Wickham. Now unhand me or I shall scream for help."

He knew the timing could be premature but he went in for the kiss. He grabbed her shoulders and kissed her lips hard and furiously. He felt her pushing at his chest but he was stronger. Her struggles were in vain, and it almost made him enjoy it even more. He pressed harder and more forcefully in to the kiss and wrapped his arms around her shoulders to prevent her from moving. *Any moment now. Where is Denny?* Elizabeth was squirming so much he had to readjust his grip in order to lean his whole body into the kiss. *Just a minute more.*

Elizabeth couldn't believe what was happening! His hot lips pressed so hard against hers that she couldn't breathe! She pushed and pulled but to no avail! She squirmed and got one hand free and reached up and started trying to push his face away from hers. When that didn't work she started hitting him in the shoulder, but he would not stop! *Somebody help! If I do not get some air now, I will pass out!* It was with this thought that her tears started flowing. His mouth let up a little, but only enough to let her gasp for air when she heard the deep timber of Mr. Darcy's voice rescue her.

"Unhand the lady, Wickham!" Mr. Darcy bellowed. He took three giant steps towards them and gripped the back of Wickham's coat and yanked hard backwards.

Wickham stumbled a little, but was still holding Elizabeth tightly causing both to nearly fall to the ground. Wickham's arms let go of Elizabeth in order to catch his own balance and also because he was so shocked at who it was. *Darcy? It was supposed to be Mr. Bennet!* Suddenly fearful that Darcy would hit him, he stepped back a few steps. He quickly surmised that he had better get out of there, and fast. He knew that look in Darcy's eyes from when they were children together. He would tease Darcy mercilessly until Darcy reached his breaking point and struck him. Now that they were two grown men, he suspected Darcy could now do far more harm. He turned and quickly strode back through the ballroom and left in a very angry state. *Denny, your job was simple! All you had to do was get Mr. Bennet to witness Elizabeth being compromised! Then I would be in the perfect position to negotiate with Darcy on her behalf!*

Mr. Darcy saw that his pull on Wickham had nearly made Elizabeth fall as well, and he reached out for her shoulders to steady her. He watched as Wickham rapidly exited the house, leaving Elizabeth shaking and crying. From what he witnessed, Elizabeth had been resisting Wickham's advances but he couldn't be sure. With her head still bowed, her shoulders started to shake worse in his hands. Darcy was overcome with concern for her. She had always seemed so strong, confident, and sure-footed. He had never imagined her in this tearful state. There was only one thing he knew to do with a crying lady, and God knew he had plenty of experience with Georgiana. He carefully pulled her into his chest and held her. Her tears continued and he carefully drew her closer. His head rested perfectly on the top of her head, as if it was meant to be there, and he said, "Shhh, Elizabeth, it is over now. He cannot hurt you. I will never allow it." He felt her relax a little and take a deep breath but the tears were still flowing. When she didn't say anything, he continued, "I am so sorry." He leaned his head into the embrace and smelled her hair and kissed it. It was so soft!

Elizabeth at first was relieved that she was free of Wickham, but then even more embarrassed at being found compromised by none other than Mr. Darcy! Some part of her heard Wickham leave before suddenly she found herself in Mr. Darcy's strong arms. They were gentle and comforting. So different than being held by Mr. Wickham! She couldn't help the tears and knew being in the arms of Mr. Darcy should not feel so much like home! Why was he holding her? Shouldn't he be angry and judging her instead? *I am a fallen woman now!* She took a deep breath and realized how good he smelled. What made up that scent? It was spicy, and somewhat woodsy, but at the same time clean-smelling. She also smelled the threatening rain and felt the first few drops on her hair. Or at least she thought it was rain. She took another breath and calmed herself, which suddenly seemed a much easier task since she was still wrapped in Mr. Darcy's embrace. He whispered gentle soothing words but she didn't hear them. All she could think about was how good it felt to be held by Mr. Darcy! A part of her laughed inside at the absurdity of such a thought. She lifted her head and was face to face with him. His eyes were so concerned! They spoke volumes of fear and anxiety, yet at the same time were full of tenderness and kindness. She pulled away slightly, and yet he kept his arms around her. He looked in her eyes deeply, with such concern, that her embarrassment resurfaced. He reached his hand to the curls on the side of her face and pushed them to the side and tucked them behind her ear, resting his hand on the side of her head. She took another deep breath and her tears lessened. She was becoming uncomfortable staring at him and letting him touch her so. She resorted to her oft-used habit of letting humor relieve her anxiety and said, "I do believe, Mr. Darcy, that you promised that you would not do that again." She gave him a weak smile in response to his confusion.

It took Darcy a moment to realize what she meant by the comment, but soon recalled his lack of propriety in the gesture of touching her chocolate curls before the ball had started. *Only Elizabeth would find humor in a situation as this! My dear sweet Elizabeth!* He reached for her again and held her close. Instinctively he caressed her back and kissed the top of her head again. He knew the moment wouldn't last. In fact, he soon saw a most unwelcome face in the door of the ballroom followed by Mr. and Mrs. Long.

"Kindly unhand my daughter, Mr. Darcy!" Mr. Bennet was not amused at what he saw. His favorite daughter in the arms of Mr. Darcy being kissed and caressed in such a manner! He watched as an embarrassed Elizabeth and Mr. Darcy separated. Elizabeth sheepishly looked at her hands and Mr. Darcy stood taller and squared his shoulders. Mr. Darcy had just opened his mouth to speak when Mr. Bennet held out his hand to stop him. "Mr. Darcy, from the looks of things, and I saw plenty, I will be expecting a private meeting with you tomorrow morning." He reached for Elizabeth who looked shocked.

"But Papa . . . it was not . . ."

"Enough!" Mr. Bennet was, for perhaps the first time in his life, less than amused with Elizabeth. He may not have been the most involved and conscientious of fathers, but he had taught his five daughters the rules of proper behavior! Granted the youngest two seemed to have learned less than the older three, but he simply expected more from Elizabeth. "I will hear none of it tonight! You, my dear, have nothing to say to me that will change how I feel about what I just witnessed!"

"Yes, sir." Elizabeth immediately stepped forward towards the ballroom at her father's impatient gesture, and looked up to see the shock and horror on Mrs. Long's face. With a sinking feeling, she realized the woman had witnessed the whole thing as well. *Oh no! Now all of Meryton will know, for Mrs. Long is a bigger gossip than even my mother!* She glanced back at Mr. Darcy only to see he had turned his back and his head was bowed. She looked away and her tears started forming once again. She suddenly was grateful for her father's hand pulling her. Her tears, in combination with the darkness of the night, left her nearly blind.

Mr. Bennet's heart softened upon seeing his daughter's tears. After all, he reasoned, things could be resolved quite easily, assuming that Darcy was as decent a man as he appeared. Seeing her distress he tried to tease her into a better mood. "Well Lizzy, I do believe this ball ended up being life changing after all!" Surprisingly, or at least to Mr. Bennet, it just seemed to make her tears worse.

Mr. Darcy's Promise

Chapter 4

Mr. Bennet was sure to demand marriage after what he had witnessed. Mr. Darcy had been up all night contemplating what to do. The dawn was breaking in the east and he hadn't had a wink of sleep. He had thrown his cravat and waistcoat haphazardly on the floor, and sent his boots after them, hearing them land somewhere by the window. Still his body felt confined and constricted. Sleep was impossible given the turmoil his mind was in. One moment he was furious with Wickham and wanting to call the magistrate, but what crime had been committed? It was a man's world and all Wickham had done was work to ruin a woman's reputation. And the woman was not a faceless creature, but his Elizabeth! He chastised himself for not unearthing Wickham's plan in time. *I, who knew him better than anyone, and yet was still too blind to see his scheme!* Elizabeth's reputation would be ruined, and Darcy knew that he would be seen to have played a part in it.

And to be seen by Mrs. Long! She most likely would have sworn all her friends to "secrecy" about seeing him and Elizabeth embracing so intimately, effectively making certain everyone knew about it by the noon meal today. Certainly Darcy had no objection to comforting Elizabeth— far from it— nor did he even regret being found doing so. But to have people assuming a relationship or even expecting an understanding to take place was another matter entirely. Darcy was a private man for the most part. He hated when his personal affairs were written about or gossiped about.

But he could not bring himself to focus on that entirely. Every time he thought of the embrace in his mind, he would relive every touch, making his body react the same way it had then. It had felt so right! Her soft hair on his lips, her small shoulders in his hands, her face nestled in his chest, the way she looked up at him . . . *stop it, man! You are to meet with her father in a few short hours and you still have not figured out what to do! Stop thinking about last night and determine what you are to do today!* He went over the situation again but his mind drifted back to her tearful face and he was stricken with anger once again. Wickham! If only he knew what his original plan was. *Was he just trying to ruin Elizabeth? Why? Did he know my feelings for her? How?* He replayed that awful day at Longbourn where he had spoken with him in front of Elizabeth. What had he said or done that led Wickham to think he had admired Elizabeth? Surely one afternoon was not enough to surmise such feelings were present! He could have no doubt that what Wickham did to Elizabeth was done to injure Darcy. What else could interest Wickham in ruining a woman of little fortune? *Focus, man! What will you tell her father?* It was no use; he needed to be out of this confining room. He rang for his valet. Martin would not appreciate the earliness of the hour, and would regard his state of dress with suspicion, but it didn't matter. Let him think what he wished. Out of pride he went to the bed and ruffled the bed linens and pillows to make it look as if he had slept in it. *There, now it will look like I fell asleep in my clothes.*

A few minutes later his valet knocked. "Enter," Darcy said. Martin did so and regarded his master with marked displeasure. "I am sorry, Martin. I slept very ill and would like a long ride on Calypso."

"Yes, sir. Perhaps a shave as well?" Martin had seven years of experience as Mr. Darcy's valet. Darcy never outwardly stated his concerns or thoughts but by now his face was quite readable to Martin, and he could tell there was something deeply troubling his master. This was even more worrisome, because in the last few weeks he had seen a peace and calmness that hadn't been there since before Darcy's father died. That peace was no longer present today. He couldn't remember a time when he had seen his master so troubled. As he prepared to shave him, he spoke up. "Calypso is good for you when you are troubled, is she not?" Darcy gave him a questioning look. Martin knew he rarely spoke to his master so forwardly. He continued, "Forgive me, it is not my place to ask questions."

Darcy sighed. "Martin, you are a keen observer. You could be a bow street runner." It was his way of excusing the comment. Perhaps talking about his distress would help him out. He knew Martin would be discreet. "I do not know what has come over me; my mind will not focus on the task at hand! I am afraid my heart and mind will not be settled easily this morning."

His heart? Was he speaking of Miss Elizabeth Bennet? Martin wasn't a gossip, but had knew all the same that his master was partial to her. He summoned his courage before speaking again. "Yes, the heart is a delicate thing. I have learned, though, that one must listen first with the heart, and then use the mind to create roads of opportunity."

Roads of opportunity? Darcy would have to think on that a little. "Yes, well, although you are a man of few words, I thank you. I do not know what roads of opportunity could be found in this situation. You may continue with the shave." It was his way of dismissing the topic. No. This situation was far too delicate to be discussed with his valet.

*****

Mr. Bennet had been listening to Elizabeth try to get him change his mind all morning. He certainly did not want to force her into a marriage. He always wanted her to marry someone she could respect and admire. But he felt her resistance to this marriage was somewhat dramatic. He remembered her blushing brightly when he teased her about Mr. Darcy after she came home from Netherfield which only confirmed that she at minimum, had the buddings of regard for him, if not already loved Mr. Darcy. And to witness Mr. Darcy brush back her curls at the entrance of the Netherfield Ball only confirmed to him that these two had a much more intimate relationship than they let on. He was sure that was the case since he saw them embracing so intimately at the end of the ball. Yes, this would be a love match, even if Elizabeth was unsure of her feelings overall. She was scared, like all young brides were. He would listen no further to her objections to the marriage. After such a display in front of Mrs. Long, her reputation, as well as those of her sisters, would be ruined if she did not marry him. Her objections were simply not valid. Any woman would be nervous, especially when the marriage was hastened, but what else was there to do? Mr. Darcy compromised her, with at least one loose-tongued witness, and therefore there was no other option. Elizabeth would come to understand that it was in her best interest to follow her heart on the matter.

"But Father, you must hear what I have to say!" She didn't call him "Papa" this time. That kind of endearment was saved for happier times. Elizabeth had spent the morning trying to explain what had happened the night before, but he would not listen. She had never seen him behave so stubbornly. Mr. Darcy would arrive at Longbourn any minute and she was desperate. She tried a different approach and sweetened her voice. "I know it was hard for you to witness what you did. You have taught me good principles and I have learned what you wished to teach. I beg of you, listen to me before you start making decisions that will affect me for the rest of my life!"

He had already made up his mind. Hearing her make excuses was nearly heartbreaking. Mr. Bennet simply could not stop the images of his favorite daughter being held in such a manner and couldn't stomach hearing his daughter try to explain herself. He felt frustrated with her pointless efforts but more importantly, he was getting irritated and angry. This marriage was not what he had planned for her either, but it was a very good match. Her protests only made him angrier, as it seemed she was taking no responsibility for her actions. He may have all five daughters at a marriageable age but he expected them to be properly courted and with his permission! That was not how it happened last night. He simply could not bear to hear of other behavior that he may not have witnessed. He knew he should not be so stubborn; he should listen to her very determined pleadings, but this was his daughter after all, his favorite daughter! The images flashed once again through his mind. The only thing to do was to insist upon marriage. It was the only way, and it would be a good match for his dear Lizzy. Whatever she had to tell him was of little consequence; they must marry. He still could not believe his Elizabeth would behave in such a way in public! After listening to her attempt to change his mind for the tenth time that morning, he turned a deaf ear to her pleadings and motioned with his hands for her to leave his study.

She nearly stomped her foot as she left the study. How was she going to stop this incident from snowballing? She turned on her heel and nearly ran right into Mr. Darcy. Hill's announcement of his arrival must have been drowned out by Elizabeth's pleadings to her father. She averted her eyes. She could hardly risk looking at him.

"Good morning, Miss Bennet," he said politely.

So it was "Miss Bennet" now? Last night he used her Christian name while holding her in his arms, but today it was back to the formality of "Miss Bennet." Surely after the events of last night they might share some more intimacy than that. She glared at him, and his gaze met hers. His eyes seemed to be searching for something, but he bowed slightly when she did not respond. She turned and left, not giving even the slightest curtsy or nod of the head in acknowledgement of his presence.

"Come in, Mr. Darcy. My daughter is not in the best of moods, I confess, but it is a strange situation indeed. It seems all her manners have been forgotten. Close the door behind you."

Darcy entered the study and stood there silently. He had been hoping against hope to encounter Elizabeth before the meeting with her father. He was hoping for some kind of indication of what Elizabeth felt about all this and what it entailed. She had to have known that they would be expected to marry. Was their union acceptable in her eyes? Did she still have feelings for Wickham? He flinched at the thought.

Last night his attention had been divided between Georgiana, Elizabeth, and Wickham, and it had nearly exhausted him. He had missed the disappearance of Wickham at first, and it was some time before he noticed that both Elizabeth and Wickham were gone. He had never dreamed that he would find them kissing.

His first reaction had been nausea, then anger, then fear. The nausea was because his greatest enemy was kissing the woman he loved. The anger came when he realized it was Darcy's fault: he had known Wickham's nature, but had not openly exposed him. His warnings to Elizabeth and Mr. Bennet had been too cryptic, too vague. Was there more he should have done? The fear followed at the memory of Elizabeth's words: "Perhaps then I would not have to choose between a man with selfish disdain for others and a man who is charming and handsome." Was this Elizabeth making her choice right in front of his eyes? When he relived the scene, it seemed like Wickham's advances were unwanted. But did Elizabeth regret them wholly? Her heated look gave him no hope from her regarding a positive preference towards marriage. If anything, she was angry and did not want to be forced to marry him. Darcy cleared his throat and resisted the strong urge to vomit.

"Well, Mr. Darcy? Are you going to stand there and look ill? Or can I offer you some brandy?" It was before noon, but Mr. Bennet thought the situation called for a bit of brandy. Arranging the marriage of your favorite daughter when she does not wish it took a little courage.

Darcy knew his nauseous stomach was just nerves, but he also knew alcohol would not be helpful. "No, thank you, sir."

"Well, then, sit down." Mr. Bennet poured himself two fingers of brandy and swirled it in his glass. He didn't quite know Mr. Darcy's intent, but he was here and that was a start. Mr. Bennet began innocuously, with a few questions about his estate in Derbyshire. He then probed about his views on the Corn Laws, and asked about the health of his parents and learned that both were deceased. He had begun to ask about his education when Darcy finally interrupted him.

"Sir, I doubt you truly care about my views on the Corn Laws. Perhaps we should both address the matter at hand?" Darcy was nervous. He had never asked for a lady's hand in marriage before. In fact, he had never even wanted it before meeting Elizabeth. Should he have paid Mr. Bennet more respect?

A frown came slowly to Mr. Bennet's face. He didn't want to insist his favorite daughter marry without fully knowing the man, in spite of all that had happened. All he knew about him was what his family had gossiped about. Mrs. Bennet said he earned ten thousand a year. Lydia thought him boring. Jane had stood up for him several times claiming that Bingley liked him "so he must be good." And he had heard too many times to count how Mr. Darcy scorned Elizabeth at the Meryton Assembly by saying how she wasn't "handsome enough to tempt" him. It was obvious after the display last night that she must tempt him a little! He opened his mouth to speak, but then took a sip of the brandy instead. After the burning in his throat subsided, he said, "It was quite the scandal last night when right in front of Mr. and Mrs. Long that Denny officer came and told me Elizabeth was kissing a man in the most provocative way out on the balcony. If I recall it rightly, Mr. Denny's exact words were, 'Come Mr. Bennet, Miss Elizabeth has been compromised! She is kissing a man in such a way that you must stop her! Make haste!'" He gauged Mr. Darcy's reaction carefully. Did he feel remorse? Was he proud of his actions? From what he could tell Darcy's lips tightened, his shoulders squared, and he seemed to grow taller in his chair. It wasn't remorse he was witnessing and it wasn't pride. Anger? Why would Mr. Darcy be angry?

So Mr. Denny was in on it? Wickham had planned this from the beginning? If only I knew why he would do such a thing! What was he after? Mr. Darcy knew he couldn't stay silent for long as his nausea had turned to dangerous levels. He quickly poured over this new piece of knowledge. Denny was to get Mr. Bennet to witness what Darcy himself had witnessed. *Somehow compromising Elizabeth in front of her father was supposed to either benefit Wickham or hurt me. Which was it?* Wickham would do anything for money; he knew that all too well by experience, but the Bennet ladies did not have dowries to speak of. Did Wickham suspect he had feelings for Elizabeth? If he was trying to hurt Darcy, then ruining Elizabeth's reputation could be a way, however indirect, of attacking him. But was it money he was after, or the chance to damage Darcy's own chances with Elizabeth? Suddenly he knew he understood; it was both. Wickham intended to be the man in this very chair being forced to marry Elizabeth! And in doing so, Wickham would take Elizabeth away from Darcy forever. Unless, and this seemed to be a real possibility, he was going to try to negotiate money from Darcy.

Wickham was smart enough to realize that if Darcy wanted Elizabeth, he would pay handsomely to keep Wickham from marrying her. Of course! It was all too clear now. Wickham wanted to compromise Elizabeth and had hoped that Darcy would pay Wickham *not* to marry her, but instead to allow Darcy to salvage her reputation by marring her himself. It was an interesting plan, one that would have risked Wickham losing his chance to marry an heiress. He must have been quite confident in Darcy's admiration as well as his wiliness to pay anything to keep Wickham from marring Darcy's true love. But things didn't pan out for Wickham like he had planned. Darcy's mind and stomach felt a sudden wave of relief. He had spoiled Wickham's plan and now Darcy was the one being asked to marry Elizabeth. He knew now how lucky he was to have come across them when he did. For not only was Darcy willing to offer marriage, but it looked like Mr. Bennet thought it was Darcy all along who had been kissing Elizabeth in that "provocative way."

"Well, Mr. Darcy? You have sat there silent now for a good five minutes. I have watched you go from anger, to confusion, to what now appears to be excitement. Do you mind sharing what seems to have gone through your mind?" Mr. Bennet was all curiosity now.

"No, sir."

"No? I believe this meeting requires at least some disclosure of your thoughts." Mr. Bennet saw Darcy start to smile.

"Sir, on that topic I would be happy to inform you of my thoughts and intentions. I am fully aware that my actions," *and those now-thwarted actions of Mr. Wickham, thank goodness,* "now imply that I must offer marriage to your daughter. I am a man of honor and will stand by what is appropriate. If you insist on me marrying Eliz . . . Miss Elizabeth, I am willing and able to offer a comfortable home and will give you my word that she will be well cared for. I was raised a gentleman and will treat her as a lady ought to be treated."

Mr. Bennet didn't know whether to be pleased that he was offering marriage or displeased that love and admiration was not part of the speech. "Well, I am glad to hear you and I are on the same page. I must tell you, though, that I fear Lizzy is not of the same mind. She is headstrong and has tried to voice her opinion several times in the last twelve hours. How best to inform her?"

Mr. Darcy was more than a little disappointed to hear that Elizabeth did not want to marry him. He assumed her opinion of him had not changed much from what he overheard on the road to Meryton. His nausea came back again as he realized that she might really prefer to marry Wickham. Nevertheless, he loved her, and would take part or all of her heart in any way he could. He knew that if given the chance, she would eventually soften towards him and hopefully learn to at least respect and admire him. "Mr. Bennet, I feel you know your daughter best. Perhaps that is a decision for you to make."

"If our domestic peace is upset much longer, I fear it shall never be restored to this house. What do you think about getting a special license and getting this done quickly; say, in two weeks? The incident I am sure has been widely spread by now, knowing Mrs. Long's tongue. I admit that I am surprised Mrs. Bennet has not found out yet." He heard a knock on the door. "Just a moment!" He then lowered his voice and said, "If I were you I would leave soon or you will see one of my wife's nervous attacks when I tell her she will have a daughter married in two weeks!"

"I understand and I appreciate your thoughtfulness. Perhaps we should speak to Miss Elizabeth first?"

Another knock sounded at the door. Mr. Bennet smiled, "If I am not mistaken, that is probably her right there." He raised his voice, "Come in, Lizzy dear!"

Elizabeth opened the door slowly. She had waited long enough. If these two men were going to discuss her future, she wanted be a part of it. Her first glance told her that her father's wrath and stubbornness were lessened. She also saw Mr. Darcy looking at her with an expression that she couldn't quite determine— was it concern or distaste? She understood all too well that she was too late to influence the decision.

"So it is decided?" she asked her father before turning to Mr. Darcy. "We are to marry?" She raised her chin and looked him directly in the eye until her strength wavered and she looked away, tears threatening her composure. Her head turned before she saw the look on Mr. Darcy's face change to the same compassion she had seen the night before. She also did not see him blink back tears of his own from seeing her displeasure at the thought of marrying him. All Elizabeth could do was look out the window and ask, "When?"

*****

Looking back, the two weeks passed by quickly for Elizabeth. Mr. Darcy only called on her a few times and usually with Georgiana. The only liberties he requested was his offered arm when they went on chaperoned walks. He had also traveled to London for part of the time to get the special license. She was relieved that he seemed to be just as anxious about the wedding as she was. Even Georgiana, who at first seemed to welcome the union, seemed anxious and distracted. It was now, alone in the carriage with him after the wedding had taken place, that it all caught up to her.

She had been too proud to show her shock when her father relayed that she would be a married woman in two weeks. She had also been too proud to show her frustration with Mr. Darcy. He had been so kind and comforting the night before, yet that morning in her father's study he was anxious and his actions and words seemed forced. She remembered how rote and rehearsed his unnecessary proposal was. After all, it wasn't as if she could say no. What made her the most upset was that she knew there was part of her that wished Mr. Darcy wanted to marry her, but each pained expression on his face told her that he was being forced into his marriage. She had been right all along. Mr. Darcy did not admire her in the slightest. Recalling this realization while in such proximity inside a carriage only brought fresh tears to her eyes. She tried not to think of the wedding vows she had repeated just hours before, those vows which she had once imagined as sacred, but had been said without hope of a happy marriage. Her tears flowed freely as she thought of how he had said his vows with a strained, pained voice. He had glanced quickly to her as he said them, the expression in his eyes revealing the mockery and falsehoods of the vows. *Oh, how he must hate me to have placed him in this position!* She glanced in his direction to where he sat across from her in the gently rocking carriage. He seemed on the verge of speaking yet he did not.

She remembered telling Jane of her engagement and Jane's initial excitement that lasted until she saw the look on Elizabeth's face. Her tears flowed further and she did not even try to wipe them away. Her thoughts kept returning to these moments in the last two weeks, which only brought on more tears in return. She tried not to think of Jane's engagement to Bingley which had occurred only two days before. How different Jane's feelings were than hers. Jane's was a love match, but hers was clearly not. But she kept her sobs from escaping from her tightly constricted chest by holding her arms around herself, as if physically trying to hold in the pain. *If only he cared for me! Then things would be so different.* She had always told herself that if she were to marry it would only be for love. Now it was evident that her husband— a word that she still had a hard time associating with

Mr. Darcy— didn't love her. If only she could let go of the expectation that a husband should care for his wife, things would be so much easier. If her heart could just be content and not give into hope! Hope that his pained expression was concern, hope that their dances at Netherfield were as enjoyable for him as they were for her, hope that she could be comforted in his arms once again, and hope that she mattered! The tears flowed further and she very nearly let out a heart wrenching sob.

Darcy could not take it anymore. Her tears were silent but they wounded him deeply. He took out his handkerchief and offered it again, hoping she would finally take it. She looked at his face and sighed, then reached out her hand and took it this time. She did not, however, wipe her face with it, instead she just held it in her hands and turned her tear stained cheeks away from him. It was simply too much. He leaned forward and took the handkerchief from her hand and wiped her tears on her cheeks with it. He gently wiped and dabbed at the corners of her eyes. She let out a small sob of pain, her chest jerking in spite of her attempts to remain silent. *Oh, dearest Elizabeth! If you would just tell me what troubles you most. I will do everything in my power to your ease your pain!*

He hated the direction his thoughts kept leading him towards. Why was she so forlorn? Was it out of lost love for Wickham? He prayed not. She was surely too clever to be taken in by his schemes. But that kiss! He wished he could make up his mind on whether or not she was a willing participant! Then he would know for certain. Was she missing her family? Did she regret being forced into marriage with such a "proud" man? Or was she most anxious about the wedding night? He understood many women feared what would happen in a marriage bed. Growing up in the country she surely knew the particulars of what it entailed, but he couldn't be certain even of that. Nor could he imagine that her mother had given her any great reassurance on the matter. Yes, he decided, she was probably worried most about the expectations of being intimate with him. This last thought was the only one he felt he had any power to control. He would do anything to ease her anxiety and pain.

He dabbed her eyes once again. "Elizabeth?" he said softly. She slowly turned her head towards him and met his eyes. Her own were swollen and red from crying. "I do not know all that troubles you, but I can assure you that you need not worry about tonight." She looked at him, confusion clearly written across her face. *How do I speak of this with her?* "What I mean is . . ." He tried to speak delicately. "I promise not to make any demands of you as your husband until you wish for it."

There was a point in Elizabeth's thoughts where she felt she could not hurt any more than she was. All she heard him say was that Mr. Darcy did not wish her in his bed and it was too much. She let out a sob of pain, new tears forming with each word he said. *He does not wish to even share my bed?* She thought again of her first encounter with him. *"She is tolerable, but not handsome enough to tempt me."* And yet there were those engaging eyes during the dance at the ball! She swallowed her pride and tried to speak. "Mr. Darcy . . ." she began. It came out high-pitched and clipped.

"Please Elizabeth, call me Fitzwilliam or William. I would prefer it."

How could I use such a familiar name when he seems so reluctant to even marry me! And why does he keep calling me Elizabeth? I never gave him permission to do so, not at the ball when I was in his arms, and not now! She took a deep breath. They were married now and he could use her Christian name. He could call her anything he wished. She rallied her strength and cleared her throat, "If that is what you wish, I will abide by both your requests . . . I am your wife and I vowed to obey you . . ." It was all she could do to speak calmly, and she looked away again, gazing out the window in an effort to regain control over herself.

"Dearest Elizabeth, I do not wish for you only to obey. I want you to be happy!"

Why was he speaking so intimately with her? Dearest Elizabeth? She let out another sigh. It was only appropriate now that they were husband and wife. But all it did was confuse her more. His voice was soft and caring, but his eyes anxious and sad! Oh, how frustrating! If only she knew why her father insisted on them marrying when it was Wickham who was so inappropriate! Perhaps her father had refused to listen to even Mr. Darcy as he had refused to listen to her. Now he was in an arranged marriage to a woman who couldn't stop crying!

She took a deep breath and collected herself. *This will not do! I am stronger than this! I know he does not care for me but I must get control of myself.* Although the pain was raw, and she felt like unleashing her sadness, she knew her fate now. She was married to a man who did not love her.

Regardless of how comforting it felt to be in his arms or the stirrings inside her that she felt when she danced with him, he had promised not to force her into his bed. How much she even wanted such a thing was still unknown. What a strange promise to make. Certainly he could demand his rights as a husband. What man has the fortitude to avoid such a thing when they will be in each other's presence regularly? She pondered on this promise for a while. If it was true that Mr. Darcy was not attracted to her, perhaps it would be an easy thing to avoid her presence. If he was indifferent, she reasoned, he would not have made such a promise. If he cared . . . no, Mr. Darcy could not truly care for her, in spite of his professed endearments. Once again she felt overcome with emotion but bit back the tears that sprang to her eyes. This moping was not in her nature. She was what others would call a strong, confident lady. It was not in her nature to focus on the sorrow she felt. At some point she would have to learn to accept a loveless marriage. One thing she knew for certain was that she did not want to continue to hurt this way. She committed herself to try her hardest to preserve or merely erect a certain level of companionship with Mr. Darcy. If nothing else, she would be a good wife to him. She turned her head back to him and gave him the best smile she could create under the circumstances. *Yes, companionship I can live with; it may not be love, but what more can I expect?*

Darcy was so relieved. *She smiled! Thank goodness! I must have been right! She was worried about the wedding night!* He dabbed at the single tear running down her cheek and placed the wet handkerchief back in her hand. He gazed in her eyes and smiled back. He then settled back against the back of the carriage and prayed that this was a good sign. *Perhaps she might even start teasing me again!*

*****

In spite of her self-consciousness in doing so, Elizabeth reached for her reticule and took out her mirror. By now London was all around her, and by the way Mr. Darcy was acting, it would only be a matter of minutes until they reached Darcy House. She examined her reflection with consternation. "Oh dear!"

Mr. Darcy looked more concerned than the matter called for. "What is the matter?"

"I am hardly presentable! How much time do we have until we arrive?"

"Five minutes or so." In spite of Elizabeth's attempts to do so discreetly, he closely watched her pull out pins and section by section repin her hair. She folded up the handkerchief and patted at her eyes before she surreptitiously pinched both her cheeks. He had heard of women doing so to bring some color to otherwise pale complexions, but never actually witnessed it. "You are quite presentable," he said, and then added after a moment, "In fact, you look lovely." He watched as his second comment made her glance his way briefly. When her eyes met with his they fluttered before a charming blush suffused her cheeks. *Now that is how one puts color in a lady's face!* She looked back out the window and they sat in silence until they arrived.

Mr. Darcy's groomsman was waiting faithfully to open the door. "Welcome home, Mr. Darcy."

"Thank you, Anderson." Mr. Darcy exited the carriage, handing Elizabeth out before tucking her arm into his. They walked in silence to the front door where he introduced Elizabeth to the waiting butler. "Mr. Taylor, this is Mrs. Elizabeth Darcy, my new bride. Elizabeth, this is the butler, Mr. Taylor." He turned to the butler. "Would you be so kind to collect the servants so I can introduce them to their new mistress? I will just show her around a little."

"Certainly, sir!" He took the gloves and hats from them, bowing once more to Elizabeth and left immediately.

It took Elizabeth a moment to realize how firmly she was holding onto Mr. Darcy's arm. She released it slightly, but he placed his other hand atop hers. She didn't know what to make of it, but realized that he was probably putting on a show for the servants. *I am his wife now and I must remember not to embarrass him.* She was too embarrassed herself to even look around until they were half way down the hall and he began pointing out different rooms to her. She was shown the sitting room, the music room, the door to his study, and then he stopped in front of a large door.

Mr. Darcy let go of her arm with one hand while he opened the door to the library. "This is the room I most hope you will enjoy. I have great pride in it." He tried to guide her in while still holding her arm. It was a little awkward as the frame was too narrow for both to pass comfortably, but he wasn't ready to give up this simple pleasure quite yet.

Oh my! Look at all these books! Each wall was filled from floor to ceiling with books. The room itself was bigger than Longbourn's sitting room and dining room put together. There had to have been thousands of books! She could smell the leather and the aged paper. The smell filled the room and calmed her a great deal. It also helped a little with the headache that had been forming for some time. She reached her hand out, brushing her fingers against the rows and rows of books. Mr. Darcy finally dropped her arm. *Of course, now that there are no servants to watch, we do not have to perform our roles. I will have to remember that in the future and perform as a good wife should.* She fingered the bindings and looked at the many titles, most of which she had not heard of. Each book had a series of numbers and letters on the bottom. "Mr. Darcy . . ."

"William . . ." He corrected her.

She was too impressed with the sheer number of books to be disgruntled by the reminder of his request to call him by his Christian name. "What are these numbers and letters engraved on the base of each book?" She looked at him then. His eyes lit up. For a moment she could imagine what he looked like as a schoolboy.

"It is a method I heard about in France that allows one to organize and find any book in your collection. Here, come over here." He walked over to a cabinet and pulled out a drawer. She leaned over and was surprised to see that the drawer held hundreds of cards, each filed one right after another.

He pulled out one such card and showed it to her. "Each book I own has two sets of cards in these drawers. One card is filed under the title and the second is filed under the author. See here, this card in the J's is filed as *Julius Caesar* and at the bottom is the name of the author, William Shakespeare. You will find an identical card under the S's for the name William Shakespeare for *Julius Caesar*. You can find any book as long as you have the name of the book or the name of the author."

Elizabeth felt as if she should say something. "Such an impressive way to catalog what books you own," she commented.

"It is more than that. See, on the right of each card is a series of numbers and letters that correlate to the numbers you see on the books themselves. Over by the door are the smaller numbers and as the books wrap around to the fireplace they get larger."

Elizabeth was stunned. She could spend hours just reading the titles, but to have the ability to find the exact book she was looking for in a matter of minutes in a library this large was thrilling! "I am thoroughly impressed! I do not think I have ever seen a library quite this large! I am afraid if you cannot find me you should look here first. It is sure to be my favorite room."

Mr. Darcy was overjoyed at the spark of light that appeared in her eyes as she said this. "Then I shall have great pleasure in bringing you to Pemberley. The library there is three times as large."

Her eyes widened. "Truly?"

He walked over to her and took her hand in his, "Truly, but I admit you might not be as impressed as you are here. We have just started the cataloging process and it is not in any way a sanctuary. This room took nearly three months to catalog. We just started Pemberley's right before I left for Hertfordshire. I am assured that in spite of everyone's best efforts, it is still greatly in need of work."

Elizabeth offered him a quiet smile. "Perhaps I can look forward to being of assistance."

A knock was heard at the open door and Elizabeth was suddenly aware that Mr. Darcy was holding her hand. She pulled her hand away in embarrassment but then regretted it because the butler— Mr. Taylor if she remembered correctly— saw her. It would be perfectly acceptable for a husband to hold his wife's hand! Elizabeth's headache returned in full force. Each new situation seemed to draw some additional amount of strength from her.

Was it only two weeks ago that she knew who she was and how to behave? Then she had woken up each morning knowing what to expect, the only variable being the weather and her mother's nerves. Two weeks ago her shoulders were held high and proud, not tight with tensions. And two weeks ago, Mr. Darcy was just the friend of her sister's suitor. She realized she was being led back out of the library and took one more look back at the amazing scene behind her. Two weeks could change a lot of things.

She was somewhat in a daze as they walked back towards the front door. Her head was throbbing mercilessly. She let Mr. Darcy guide her and she could tell he was saying something to her but try as she might, she could hardly hear what he was saying. She realized they had stopped walking and she was being presented to an incredibly long line of smiling servants. Each time she was introduced to a servant, Mr. Darcy would say, "This is my wife, Mrs. Elizabeth Darcy." *I am sure they heard you the first ten times, why must you keep repeating it?* She tried to smile and acknowledge each servant, but they all blurred together. Mr. Darcy's speech to his servants was friendly and kind, and he seemed aware of each of their preferences and background. He would say things like, "He has served the Darcys since 1801 and has a love of apples," or "She first started as a house maid but now runs the entire first floor but I cannot get her to let me see that darling new dimpled baby boy as much as I would like," or "He may be a groomsman but you will never find a more avid reader."

His kindness to his servants was almost unnerving, but remarkable all the same, as if they were a part of his family. She had never seen such a loving and kind, almost intimate, relationship between master and servant. She didn't think she knew anything personal about Mrs. Hill back at Longbourn. At Darcy House, he seemed different. He seemed comfortable and . . . perhaps even charming? Was that what she was seeing? Her head spun a little and she held Mr. Darcy's arm a bit more tightly. She was relieved to see the end of the row of servants. She had a new home, and saw a new side to the man she had once thought she had known as much as she wished to. She touched her hand to her aching head, forcing herself to draw in a deep breath.

"Mr. Darcy," she said after the staff had all been introduced, "I should greatly like to rest before dinner."

"Of course. I will show you to your room." He dismissed all the servants but one. "Serafina, would you mind coming with us?" He turned to Elizabeth. "Serafina will be your personal maid while you establish yourself here. Of course, if you so desire, she can accompany us to Pemberley."

Elizabeth nodded. She fingered the beautiful intricate bannister on the stairs. The white and grey marble floor went from the entrance all the way up to the triple wide curving staircase. The hand-carved dark mahogany floor boards shone as if just recently polished. She felt the textured walls against her fingertips. The pattern seemed to be mesmerizing. *All this beauty is now mine?* When she reached the top of the stairs she realized her gaze was fixed on the floor. *Much like my mood has been.* The stress of the last two weeks made itself known on her shoulders worse than ever. She felt so very weary after the trying day and travel. Was it really just this morning that she married Mr. Darcy? She tried to respond to something Darcy was saying, but felt a sudden wave of fatigue overcome her, causing her vision to blur. She reached out for something to steady herself but found nothing.

Darcy saw her face pale and her form swaying at the top of the stairs. He instinctively reached out for her. "Elizabeth, are you ill?" When she didn't say anything he gestured towards Serafina. "Fetch some water and some towels. Immediately!" Darcy reached under Elizabeth's arms and legs and lifted her up quickly into his arms.

The feel of the closeness of his person, the spice and warmth of his scent, and the strength in his arms sent a tingle through her body. Suddenly she felt very much awake again, as if every sense were heightened. Her heart beat sharp and fast, and she felt suddenly far too warm. She could even hear the steady rise and fall of his breathing. It did not seem to tax his strength to support her so. She wanted to put her hands to her cheeks, which now seemed to be blazing with embarrassment. "Ah, Mr. Darcy? I feel I am recovered, you may put me down now."

At first, he had wanted nothing more than to catch her during her faint. But as Elizabeth's color returned, her eyes brightening, all he desired was to continue to hold her. He reasoned, if he put her down, she might very well collapse again. But truthfully, it was that the absence of her in her arms would be wretched. But he must. He didn't wish her to feel that he would take liberties with her at any possible moment. He pressed on towards her room, his gaze fixed on her pink cheeks, his hand trying to memorize the feel of her slender waist. He should have honored her request, but instead he relished in his selfish desires. Nevertheless, it was too late now. They had reached her door. He should at least say something in recognition of her question, but what? "I believe we have made it to your room safely." His hand let go of her waist only enough to turn the handle and enter the room.

He could place her anywhere, he knew— on the armchair by the window, at the writing desk, at the dressing table, on the fainting couch, or, of course, the bed. Almost by instinct, he stepped forward and gently placed her on the bed.

Elizabeth could not resist the temptation to laugh. *After his promise not to take me to his bed, he of course carries me to my own!* "I do believe, Mr. Darcy, that there will be talk among the servants that you carried me off to my bed the moment you had a chance!"

A smile crept to the corners of his eyes. He stepped back and looked at that beautifully arched eyebrow and teasing smile that she was obviously trying to hold back. He couldn't think of a thing to say in return to her lively comment, but he felt a wave of gratitude that she felt comfortable enough to speak so lightly.

Elizabeth glanced down at the floor in silence. Had she offended him? She was about to speak again when Serafina rushed in.

"Sir, the water and towels."

Elizabeth, grateful for the distraction, turned to look at the new maid. She was strikingly beautiful, but not in a way like Jane or any of the pretty girls at Hertfordshire. Her hair was rich and dark, and piled on her head in a simple bun. She moved gracefully, placing the towels and water down with ease. Did she detect a hint of French in her accent? She looked to be a bit older than Charlotte, Elizabeth decided, and was somehow comforted by the thought. Her thoughts were interrupted by Serafina placing a chilled towel against Elizabeth's brow. Elizabeth let her fuss over her, her mind traveling back to a few moments ago, when Mr. Darcy had held her. She was so preoccupied that she didn't notice Serafina removing her boots until one was fully removed.

"Oh no, you do not have to do that!" She felt a stab of panic at the idea of being undressed right in front of Mr. Darcy. Serafina was surely not aware of the particular arrangement between the two.

"Madam, you must lay down! You will be far more comfortable without your dusty shoes on."

Elizabeth was quite determined that she did not want to lay down. Her heart was most definitely not weak at the moment. She looked to Mr. Darcy for help. His eyes were on Serafina's hands nimbly untying her laces of her other boot. *I must stop her!* She stood up quickly and said, "I am fully recovered, thank you. I do not wish to lay down." She set her jaw and folded her arms in front of her.

Darcy had been so entranced in watching Elizabeth— even her foot was delicate and small, and beautifully shaped— that he hadn't seen her evident discomfort with him being in the room. Recognizing her silent demands that he leave her to her privacy, and knowing she should really lay down, he bowed and said, "Miss Elizabeth— I mean Mrs. Darcy, I will leave you to your maid. She is greatly experienced in service to the Darcy ladies. She even assisted with my own mother before she passed." A pained expression came across his face before he bowed and left, closing the door behind him.

Elizabeth didn't know if she should feel relieved that he was gone or confused at the strange loss she felt in his leaving. She obediently sat back down on the bed and let Serafina continue. "Is it true, Serafina?"

"About laying down? Yes, most definitely."

"No, I mean did you help with his mother before she died?"

"Oui, it was many years ago and I was quite young. I had just started in service for the late master. Now you must lay down and recover before dinner. Is there anything I can fetch you?" She slipped

Elizabeth onto the bed and laid a lap blanket on her, tucking it ever so carefully around her hips.

It was odd, Elizabeth thought, being so nurtured. Jane and she would comb each other's hair frequently but in a family of five sisters there was hardly time for any of them to be so doted upon. The changes in her new life were going to take some getting used to. "I have to admit that I have a headache. It has been there for quite some time. Is there some chamomile tea in the house?" Reminded of the soothing sensation of Jane combing her hair, she added, "And perhaps we could comb out my tresses for a time. It seems to help with my headaches."

"Right away, madam." She left, but returned in what seemed like no time with the tea.

Elizabeth sat up to allow her access to her hair. She sipped on the chamomile as Serafina began to unpin her hair. Serafina began to brush rhythmically, smoothly drawing the brush through Elizabeth's hair. Soon her tea was gone, and Elizabeth closed her eyes, letting herself surrender to the gentle pull against her tense scalp. Then Serafina put the brush down and her expert fingers helped soothe her tight shoulders and chaotic thoughts with just the right amount of gentle yet firm massage. The tension melted and her eyes became heavy. Without a word, Serafina gently guided her shoulders down to the pillow and lifted her feet to the bed.

*****

Elizabeth dreamed of a forest of cedar trees with a giant swing hanging from one of the aged branches. She felt large hands push her waist from behind, and heard herself laugh naturally in delight at being pushed. It was spring and the birds were singing. She couldn't place where she was but knew without a doubt who was pushing her. She didn't look back behind her but could hear his laughter as well and could smell that familiar scent of wood and spice. His hands were firm and yet gentle against her back. "Dearest Elizabeth . . ." he said, stopping the swing. He wrapped his arms around her from behind and placed his hands on her lower abdomen. Elizabeth looked down as well, realizing with distress that it was swollen!

Suddenly Elizabeth was wide awake. She lay in the room, overwhelmed by the newness of everything. Even the curtains were unfamiliar, with nothing here to remind her of home. She reached for her stomach. *Flat! It was just a silly dream!*

The motion reminded her, though, of how hungry she was. She looked around the room for a clock— surely it was late. It was quite dark and she could find nothing to gauge the time or how long she had been asleep. Her stomach growled loudly. Where was Serafina? She decided she would venture out to find her.

She opened the door and headed for what she hoped was the staircase when she saw a faint light under one of the doors. It flung open and she found herself standing face to face with Mr. Darcy.

"Elizabeth, how are you?" He reached for her hand. "Can I get you something?"

Right then her stomach growled again and her other hand reached to quiet it.

"Let me fetch you some food." He turned to leave when Elizabeth spoke.

"Mr. Darcy . . ."

"William."

Elizabeth once again ignored his request. The moment felt all too intimate as it was. "I was wondering how long I was asleep?"

"It is nearly midnight. So I would say about five hours. You did not answer my question, How are you? I have been very worried about you."

The look of concern on his face was distracting. Could he really mean it? Could he care? She felt her heart flutter and the heat rise to her face. No, she told herself sternly. Hope was not healthy in this area. Companionship was all she dared hope for. She may think him handsome and at times kind, but he did not feel the same for her. A wave of emotion overcame her once again. She tried to collect herself and schooled her features. *I cannot let Mr. Darcy know he affects me so!* "I thank you, but a little bread and cheese is all I need." He consented and promised to return shortly. She turned back to her room and flopped herself on the bed again. She wished she didn't have to face Mr. Darcy so often. *No, what I really wish is that he did not affect me so!*

The time ticked on as she sat in the darkness. Her headache was gone now but a different ache was starting deep in her chest. She began to realize that he would be returning soon with the food and they would have another awkward moment in her bedchamber. She could only think of one thing to do to avoid him making her heart flutter so. She quickly made up her mind and laid back down on the bed and pulled up her covers. She hadn't realized until then that her hair was still down and she groaned realizing that Darcy had witnessed her in such a state! *Being married to him will be harder than I thought.* She heard soft footsteps coming up the hall and she closed her eyes and slowed her breathing.

Darcy saw her open door but gently knocked anyway. He could make out her figure on the bed but she didn't stir. Her back was turned to him. "Elizabeth," he whispered. He could barely make out her curls splayed across her pillow. He placed the tray of food and candle down. He whispered again, "Elizabeth, your food is here." When she didn't stir he knew she had fallen asleep again. He didn't want to wake her. Just then a curl fell across her face. He reached for it, paused, and then continued. His hand had a mind of its own as it reached for that curl and gently placed it back towards her ear. He could see the shimmer of her profile dancing in the candlelight. He let out a sigh. *Being married to her will be harder than I thought.*

Mr. Darcy's Promise

Chapter 5

The next morning Elizabeth stirred slightly, her mind still foggy with sleep before she was struck with the memory of Mr. Darcy touching her hair last night while she pretended to sleep. What possessed him to do such a thing? She had stayed up hours just contemplating it. That had been the third time he performed such an intimate gesture, and he had made a promise not to do it again. Were there other promises he has made that he planned on not keeping, specifically the one he made in the carriage yesterday? And if so, why make such a promise in the first place? She found herself feeling apprehensive at the thought. Nevertheless, it was a new day and she would continue with her commitment to be a good wife and build a companionship with Mr. Darcy, starting with dressing for breakfast! She had hardly pulled back the covers when she realized Serafina was in the room and had already started to attend to her. *Had she been watching me sleep, just waiting to serve me?* She couldn't help but be impressed by the thought. She let Serafina help her out of her wrinkled gown and into her best morning gown of sprigged muslin. Her mind wandered to their travel plans as Serafina fixed her hair into a very beautiful knot. Her thoughts wandered. Did they have to leave London so quickly? Perhaps she could visit her aunt and uncle while they were here, if Mr. Darcy could bring himself to visit Cheapside. She mentally chided herself for the thought. He would at least allow her to visit them on her own. She would ask Mr. Darcy at breakfast.

Elizabeth looked one last time in the mirror and smiled. "I have to compliment you, Serafina," she said. "I have never achieved such results in such a short amount of time. You are truly an artist." Serafina curtsied and turned to put away her toiletries. Elizabeth took this as her cue to go downstairs.

She descended the stairs slowly, her gaze fixed on the ceiling above. Its dome was inlaid with gold leaf, and circled with the same dark, intricately carved mahogany she has seen on the floor boards. The rest of the ceiling featured delicately painted ivy and pale pink berries; surely a master artist at work. She knew he was rich but this was beyond anything she could have imagined; even Netherfield was outshone by this elegance. She realized this was just the London house, she could only imagine how beautiful Pemberley will be. Her mouth was slightly agape when she heard someone call her from the bottom of the stairs.

"Mrs. Darcy, I thought perhaps we might have an early breakfast. Allow me to escort you, as last night's tour didn't extend to the dining rooms or kitchen." Mr. Darcy couldn't resist a smile at the memory of how last night she had been wandering the halls in the dark trying to find the kitchen.

She smiled in spite of herself; she was hungry, she had to admit, and his deep voice was smooth and welcoming. "Thank you, I am quite famished."

They didn't even have to ring for breakfast as it was brought in as soon as Mr. Darcy had led her to her chair. Her stomach growled quietly at the display of food in front of her. Normally, her breakfast was a simple repast of toast and tea, but when she gazed at the table saw a veritable feast. Here she saw oatmeal with sweet cream, a cold veal pie, a rasher of bacon, plum and pound cake, hot and cold rolls, freshly made marmalade, and both tea and coffee.

"Forgive me," he said in response to her gaze. "I did not know what you like to eat in the mornings so I asked them to prepare a few of my favorites. I hope there is something to your liking." He relished the sight of her lovely form in a simple day gown. *And now I can see her every morning!* For the first time ever he thought, *thank you, Wickham, for being so evil to allow me this pleasure!*

The simple act of kindness made her smile and sit more comfortably. "Mr. Darcy," she said after a moment, lifting a slice of plum cake onto her plate. "Do we need to go to Pemberley right away?"

He glanced up at her with some surprise. "No, as I said before we may do whatever you prefer. Do you have a preference?"

She set her fork on the side of her plate. She knew he did not handle her relations well, but she longed to see her aunt. "I have an aunt and uncle here in London," she cast her gaze up at him, but continued, "in Cheapside, and it would be nice to spend some time with them before we leave."

A small smile graced his features. It was a good sign, he reasoned, if she felt comfortable enough to make that request. And, on a more selfish note, he had wanted to take her to the theatre and show her around a little as well. "I would be pleased to meet your aunt and uncle." Off her answering smile, he continued, "I am anxious to reconnect with a few people here in London as well, and would be pleased to introduce you to several of them. In fact, if we stayed through Saturday we could go to the theatre. Lord and Lady Matlock, my aunt and uncle, are eager to make your acquaintance."

Elizabeth wondered what the wife of Fitzwilliam Darcy wore to the theatre. One thing she knew was that nothing she had was likely to be appropriate. She looked up at him feeling lost as to what to say next, and took a sip of her tea. He seemed equally lost for words, and she devoted herself to the meal instead. What can be said between new spouses when there is no affection?

*****

She spent all the morning in the library, absorbed in books. There was a pianoforte, she knew, in the east parlor, but she couldn't bring herself to step outside of the one room she felt most comfortable in. She wondered what Mr. Darcy was doing. Working, no doubt. Or perhaps bemoaning this unfortunate marriage. She set her book down. All this idle time was not good for her mind. Elizabeth was really beginning to worry about what she would wear to the theatre. There had been no time to buy wedding-clothes, and the longer she thought about it, the more formed her idea became. It was better than sitting around doing nothing. It was London after all!

She asked the butler where she would find Mr. Darcy and was told he was in his study. She knocked on what she hoped would be the correct door and heard "enter" spoken loudly in his deep voice. She turned the knob nervously and stepped inside. He was sitting at his desk but stood when he saw it was her. His jacket was folded on the side chair and he was just in his waistcoat which was unbuttoned. She had never seen him dressed so casually. She eyed his broad shoulders and watched his cravat rise and fall with his breathing. He bowed and asked how she found Darcy House. She gave her glowing impression. They stood in silence for a spell and then Elizabeth lost her resolve and turned to leave. *Perhaps it was not such a good idea after all.*

"Elizabeth? Was there something you needed? I am really not that busy . . ."

She turned around and collected her nerves. "I was just wondering if . . . well when we go to the theatre . . . I must confess that I do not have anything grand enough for the occasion . . ."

He saw her discomfort and interrupted, "Perhaps I could show you around town and look at some of the shops. Perhaps we will find something you like. It is just under a week and I am sure they could fit a gown in that amount of time." He stared at Elizabeth for a minute but she didn't say anything. *Certainly she knows she can ask for a new dress!* He watched as her eyes still showed the anxiety of before. He thought maybe he should have been clearer.

A dressmaker would have to be paid handsomely to make a formal gown in less than a week. She was truly troubled. "I do not have my accounts ready," she said hesitantly. She knew that she had some pin-money settled upon her, but could not remember the amount. The time before the wedding had been such a blur.

"No, no," he said quickly. "I must clarify myself. Whatever you need, whatever you want, it is yours. As my wife you will be free to spend whatever you need. In fact, I will go with you today and we will get accounts set up in your name. I am ashamed I did not think of it myself. I have to admit I am not the most experienced man at dress shopping, but I could give you my input. Expense is not an issue. What was once mine is now ours."

She couldn't think of what to say! She thought of how Georgiana had claimed the servants felt him generous but she had not understood it until she saw his generosity firsthand. She was embarrassed to have asked for such a thing but truly, she had not brought anything appropriate. Feeling his generosity didn't make the blow to her pride hurt any less.

He started buttoning his waistcoat and took his jacket off the chair, "Shall we?"

"Right now?" She was hardly prepared to go out into London.

"The week gets shorter as we wait. Come, London has a great deal to see." He was ecstatic that he could spend a whole afternoon together with her. "Let me check on something first."

Elizabeth glanced around his study as he stepped out and called to a servant, speaking quietly with him before he busied himself with his watch. Soon she saw Serafina come from what she thought was the servants' quarters and addressed Mr. Darcy. Curiosity prompted her feet forward to hear the conversation but she tried to be discreet. What would he want with her maid? She listened closely as they spoke.

"Mrs. Darcy and I are going shopping for her wardrobe. I need to know what my wife might need."

Serafina started discussing what she knew she had brought from Longbourn and then offered suggestions for three day dresses, two or three evening gowns, a ball gown, new evening gloves, a nightgown, a set of ballroom slippers, and a new brush. Elizabeth could not believe her ears! That would nearly double the wardrobe she had brought with her! She was sure Mr. Darcy would not buy all of that for her! And a nightgown? Surely Mr. Darcy would not take her shopping for a nightgown! She looked away trying to appear that she did not eavesdrop but she was mortified! She blinked back tears and retrieved her pelisse from the butler who looked at her with what appeared to be sympathy. She met his gaze boldly and thought, *I do not want your sympathy!* If Mr. Darcy felt his wife's wardrobe is in need of replacement then she must accept it. She recommitted herself to the idea of being a good wife. And a wife of Fitzwilliam Darcy must look the part.

"Shall we? It sounds like we have a bit of shopping to do." He offered his arm and when she placed her hand on his arm he placed his other hand on hers.

Her embarrassment seemed to ease as he placed his hand on hers. His very touch seemed to calm her; well, all but her heart. It was beating fast and she had to focus on controlling her breathing. He handed her in the carriage and sat across from her.

They must have gone through every store on Daggett Street, a street she and her aunt never shopped on because of the prices and quality were higher than what Elizabeth could afford. In each store he introduced her as his "new bride, Mrs. Elizabeth Darcy." *Would he ever get tired of such an introduction? It is like he is proud of it!* Several shop owners greeted her with kind words, but she felt their eyes looking her up and down, evaluating who the lady was who finally caught Mr. Darcy in the parson's mousetrap. She overheard Mr. Darcy on several occasions set up an account for her personal use at any time, insisting on "no limits." She tried to express her gratitude several times, but he would not hear it. They found several dresses already made but had to peruse fabrics and patterns for the ball gown and the evening gowns. Each time they brought their packages into the carriage and headed to the next store the carriage got fuller. On the next stop, Elizabeth was measured and sized up right in front of Mr. Darcy. He sat with his legs stretched out in front of him as if he was actually enjoying shopping for women's clothing.

He watched with amazement as the dressmakers stretched measuring tapes around her shoulders, arms, chest, waist and height. He was entranced in watching her form. He noticed she kept looking in his direction and each time would look away quickly and a brief blush would come to her face. Once when this happened he gave her a grin and she in turn returned the look with an impertinent lift of her eyebrow. He had only accompanied Georgiana a time or two before, and it had offered him plenty of that experience for his tastes. But this was entirely different. Rather than watching his sister vacillate between a sprigged or plain muslin, he was watching Elizabeth select whatever gowns she would need for their life together. She was building a future as Mrs. Darcy. He had to admit, he was actually enjoying it. He went through the list in his head of what Serafina had suggested. All that was left was the slippers, gloves, and nightgown. The slippers and gloves would easily be found at the milliner's shop but he had no idea where to shop for woman's nightwear. Would it even be appropriate for him to buy such a thing? He was certain she would neither need nor desire his help with that. But Serafina had said she needed it.

The shopkeeper interrupted his thoughts. "Mr. Darcy, I believe I can have the gown ready by Friday morning but I will need to do a fitting Thursday. If the other two gowns are not needed right away I can have them ready in two weeks."

"Very well," he said. It seemed that Elizabeth was immersed in a selection of ribbons, and he took the opportunity to privately ask a question of the shopkeeper. "Where might we find a lady's nightgown?"

The shopkeeper smiled knowingly and said, "That kind of thing can only be found at Ellen's. It is around the corner to the north off Hawthorne Street."

He thanked her and then went to retrieve Elizabeth but then something the shopkeeper said tickled his brain . . . "that kind of thing . . ." *Oh no! She thought I meant something far different from a simple nightdress!* He turned quickly back to the shopkeeper and clarified himself. "I fear my wife is quite modest and prefers simple attire at night. Is there another shop that might be more appropriate?"

Her forehead furrowed up with confusion before she frowned slightly. "A new bride should shop at Ellen's. But if you feel strongly about that, then try Everette's Depot and Clothing."

"And where might that be?"

"Next to Ellen's." Her frown deepened as Darcy only thanked her before leaving to collect Elizabeth.

This time when he handed her into the carriage the packages seemed to dominate his side of the carriage. He gestured at the seat next to her. "May I?" he asked, and she nodded her assent, slipping over towards the window, leaving plenty of space for him. "Thank you." He cleared his throat. "There are only a few things left, and they should be easy to find."

Elizabeth's fears of shopping for a nightgown with Mr. Darcy resurfaced. Was he actually going to watch her shop for such a thing? The carriage went around the corner and stopped in front of a store called "Ellen's." When she peered at it, she realized with a flash that the windows were white-washed so one could not see what was inside. She had heard whispers of these sort of stores that sold scandalous clothing they couldn't advertise in their window because of what they sold. *Oh no! I have endured him watching me measured and try on dresses but I will not do this with Mr. Darcy!* Luckily he spoke up.

"I have a few purchases to make across the street at the bookstore, but I am confident you will find what you need at this store."

He handed her out of the carriage and took her arm, which she gave only with the greatest reluctance. *How dare he assume he can take such liberties and bring me to such a shop!* Her resolve to be a good wife was dwindling fast. He had promised he would not demand his rights as a husband until she was ready and she was definitely *not* ready. Just as she opened her mouth to protest, he passed the entrance to "Ellen's" and headed for the next shop. She could see from its windows that it was a simple sort of shop. He held the door open to it and she sheepishly went in. *Perhaps he is more trustworthy than I had just thought.* He introduced her once again just as before and then he left, claiming he wanted to get the book he had been waiting for. It was most certainly an excuse, but one that she was all too willing to believe. She looked over at the shopkeeper.

The shopkeeper introduced herself to Elizabeth, "Miss Tamara, madam. What can I help you find?"

It took a minute to recover from the mingled outrage and embarrassment that she had just felt. She took a deep breath.

"A nightdress," she said, and then paused before Tamara stepped towards the corner. "A dressing gown as well." She was guided to the corner of the shop where a pile of silk gowns were neatly folded. The shopkeeper showed her one and Elizabeth just shook her head. Another one was unfolded and displayed. It was a lovely ivory silk, and the bodice was trimmed with Ile d'Aix lace. She reached her hand out to it and touched the fine, smooth fabric. She had never owned such a thing. It was what she imagined herself wearing on her wedding night if she married for love. But she didn't have that kind of marriage. She shook her head. A simpler batiste gown was held up for her examination next. It was far less ornate, but the fabric was still good, and the neckline was gathered near the neck modestly. "This one will do."

The shopkeeper started wrapping it up in brown paper before she looked up at Elizabeth. "Perhaps that second one too? I am sure Mr. Darcy would be pleased."

Elizabeth truly loved the second silk one more, but when would she wear it? It was too fine for every day wear. She knew Mr. Darcy would not mind her buying two. He had been quite clear all day as he refused her protests time and time again. She looked around the store to make sure he hadn't returned. "Perhaps I could see it again?" She was embarrassed for even thinking it, but there was a spark of hope that flickered into life. Perhaps one day he might desire her and then they might have a real marriage. Hope. It felt good for a change. Relishing the feeling, she followed Miss Tamara back to the corner. She held it up to her again. She decided to buy it simply because if offered her hope. "I think I shall take it as well. If you could wrap it together?" She didn't want Mr. Darcy to see two packages.

Miss Tamara showed her the only dressing gowns she carried. There wasn't anything that seemed to catch her eye and decided that her old robe would do for now. Perhaps Serafina could mend the torn ribbon that made it difficult to fasten in the front. She took her wrapped package and headed out the door. She found Mr. Darcy leaning against the carriage with a book. He looked up and bowed to her. She flushed upon meeting his eyes, thinking again about that second gown. Someday she might be able to wear such a thing and he would see it.

"I see you found something you needed. May I take it?" He reached for the package.

She pulled back instinctively. "No!" She was not about to let him touch her nightclothes! She then flushed deeper at the intensity of her reaction. *For goodness sake! It is wrapped in paper!*

"I was just offering to put it in the carriage." Mr. Darcy flushed himself as he absentmindedly had reached for what was probably her nightclothes. "I apologize."

They made a brief stop at the milliner's and Elizabeth found a set of slippers and gloves quickly. Perhaps too quickly, she thought, selecting the first pair of embroidered slippers that were offered to her. Her heart was ready to be done shopping and ready to have

Darcy out of her constant presence. She couldn't quite say she wished to go home, because she couldn't quite think of the Darcy house as home yet. All she knew was that her emotions were nothing but tumultuous with Darcy by her side. She moved from feeling nervous, to grateful, to embarrassed, to fearful, to feeling an element of pride as he introduced her, irritated, and then finally feeling her first glimpse of hope. But right now she was at the end of her emotional fortitude. She needed to be away from Mr. Darcy. *Out of sight, out of mind.* Or at least she hoped.

*****

During breakfast a few days later there was some voices heard in the vestibule before Mr. Taylor came in and announced, "Colonel Fitzwilliam, sir."

Darcy let out a chuckle at the introduction. "Well, it sounds like we have our first visitor!"

Elizabeth looked curiously at Mr. Darcy. Who was their visitor that inspired such outright pleasure in her husband? A man entered— he was neither as handsome nor as tall as Darcy, but he had the most engaging grin. He openly and unashamedly eyed Elizabeth up and down. Who could he be? She stood to greet him.

"You must be Mrs. Darcy. Colonel Richard Fitzwilliam at your service." He bowed, and then said, "I must confess, Mrs. Darcy, it does not surprise me that he picked you as his bride. If I know anything about Darcy, it is that his taste in beauty is impeccable!"

Elizabeth colored at the forward statement. Was he a friend? A relative? She watched as Darcy and Colonel Fitzwilliam gave each other hardy slaps on their backs before exchanging teasing jests and pleasantries. He seemed to bring out the smiling eyes of Mr. Darcy.

Colonel Fitzwilliam turned to Elizabeth and said, "I hope the old man has not been too boorish for you. If you ever need a little lively company, just call on me. My cousin is far better-connected than I am, but I admit that I still cannot seem to find why others might prefer him!"

Cousin? "Well then, I shall call you Cousin!" She liked him already. It was a relief to know that not all of Darcy's relations would look down upon the daughter of a country gentleman. And besides, Colonel Fitzwilliam was so engaging. He seemed to have captivated their morning parlor with his presence and jovial laugh.

"Oh, please no, call me Richard. Only Darcy calls me Cousin and knowing him he might just not share me with you! If you have not noticed, he is a very devoted friend, cousin, brother," and while leaning towards Elizabeth and giving her a knowing smile said, "and I am sure husband." He grinned back at Darcy, who had the grace to look flustered at the statement.

"Yes, well, Cousin, thank you for your flattery. I am sure Elizabeth will make up her own mind about me." He briefly saddened at the thought that she probably had plenty of opinions about him already, and none of them were what he wished them to be. "Richard, you have come at a great time. Come, have some breakfast and catch me up on the things going around town."

"Sorry chap, I just came to give you this." He handed a letter to Darcy. "My mother would like to meet your new wife for tea today. And I must warn you that she insists you both accompany us all to the theatre Saturday."

Darcy looked to Elizabeth for her preference but she gave no sign of an opinion. "We were planning to go to theatre Saturday anyway. If it acceptable to you, Elizabeth, I would love to accept Lady and Lord Matlock's invitations."

"As you wish, sir." Elizabeth saw Darcy's smile broaden and reach his eyes. *There, that was the smile I like so much.*

Colonel Fitzwilliam turned to leave, then turned back around, "Oh, Mrs. Darcy?"

Elizabeth laughed softly. "If you insist I call you Richard, my dear cousin, you must call me Elizabeth in turn."

"Well then, Elizabeth, what do you call a cow that jumped over a barbed wire fence?"

She looked puzzled. What on earth could he possibly mean? She glanced at Mr. Darcy for an explanation, but saw only her husband shake his head and groan perceptibly. "I do not think I could say, Richard. Perhaps you could enlighten me?"

"Udder destruction!" He turned and laughed manically as he left the room.

*****

Her tea with Lady Matlock went more smoothly than even Elizabeth could have hoped for. She was very kind and graciously hospitable, and kept her conversation to light topics that were easy enough to discuss. Thankfully, Elizabeth thought, Lady Matlock had the courtesy to avoid any but the easiest discussion of her marriage. Lady Matlock insisted on confirming the Darcys' attendance at the theatre. After the pleasant afternoon, Elizabeth found it easy to consent. But, she had to admit to herself, as she left the richly furnished sitting room, she felt a little underdressed in spite of wearing her best day gown.

Elizabeth had also visited her Aunt Gardiner twice in that week, and had requested she come to the final fitting for her theatre gown. She was much more comfortable having her aunt there for that kind of thing rather than Mr. Darcy, although he did offer. It felt good to be with family and have her worries lessened. She discussed everything but Mr. Darcy with her aunt because she felt that she would have nothing but a jumble of confusion to tell. She did tell her about their day trip to the Chinese gardens and the art museum that Mr. Darcy insisted on taking her to, but she did not tell her about how holding his arm seemed to both calm and alarm her at the same time. She told her aunt about Colonel Fitzwilliam and his jokes, but she did not tell her how she was beginning to like being introduced as Mrs. Elizabeth Darcy. She told her about the delicious fine food the French cook prepared for them, but she did not tell her about how when his eyes smiled it made her heart flutter. She told her about the plans to go to the theatre and how they were to sit in the balcony in his personal box seats, but she did not tell her about her hope to look spectacular and "tempting" to her new husband. Yes, she told her aunt about everything but the stirrings in her heart. For that was both confusing and at times painful, as she was often reminded of the kind of marriage she was now in.

She now sat in front of the mirror letting Serafina create what looked like a masterpiece on top of her head. She was placing the last of two silver combs in the crown and adding sprigs of baby's breath behind them.

"I do think, madam, that the master will not be able to take his eyes off of you tonight and he will not be able to recall one thing that happened on the stage." Serafina's words were lightly accented, but the meaning was still clear.

Elizabeth appreciated her words, but still doubt overcame her as she gazed at her reflection. Would he like the dress? Would he appreciate the efforts she was taking to impress him? Would he even look twice in her direction? Serafina tightened the corset one more time before helping Elizabeth into her new gown. Elizabeth gazed at the wall, not daring to look in the mirror. *What if he doesn't like it? Will I embarrass him in front of his family and friends?* She shook her head to herself. Mr. Darcy was at the least indifferent to her appearance, and a change in her dress and hair would hardly change matters. Just then a knock was heard on the door that led to the master suite.

"That would be the master."

Serafina went to open the door but Elizabeth held a hand out to stop her. "Wait, do I look acceptable?" She knew her face betrayed her fears but she couldn't help herself.

"Oh yes, madam! You have never looked as beautiful as you do now." She then opened the door and Mr. Darcy walked in.

He entered and immediately found himself speechless at the sight of her. *Elizabeth, you are truly breathtaking!* His gaze traveled from her head to her slippered feet and back again. The skirt of her silk gown was a forest green interwoven with thin gold thread, while the bodice was made of shimmering gold silk. The neckline scooped becomingly into a point at the center. The high empire waist fit snugly under her breasts, accentuating her natural curves of her chest and waist. The rich green of the gown made her complexion gleam ivory and rose. Her hair was pulled up, and in the mirror behind her he could see several small braids looped around each other in a most flattering array of curls and braids. The combs held back the curls that often framed her face and for a moment he was saddened to not see those curls fall around her face. He then saw her eyes. He expected them to be bright and excited but there was anxiety and fear in them. He cleared his throat and tried to speak but only a croak came out. He tried again, "Have you seen yourself in the mirror?" He watched her shake her head silently. "Well, I suggest you turn around and look at what I have to endure tonight." He had meant it as a compliment but he saw tears forming in her eyes. *What did I say?*

Elizabeth bit back the tears of disappointment that sprang to her eyes. He would need to *endure* her appearance tonight? Soon anger replaced the disappointment and she opened her mouth in rebuttal. "Well, perhaps I should not go if my appearance is not *tolerable* to you. I would not want to embarrass you in front of all your friends and family." She bit her lip, stopping herself before she said more.

Darcy was confused. She was obviously offended by what he said. Not tolerable? He knew she was referring to his comment at the Meryton assembly. *Will I ever live that down? She is everything beautiful and perfect!* "Let me explain myself . . ." he began.

"No, Mr. Darcy, I believe you have made yourself quite clear." She turned around and for the first time saw herself in the mirror. Never had she even hoped to be wearing something so fine. She brushed her fingertip against her puffed sleeve, marveling at the careful construction of the pleats. She watched in the mirror as Darcy approached her from behind. He reached into his waistcoat and took out a gold chain. Careful not to disturb her braids, he reached around her neck to place a necklace there. In the center of the necklace hung a simple emerald, with a pearl dangling beneath. The shape of the chain was perfectly matched to the neckline of her gown. His hands worked to fasten it securely behind her neck, so she stood in silent awe, watching his head bent behind her. It seemed to take an enormous amount of time to clasp the necklace and she felt his breath on her neck giving her chills. His hands seemed to have their own pace as each touch or brush of his fingers on her neck seemed to extend the moment into eternity.

Mr. Darcy was having a difficult time fastening the necklace as he had never done such a thing before. The clasp was so little and his hands were shaking! *Good Lord! Just finish it already!* His gaze kept wandering back to the smooth feminine line of her neck and the loose ringlets that escaped Serafina's careful work. His hands finally accomplished the task and he stepped back, clasping his trembling hands behind him. "If I may clarify, you have never looked so tempting before and that is what I must endure tonight." He then bowed before he turned around and left the room.

*****

Mr. Darcy returned to his room feeling the heat of embarrassment. *Why did I let my guard down with her again? Her feelings for me obviously have not changed.* The flash of anger in her eyes, her silence as he fastened the necklace around her neck, and her scornful response all told him that she did not wish to go to the theatre tonight. At least not with him. Could she still be pining over Wickham? *By gads! How beautiful she looked!* His valet was waiting with his cufflinks and his everyday pocketwatch. "No, Martin, tonight I will wear the gold watch."

Martin looked at him and then cleared his throat. "Sir, I cannot find it."

"Cannot find it? Whatever do you mean?"

"I mean it is nowhere to be found. I went to retrieve it this evening, but it is not where I usually store it. I am sorry, sir, but I realize I do not remember unpacking it from Netherfield and to be honest, I do not remember seeing it after the Netherfield Ball. You did sleep in your clothes that night and I did not assist you, so I do not know where it was placed. I apologize, sir. I should have been more careful."

"Truly? We have lost the watch my father gave me when I graduated from Cambridge? It was solid gold!"

"I know, sir." Martin waited for a moment. "Perhaps the staff at Netherfield has found it when they cleaned the room."

Mr. Darcy promised to write to Bingley right away in case it had been discovered. He let his valet fasten his cufflinks and brush his coat before dismissing him. "Tell Mrs. Darcy I will be detained a few minutes," he instructed, before sitting down to pen a quick letter to Bingley.

*****

After they returned, Mr. Darcy walked Elizabeth back to her room. In spite of his best efforts, he had not been able to shake the foul mood that had descended upon him. Elizabeth had been quiet for much of the play, and every time he checked his watch he was reminded that one of his most precious possessions was missing. The watch had been one of the last gifts his father had given him. All night he had tried to pay attention to the stage, but he was too easily distracted. The few precious times Elizabeth did laugh, his eyes betrayed him and went to look at her beauty once again.

He reached for her hand before she could open the door to her bedroom. "Elizabeth, I feel I must apologize for my mood tonight. I got some distressing news prior to departure and it has affected me more than it should. You were everything lovely tonight. I hope you had a pleasant time."

She was grateful for the opportunity to speak to him in private, "I did, thank you. If I may say, the necklace is exquisite and matched my gown perfectly. Thank you."

"It was my mother's but when I saw the fabric you picked I knew it belonged on your neck." He raised her hand and turned it over and kissed the tender flesh on the inside of her wrist, his lips lingering a moment longer than necessary.

Elizabeth breath caught in her throat. He had bowed over her hand and kissed it many times, but not like that! She watched as he turned and walked to his own door. His hand reached for the handle but paused. He then looked back at Elizabeth and smiled. She gave him her best smile in return. She watched him as he entered his room and closed the door. Her heart was still pounding and she flushed pink once again as she felt the kiss still lingering on her wrist. She entered her room and rang for Serafina.

Serafina made quick work of removing the gown and undoing the masterpiece on top of her head. Elizabeth sat docile as she did so, silent pondering all that had occurred tonight. *"You have never looked so tempting before and that is what I must endure tonight."* And yet after that, he had seemed distant and quiet during the play. She hadn't even had the chance to tell him how nice he had looked in return. The news he received must have been difficult indeed.

"Serafina? Mr. Darcy received some troubling news prior to leaving for the theatre but he did not mention the details as we were so preoccupied. Do you know what it was?"

"Yes, madam, his valet could not find his gold pocketwatch. It upset the master because his father had given it to him." Serafina began unlacing her corset.

"Has it been stolen?"

"I cannot imagine it has been, madam, just misplaced. Martin takes very good care of the master's things."

She let Serafina finish her work in silence. Her mind went again to Mr. Darcy's words when he gave her the necklace. Her hand absently went to her neck but Serafina had already removed the necklace and it lay gleaming in its box on her vanity table. *I was tempting?* The thought was foreign. Her mind wandered to the many moments in the last week where they interacted. Had it only been a week? Her body felt weary, but she knew that sleep would not come easily tonight.

"Goodnight, madam," Serafina said, curtsying and interrupting her thoughts.

"Goodnight," Elizabeth said. She tried to push away the feelings she felt when he kissed her wrist but they would simply resurface unwillingly. No, sleep would not come easily tonight. She reached for her book and tried to read but her heart would start fluttering every time she remembered his hands at her neck and the breath that had sent chills down her spine. Even more disturbing were his kind eyes as he said those words.

She put the book down and walked the room, hoping to tire herself out without avail. Tomorrow was Sunday and they would be in each other's company more than they had been for the last few days. That morning they had agreed that a week from Monday they would depart for Pemberley. Elizabeth's gowns would be finished and that would be the end of their social obligations here for now. From what her aunt and Miss Bingley had told her of Pemberley, there would be plenty of places to hide. Aunt Gardiner had grown up not five miles from Pemberley in Lambton and had toured the estate several times over the years. She talked about the sculpture room, the ballroom, the painted vaulted ceilings . . . but what she had praised most of all was the gardens. Elizabeth couldn't wait to walk among the many trails and lakes she had heard about. It had been a good week since she had gone out walking, and she felt the lack of fresh air in the confusion of her thoughts. She finally settled down to sleep. Before she closed her eyes, her thoughts veered back to what Mr. Darcy had said. *"You have never looked so tempting before and that is what I must endure tonight."* She remembered once reading a book that had reminded her that "hope sees the invisible, feels the intangible, and achieves the impossible."

Well, Mr. Darcy, she thought before she closed her eyes once more. *Dare I hope?*

Chapter 6

"We should get our first glimpse of Pemberley in a few minutes," Mr. Darcy said.

Elizabeth turned to him. They had sat in silence for much of the journey, and now the window was cracked open, filling the carriage with the sounds of the road and the scent of fresh country air. Something about the place felt oddly familiar, but she couldn't imagine why. She had never been this far north. They passed by magnificent hills and cliffs, lush with greenery and groves of cedar, sweet chestnut, beech, and sycamore trees. The warm scent of cedar and sage filled the air. Although her gaze was ostensibly fixed on the land outside, she couldn't stop glancing back at Mr. Darcy every few moments.

She would have thought another week together would have clarified their relationship, but the events of last week had done nothing but confuse her further. She had watched him interact with the servants with nothing but kindness and respect. He had insisted that they invite her Uncle and Aunt Gardiner to dinner, and had been nothing but amiable and considerate in their presence, and had declared that he already considered them family. Her aunt had even commented about how "charming" he was, and had praised his intelligence and warmth. Elizabeth had to admit he wasn't the prideful and quiet "Master of Pemberley" that she once thought him to be in Hertfordshire. She didn't know what to make of this change. When had this first begun? She had to credit her shift in thinking to when Georgiana came to Netherfield. His loving embrace and kindness towards her was so endearing! Her coming had seemed to transform Mr. Darcy, and the cold man Elizabeth had met at the Meryton Assembly had become someone who smiled at her often, and was perhaps even a little charming. As she listed all of these changes, her mind seemed to protest, urging her back to her first impressions of her husband. For example, when he asked for her hand in a private audience, he had been so stiff and cold! She concluded that surely he hadn't changed too much.

Although he had been distant during that moment, he had still been kind to her. Even in the shock of realizing the marriage must take place, Elizabeth had still been determined to make the best of it. After she had given her assent, she had then paused and asked him to humor a request. She remembered keenly his words. "Whatever you wish." Those were not the words, she realized, of a man who thought only of his own pride. And when she then asked that he openly support Bingley's preference for Jane, or at least not hinder his advances in any way, he had immediately agreed. It was the only positive result of such a forced marriage that she could think of at the time.

She had once promised herself that if there was anything she could do to ensure Jane's happiness, she would do it. If marrying Mr. Darcy had any benefit, his blessing on Bingley and Jane's marriage would be enough. She had not thought much of his agreement at the time; after all, how could he oppose such a connection if he himself was marrying into what she knew he felt was a wretched family. And now Jane and Bingley were engaged. Yes, she knew why she "agreed" to marry him, or at least accepted the inevitable. It was for Jane's sake, and she hoped her sister's marriage would bring her nothing but happiness.

The question that kept eating at her, though, was why did *he* agree to marry *her*? A man of his wealth and status could have simply said no without much consequence to his reputation. She had been sure he would have told her father about what really happened, and therefore absolved Darcy of any responsibility. Still, he had offered his hand without hesitation! She would find an opportunity to ask him outright, regardless of propriety.

Elizabeth studied him, watching him look out the window of the carriage. So far he had been the perfect gentleman, and quite trustworthy in keeping his promise. He hadn't made any advances towards her or invaded her privacy. The long trip to Pemberley from London required an overnight stay at an inn and he had procured two rooms. What did the servants think about it? *Surely Serafina has noticed that I wake up in my own bed every morning and his valet, Martin, I am sure, suspects something. They have to! How could they not?* After their day of shopping, Serafina had unpacked her purchases. Although she admired all of them, it was the silk nightdress that earned the most praise. Serafina had suggested wearing it that night but Elizabeth refused, saying "perhaps another night." Twice she had set it out for her, and twice Elizabeth picked either her old nightgown or the more modest batiste gown. Serafina had seemed to take the hint and had stopped laying it out.

"Elizabeth, look, there it is!" Darcy's voice interrupted her thoughts, and she looked up in surprise as he tapped the carriage roof and they drew to a stop. "It is tradition to stop here and look at my home," he explained, and then felt brave enough to continue. "And now it is our home!" He stepped out of the carriage and handed her out, but did not release her hand afterwards. He tucked it into his arm and held it close.

The now-familiar tingling sensation caused by the touch of his arm began, and Elizabeth felt her heart beat faster. *Why does he affect me so? Will this ever get any easier?* She gazed out in the direction he indicated, delighting in the sight of a large, tranquil lake. A forest sat to its left, but what drew her attention was the grandest house she had ever seen, sitting just beyond the water. The stone building was at least four stories high and one, two . . . she stopped to count, fifteen windows wide! Decorative stone pillars framed the main door and then extended all the way to the roof. She took in the hills and boulders that surrounded the lake, amazed by the naturalness and taste of the landscape. How badly she wanted to explore all of it! *It is so large,* she thought, *I might not ever find the same path twice to explore!* Her "walking legs" itched to seek out all that Pemberley's grounds held for her.

"Welcome home, Elizabeth." He turned to look at her face.

She looked up at him, his face closer that it had ever been, seeing his dark, brooding eyes fixed on her. She had a fleeting thought that for a moment he was going to kiss her. She drew back a little. As much as she might have wanted Darcy's love, the idea of being kissed by someone who didn't love her remained painful. She drew in a deep breath to steady herself, and then was struck by a realization.

Cedar! That is what he smells of, cedar and sage! She smiled widely at her new realization.

Darcy took both her hands and held them to his chest. "You are smiling," he said, feeling a sense of wonderment. It was more a statement than a question, but she nodded at him. He felt encouraged enough to continue. "You must tell me what you are thinking."

She let out a giggle and pulled her hand away to cover her mouth, as if astonished by the sound. "You sir, do not want to know what I was thinking!"

His eyes brightened. *That is the first laugh I have heard since the Netherfield Ball!* "You are mistaken; there is nothing I want more than to know what has made you laugh. I always want to know what you are thinking." He looked more intensely at her, but then smiled broadly as well.

She laughed softly for another moment before she shook her head. "No sir, I promise, you do not!" He took her hands again, kissing each one before he held them again to his chest. Her face flushed a bright pink.

He couldn't resist; he reached up and brushed her rosy cheek with the back of his fingers. "You are blushing . . ."

How could she tell him such thoughts? As she looked as his smiling eyes that she adored, she grinned and said, "If you insist . . . but I will not explain myself!" She let out an uninhibited laugh once again and said, "You smell like Pemberley!"

*****

"Welcome home, sir. I hope your journey was most pleasant." Mr. Reynolds walked with him down the hall. "There are two letters from Georgiana in your study. One was sent by way of express two days ago, but you were on the road and we could not forward them."

"An express? From Georgiana? Thank you, Mr. Reynolds." Darcy picked up both the letters with concern. He had left Georgiana at Netherfield with her companion and the Bingleys. Late at night, he had conveyed the whole story of Ramsgate and Wickham's doings at the ball to Mr. Bingley. It was prudent, Darcy had decided, that Bingley know what had truly happened in order to protect

Georgiana. He would have taken Georgiana with him but she had insisted that he take his honeymoon alone. During the two weeks of his engagement he had found out that Wickham had asked for leave and no one would admit to knowing where he went. Colonel Forster had said he asked for five weeks. He counted it out in his head. Between the two weeks of their engagement, and the fifteen days since their marriage, Wickham should still be gone. It still worried him as he opened up her letters.

He read over the letters quickly, but the gist of it was she wanted to return to Pemberley immediately. He reread it, this time more slowly, wondering if there was something he was missing. The only thing that could account for his uneasiness was that her tone was all too familiar, she was self-conscious and anxious all over again. Just like after Ramsgate. He immediately sat down to instruct her to come home. He was a newlywed, but not in any real sense of the word. If it was up to him he would spend every waking hour with Elizabeth, and with a sigh, thought, *and every sleeping hour as well.* But he knew Elizabeth didn't feel for him as he did for her. Not yet. Two weeks was a very short time to change someone's opinion as decided upon as Elizabeth's was of him. She hadn't been herself since his proposal and rarely teased him or challenged him anymore. But Pemberley would change that. It was a wonderful place that offered everything he knew Elizabeth loved: a wealth of nature, an extensive library, elegance and warmth. Yes, she would fall in love with Pemberley soon enough. He had already seen its healing powers bring the first sign of laughter from her. He smiled to himself, recalling her lighthearted banter and her laughter as she told him he smelled like Pemberley. Although she had said she wouldn't explain herself, he had insisted he tell her what Pemberley, and himself smelled like. Cedar and sage? His clothes were hung in cedar closets but the sage? He had never considered before what his person would smell like. He made a note to ask Martin what his shaving soap was made from. His thoughts drifted once again to her bright pink cheeks. He had very nearly taken her in his arms and kissed her right there! He had many moments where impulses to do so were strong, but he refused to let them become overpowering. It took the sound of her laughter to turn his thoughts towards a safer, less impulsive end. And, he reminded himself, she never did say whether or not she liked

"Pemberley's" smell. But upon remembering the depth of the blush, he could hope that she did.

*****

Elizabeth's welcome at Pemberley had been everything and more than the warm greeting she had received in London. The servants were introduced just as before, and she couldn't help but be in awe at how kind and endearing Mr. Darcy was with them. There were so many new faces, though, that she was grateful that she agreed to bring Serafina to Pemberley. It was surprisingly pleasant, she had to admit, to have her own personal maid. Serafina was so talented in managing her unruly curls, even on the most humid of days when Elizabeth would have given up in despair. Serafina seemed to have the gift of fading away when Elizabeth needed privacy, but was there the moment her opinions were needed. One night, as Serafina took her hair down, Elizabeth had found that Serafina grew up at Pemberley, and was in fact the daughter of the late Mrs. Darcy's maid. From a young age, she had been taught how to care for a mistress of such an estate, and it only seemed natural that she would assume this position. And yet there was a natural liveliness and humor about her that Elizabeth appreciated. She did not want a maid who never spoke but to mark the bounds of propriety.

There were a number of things she needed to do as Pemberley's new mistress, the first of which was a meeting with the housekeeper, Mrs. Reynolds, but upon waking up, Elizabeth stood and walked to the window. A walk was nothing short of necessary. How could she not explore the riches before her at the first possible moment? She rang for Serafina and asked to be readied for a walk. She waited impatiently as Serafina carried in her new pelisse, a fine forest-green wool that seemed to be made for walking in Pemberley's woods, and fastened her bonnet over her hair. She found her way to the front door easily enough and found the butler, Mr. Reynolds, busy at his work in the entryway.

"Good morning, Mrs. Darcy," he said with a bow. It was a surprise to her that the name no longer sounded quite so strange. She remembered that he was the husband of the housekeeper, and nodded to him before he opened the door. Soon enough she found herself faced with the beautiful grounds of Pemberley.

She at first thought she would stay close to the building but a certain picturesque cliff to the north begged her to come hence. Once she reached the top, she knew she would have a very good view of the entire estate. As she walked she came across a faint trail that seemed to lead her in the right direction. It wound around trees and led her to a shallow trickling stream. Laughing, she picked up her skirts and jumped. She felt more carefree than she had in a very long time.

The weather was quite warm for autumn, and she assumed warmer than usual for Pemberley as many trees were already turning crimson and orange in a riot of color. She scrambled over several boulders, but finally made her way to the cliff. A spot on the ground was worn with hoof prints etched deep in the dirt. Someone else seemed to like this view as well. She surrendered to the temptation to sit in a grassy area in the sun. Beneath her she could see the top of the house, the garden maze, and delighted in imagining making her way through its secret passageways. She shed her bonnet to feel the warmth of the sun on her hair.

The stables were nearer to the gardens, with a barnyard just to the south. She could make out a whole flock; nearly fifteen to twenty chickens, and perhaps more of those that she could not see. She would need to visit them later, she decided. As a child, she had been mesmerized by the constant pecking and scratching whenever they were fed. She had to concede that chickens were the silliest animal she knew, but she took every opportunity at Longbourn to feed them whenever possible, even saving her scraps for them. She had needed to be secretive since her mother did not approve of such behavior. She could hear her now. *This is not the sort of thing a gentleman's daughter does, Lizzy! Whatever will I do with you?* The memory made her laugh. She was so content at the moment, more content than she had been in many weeks. She took one last glance at the estate and then stretched out to soak up the rays of sunshine. She hadn't had a single confusing thought about Mr. Darcy on her entire walk. *I knew a walk was what I needed!* She closed her eyes— just for a moment, she told herself— and promptly fell asleep.

*****

"What do you mean she is missing?" Darcy started to pace in front of Mrs. Reynolds. He had assumed she slept in after yesterday's long journey and had asked for a tray to be brought up to her. And, he had to admit, he had also assumed that she was avoiding him after the near-kiss yesterday. He should be more careful, he told himself firmly.

Mrs. Reynolds cleared her throat. "Serafina was rung for several hours ago and readied Mrs. Darcy herself. Serafina said she was especially in good spirits and asked for her pelisse and bonnet."

"Well, does Serafina know where she is? Did my wife give any indication where she went?"

"Mr. Reynolds attended her at the front door but she gave him no indication of where she was going."

"Well, search the house; I want every servant looking for her inside and out! She is new to the area and could easily be lost. And tell Roberts to fetch my horse!" He went searching for Mr. Reynolds. He was certain Mrs. Reynolds had reported all that she could, but he was going to ask him himself.

"Reynolds!" he barked. "What time did my wife leave? Do you know which direction she went? Did she say anything? Did she give any indication at all where she was heading?"

"Sir, it was just after seven, and she headed north towards the gardens. She gave no indication of where she was going or even why she was leaving, sir," Mr. Reynolds said.

"Seven? That was over three hours ago! And you have not seen her since?" Darcy's heard his voice crack slightly with worry.

"No, sir." Reynolds looked at him. "I am sure that we will find her very soon, sir."

Darcy ignored his reassuring words. His mind was busy imagining the worst: Elizabeth lying somewhere injured, lost, or even attacked by an animal. He started pacing at the front door, praying that Elizabeth would simply walk through it. For a moment, he could almost see her laughing at all the commotion and then chiding him for his worry. When she did not appear, his hands tightened so much that he could feel his rapid pulse in them. "Where is my horse?"

Mr. Reynolds did not offer an answer, wisely discerning that it was not truly a question, only Darcy's method of regaining some control of the situation.

Darcy stepped out the front door and headed towards the stable. *If I have to ready the horse myself, I will!* He could see the servants running around the estate calling Mrs. Darcy's name. His eyes darted every which way for a glimpse of her skirts or a flash of her curls.

Much to his relief, he could see Calypso being led up the path. He closed the gap and mounted her. He headed north, barking out further orders to the servants he passed. He passed the gardens, scanning the landscape that he knew so well. Where would she go? There were a number of well-marked gravel paths that led around the estate, but knowing Elizabeth, she would take the path least marked. He needed a better view. There was a great cliff that rose high enough to see the entire estate, a favorite of his, and he led Calypso in that direction. To his relief, he saw the delicate impressions of a shoe that must be hers.

"Elizabeth!" he called. Did she cross the stream? She would have had to jump, but he couldn't imagine that deterring her. Sure enough, the footprints began on the other side of the water. Of course she would jump! He kicked Calypso on. "Elizabeth!" he called again. The footprints died off as the ground dried, but he pressed on, hoping to find her nearby. He stopped the horse for a moment. Just ahead was a flash of yellow skirt beneath a green pelisse. He recognized the gown immediately and dismounted. "Elizabeth!"

"Mr. Darcy!" She turned in astonishment. He was rushing towards her, his face tight with anxiety. His long strides quickly closed the distance between them.

He reached out for her and embraced her tightly. She looked to be in good health; no limp or blood, no dishevelment besides a hint of windblown curls. He held her so tightly that her bonnet slipped to the ground. She was safe! A moment later, however, he realized that not only was she safe, but she was pushing against him quite forcibly.

"What is the meaning of all this?" she demanded. She reached for her bonnet and fastened it securely back on her head.

"We could not find you and we feared for your safety!"

"We? Who is 'we'?" Her eyes narrowed suspiciously.

"The whole household! Everyone is looking for you! Where have you been? You left over three hours ago!" He heard her groan loudly and saw her grimace. Her hands went to her hips, and he found his relief at finding her had settled back into anxiety as he suspected he was about to be privy to a very strong reaction from her.

"Mr. Darcy, I simply went on a walk! You sent the whole household looking for me because I did not show up for breakfast? Must I be at your side at all times? Is that what a good wife should do?" In spite of her vows to obey and be a good wife, she found she was furious at his presumption.

He felt heat rising in his own chest. If she knew even the slightest amount of fear he had experienced in the last half hour she would not be so belligerent and flippant about what had happened!

"A good wife? A good wife?" What was this she was saying about being a good wife? All he cared about was her safety! "Is leaving and not telling anyone where you are going, and taking unescorted adventures to areas unknown to you what you call being a good wife? Try starting with a little consideration for what others are feeling before you give your opinions about what a good wife should be!" He watched her eyes widen at his heated words and he regretted them immediately. He wanted to explain that he was only speaking out of the sheer worry he had felt since he could not find her. He took a deep calming breath before gently grasping her shoulders. He leaned into her, lowered his voice, and whispered, "Dearest Elizabeth, I only feared for your safety. You worried me."

His voice was soft and she could feel the heat of his breath on her ear. It sent shivers up and down her spine, and she felt her anger dissipate with the sensation. His hands released her shoulders and she let out her breath. Her heart was racing and she couldn't imagine it slowing anytime soon. She looked up to see his eyes were looking cautiously at her. She remained silent; she couldn't say anything for fear that her voice would tremble.

"Please Elizabeth, let me escort you until you know your way around the area." Then seeing her bite her lip, most likely because she did not want to be escorted by him, added, "At least tell someone so we can have an escort, anyone, to ensure your safety."

She could see the plea in his eyes and whispered her meager excuse, "I simply fell asleep. I am sorry. I have not been sleeping well lately." Concern etched deeper lines into Mr. Darcy's brow.

"May I ask why you have not been sleeping? Is the bed not to your liking?" Mr. Darcy had never thought to ask her if she had slept well. The topic felt somewhat inappropriate, to say the least, when speaking to a wife whom he promised not to take to his bed.

How could she tell him that thoughts of him kept her awake each night? How could she tell him that she couldn't stop recalling each and every encounter between them, and every time, her body would react as if it were happening at this very moment? How could she tell him that he seemed a totally different man than what she expected to marry? How could she tell him of the repeated dreams in which he appeared, some of them more intimate than others? She couldn't. Not when she did not know why he offered his hand in the first place. "Mr. Darcy . . ."

"William . . ." he corrected her.

She felt a prickle of embarrassment at having causing all this trouble by falling asleep, so she partly appeased him. "Fitzwilliam . . ." His eyes started to smile.

"That is the first time you have used my Christian name." He smiled gently at her. "I am sorry that I interrupted you. Please continue." A shiver ran down his neck and shoulders at the beautiful way she said his name. He felt as if, having been deaf all his life, he was now hearing music for the first time. The only thing that would make it better was if he didn't have to remind her to use it. *Time*, he told himself, *it will come in time.*

"Sir, being married has not been easy for either of us, I am sure, especially considering our . . . special circumstances. My mind has been preoccupied with a particular problem. I find this difficult to address but I must beg of you to answer a question."

"Anything."

She swallowed hard and cleared her throat. It was not in her nature to mince words. "Why did you marry me?"

He took a step backward almost out of instinct. He had not been expecting that kind of question. Didn't she know? How could she not see the depth that he felt for her? He had time after time found himself gazing at her longingly, he sought opportunities to be near her both emotionally and physically, he looked for ways to give her all that he had. Was that not enough? *Could she really not know that I ardently love and admire her? If not, why not?* What was stopping her from seeing his complete devotion? A chill ran through him. What was she really asking? Was she asking his motives in marrying her or was she asking him to explain why he didn't allow Wickham to marry her?

Bile rose to his throat as he thought of the sight he had seen that night at Netherfield: that scoundrel with his arms around Elizabeth, kissing her in a way that declared nothing but filthy intent. If Wickham's advances had been welcomed, then that could only mean Elizabeth admired Wickham and not him. His stomach tightened. He needed more time to change her mind and fall in love with him. He needed to allow her enough time to forget Wickham's charms. *Time, it just takes time.* It was a thought which seemed to repeat itself quite frequently these days. *She needs more time to learn to love me.* "I promise to tell you, but not now. We must be getting back."

"More promises? Give me at least a little insight into your reasoning, for I will not move an inch unless you do so." She brought her hands to her hips once again. This time she would not let him escape her questions by making a vague promise. It had taken great courage to ask such a bold question and she expected an answer in return.

He stepped forward and lifted her left hand off her hip and examined it. It was so feminine: the fine white palm, the beautiful slim fingers, and the half-moons of her nails. He turned it over and looked at the ring he had placed on that very hand, his fingers absently caressing the back of the hand as he did so. He brought it to his lips and kissed the back of her hand, before he looked at her and then kissed the inside of her wrist. He had promised to tell her later, yet she demanded a little insight into his reasoning. She hadn't specified that it had to be a verbal insight. He continued in silence as he took that hand and tucked it into his arm before starting to guide her back down the hill. Surprisingly she came willingly and silently. *Was that enough insight for you?* he wondered. *Because I would be more than happy to attempt to be more insightful on your lips!*

*****

True to her word, she always let someone know when and where she would be walking. She tried to avoid telling Mr. Darcy directly but he always seemed to unearth her plans, as well as to find the time to accompany her. By the fourth day in a row she started suspecting that the servants were under strict orders to notify Mr. Darcy whenever she would go out walking. She was surprised to find that she didn't mind this as much as she thought she would. He was pleasant company, as well as very knowledgeable about his land and the surrounding villages. It became natural to accept his offered arm and guiding hand on the back of her elbow as they walked over more difficult terrain. It was usually easy conversation as well. It had been a week since they had come to Pemberley and Georgiana was due to join them today. Because of this, Elizabeth decided to tell Mr. Darcy directly of her plans to see the stables and barn, knowing he would accompany her, thus allowing him to be nearer to the house than their usual walks so he could watch for Georgiana's arrival. He had been working with his steward all morning but he dismissed him as soon as Elizabeth entered the room.

"I understand you keep chickens," she said as soon as his steward, Livingston, had left the room. Some part of her laughed at the plan she was about to carry out.

He looked at her quizzically. "Yes, they are out by the barn on the south side. Why do you ask?"

"I thought I would feed them some scraps the cook saved from yesterday," she paused. "I thought perhaps you might like to join me."

He did not know if she realized the import of it, but this was the first time she had invited him on any of her adventures. Usually she just informed him of her plans— or he was informed of them— and

Jeanna Ellsworth   127

he would offer to accompany her. His heart skipped a beat. Did this mean they were making progress? "I honestly do not think I have ever fed the chickens myself. I believe I must see how it is done." He closed his estate book and took up his greatcoat. He reached for her arm out of habit, but realized after a moment that her hands were holding a soiled linen bundle. He looked at the bundle with puzzlement.

She smiled and arched an eyebrow at him. "Your eyes are asking a question for you, Mr. Darcy. Perhaps you should let your lips relieve their curiosity."

"Forgive me, but what are you holding? It is filthy!"

She let out a laugh. "I did warn you we would be feeding the chicken scraps! Do you doubt my honesty? Do not worry, for I assure you the very proper Mr. Darcy will not need to get his hands dirty. I know my way around chickens."

He raised his eyebrow in return, but followed her out the door. Rain clouds threatened dark and heavy above them. He followed her until her pace slowed, and then caught up to her. He couldn't contain his curiosity any longer, "May I ask how you know your way around chickens? I thought I married a gentleman's daughter." He smiled at her teasingly.

She pursed her lips together and "shushed" him. "Listen! Do you hear that?" She watched him halt and lean his head forward in silent contemplation. He then looked at her suspiciously, as if suspecting that she was only working to make a fool of him. She whispered, "Scratch scratch, peck peck. Scratch scratch, peck peck. Is it not amazing?"

What was amazing was how those lips looked so adorable as she shushed me! He could hear the chickens, but what made them so interesting? She must have seen his confusion, for she took his hand in hers before pulling him closer. He could see them now. He watched as she took his hand and maneuvered his fingers into a pointing gesture before she aimed it right at a black and white speckled chicken.

"That one, see how it found something in the ground? It is very determined to get what it wants. Hard work and fortitude eventually pays off," she said.

Hard work and fortitude? Wasn't that his personal motto he used in his own life? He was struck with a memory of using those exact words while he was riding Calypso at Netherfield. He watched her as she started calling out to the hens.

"Here chick-chick-chick! Here chick-chick-chick!"

Her voice was high and clipped, which made it sound more like a bird call than human words. He was amazed when all the chickens' heads perked up and the scratching at the ground stopped. She called them again and they started running towards her. She opened the soiled linen and he saw pieces of meat, carrot shavings, potatoes, and cracked egg shells. "You are going to feed them egg shells? Is that not somewhat morbid?"

"Not at all," Elizabeth said briskly. "They love it. It makes their shells stronger if you let them eat them. Watch, this is the part I love." Elizabeth tossed the scraps out into the pen. She watched them peck at the food and shells, the rhythm of the eating calming her like it always did back home. She listened to the cooing of the hens and the occasional flap of the wings as a rooster threw its head back and displayed its colors and size for all to see. "See the rooster there?" She pointed him out to Darcy. "He is very proud and protective of his hens and sees you as a threat."

"Me? Why me? Why aren't you the threatening one?" he teased.

She turned her head towards him, surprise startling her out of her focus on the chickens. *Is Mr. Darcy teasing me? Does he have a sense of humor underneath that stiff exterior?* But then his kindness and generosity had taken her by surprise as well. "Because, sir, you are the Master of Pemberley. I have never known such a man who would stoop low enough to throw his chickens food and shells." She smiled brightly at him. She no longer believed he was that proud man she had first met; however, it still didn't surprise her that he had never fed the chickens before, not even as a child. "Or do you dare attempt such a task?"

"I would, but you seem to have thrown them all the food already." He so enjoyed watching her tease him. The mirth in her eyes and mouth was balm to his battered heart. He was then not surprised when she challenged him.

"Fair enough," she said with a smile at the corner of her mouth. "Come with me. The corn is in the barn and we shall see Fitzwilliam Darcy feed his chickens." She took his hand to lead him into the barn.

"You obviously know the way," Darcy said, amused at her confident direction. "How long have you been coming out here?"

"Every day, really." She glanced back at him. "A few times a day. Do not fret, I can see the house from here and I did not get lost once!"

"Well, that explains why they know your . . . what would you call the sound you make when you call them?" He teased further.

"Oh no," she said, "you shall not divert the attention to me, sir. This is your time to prove you can get your hands dirty. Here, pull out a handful of the corn and bring it over." She waited for him to follow her command before she brought him to the gate and then inside. She laughed inwardly as he gingerly picked his way around in favor of clean portions of the ground. "Now bend over and hold your hand out."

"Will they bite?"

"If they do, I would not worry, for my bite is worse than theirs." She smiled saucily at him.

Was she openly flirting with him in the middle of a chicken pen? Who knew that chickens could be so interesting! *Perhaps it is not the chickens that have got my attention!* He saw she was waiting for him to do as he was told. He stretched out his hand to the nearest chicken but nothing happened. "I would wager it is you they love after all. They do not seem to like me."

"You have to call to them." She gave him the most sober expression she could muster. Would he take the bait and call to the chickens?

"Do be serious." He saw her mischievous eyes and took a deep breath. *Fair enough, I can do this.* He made his deep voice mockingly rise to a falsetto pitch. "Here chick-chick-chick!"

She let out a hearty laugh then, wrapping her arms around her stomach in an attempt to contain it. All the chickens scurried over towards them. Mr. Darcy took a hasty step back. She reached out for him. "No, no, put your hand out and feed them, do not back down now! They are expecting food!" She spoke in between fits of laughter.

Darcy leaned over and put his hand out, watching in amazement as the chickens started pecking at the corn in his hand. Most of it was knocked from his palm and fell to the dirt. Soon the chickens were ignoring his hand and pecking at the dirt below it. He looked at Elizabeth and smiled. Never before had he felt so comfortable with her; he was having quite a bit of fun. She was watching the chickens intensely. Then she looked at him with all seriousness.

"I find it relaxing to come out here. It is mesmerizing." She turned her gaze back at the chickens.

"Yes, it is." Mr. Darcy said. His gaze, however, was fixed on Elizabeth, watching the curve of her delicate cheek as she smiled.

"I want to show you one other thing." She reached for his hand again, not caring in the slightest that it was covered in corn dust. She led him into the barn again and lifted up a small nest box door.

"Are we harvesting eggs now, Mrs. Darcy?" He couldn't believe how alive this made him feel. He could roll around in the muck with her by his side and he would still be this happy.

"Oh no! Not these eggs," she whispered.

She shushed him again with her perfectly plump lips. He found it difficult to focus on the task at hand, chickens or none. He lowered his voice to match hers. "Then what are we doing looking in a nest box?" She pointed inside the nest box and he could see a yellow hen sitting placidly. She then reached in and lifted the hen up, just enough to let Darcy see that there were about half a dozen eggs nestled under her. Elizabeth carefully lowered the hen back down on the eggs and closed the nest box door.

She walked a few feet away before she spoke in normal tones. "She is broody and does not leave the nest box except two or three times a day and even then only for very short periods of time. There are seven eggs."

Darcy could feel the moment coming to an end. She had shown him everything. They had laughed, and teased, and flirted, and he had learned about something that was precious to her. He did not want it to stop, but could hardly think of what to say. "I was under the impression that chicks hatch in the spring. It is nearing late autumn."

Her smile faded slightly. "You are correct, but that hen in there wants to raise chicks right now. It is an instinct that cannot be stopped. Nature has guided her to this place, and her own convenience or the fact that it has happened not on her timetable does not matter. She is literally forced to sit on those eggs until they hatch. The real question you are asking is, can baby chicks survive the winter?" She watched as he silently shrugged his shoulders. "The answer is yes, but only if they get their feathers before the winter storms hit."

She looked at him intensely. He had the feeling that they were no longer discussing chickens. If they weren't, then what were they talking about? He felt like he had missed some crucial moment. Sure enough, the moment had concluded and he watched as Elizabeth turned to head back to the house. Her head was down slightly and she was silent. He turned over the last things she had said, but none of it made any sense to him, except directly relating to the hen and the chicks. He calculated how long they had until the winter snows came. It was probably less than two months. He wished he could ask her more about the chicks but the moment had passed, and she was well on her way back to the house. What else could she have been talking about?

*****

The rains came hard and fast that afternoon. Mr. Darcy stood in his library, pondering the education on his own chickens, the enigma that was his wife, and the upcoming arrival of his sister. After some time, he walked to the window, feeling a twinge of worry at how hard the rain was coming down. Georgiana was on the road but how early they left he did not know. These kind of rains, he knew, slowed travel quite a bit. It was getting dark outside and he briefly considered heading towards town to make sure everyone was safe, but that wouldn't help anyone. It would only mean there would be two carriages rolling through the mud.

A knock came at the door, interrupting his anxious thoughts. "Enter."

His butler came in and bowed. "The carriage has been spotted, sir, and it should be here shortly."

"Thank you, Reynolds," Darcy said, glad for an excuse to close the book he had been attempting to read. He pulled on his jacket and fastened it as he walked to the front door that Reynolds already held open. He had about two yards of covered porch to stand under or he would be fairly drenched. He could see the carriage now as it wobbled from side to side significantly under the influence of the rain, but the driver guided it away from the more difficult areas of the road. At last it pulled up to the front. The groomsman sprang into action with an umbrella to shield Georgiana and Mrs. Annesley. Darcy waited anxiously as she came up the steps.

Georgiana looked up at him. She had never been so relieved to be home. "Brother!" It was as if her arms had a mind of their own, for it was barely two seconds later that she flung them around his neck. She clung to him as if he was the only thing that mattered in the world. He was! Her shoulders started to shake and her chest hurt as the tears burst forth. She was home, and now he would make everything right. She was sure of it.

"Georgie, I have missed you as well," he said soothingly, but as she continued to sob, he frowned. "But we have not been apart much more than three weeks! Why all the tears?" He wrapped his arms around her. Would he ever understand the mind of a lady? It seemed Elizabeth spoke in nothing but confusing riddles, while Georgiana said nothing at all! He heard the front door open again.

Elizabeth pulled her shawl around her shoulders. "Welcome home, Georgiana!" Why were they standing out in the rain? After a moment she recognized the intensity of Georgiana's distress, and she met Mr. Darcy's eyes questioningly. His expression looked just as bewildered as Elizabeth felt. She stood by and watched silently as Fitzwilliam held Georgiana close and brushed her hair away from her tearstained face, then murmured kind words and reassurances into her ear. She could almost hear Georgiana's breathing slow and become calmer. Were all the homecomings this emotionally charged? After a few moments, the wind changed direction slightly, sending fat raindrops to angle in on the brother and sister. Fitzwilliam began to coax her towards the door, all the while eyeing Elizabeth pleadingly. She looked back mutely at him. *What do you want me to do? She just needs her brother, not her new sister!*

"Come Georgie, we held dinner until you arrived," he said soothingly, before trying to lighten her mood. "Are you going to make me go hungry? You know how I get when I get hungry." He brought her into the dining room. Georgiana reluctantly sat down, but her hands refused to let go of his waistcoat. It was only when he reached in his pocket and took out his handkerchief that her hand finally released him. She held the handkerchief tightly in her hands as her tears continued to roll down her face.

She looked up at Elizabeth and offered her a weak smile. "I am so sorry, Elizabeth. I do not mean to be such a watering pot! You must not think too ill of me. My brother has often seen me in this state, but I am afraid you have not and I am terribly embarrassed."

Elizabeth put a hand on her shoulder. "The road must have been terrible on that last stretch, for it has been raining this hard here for over an hour." Elizabeth took off her shawl and placed it on Georgiana's shoulders, bringing it together under her bowed chin. She used this opportunity to lift the sad face and look at it. Georgiana's eyes had dark bags under them and she was pale. She looked like she had not eaten well nor slept well and the usual shine in her eyes held only the gloss of tears, not true happiness. *What has happened?* Elizabeth became quite concerned the more she evaluated her face. New tears slipped out of the corner of Georgiana's eyes. Elizabeth took the handkerchief out of her hand and dabbed at her cheeks with Mr. Darcy's handkerchief. She suddenly remembered Mr. Darcy doing the same thing to her just a few weeks ago. Had her emotions been so intense on the day of her wedding that she didn't recognize what such a kind and loving gesture it was? She looked at

Fitzwilliam. For a moment their eyes met and she was overcome with an urge to tell him thank you for his sensitivity during such a dark moment in her life. *Oh, how he must think I hate him!* She promised herself that she would express her gratitude in the next possible moment.

Georgiana seemed to get more control of herself and dinner was served. Both Darcy and Elizabeth kept trying to engage Georgiana in conversation but she still seemed low in spirits and did not offer much back.

Mr. Darcy started telling Georgiana all he learned about chickens today and embellished the story a little to see her smile. She only nodded and murmured sporadically. He then decided since she wasn't eating anyway, that dinner was over. "Georgiana, I have not heard you play the pianoforte. I would be delighted to hear what you have been working on."

"William, I fear I am not in the mood to play tonight. For if I did, it would be very depressing music, indeed. I think I will retire early, thank you." Georgiana got up from her chair, placed her napkin on the table, and removed Elizabeth's shawl. She turned to Elizabeth, "Forgive me my rudeness. I am very weary."

After she left, Darcy stood and escorted Elizabeth to the music room, his worry evident on his face. Elizabeth took his arm, relishing in the sensation it gave her to be close to him. "Fitzwilliam? What is wrong with Georgiana?"

His heart leapt for joy for a moment; she had used his Christian name without being reminded! "I do not know. Her last letter begged to come home to Pemberley and yet she behaves as if she does not wish to be here."

Elizabeth didn't get that impression at all, "On the contrary, I feel she clung to you quite forcefully. I do believe she missed you."

Darcy's eyebrows furrowed. "She is always in the mood to play for me when I request it! Something is troubling her. Perhaps I should go to her."

Elizabeth sat down on the chaise next to him and patted his arm. "Sometimes it takes a woman's touch. I will try to talk to her soon and find out what is the matter. Now in the meantime, your mood is so dark right now I believe a good wife would try to lighten it." He looked up at her, wondering what she could mean. "Since I do not play well, I am sure to make you laugh as I attempt to play something on the pianoforte. But I must caution you, you may smile like you are now, but if you openly laugh at me I may never touch the keys again!"

Thrilled at the idea that he could listen to Elizabeth play for him, he nodded his head. "I shall do my best to control my inner laughter, for it would be a tragedy for you to stop playing. Well, my dear 'good wife,' I believe I must insist that you lighten my mood."

*****

Elizabeth played for him for some time, and he found that her protestations of being unskilled to be a gross exaggeration. He requested a song as well and she sang for him. He sat back with a peculiar look on his face, and afterwards pressed a kiss to her hand before they retreated to their various spaces.

It was getting late, but Elizabeth kept thinking about the eggs in the barn. Now that the rain had stopped, she concluded she would slip out and check on them, but first she needed to gather her supplies. She found her way to the kitchen and found a whiskey glass. She put her shawl around her shoulders and used the candle to light her way to the front door. Most of the servants had already gone to bed, and she had thought she was alone. The sound of Mr. Darcy's deep voice startled her as she reached the front door, and she nearly dropped the candle on the floor before straightening.

"Where are you going at this time of night?"

"I was going to check on the eggs."

He looked at her with a small grin, recalling the wonderful time they had shared that afternoon discussing chickens. "In the dark? Do you mind if I accompany you?"

"Night time is the only time I can do what I am wanting with them." She saw his eyebrow rise in puzzlement and she added, "You will see, you may come if you desire to. It will not take long." It was late and wet outside, but she knew she wouldn't be long so she just wrapped her shawl around her more tightly. The pathway that led to the barn was familiar enough, but she had not counted on the slipperiness of the ground. She felt her boots slip a few times and Mr. Darcy reached out for her to steady her, remaining close all the way.

When they reached the barn Elizabeth put the candle and glass down on a shelf. "What are you doing with a whiskey glass?" Darcy asked. His interest was piqued now. Here they were, together in the barn with nothing but a single candle making shadows dance along the walls. He took a moment to appreciate her beauty, a habit that he quite enjoyed. She moved so gracefully around the barn, and the candlelight showed the brightness and loveliness of her eyes.

Elizabeth saw him examining her, and glanced away briefly, feeling conscious of the intimacy of the moment. She smiled at him. "You will see. I am going to see how far along the eggs are and it will tell me when to expect them to hatch." She lifted the nest box door and slid her hand in carefully under the hen and pulled out two eggs. She placed them on a pile of hay. He motioned to Darcy to bring the candle over. She reached for the whiskey glass, held it up to her face and inverted it. "Now, if you do not mind, it will help if you hold the candle while I hold the egg and glass. Once I have the egg on top of the bottom of the glass, put the candle inside the glass, but only for a few seconds at a time; the candle will go out if it stays in too long."

He nodded in assent. He stepped closer and watched her pick up an egg and then cup the lowest portion of it between her thumb and forefinger. She wrapped her other fingers over the base of the inverted glass, therefore sealing the gap between the egg and glass. The egg was held in place above the glass by her slender fingers.

"Now put the candle inside the glass and look at the egg." He did as she instructed and the lower part of the egg started glowing in her hand. She pushed her face closer to the egg. "There in the center, do you see that dark spot and the spiderlike vessels?" He leaned in and examined the egg for an extended moment. The glow started fading and she said hastily, "Take the candle out quickly!"

"Sorry." The candlelight lit up the barn again.

"Try again but do not forget to take the candle in and out frequently."

Her arm held up the egg and inverted glass again. His arm that held the candle was so close to hers. Their faces were close enough that if he turned his head towards her he could brush up against her cheeks. This close, he could smell the fresh lavender in her toilette water, and it was intoxicating.

Elizabeth was quite conscious of his proximity. *Perhaps this wasn't such a good idea*, she thought ruefully. *I am already having a hard time making sense of my feelings for him and moments like these make it all the more difficult.* She had begun to care for and respect him, but that was only appropriate now that they were spending so much time together. He had been quite engaging this afternoon and it was exciting to see him enjoy himself with the chickens. It was moments like this where he touched her or was close to her that her mind and heart veered in different directions. What her mind understood was that Mr. Darcy was being kind and polite and accommodating to her needs. He proved trustworthy and generous too. He was providing for his wife, as the gentleman he was raised to be would do. This did not mean he cared for her.

But what her heart understood was that his eyes often spoke of more than kindness. Her heart remembered his gentle touches and kisses on her hands, and thought that he would not do so if he did not enjoy them. Her heart also told her of her budding feelings for him every time he touched her or was near her. She felt a sudden desire to turn her head towards him and look at him. Her face was just below his as he was leaning over to see the egg. She could smell his familiar scent, and could see the day's stubble forming on his face. She could hear his breathing and felt it move her hair as he exhaled.

She forced her attention back to the egg. "That dark spot in the middle is the chick forming. It looks like it is growing well, but this is the first time I have candled them."

He had been consciously reminding himself to breathe. Every time he placed the candle inside the glass his arm would brush against hers and his heart would skip a beat. It took the candle flickering to remind him to remove his arm and allow the flame to grow bright again. He wondered if they would hatch and grow their feathers in time before the winter storms hit. He knew from the confusing words she had uttered this afternoon that these eggs meant something more to her than simple farm animals. "Elizabeth, how long before they hatch? It looks like there is still quite a bit of light area."

"If I remember correctly the hen only sits on the eggs for twenty-one days. I have only candled them towards the end so I do not know how far along they are now. Perhaps they are less than a week into it? Maybe more."

"So that means two more weeks before they hatch?"

She nodded. "The egg will be entirely dark when it is time to hatch except for the base. Have you ever watched eggs hatch?"

He was overcome with admiration for her brightness and inquisitiveness. He had done the right thing in marrying her. *How could I live without her?* She looked as if she were awaiting a response, so he refocused his mind. "If I have never fed chickens before you cannot expect me to have witnessed eggs hatching. But I confess I am overwhelmed with the desire to see it with you. Promise me that you and I will watch them together." She looked back up at him and their eyes locked. He was just inches away. He leaned his head forward and his forehead rested on hers. She held her breath. He reached with his only open hand and placed it gently on her waist. "Promise me, dearest Elizabeth." His voice was barely a whisper.

She could barely hear his last words over the sound of her racing heart. "I promise." She whispered. Her waist was tingling where his hand was. She closed her eyes. *So he is to kiss me now? Am I ready for this?* Her heart beat faster as she waited for her first kiss. *Yes, I want him to kiss me.* Suddenly he raised his head and stepped away, his hand still on her waist. She opened her eyes to the dark surrounding them. The candle had gone out. She pressed her lips together, thankful for the dark that cloaked her disappointed face.

Darcy tried to find his voice. They now had far more privacy than he could have wished for. The candle had blown out just as he was leaning in to kiss her. Although he desperately wished for this, and had imagined numerous times, the impulse was premature. He didn't want to rush her, and, after all, he had made her a promise. He was finding keeping that sort of promise to be very trying indeed. His hand remained on her waist and couldn't find the strength to remove it. He cleared his throat. "Elizabeth, I fear we will have to try to make it back without any light." His voice was shaky and soft. He didn't really want to leave; what he really wanted was to pull her close and take the time to find her lips and cover her in kisses. He wanted to feel her next to him here in the dark, and to taste that beautiful impertinent mouth.

Her eyes were trying to find his form in the darkness but she could see nothing. She put her eyes in the direction of his soft voice. There would never be a better time to say what she desperately wanted to say. Here, in the dark, it felt like she could speak honestly. She placed her hand over where his still rested on her waist. He pulled away slightly but she held it. "I need to tell you something. And if I do not tell you now, I do not know if I will find the courage later." He gave her waist a subtle squeeze and she continued. "That day in the carriage, our wedding day, I was not in the best of moods. I fear I am a woman with decided opinions, and I could not bear the thought that I had lost my ability to choose whom I would marry. My mind was quite decided against our marriage."

"Elizabeth, do not . . ." He did not want to hear from her lips how she hated him. His heart could not bear it, not after having seen such positive indications over the last few days and weeks. Not after today.

"No, please, I beg of you not to interrupt." She took a deep breath and ensured his silence before she continued. "My mind was quite decided against the marriage and I felt forced into doing it. You looked so anxious at the wedding that I knew you felt the same way." She heard him take a deep breath filling the darkness. This was going to be harder than she thought. "And in the carriage, I could not stop crying, no matter what I did. I was in a very dark place. It was not until today that I realized how kind you had been to me to wipe away the tears when I had not the energy to do so. I must thank you for the kindness and generosity you have shown me. I did not know what to expect when we married, but I have been treated fairly and for that I must thank you." She lifted his hand off her waist and kissed it before she held it in her own.

Darcy was grateful for the darkness as well, for his eyes had tears forming in them. He thought about her words. He wanted her to feel more than his kindness and generosity, and he wanted more from her than her thankfulness. He did not trust his voice, for his eyes were treacherous already. He started leading her through the darkness but only got a few steps before she cried out.

"No, wait! We must put the eggs back!" She was still cradling one in her palm, and let go of his hand to search for the other on the hay. She could not find it. She knelt down and felt around, careful to move lightly. "I cannot find it, Fitzwilliam!" Her voice was frantic. She heard him step behind her, making his way in her direction.

"Where did you put it?" He could hear her hands rustling the hay. From where her voice came from, he could tell that she had bent over or was kneeling. He followed the sounds until his hands found her shoulders. He knelt beside her and started feeling around for the egg. He heard her sniffle and knew that she had begun to cry. Yes, these eggs meant something more than simple farm animals or even a hobby of hers. His hand touched something round and warm. "I found it!"

She reached her hands over to where his voice was and found his shoulders. In spite of any hesitation, she pulled him close to her and cried, "Thank you! You do not know how relieved I am!"

His arms wrapped around her and held her close. He relished in the warmth of her body but then realized she was shaking. "Are you chilled?"

She pulled away and said, "I only brought my shawl because I did not think it would take this long."

He released her completely and took off his jacket. "Now, where are you? If I may, I will place this coat on your shoulders, but I fear I cannot see what I am doing."

She spoke then and felt the warm coat being brought around her shoulders. She tilted her head down and smelled the comforting cedar and sage, grateful then that he couldn't see her do it. They picked their way back to the nest box and slid the eggs under the hen. He took her hand and started making his way out of the barn. It was slow work, not only because he couldn't see anything but because he didn't want the moment to end. Once outside, the moon shone through the clouds enough to help them find their way back to the house. Even when they were inside, Darcy couldn't find it in himself to let go of her hand. They found the halls were still lit up with one or two candles. He took one of the candles with his free hand and continued to walk with her. He knew she should get warmed up soon or she would risk a fever. He led her to the library and set her down on the chaise while he stoked the fire.

Elizabeth, still shivering, looked around curiously. She hadn't spent much time in the grand library at Pemberley because of the cataloging being done. She had lingered in the front room, and sometimes ventured down a time or two to get a new book but that was it. The walls were lined with books, and two aisles of books reached halfway out into the room. Books were everywhere, in piles, on the floor, on the tables stacked five high, and in the corners.

Darcy saw her looking around the room. "Forgive the disorder. If we can but endure it a little while longer, the cataloging will be complete and it will be the most organized room in Pemberley."

"Oh, I do not mind," she said with a small smile. "Papa's study looked much the same. Although he suffered from an excess of books and a scarcity of shelves. It reminds me of home." The heat of the fire began to grow, and she stood to approach it. He knelt with his back to her, still adding wood to it. She hesitated at the sight of his broad shoulders and the shape of his arms in his fine linen shirt. Her hand reached for his shoulder before she knelt beside him. The fire was burning merrily, now, and she held her hands out in front of the flames. She sat wrapped in his jacket, leaving only her fingertips visible in front of the fire. They sat in silence for some time.

He remembered that she called Longbourn home. He had hoped she felt comfortable at Pemberley. "Do you miss Longbourn?"

She contemplated the question. "Not as much as I thought I would. Jane is faithful in her letter writing and tells me all I am missing. My father is much the same." She laughed softly after a moment. "My mother does not stop telling all who will listen about how I managed to find 'such a fine husband' with my impertinent ways. And when she is not doing that, she is making wedding plans. Jane tells me all about Mr. Bingley and their engagement." Elizabeth didn't tell him about how Jane told her of her first kiss.

"She is happy," she continued, since it seemed that Mr. Darcy was still listening curiously. "And it seems Lydia and Kitty are just as preoccupied with the officers as they always have been. Mary found a new book on sermons and has started spouting her newfound opinions on the role of the woman in the home. It seems she is displeased with our mother's long-fixed habits. Oh, and Charlotte Lucas has had a new suitor visiting regularly. He is much older than she is, but he has been kind to her."

"Indeed! Well, she is a fine lady and would make a fine wife."

She smiled brightly at him. "And now you know all the happenings in Longbourn."

"For which I am very grateful, I assure you," he said with a smile back to her.

They sat there in front of the fire talking. The fire burned hotter, forcing both of them to step back in turn and sit down on the floor. The conversation was invigorating and helped both, although sporadically, to divert their thoughts of their moment in the barn an hour ago. Each one would play out the scenario differently. Darcy would chastise himself for almost kissing her one moment, then the next he pictured himself kissing her freely and passionately. His imagination was quite keen.

Elizabeth was reliving the feel of his hands on her waist and the intimacy of their foreheads touching. Had she imagined their almost-kiss? She wondered if he was starting to have feelings for her like she was for him. She understood now that she would welcome his kisses, and blushed at the thought.

Darcy stopped in the middle of the conversation to touch her cheek. "You are flushed. Is the fire too hot?"

She blushed deeper, as embarrassed as if she had spoken her thoughts aloud. "No, but perhaps it is time to retire." She started to rise but he was quicker and assisted her up. They walked in silence up the grand staircase, walking slower than usual. It seemed that neither one wanted the moment to end.

He escorted her to her room and then stopped her outside the door. "Elizabeth, you were wrong in the barn about something."

Fears that she really did imagine him wanting to kiss her resurfaced and she stood taller. *Why is it that in the moment I find him most intriguing, I set myself up for embarrassment?* "About what, Mr. Darcy?" She asked coolly.

Mr. Darcy noticed her cold tone and faltered in his resolve. She had returned to calling him Mr. Darcy. He decided he must tell her anyway if she were to feel more than kindness and generosity from him. "You said you thought I felt forced into the marriage. I just wanted to clarify that I did not, and do not feel that way. It was the best thing that could have happened to me." He gave her hand a gentle squeeze and went to his own room. He resolved not to look back for once, and missed seeing Elizabeth's mouth open in shock.

Chapter 7

Elizabeth removed Darcy's jacket and looked at it. She should give it back to him this very night, she knew. But still . . . she brought it up to her nose and inhaled that wonderful smell. *He did not feel forced into the marriage!* She couldn't help but laugh out loud. Perhaps her hope of true companionship was possible after all. The whole day had held so many moments where she had felt close to him. She folded the jacket thoughtfully before ringing for Serafina. While waiting, Elizabeth began to take down her hair. She mused over his parting words. He had said, "It was the best thing that could have happened to me." If it hadn't been for the softness and warmth in his tone, she might have doubted his sincerity.

No. He had meant what he said. But did he mean marriage in general, or did he mean marriage to her? Their marriage wasn't typical; at least not yet, but they shared plenty of time together. Granted, their newfound affinity had not been her intention initially, but she quickly discovered she didn't mind it; and even found herself anticipating their time together. Her feelings for him had grown with a force beyond anything she could have predicted. It was just like the hen, she thought with a quiet smile. She had no control of the situation she was in; something outside of her decided it. True, it hadn't been what she wanted, or even at the time in her life that she had thought it would occur. But as she was forced to spend time with him, something deep in her heart urged her to continue. It was an instinct that she was unable to control, just as the hen was compelled to make a nest and nurture her eggs. Elizabeth just hoped that whatever blossomed between them could weather the storms of life, just as she hoped the chicks' feathers would come in before the winter storms. She hoped, and realized how good it felt to hope that perhaps someday there would be more than companionship in her marriage. She felt herself smiling again at the thought.

Elizabeth looked over when Serafina entered. "I am ready for bed," Elizabeth said. She pulled out the last hairpin and set it on the vanity. Although with these new thoughts racing through her mind, she doubted she would sleep until far later this evening.

"Yes, madam." She took the brush from her mistress' hand and began to brush Elizabeth's hair. Serafina looked over at the master's jacket on the bed with a smile. *So they are finally together?* It made her heart happy, for she had learned to love her mistress deeply, and could see the changes in her eyes over the last few weeks. "Perhaps a bath before the master comes back?"

Elizabeth had been sitting with her eyes closed, enjoying having her hair brushed but they flew open in surprise! Why would Serafina say such a thing? Had he told his valet that he was coming to her room tonight? She couldn't ask such a question of Serafina because a servant would, or at least should, know less than her. Would she accept him if he did? She knew she wanted him to kiss her but that was much different from being man and wife in truth! She would have to be discreet in her search for information. She schooled her features before she replied, glancing at herself in the mirror to make certain that she appeared composed.

"No, if I am not mistaken he has retired for the night; he did not say so exactly, but he appeared fatigued when he left." She watched Serafina closely. Sadness, but not confusion, was portrayed through her eyes. So Serafina had hoped he would come again? Why? She decided one of Serafina's greatest virtues was her honesty and willingness to voice her opinions when asked. "You were hoping he would come back?"

Serafina blushed in embarrassment before examining her mistress' face. Earlier she had seen surprise that had now transformed into anxiety. "He is always happier when he has been with you. That is what Martin says. And you seem much more content tonight than any other night."

Relief that Mr. Darcy was not coming to her tonight washed over her. "It was a good day," Elizabeth said after a moment. "We spent a great deal of time together. I . . . . I enjoy his company very much."

Serafina's eyes brightened and she smiled. "Then tomorrow we will make you look spectacular and you shall have another wonderful day." She helped her change into her nightdress. "Will there be anything else tonight, madam?"

"No, thank you, I am just going to finish writing a letter to my sister Jane and then I will retire." She felt suddenly exhausted and wanted to crawl right into bed. She forced herself to her desk, intending all the while to write before hesitating. She was just too tired. Jane's letter would have to wait.

She crawled under the covers but her eyes refused to close. She reached back to fluff her pillow and got a whiff of something familiar. She sat up abruptly. Had he come in her room after all? Although she hadn't heard anything, the scent of cedar and sage wafted through the air. She looked all around, blinking against the darkness before she decided to light a candle, but couldn't see him in the darkness. No, no one was in her room, and certainly not him. *Then why can I smell him?* She blew out the candle and rolled over, her face hitting something cold and hard and round. It was the buttons on his jacket! She laughed out loud. *This is the composed and calm Mrs. Darcy!* She gathered up the coat and smelled it once again. She still had it in her arms as her heavy eyelids drifted shut, and she slid into a very restful, but familiar, dream-filled sleep.

*****

A few days later, Elizabeth decided it was time to start acting like the mistress of Pemberley. She had explored it every day for almost a fortnight, but knew very little about what made it run. She definitely did not know what her role was or the expectations Fitzwilliam had for her. She could not, however, forget the fact that he had not said he didn't feel forced into the marriage. Her mind had turned it over and over, trying to decipher what he meant. Each day she spent at Pemberley, she felt a slowly forming pride in the fact that she was married to the master of Pemberley, and a growing need to act the part of its mistress. Armed with these thoughts and feelings, she asked to meet with the housekeeper, Mrs. Reynolds.

"Thank you for meeting with me. I must admit I have enjoyed being here, but feel like I have benefitted too long and am ready to take up my responsibilities. You were here when Mrs. Darcy, Mr. Darcy's mother, was still alive, correct?"

"Yes, madam. She was a fine woman," Mrs. Reynolds said.

"I first would like to enquire into my duties and what might be expected of me. I am new to this position and know that you have managed it successfully since her passing. I suppose I will need to know what Mrs. Darcy did and how to best do it."

"Certainly, Mrs. Darcy. May I ask first what kinds of things interest you? I have found that a woman is happiest when she runs her house based on her own convictions, rather than what other great women have done before her."

Elizabeth was impressed with such wisdom. She could tell she would have much to learn from this housekeeper who had been here for so long. "I enjoy the outdoors a great deal. The grounds have captured my interests so far, and I confess that I have neglected the household completely in comparison. But that is not to say I do not enjoy or value the proper running of the house. I also have a great desire to know more of the people here. I have been very impressed with the staff so far."

"Well madam, I suggest we start with your two interests: the grounds and the people. I think these are very wise places to begin. I can have the groundskeeper meet with you this afternoon so you may learn and discuss your desires with him. He has been in service here for years and his son has followed in his father's footsteps. You will find him very knowledgeable and obliging. I understand Hertfordshire has different terrain and a slightly warmer climate, but if there are native plants you would like to grow that remind you of home, he will be able to tell you if they will do well in this soil." Mrs. Reynolds evaluated Elizabeth's face, and decided that the master's new wife did not seem to be too proud. She would even accept guidance from a servant.

"Thank you, I will take that into consideration. And what of the people? I am very anxious to know the staff and tenants but I confess I do not know where to start." Elizabeth knew Mr. Darcy cared for each servant and treated them with respect. This was one area where she knew their feelings were in perfect accord. She wanted to know them individually, just as he did. She did not want to dismiss them as faceless entities who served her.

"The mere fact that you care to know them will be all the start you need," Mrs. Reynolds assured her. "I am sure it will not take long for you to feel absolutely at home as the mistress of Pemberley." She paused. "It is a great pity; I know Georgiana had started to visit the tenants before she left for London but she seems to be so out of sorts lately."

Elizabeth could see a motherly concern come across Mrs. Reynolds' face and reminded herself to find some way of speaking with Georgiana. Georgiana had been anxious and frequently tearful since her return, and although Elizabeth hadn't found the right moment to approach her, it was always at the forefront of her mind. She made a mental note to find a moment today. Perhaps some service visits would cheer her up. She had a thought and posed the question to Mrs. Reynolds. After all, the housekeeper had known her since Georgiana was a babe in arms. "I too have noticed she is in a poor mood, quite withdrawn and even a bit fearful. Do you know of any way I might be able to lift her spirits?"

"Well, we have hosted an Autumn Festival in years past for all the tenants and servants. It might be something to consider. She would probably enjoy it as it has been a favorite of hers in the past. It might be an excellent way for you to get acquainted with the tenants as well."

"We held a ball after summer at Longbourn, but what exactly is Pemberley's Autumn Festival?"

"Oh, I am sure it is much the same. It is somewhat like an informal ball with a lot of music, dancing, and wonderful food. We usually get quite a turn out."

Elizabeth spoke with Mrs. Reynolds about the Autumn Festival for a few more minutes, all the while feeling her excitement grow at the thought. Could she really preside over a festival like the one Mrs. Reynolds' described? She was reassured by the thought that Mrs. Reynolds was all kindness and discreet guidance, and Elizabeth would have months— even years— to fully take on all the responsibilities that were now hers. Afterwards, they discussed the menu for the dinner meal. Elizabeth felt for the first time that Pemberley was beginning to feel like home. A feeling of peace overcame her.

"Thank you, you have been most helpful."

Mrs. Reynolds nodded, hesitating before she continued. "Mrs. Darcy, I feel I need to inform you of something. The kitchen maid has reported some missing silver. She was putting it away after dinner last night and there were several pieces out of place. She and I together thoroughly searched the kitchen this morning right before this meeting, but I am afraid there are four sets of spoons, forks, and knives that are unaccounted for."

Her eyes opened wider. "Have they been misplaced? I cannot imagine that anyone would steal them."

"No madam, you can trust the staff implicitly. I am sure they were just misplaced. I just felt you should know." Mrs. Reynolds didn't feel the conviction that her words portrayed but hoped not to cause Mrs. Darcy any unnecessary worry.

After asking if Mr. Darcy had been informed, Elizabeth thanked her. Apparently he had been. Not knowing what else she could do at the moment, she then dismissed Mrs. Reynolds.

The weather had remained rainy through the morning and into the afternoon, so feeding the chickens with Mr. Darcy was not an option. Since he was busy with his steward, she thought she would venture to the library. They had gone out every morning for a walk, and every day after lunch to feed the chickens. She found herself disappointed that they could not today.

After the night that they had candled the eggs together and she had imagined that he might kiss her, he seemed changed somehow. She couldn't quite explain why, but knew for certain that he seemed . . . different. It was like being near her was great, but to talk to her and engage her in conversation seemed to please him more. It seemed like their first few weeks of marriage had been akin to their first dance at Netherfield; no one spoke, but each touch and look exchanged was physically moving. But these last three days was more like their last dance where they talked and laughed, each time feeling a little more acquainted with the other.

She couldn't decide which "dance" she preferred. She might enjoy a brief touch of his hand or a kiss on her hand, but it created such turmoil inside of her. And their conversations impressed her with his strength of character and thoughtful, educated speech. One thing was certain, however, and that was that she felt like they were becoming friends. They were no longer mere strangers fated to live together. She smiled at this thought. Companionship was all she had hoped for and it looked like it had already passed that.

These thoughts kept her company on her walk to the library. She had finished the book she was reading and was in the mood for a good, intriguing book that would reflect the stirrings and hope that she currently felt.

She looked admiringly up at the two-storied wall of books as she entered. A ladder rolled around the room in order to reach the upper shelves. She had wondered what it would be like to glide around the room high up on the ladder. The servant, who was usually here cataloging the books, was not present. She glanced around at the empty room before she hiked up her skirts and climbed about half way up. She pushed her hand against the shelves. The ladder only moved a few feet. *Well, I suppose I will need to put a little more heart into it.* She gripped the ladder before stretching out her leg and kicking hard against the shelf. The ladder rolled easily some fifteen feet away at great speed, making her hair catch in her open, smiling mouth. Elizabeth laughed, pulling her hair back before she did it in the opposite direction. This time she went even further. She continued to do this, learning along the way that she needed to hold onto the ladder with both hands or risk falling to the floor when it jolted to a halt. She had nearly taken a tumble, but now found herself enjoying the challenge of making it all the way to the end. She was absorbed in attempting to go further and faster when she was interrupted by a voice.

"I believe that is yet another thing you have found at Pemberley that I have yet to do," Mr. Darcy said. She looked down to see him smiling impishly at her.

"William! Oh dear, how long have you been watching me?" . . . *and seeing that unladylike behavior?* She started her descent down the ladder.

She called me William! He grinned. "Only a moment or two. Long enough to learn what was making the sound I heard on the other side of my study. Did you enjoy yourself?" He knew she had. He had watched her for longer than a moment, but couldn't bring himself to confess that he had been watching for a full five minutes. He wanted to laugh as he had not laughed since childhood, watching her stretch her leg out and kick hard. There was a moment or two that he feared he would see her fall, but she held on quite well. Elizabeth's strength was not confined to her mind and will, but extended to her body as well. In his arms, she felt slender but firm, with hints at the strength she had acquired from walking over the country hills. He wondered again how it would feel . . . *Stop it! Her mind is what you fell in love with. You must keep your thoughts in control or you will be controlled by your impulses!*

He had learned that the more he reached for her arm, kissed her hand, or let his eyes drift to her feminine neck, the more that he would struggle with his resolve to let her choose when they became intimate. He had been half a second away from kissing her when the candle went out a few nights ago. That had been too close a call. The more he let himself remember her touch or the smell of her hair, the more he longed to be near her. If he went to bed thinking about her being in his arms, the more restless a night he had, and therefore the less control he had the next day. Yes, if he was going to be the gentleman he promised he would be, he would have to keep his hands to himself, his eyes on her face, and keep from becoming distracted. What he hadn't expected was to learn that his heart would still gallop when she laughed, and yet he couldn't quite control his ears from hearing it. It was the one indulgence he allowed himself. Hearing her laugh brought up all his suppressed desire, but at least it was not overpowering like it was when she was physically touching him. Yes, enjoying hearing and making her laugh was his latest quest and pleasure. That is why he didn't confess to how long he had been watching her enjoy herself on the ladder.

She jumped from the last rung of the ladder before she smoothed her skirt in an attempt to appear dignified. The smile on his face said he had seen plenty of the undignified behavior in which she had just partaken. It was no use denying her pleasure. "I did enjoy myself, thank you. It was a bit of exercise, however. Would you like some tea?"

"I would love some." He wanted to reach for her and tuck her arm around his but he resisted. The sight of her smile and the faintest blush made things difficult enough. He rung the servants' bell before he moved a few books off the couch, motioning for her to sit down. He wasn't quite strong enough to take a different seat, and so found himself sitting next to her. "So what brought you to the library? It is in such disarray that I am sure you were not looking for a specific book."

She gazed around at the stacks of books all over the room before she smiled. "I was hoping to find a romance novel, but I doubt the great Pemberley Library has many of those. I admit, though, that I was immediately distracted and did not do much looking."

He let out a laugh. "I may not own too many, but Georgiana has plenty! I must admit not all of them are that bad."

"You read them?" She was sure her shock was evident on her face.

He cleared his throat and did not meet her eye for a moment. "William Cowper says that 'variety is the very spice of life, that gives it all its flavor,' so yes, I read a wide variety of things. I find myself a little— some might say too much— protective of the people I love and I do not want Georgiana to be reading things that are inappropriate for a young girl's eyes."

Something he said tickled at her brain, but she couldn't quite place what it was. Why couldn't she unravel the mystery? The way he spoke made her blush slightly. *Why am I blushing? I knew he was a devoted brother!*

The tea came in and they talked all the way until lunch. The time seemed to pass quickly in each other's company. Mr. Darcy knew the servants were probably holding the lunch meal for them, but he wanted to address a question with her first. "I was wondering if you have gotten a chance to talk to Georgiana yet. She seems uncomfortable in my presence lately, and although we are close, I am under the impression she does not want to confide in me what troubles her."

His brows were furrowed and she felt a little guilty that she hadn't found the right time to approach her yet. "I did ask Mrs. Reynolds for some help with it. I planned on speaking with her today. Mrs. Reynolds mentioned that you usually hold an Autumn Festival and that Georgiana enjoyed that sort of thing."

"I confess I had not thought about it, but that sort of thing may very well help lift her spirits. How do you feel about taking on such a project so early on in our marriage?"

The way he so casually said "our marriage" made goosebumps form on her arm, and she raised her hand to rub them away. It took a moment to refocus her mind on his question. "I feel I am probably inadequately prepared to take it on by myself, but Mrs. Reynolds will be an invaluable asset. I think we should host an Autumn Festival, if that is acceptable to you."

"I think it sounds wonderful!" He thought of how he would be able to dance with her again, but forced his mind back to the question at hand. "Come, Georgiana is probably waiting to eat, and I imagine that the servants have lost us. I doubt anyone would think to look for us here."

Elizabeth stood and Darcy handed her a book from a pile on the table. *Sense and Sensibility*, by a Lady. *This should do*, she thought, and rewarded him with a smile. "Thank you," she said.

*****

After lunch, Elizabeth walked to the music room where she heard Georgiana playing halfheartedly. Now was as good a time as any to approach her about her mood. Elizabeth still had her new book with her but didn't want to miss being able to discuss whatever was bothering her by putting it in her chambers. She walked in, gazing around the room before she took a seat next to Georgiana on the piano bench. Although Georgiana shifted over, she still continued playing. Elizabeth set her book in her lap before she reached over and turned a page of the music.

Georgiana hadn't intended to play long, but she sensed that Elizabeth had a purpose in coming in to hear her play, and she didn't want to talk yet. She urged more feeling into her fingers, letting them dance across the ivory keys. Soon she was feeling the release from concerns that she usually did when she played. It had been so long since she felt that emotional release she got from delving into her music with all her soul. When she finished the first piece, she immediately began another. She hoped that Elizabeth would get the hint and leave her to her music. As she played, however, Elizabeth simply turned the pages or listened quietly when it was a piece known by heart. She didn't open her mouth once to interrupt or give praise. She simply listened. Georgiana found herself appreciating Elizabeth's silence and listening ear. *Would she listen as attentively if I talked to her about him?*

Elizabeth had sat with Georgiana for over an hour and patiently waited for her to finish. This would take time, she knew, but what else did she have? The weather was still very wet outside and William was busy again in his study. As she listened she felt Georgiana change from restless and agitated, to soulful and intense, and now, as she listened, she could tell her new sister was relaxing into the song.

Georgiana's fingers rested momentarily at the end of a piece, letting them decide on their own whether or not to continue. It was not a choice she intended or even desired to make, but they stopped playing. She sighed. *If I must talk, I might as well get it over with.* "Elizabeth, I know what you are going to say, and the answer is that I do not know if I can tell you."

Elizabeth silently reached for her hands and held them.

Years of being a motherless child made opening up to someone difficult for Georgiana. It was even worse when her secret had to do with the shameful secret of Wickham. Elizabeth would listen, though, and hopefully understand. No matter how she divulged what was worrying her, Georgiana knew it would hardly cast her in the best light possible. "I received a letter from Mr. Wickham before your marriage." Georgiana looked at Elizabeth, but Elizabeth's face remained unchanging, still intent on simply listening to her. "I have it with me. I am too afraid to put it down and have someone, especially William, find it. He would be so upset." She reached into her pocket and drew out a crumpled, tearstained letter.

Elizabeth's brow furrowed up. She could tell the letter had been read many times and was crumpled and torn in some areas. She hadn't thought much about Wickham since that dreadful night at Netherfield. She hadn't seen him since then either. In truth, now she thought him nothing but a rake. She attempted to keep her face still. She did not immediately criticize Wickham, not when it seemed the girl still had feelings for him. Why else would she want to keep a letter from a former suitor— a suitor Mr. Darcy refused to give consent to, no less—so close to her for so long? This was going to be more complicated than she had initially thought.

"I know what you are thinking. It is not proper for me to accept a letter from a gentleman whom I have no understanding with, but it was not like that. I did not know who the letter was from. It just came one day while William went to get the special license in London. I would have never accepted a letter, and especially not one from that weasel. I should have handed it right over to William, but what he wrote worried me so much that I got confused about what to do. Promise me you will not show my brother?" She handed the letter over to Elizabeth.

Elizabeth's frown etched itself more deeply into her brow. Mr. Wickham had claimed that they were in love and were going to get married, but it did not sound like Georgiana liked him in the least if she thought him a weasel. She remembered Georgiana's fear at the ball, and the pieces began to fall together. Had Wickham tried to force himself on Georgiana? Or had something even worse occurred? "Dear, I am afraid I do not know your full history with the man. All I know is what he told me. He said you were in love and Mr. Darcy would not give his consent for you to marry."

Georgiana let out a faint cry, her hands crashing against the keys. A discordant series of notes sounded. "Then you know nothing of Ramsgate? You know nothing of his conniving, evil, mercenary, selfish ways?" Elizabeth shook her head. Georgiana took a deep breath then told her of the near-elopement and how he wanted only her thirty-thousand pounds. Her voice cracked as she even told Elizabeth of the hateful things he said about her once it was made clear he would not receive any of the dowry. She focused back down on the keys again, feeling tears threaten, but Elizabeth needed to know precisely what sort of man Wickham was. She would need to know to understand the letter. She nodded towards the letter and said once again, "Promise me you will not show my brother?"

Why must the Darcys insist on all these promises! What if what is in the letter requires me to tell Mr. Darcy? "I told you I did not know his evil ways, but that was not entirely true. I confess that at first I found him charming, but later understood him to be nothing but a scoundrel. I have had my own encounter with him, and I assure you my opinions on the man are not good. It pains me to hear of what he did to you but it pleases me to hear you no longer care for him. It must have been a very difficult thing to experience. I must tell you though, that if you do not want me to tell Mr. Darcy, I do not know if I should read the letter. I am his wife . . ."

"Oh, it is not anything like that. I certainly do not want you to keep secrets from your husband, but I know how William feels about the man and it would only upset him." Even as Georgiana sought to downplay the letter, she knew that it was nothing of the sort. If William knew about it, he would track Wickham down and perhaps even challenge him. She couldn't risk her brother taking such a risk. For a moment, she contemplated snatching the letter from Elizabeth's hand as her new sister opened it.

"I will read it," Elizabeth said, and gazed steadily at her. "But would you mind giving me some time to think on whether or not Fitzwilliam should know about it?"

"Only if it is necessary . . . but I do not think it will be so. Will you please tell me first if you are going to show him the letter?"

Elizabeth unfolded the paper she held and turned it over in her hand. There were no markings on the outside of the letter. "Of course I shall tell you first what I decide. How did you receive it? It is not addressed to anyone in particular."

"It came inside a separate paper which I have thrown away now. It was definitely addressed to me."

Elizabeth nodded her understanding and read the following:

I find myself thinking about our time together not too long ago. Your eyes that last night together told me you think about me too. I must say that your body language that night spoke volumes. You need to know that I do not give up easily. You may be with Darcy now, but eventually I will come claim what should have been mine all along. I am sure you can find a way to stay my hand. If I remember correctly you have an active and creative mind. I look forward to hearing from you and seeing how much your heart can give. For now, you can send any correspondence through Mrs. Forester. She is a favorite of mine, and owes me a great deal. Do not fret too much on the issue; just do what comes naturally in your blood.

Until I hear from you, sincerely,

Your dear Mr. Wickham

"Oh dear, and you have kept this threatening letter all this time? When did you say it came? There is no date on it either." Elizabeth let the letter drop to her lap. She did not know what to do in the matter. From her experience, Wickham could be quite forceful in his pursuits. She was reminded again just how forceful his lips had been that night on the balcony.

"It came a few days after the ball, after you and William got engaged. Oh please do not tell him about it. It has caused enough anxiety with me. We do not need to tell William about it!"

"Tell me what?" Mr. Darcy said lightly as he walked into the room. He assumed from their hushed tones that they had finally had their discussion. He could also see Georgiana look frantically from him and back to Elizabeth. He wished he could see Elizabeth's face but her back was to him.

Elizabeth quickly slipped the letter into her book and winked at Georgiana before she turned and said, "Dear, you do not expect to be privy to your birthday present plans do you?"

She called me dear! He smiled brightly. "My birthday is not for two months! What can you possibly need two months to plan for?"

Georgiana had seen Elizabeth hide the letter and wink, but it did not help her anxiety. What if he had heard more than he let on? What if Elizabeth told him about the letter? She was very near bursting out in tears, but collected herself. "A duet on the piano," she said weakly. She was never good at deceiving people and definitely not her brother.

Mr. Darcy did not miss that Georgiana did not meet his eyes. He knew the duet was not what they were discussing, but he also knew when to back down. He had enough faith in Elizabeth to know that if it was something he should know about then she would tell him. "Well then, I hope to hear something spectacular if you plan on practicing for two months!" He bowed and exited the room. Something was wrong, he knew, but he would trust Elizabeth in the matter.

After he left the room Elizabeth put her hands on Georgiana's and said, "Give me some time to sort out what to do. But for now, I promise not to tell him." Holding up her book, she added, "Do you mind if I keep this? I may need to study it a little, and from the sight of these frayed edges, you have studied it quite enough."

"Certainly. And thank you for your discretion."

*****

Things started to improve a little for Georgiana. Simply not having the letter on her person was a relief in itself, but she had to admit telling Elizabeth and not feeling the entire weight on her shoulders made things much better. She still felt terribly guilty, but that was something she needed to work out on her own. She even started going on a few walks since the weather had cleared up. One such afternoon Elizabeth offered to go with her.

"Elizabeth, may I ask you a question?" Georgiana said in the midst of their stroll.

"My dear sister, you may ask me anything. But I warn you my answers do not always come out with forethought, and have caught myself in terrible messes because of my impertinent tongue," she said, smiling.

"Now that you know about Ramsgate, the question I pose will make more sense. I lost a great deal after Wickham tricked me . . . mainly my faith in the goodness of people. I used to think that everyone had good intentions and always sought to better themselves in any way possible. I now know that is not the case. I once thought that money did not matter, but I have learned it matters a great deal to some people. I once thought that one should listen only to the heart, and now I recognize how much of an asset a rational mind can be. I once thought that love came easily and naturally, but after Wickham, I did not know if there was such a thing as love. But now I am even more confused. I see the goodness in your love match with William and I wonder what is it like to really be in love?" Georgiana was a pace or two ahead of Elizabeth and didn't notice Elizabeth's open mouth and stunned features.

Love match? She thinks our marriage is a love match? What in the world made her think such a thing? Elizabeth was speechless for the first time in who knows how long. Obviously playing the "good wife" seemed to be working. People were believing the charade they were playing. Elizabeth went over her experiences with William and was struck with deep concern over Georgiana's observation. *Mr. Darcy may be kind to me; he may now even think me tempting at times or even drop money on me like it was effortless. He may enjoy spending time with me, and he may even feel a certain level of appreciation for me, but he does not love me! Certainly not. If he did, he would say so! Would he not? Why would he not?*

She began to think of the coldness of his proposal which contradicted his caring gestures in the carriage after the wedding. Although he had promised not to bed her until she wished it, there would be moments where desire appeared in his eyes. Her mind couldn't make sense of his behavior. He had very nearly kissed her twice now, or at least that was what she had thought. His smiling eyes appeared more frequently than in the past, but all these things did not mean he loved her! He would have declared himself if he did! He was a very good man; indeed, a perfect gentleman. She now understood why the servants adored him, for he had a kind heart, one that reached out to the needy and less fortunate. He treated his servants like family. It struck her then.

She, too, was needy and less fortunate. He was simply treating her like any other person in the household. Her heart and mind were battling harder than ever. She thought about how he looked at her intensely with concern and kindness, but he was concerned and kind to his servants too! *But*, her heart argued, *he says such nice things to me!* Her rational mind reminded her that he said nice things to the servants as well. It was much easier to reason that he was simply being flattering and kind, rather than let her heart take the leap of faith that he loved her. Would he not have already declared himself if he loved her? There was no reason why he should not tell her if he felt such feelings for her. And he had not declared himself in any way. She had even asked why he married her but he refused to give an answer. *Yet. Would this not have been the ideal moment to confess his love— if that love existed in any form?*

Not only did he not love her, but she was no better than any other household member in his eyes. And being the gentleman that he was he would never take a servant to bed. It all made perfect sense now. Although she tried to remain composed, the painful reminder that she was in nothing near a *love match* sent a stab to her heart. She bit her lip and wiped at her eyes. Any moment now Georgiana would want an answer from her about what it was really like to be in love. She reached for her handkerchief but was too late. Georgiana had turned around and seen her tears. *I had been doing so well, even hoping that a friendship was forming! And now I realize that it was simply Mr. Darcy being kind and generous to me, just like he is with his servants.* "I am terribly sorry, Georgiana. I fear I have a headache and cannot go on. Please forgive me."

She turned abruptly, feeling tears slide down her cheeks as she walked back to the house. Her lack of attention meant that she soon found herself in the garden maze. She was two turns into it when she realized it. So far on her walks with Mr. Darcy they had not walked the maze. *At least he will not think to look for me here.* She continued to walk and make random turns, not paying any attention to the direction she was going. It was a direct reflection of the path her thoughts took. She reached a dead end and saw a bench. Tears stung her eyes and her chest felt unbearably tight. She had let herself begin to hope and that was turning out to be a very dangerous privilege. This is what it felt to hope, and then to be disappointed in that hope.

How could she have let herself expect more than companionship? And why did her heart hurt so deeply when it had only been a short time ago that she learned to value his friendship? Did she love him? Was that why understanding his motives in attending to her seemed to hurt so badly? She would not let her heart dwell on the inevitable. She had committed to herself on her wedding day, and would recommit herself now; she would be a good wife and only expect companionship. She would not set herself up for this kind of pain again. Unmet expectations were painful. It was easier said than done. Her chest convulsed with the movement of a sob. She began to talk quietly to herself to help her make sense of her thoughts and feelings. Of course, she came to no new conclusions, and soon her handkerchief was soaked through with tears. Mr. Darcy did not love her. If he did, he would have said so. There was no reason he should not. Why did this old knowledge feel so fresh and new?

*****

Georgiana knocked on her brother's study door and waited to hear him speak "enter." She took a deep breath and turned the knob.

"Come in, Georgie, what can I do for you? I was just finishing up with a few things." He frowned. Her spirits were clearly down again.

Georgiana looked at her hands before she spoke. "Brother, I fear I have made your wife upset, but for the life of me I do not know why. One minute we were talking and I asked her a question and the next she was crying and complaining of a headache and then she ran off. I am so sorry, but I do not know what I said."

"Tell me exactly what you said." He thought back on what her mood had been the last time they were together. She had seemed everything positive and engaging.

"I was telling her how more mature my outlook on people and love was since that awful experience with Wickham. I have learned a lot, William. But I was explaining that there was a part of me that stopped believing in love until I saw you two together. I was going to say how I now believed a love match was possible as I have witnessed it with the two of you."

"What did you say *exactly*?" He did not wish to place blame, but Georgiana didn't know their marriage was precarious for Elizabeth. He knew he loved Elizabeth, valued her more than his own life, and was fairly certain that she did not return his feelings. At least not yet. *Time, just a little more time.* He had hoped that things were changing but he couldn't be sure.

"I do not know for sure. I think I said something about your marriage being a love match and then I asked her what it was like to be in love. Did I say something wrong?" She started wringing her hands.

"No, no," Darcy assured her. "Do not fret, I am sure something else upset her. Did you see where she went?"

"Do not patronize me, William! She was fine before I asked her what it felt like and then she started crying. She entered the maze." Georgiana had not the emotional fortitude to endure her brother making her feel like a little girl. She turned to leave.

"Wait," her brother said quickly. "I am sorry. There are circumstances that complicate me explaining things, but at the moment I do not know the answers to the questions I know you have. Forgive me, Georgiana. I do not mean to patronize. It is hard for me to see you so grown up. Thank you for coming and telling me. I will go find her now." He didn't even bother to take his jacket. It was a warm afternoon out and his jacket would just make his chest feel tighter than it already was.

The maze wasn't difficult to navigate. If one ever got lost, the architect had arranged it so that they could stand on the many benches to determine their position. But her being lost was not what he was worrying about. What he was worried about was whether or not she wanted to be found.

He entered the maze and walked quickly but quietly, listening for her all the while. He was deep into the maze when he heard sobbing. She was mumbling something as well. He couldn't quite make it out . . . *The new and the old . . . companions . . . or was it companionship?* She was probably two hedges away, nestled in the heart of the maze, but he would have to veer away from her first in order to get on the right path. He decided it was not such a good idea to eavesdrop on her.

The bits and pieces of what he heard were not making sense anyway. When her heart-wrenching sobs began anew, he turned to leave to find the right path.

In one more turn he should see her. He could hear her better now. He pressed on, only wanting to comfort her. Every bone in his body wanted to hold her and he would permit it this time. When she cried on the way to London on the day of their wedding he felt he couldn't, but they had built something over the last few weeks. That had to count for something. He saw her now. She sat with her shoulders slumped and her head in her hands, looking impossibly fragile in her grief. She looked so fragile and breakable. He focused on the few stray curls that framed her face, and closed the gap cautiously as if she was a frightened wild animal.

"Dearest Elizabeth," he murmured. Her head jerked up. "Georgiana said you were upset, and I can see she was correct." He slowly took a seat on the bench next to her. He ached to reach for her hand. *Oh who cares, by gads! Take her hand already. It is not going to bite me. So I will have to endure the impulses that are all too appealing! But this is not about what I want. She needs me!*

"Mr. Darcy, I fear I am not in the best mood, and I suspect I will be poor company." She heard the sadness in her own voice. She twisted the handkerchief she held in her fingers.

He took both her hands in his and held them firmly. Her fingers stilled briefly, but then began to move again. He tried to speak as gently as he could. "I believe I told you once that I always want to know what you are thinking. Will you not tell me? Perhaps I can make it better."

The only way Elizabeth could see how his knowing her thoughts would improve the situation was if he truly cared for her. Since she knew that was not possible, she only saw the folly in his logic. Even so, she could sense his sincerity and dared to glance up to his face at his kind eyes. His warm hands caressed hers rhythmically. Her aching heart calmed slightly at his touch. She reminded herself that this was nothing more than simple kindness. He simply saw her as a damsel in distress in whom he felt obligated to offer his services. She felt a flash of anger.

Before she could bite her tongue, she spoke those awful thoughts. "I am more than a damsel in distress that you feel you need to rescue or your honor will be damned!" She read several things in his face at once. First she saw surprise, then confusion, and then something that looked like pain. *Why did I have to open my mouth and say such an awful thing?* She broke down in fresh tears and tried to free her hands from his in order to wipe her eyes.

He reluctantly released her hands, but at the sight of her demoralized pose, could not help himself. He reached around her, putting one arm around her back and shoulders. The other he wrapped around her and lifted her chin and pulled it up towards his shoulder. He knew what he wanted to say but struggled to find the strength and courage to do so. *She may not be ready to hear my feelings for her.*

Her words echoed in his mind once again. He wanted to say she was more than a damsel in distress, much, much more; she was his very reason for living. Instead all he could say was, "I used to worry about duty and honor, but a certain lady I met helped me see that one's heart is all that matters. Your heart matters to me, Elizabeth. It is not out of duty that I am here."

He held her closer and felt her tears stain his shirt where his waistcoat was unbuttoned. He felt courage in the fact that she didn't pull away so he continued, "If rescuing you is my plight, then I will gladly do it." He felt her hands against his chest through his shirt. It should have driven him wild, but his concern for her emotional wellbeing was far greater than the fulfilling of such fantasies. He kept holding her and she started to relax a little.

He took this as a good sign, so he continued, "I do not know what made you need rescuing, but it is my every wish to help. You are giving me the opportunity to show you who I really am." She sniffled. "Take a deep breath, people around here love and ardently admire and appreciate you." It was as close as he dared come to saying that he loved her. He did not want to push her or make her feel obligated in any way towards him. He kept his words coming. Although he was careful to speak in somewhat cryptic and guarded terms, he was opening up his heart to her. He listened as her breathing slowed and she relaxed further into the embrace. He kept whispering his thoughts.

Moments passed that felt like hours, until he did not know how long he had been holding her. He had only hoped to hold her until her tears stopped, but that was a while ago and she was not putting up any more resistance. She seemed to have relaxed deeply into him. Her weight was fully on his chest now, and he had to adjust his posture a little to be more comfortable. When he did this one of her hands fell from his chest down onto his lap. Could she have fallen asleep?

"Elizabeth?" There was no answer. He looked down at her face which was covered with her lovely curls. Her eyes were closed and her breathing deep and regular. She was beautiful, and it was clear she was asleep in his arms. He carefully shifted so his back would lean against the bench and guided her head down to his lap. The late afternoon sun was just reaching the horizon and tall shadows were dancing in the maze. He looked down at her sleeping face and smoothed her perfect curls away towards her forehead and neck. He continued to caress her hair for some time. He let his hands and fingers run through them, even taking out the last of the pins which were not doing much good anyway. He realized he would pay dearly for succumbing to this fantasy, but she was asleep and he could not help himself.

The warmth of her face on his lap and his fingers in her hair became distracting, and so he tried to steer his thoughts into appropriate avenues. Like her laughter that he so longed to hear. Her impertinent looks that drove him wild. He thought of those conversations he had had with her that only proved she was the only one he could have married. He remembered feeding the chickens together, and the way she was so at ease in those moments. They had candled the eggs last night and the chicks were growing nicely. He chuckled at the memory. The last time he had made sure to bring two candles. She had estimated that the eggs would hatch in about nine or ten days. Together, they had promised to candle them every other night to track the progress. His eyes began to be heavy as well, but only because he felt such peace at having her so close to him. Would she become cold soon? The sun was setting and he could no longer feel its warmth on their bodies. He did not wish to lose the moment, and so he waited. Soon the dusk was nearly dark, and still she did not move. Her breathing was deep and regular. He was getting chilled without his jacket. If he was cold, she must be too. He took off his waist coat and put it over her arms. He knew it wasn't much, but it would help.

Elizabeth had been dreaming again. It was the same dream that she had had for many of the past weeks. She was on the swing under the cedar tree being pushed my William. She knew the scene felt familiar but she patiently waited it out knowing that soon his hands would reach around for her lower swollen abdomen. One minute she could feel him push her, the next she would see him pushing her. His face was bright and cheerful and it had a look of peace that was genuine. He looked older, more distinguished than the dream had shown him before. She felt him stop the swing and knew soon she would feel his arms wrapped around her body. She waited for that moment but instead she heard squeals of laughter off to the side. She let her eyes veer in that direction and saw two little boys playing. The oldest was near the water's edge with a paper boat. The youngest, about two years old was following the oldest example. The oldest was getting irritated at the youngest and pushed him away. She called out to them, "William, no! No pushing!" The sound of her own voice woke her up.

"I did not mean to push," Mr. Darcy said, feeling a sharp jolt of shame. "I was just readjusting myself. I am sorry," Mr. Darcy said. Was she finally awake?

It took a moment to understand her surroundings. Mr. Darcy's voice had come from above her and what little she could see she was horizontal. Her face was warm but everywhere else was quite cold. "Mr. Darcy? Where are we?" She tried to sit up and felt his hands assist her. Had she been sleeping in his lap? She looked up at his face. He was evaluating her face but even in the darkness his eyes were dark and penetrating.

"We are still in the maze, but I fear we should probably get back or we might have to spend the night in here." He hesitantly joked. He didn't quite know what her mood was now that she was awake.

Memories of him coming to her and seeing her crying flooded her. She recalled his sweet comforting words in her ears all over again. His very touch had been so soothing. The last thing she remembered thinking was: *He would not hold a servant like he is now. And he would not say such sweet things to a servant. And his heartbeat she felt in his chest would not be quickened like it was if he felt she was nothing more than a servant.* It had been a sweet moment but she never expected herself to fall asleep so quickly. It was as if all her stresses and fears had seemed to dissipate as his comforting words continued. He didn't exactly say he loved her, but now she knew that he cared. She knew she was more than a servant to him. *Perhaps not quite a wife, but more than a servant.*

Chapter 8

At lunch the next day, all three Darcys received mail. Elizabeth eagerly opened two letters: one from Jane as well as her father. Mr. Darcy chuckled over one from Colonel Fitzwilliam, and Georgiana perused a letter from an acquaintance.

"I am instructed by Richard to ask you, Elizabeth, 'what do you call a shoe made out of a banana?'"

"Hmmm, I do not know . . ." she looked up at him, her eyes sparkling with anticipation.

"A slipper!" Mr. Darcy shook his head. "I fear my deliverance of such jokes is not up to his standard. I also fear his jokes are getting worse, but I am happy to announce that he is planning to visit us here at Pemberley next Wednesday and plans on staying for a few weeks. Perhaps then I do not have to play the clown and deliver his jokes for him." He saw Elizabeth's face light up in pleasure, but Georgiana's did not. "Did you hear me, Georgiana? I said Richard is coming to visit."

Georgiana looked up from her letter. "Oh, splendid." She knew her tone did not match her words and saw the concern march across both their faces. She tried again. "I do so enjoy his company."

Elizabeth frowned. Something in Georgiana's letter must surely be distracting her. Wickham would not have the presumption to write her at Pemberley, would he? "Georgiana, what do you call a shoe made out of a banana?" she tested.

"I do not know." She stood up and left her half-eaten luncheon as she exited the room.

Elizabeth wondered if she should talk with her further. Georgiana seemed to have done better for a little while, but was now back to the saddened tearful shell she had been a week ago. Elizabeth met William's eyes with her own for a brief moment, and read deep concern in them. The more she thought about it, the more she knew William needed to know about the threatening letter from Wickham. She did not want to breach the confidence that Georgiana had requested, but at the same time honesty with William seemed paramount.

*****

Mrs. Reynolds had three baskets of treats, candles, and bread ready when Elizabeth came to the kitchen. "Now, little Miss Madison is one of the dearest and most sincere girls you will ever meet. Her mother, Mrs. Mae Madison has been ill, and the little miss has had to take a great deal of responsibilities on her shoulders. She may be only twelve but she is very mature and responsible. This basket is for them. This one right here is for the Petersens. They have had to struggle with their farm because it is not draining properly, and their oldest son joined the navy, leaving them without the hands they need. The last basket is for the widow, Mrs. Smith. Her husband died six months ago, leaving her with two young boys and a darling little girl of three years. The boys have not yet been able to take on the farm's responsibilities but the neighbors have been helping a great deal."

Elizabeth tried to memorize what she just heard. "There is so much heartache," she said. "I hope Georgiana's and my visit will help." She looked to Georgiana, who was gazing at the baskets, yet not really focusing on them. "Georgiana, is there anything else I should know about these three tenants before we visit them?"

"I do not think so. Mrs. Reynolds was quite thorough." Georgiana had barely listened to what was said, but did not want to admit to it. She reached for two of the baskets and watched as Elizabeth took the other one. They were handed into the carriage together, the baskets crowded at their feet.

The service visits went smoothly, and at each house she noted ways she could offer assistance. The Madisons needed wood in their wood pile before the winter set in. The Petersens had two windows that were broken and boarded up that she could ask Mr. Darcy to fix, and the Smith's little girl had obviously grown out of her clothes. She offered invitations to all of the families to come to the festival and gave them their baskets. She was thanked profusely each time as well.

By the time they returned to Pemberley Mr. Darcy was waiting for them outside. He handed them out of the carriage and he tucked Elizabeth's arm into his. *Just this once. I will hold her arm just this once.* He stopped her just before they went inside, "How did the visits with the tenants go, Elizabeth?"

She paused and looked thoughtful. "It was wonderful; well, sad, but wonderful. I feel like I am a better person for going, and yet I was the one supposed to be helping them. They were so kind and welcoming." She then told him about the needs she noticed and asked what they could do about them.

"Of course we can help. These tenants ask so little but need so much. I am sure they all appreciated your visit." He had seen Georgiana go in silently to the house but also noticed that her mood wasn't any better. "And how did Georgiana do? Do you think it helped her?"

"For a while there last week I thought she was doing better, but she seems anxious and distracted again. I do not know if the visits helped. She conversed with them but it seemed to take effort on her part." Elizabeth wondered if now was a good time to talk to him about Wickham's letter to Georgiana. She had been thinking about it quite a bit and felt he should know about it. It was so threatening, and at the very least he should know some way to ease Georgiana's anxiety. But first, she recalled, she would have to talk to Georgiana about her decision to tell Mr. Darcy.

Elizabeth felt wholly comfortable now talking with Mr. Darcy. They had continued their walks and conversations, and now spent a great deal of time with each other. Although she was filling her time with learning her new duties as mistress of Pemberley, and she was sure he had plenty to do as master of Pemberley, he always made time to feed the chickens every day after lunch. She giggled, thinking about his falsetto chicken call and his funny face as he did it. He would tilt his chin up and half-smile when he did it, revealing his teeth in the same moment, making each time he did it quite entertaining. She could tell he was still uncomfortable around the chickens, but he did it anyway. In fact, he still always stepped back when they came rushing to his call. One such time he stepped into mud and his foot had slipped, almost causing him to fall. She wondered why he kept feeding the chickens with her when he was not totally comfortable around them. *Perhaps it is a way to spend time with me.* The thought made her blush.

"Why are you giggling?" His hand started to reach for her blushing cheek but he tucked it back behind him. Holding her arm was enough of a temptation and tried his convictions plenty.

"Oh, I am just distracted, I suppose."

"No, I do not think so. I insist you tell me what you were thinking."

"Or what, Mr. Darcy?" She arched her eyebrow challengingly at him.

"Oh, it is back to 'Mr. Darcy'? I was getting rather used to 'William.' Well then, if you do not tell me why you were giggling then I shall . . . I shall . . . throw you in the mud!"

Her mouth popped open, half in astonishment, half in amusement. "You would not dare!"

He looked around and started pulling her towards the barn, "Yes, I do believe there was some mud in the coop . . . I am sure it would match your hair nicely," In mock-outrage, she tugged back on her arm, but he held tight. He continued to pull, gently forcing her feet to move forward.

"I do not give up easily, you know," Elizabeth warned him.

He continued to pull her, as he rather liked this teasing side of her. "Trust me, I know just how decided your mind can be."

"What is that supposed to mean? Are you calling me stubborn?" She was enjoying the lightness of the mood. In truth, she wasn't resisting all that hard. They were making progress towards the barn and for a fleeting moment she wondered if he really would throw her in the mud.

"Oh, I would not dare call you stubborn but since you brought it up, I might remind you that it came out of your perfect little mouth, not mine." Mr. Darcy unlatched the coop gate and continued to pull her into it. The chickens were out, and once they recognized them they started heading towards them, obviously expecting food.

"I shall not tell you what I was thinking because you are just being an overbearing demanding beast of a man!" she teased.

He smiled wickedly, "Then a beast I must be! Now, madam, this is your last chance, what made you giggle?" He took her shoulders in his hands firmly.

She knew he was jesting and was quite enjoying this game. "Never!"

"Well then, you have made your bed and now you must lay in it! Pun intended!"

"Oh, good one! Richard would be proud of that little joke!"

He tried to look serious. "Joke? Who said anything about a joke! I fully intend on throwing you in the mud. Last chance . . ."

She laughed. "You already gave me a last chance. I can see that you are not the beast you think you are."

He laughed, tugging gently at her shoulders, but felt a very hard peck at the back of his calf. Startled, he lifted his foot, but then immediately slipped, pulling them both down into the mud and muck. He landed on his knees, but because he had used her to readjust his balance during the jump, she landed on her side. "Oh dear! I am so sorry! The rooster pecked at me and scared me." Mortified, he reached for her shoulders again, this time in abject apology.

"You beast!" She was still laughing, unhurt and not offended. Seeing he was only on his knees, she reached up and pushed him down onto his backside.

His hands released her only to catch his fall. The mud was at least three inches deep, and squelched as he balanced tenuously against his fingers. He reached back for a handful and raised it in front of him. "I am the beast? At least what I did was an accident. Now, madam, you leave me no choice but to live up to the title. I shall be the beast you say I am."

Her eyes widened. He would not really— she flinched back, raising her arms up to protect herself. She yelled, "No! No! Somebody help! HELP!" But her cries were to no avail, for she soon found herself with a handful of mud on her face. She sputtered, gasping with laughter. He had actually rubbed the chicken mud on her skin! Shrieking, she leapt forward towards his hair with two handfuls of mud, and her body landed right on his chest.

He let out a groan at feeling her sudden weight, moving quickly to catch his breath but losing his balance all the same. He fell neatly on his back amidst all the mud, but quickly rolled over, pinning her beneath him.

"You villain! I insist that you release me!" she screamed, laughing at the same time.

Although in his most private moments, Mr. Darcy had had many fantasies about rolling around with Elizabeth, he had never once imagined that mud might come into play. It was, however, not entirely unpleasant. In truth, it was all rather exciting. He laughed as well.

"You will pay for your actions," he said in the most dangerous voice he could muster. He was nearly ready to lean down and kiss her now, in spite of all his reservations, when he heard someone behind him.

"Unhand the lady!"

He looked behind them and saw Sparks, the farmhand. Sparks raised the pitchfork and held it menacingly. Darcy let out a laugh. "Sparks it is just I, Mr. Darcy. It appears my wife and I have fallen into the mud." Sparks' eyes got brighter and he lowered the pitchfork.

Elizabeth pushed William off and said, "Do not listen to him for one moment! That beast threw me in the mud! I insist we punish him! What say you Sparks? Should we feed him to the chickens?"

Mr. Sparks had quickly learned to love Mrs. Darcy. She was so devoted to the chickens and they had spent many of moments talking about the work he did. He respected Mr. Darcy, but truly loved Mrs. Darcy. He raised the pitchfork again and tried not to smile at the scene in front of him. Now that he knew the lady wasn't in distress, he could see the humor in it. They both had so much mud on themselves that he hadn't recognized either one until they spoke. "I believe that we must! Should I stab him first so they can get at his innards?" Sparks asked.

Mr. Darcy's mouth dropped open in mock outrage. "Sparks? Is this where your loyalty lies? After all these years of serving me, three weeks with her is enough to change your mind altogether! I shall have to rethink that bonus I gave last Christmas! Better yet, I will tell your wife of your volatile heart and let you suffer her wrath! Mrs. Sparks will be loyal to me and she will insist on yours as well!" He started to get up but turned back to Elizabeth one last time. She was flat on her back in the mud, grinning. Her teeth gleamed white through the dirtiest face he had ever witnessed. He raised himself to one knee to stand and looked back at the grinning Sparks.

Elizabeth saw an opportunity and quickly rose to her feet. He was kneeling, looking away from her, still gazing at Sparks. She gave him one good push from the back and saw him fall face first into the mud. She quickly ran for the gate and closed it behind her. "Hurry Sparks, I call on every ounce of strength in your body to get me out of range from that beast!"

She laughed all the way back to the house. She had heard him call out something about "next time" but as the words were hard to hear, she chose to pay them little mind. As she neared the house, she realized that to walk into the house like this would be to invite the deep displeasure of Mrs. Reynolds. The reality of what just happened made her laugh again in spite of how improper it all was. She probably ruined her dress. She supposed she would have to answer to Serafina as well. She decided to enter through the servants' quarters and get the help she needed there. She opened the door and called out, "Could I get some assistance?"

Rebecca, a young maid, was absorbed in her task of folding linen when she heard the sound of her mistress's voice. She paused, hands still full before she stepped over towards the door. She couldn't imagine why the mistress would be in the servants' quarters.

"Oh Rebecca, please get me a wash rag and plenty of water. And please notify Serafina that I need a bath . . . maybe two." She watched Rebecca's expression transform from curiosity to alarm as she took in the state Elizabeth was in. *Whatever horror I might inspire shall not change the fun I just had!* Rebecca did as she was instructed, and soon Elizabeth heard a deep voice behind her.

"And who might this be? Could it be the woman who pushed her poor husband in the mud?"

She turned around to see a filthy Mr. Darcy and burst into laughter anew at the sight of him. He had used his fingers to wipe away the mud from his eyes and mouth, but every other inch of him was thick with mud. "Oh dear, I pushed a little hard that last time, did I not?" She giggled in spite of the twinge of guilt that came over her.

He smiled widely. *Even covered in mud she is the most beautiful woman in the world, perhaps more than ever.* "You are giggling again? Do not worry, madam, I have learned my lesson. I will no longer ask you why you are giggling."

*****

The two of them poured water over themselves over and over again until they were both dripping wet, but finally could declare themselves at least nominally clean. Elizabeth had to resist the temptation to hide behind her hands; the dampened muslin clung to her body in a way that concealed very little. But that wasn't why her cheeks were flushed. Mr. Darcy had taken off his jacket, waistcoat, and cravat, and his once-white shirt was quite thin and soaked through to the skin. She had never noticed how masculine his person was before, and she kept finding herself stealing glances at his chest and arms. Her heart beat rapidly, and in spite of the chill of the water she was very warm. She was impressed that a man who did not do physical labor with his hands could have a chest shaped so handsomely.

"Do I still have mud on me, or is there another reason you are studying me so intently?" He cleared his throat, unaware of what he was really saying. His mind was having a terrible time keeping to the task at hand.

Elizabeth's flush spread all the way to her ears. *I have been caught looking at him in such a manner!* "No, sir," was all she could say. Her eyes did not stray in his direction again. Serafina wrapped a towel around her, and without another glance, they headed up for the real washing.

She had learned to really love and respect Serafina. The time they spent together was valuable in more ways than one. Elizabeth found herself calmed by Serafina's inner strength and fortitude. Every interaction left her spirits lighter and more at ease. Serafina also had a talent for making Elizabeth laugh, even during the most absurdly dramatic situation. She also seemed to genuinely care about the relationship between her and William. Today was no different.

"He is a handsome man," Elizabeth said, and then raised her hand to her mouth in surprise. She had not meant to speak aloud. Serafina smiled widely at her, continuing to help Elizabeth out of her soiled gown. "I am afraid I was caught looking at him, was I not?" She felt a blush coming to her cheeks again.

"Do not fret, madam," Serafina said reassuringly. "It is about time you two admitted how deeply you care for each other."

Elizabeth looked down, feeling a little embarrassed to be discussing such a topic. She had been correct, then, in her assumption that the servants, or at least Serafina, knew they had a precarious relationship. But the mud fight had broken down several rules of propriety, and she found she didn't mind having Serafina talk so boldly to her. "Do you really think he cares so deeply for me?"

Serafina's hands stopped working, and she reached her hands around to turn Elizabeth's head, looking her in the eye. "I cannot imagine him loving you any more than he does. Surely you see it too?"

"I have to admit, that is," Elizabeth said slowly, trying carefully to phrase it best, "I am beginning to suspect it, but he has never declared himself." She felt like she was talking to Jane back home instead of her servant.

"Men can only do one thing at a time. Their minds are simple. If we give them instructions, we must do so directly and clearly. They do not have complicated thoughts and feelings, which is why his adoration of you is evident. Have you made your feelings known to him?"

"I have to confess that I am not sure of my feelings myself. I know that I respect him and look forward to being with him, and my heart flutters when I am near him and he makes me feel . . . warm and happy. Is that love?"

"I cannot answer that for you. But I can advise you that if you wish to hear how he feels for you, you must be direct and clear. Men need to know exactly what we need from them. I must warn you that when you do decide upon your feelings, you may need to state your wishes directly."

Elizabeth pondered this advice. Perhaps she would ask him again directly why he married her. That was a direct question, and if he loved her, than he would tell her. "You are a fount of wisdom, Serafina," she said with a quiet laugh. "Now let us get me clean. I doubt anyone could love me when I smell like this!"

*****

After a lengthy bath, Elizabeth dressed for the day anew in one of her new sprigged muslins. Just as Serafina finished with her hair, Elizabeth heard a familiar jovial laugh downstairs. She followed the sound downstairs. "Richard! I had forgotten you would arrive today!" She hurried down the stairs and embraced him. She had seen much of him in London, and had loved him from the beginning if only because he brought out the smiling eyes of her husband.

"You wound me! What could possibly be so distracting that you forget your favorite cousin?"

Elizabeth colored. "Your beast of a cousin threw me in the mud!"

He let out an enormous laugh. "That is a good one; what is the punch line?"

Mr. Darcy walked in then, hair fresh and wet. "It is no joke, I am afraid. I really pushed her in the mud in the chicken coop." He saw Richard's eyes light up with mirth.

"So you finally admit to it?" Elizabeth laughed. She reached her arm out for his and stood close to him, looking up at his now-clean face. She couldn't suppress a faint giggle at the memory of him covered in mud.

Mr. Darcy held out his hand to stop Richard from speaking. "Stop! I must warn you not to even attempt to uncover the source of her laughter, for this wife of mine is merciless in keeping her secrets!"

Richard laughed again. He could tell there was quite a story behind the words. What amazed him more was seeing how engaging they were. He had seen them in London and worried that his cousin had married someone who was mercenary. It had been clear how Darcy felt about her, but Elizabeth didn't seem to show the same level of admiration. Seeing her smile, tease, and hold Darcy's arm like she was currently doing eased his fears a great deal. Perhaps it wasn't an absence of love on her part after all. "A chicken coop? Which reminds me . . ."

"Do not tell me you have a joke about a chicken coop?" Darcy groaned. Although, in truth, as much as he might protest, he did enjoy Richard's jokes.

"No, not about a coop. Do you want to know what happened to the chicken whose feathers were turned the wrong way or not?"

Elizabeth smiled and said, "Yes, what happened to the chicken whose feathers were turned the wrong way?"

"It got tickled to death!" He let out a roaring belly laugh, and was quickly joined by all present. Even Darcy laughed.

As Georgiana hurried down the stairs, she called, "Why all the laughter? Did I miss the opening joke?" She rushed in to embrace Richard, and was quickly enveloped in his tender arms. She felt much of her tension drain away as she realized that she was now surrounded by her three favorite people. She tried to hold back the tears, but it seemed impossible to do so when surrounded by so much love.

Colonel Fitzwilliam pulled back, "Dear Georgie, why all the tears? My joke was not that bad, was it?"

"No . . . well, I did not hear it. I am so sorry, I just cannot believe you are here." She turned to Elizabeth and tried to smile. "I am such a watering pot!"

They all laughed, the worried air momentarily easing as they settled in to talk eagerly of all that had happened in the past three weeks. After a short while, Colonel Fitzwilliam and Georgiana left to freshen up, but as Darcy and Elizabeth had already done so, they remained in the drawing room.

At first they sat in awkward silence. Elizabeth remembered what Serafina had told her earlier. She must be direct if she wanted him to declare himself. Darcy sought for some neutral topic of conversation, all the while trying not to think about their afternoon together.

With both of their deeper thoughts preoccupied, Darcy opened the conversation. "So how is the Autumn Festival planning going?"

"Very well, we started handing out the invitations today. I will go out again tomorrow but the rest we will just have delivered." Elizabeth hadn't been uncomfortable in his presence for a while, but now she felt acutely aware of how her gaze kept returning to the rise and fall of his cravat. "I am excited to see how Pemberley throws a ball."

Darcy laughed, "It is not a ball in the true sense. But I am sure now that you are here there will be many of opportunities to host a real ball. I have received many letters congratulating me on my marriage and they are all anxious to meet you. I am sure when you are ready we can start having dinner parties. I have even heard from Bingley, who is known for his terrible letter writing habits. He would like me to stand up with him for his wedding in December." He saw her eyes light up. "Would you like to plan a visit to Longbourn in just over a month?"

"Oh yes! I would not want to miss Jane's wedding for anything! I have wanted to ask you if we could go since she asked me to stand up with her before we left Hertfordshire."

"She asked you before our wedding? Why have you not asked me since then?" Darcy wanted her to feel comfortable with asking him anything. The fact that she hadn't yet indicated she had not yet opened her heart fully to him, and he found himself troubled by the thought.

Elizabeth noticed the frown and her heart sank. She wanted to see those smiling eyes that she had gotten so used to. "If I am not mistaken, we have talked very little about their engagement. I also did not know what the weather is like in early December. I truly did not know it would even be possible to travel at that time." She started thinking about the chicks that would be hatching in less than a week. It was the end of October and winter storms started mid-December back home. "When do the winter storms start here?"

He understood that what she was truly asking was if the chicks would survive the winter. "Usually in the beginning of December, but some years it is earlier. During other years like this one, it seems the warm weather holds until nearly Christmas. But I do not believe I have had a Christmas in years that did not have snow." There, he had said it. Whatever these chicks meant to her, she knows now what to expect.

"So possibly before December or Christmastime? That is either four weeks or eight."

Darcy leaned forward and touched her hand, "How long does it take for the chicks to get their feathers?" There was no use dancing around what they were really talking about. Bingley's wedding had nothing to do with the topic.

Elizabeth's eyes grew tearful. "At least six weeks. But they are not due until next week. Probably the night after the festival."

Darcy didn't need his Cambridge mathematics to calculate that unless it remained unusually warm, the chicks would not make it. "Is there anything we can do to help them stay warm until their feathers come in?" If there was, he would do it. He didn't know why, but they were special to her.

"I have heard of bringing them indoors, but the risk of them not developing the winter resistance is high if we do that. It could harm them more than help them. Sometimes when we think we are helping, our actions make things more difficult. I am afraid the only thing to do is to see if the winter storms will stay away until they are healthy and strong. These things take time. I just wish there was some way to control it, but nature has its own timetable." Elizabeth squeezed his hand but looked away, her eyes glossing over tears.

More riddles about the chickens? I wish I understood what she was really talking about!

Two days later, Darcy suggested a picnic at his favorite part of the stream. Georgiana declined, and Colonel Fitzwilliam seeing an opportunity to corner Georgiana about the mood he had noticed since he had arrived, declined as well. He was one of her guardians and there was something deeply troubling her. She usually was bright and cheerful around him, but she was being cryptic in her conversations, hardly offering any information nor contributing in any way. He had tried to ask Darcy about it, but Darcy simply shrugged and said he didn't think it was anything big. Darcy told him Elizabeth had talked with her and never came to him with any concerns. *Well, if she told Elizabeth, then she is certain to tell me.* Colonel Fitzwilliam wished them well and watched them leave.

Darcy explained to Elizabeth that it was quite a walk, maybe even a bit of a hike, but the view was worth it. She followed him up into the forest to the north, weaving through trees and over boulders. They walked together for at least two hours, laughing and enjoying the landscape before they came to an open area with tall, silvery grasses.

"You have a meadow too? Now I know Pemberley has everything I could possibly want!" Elizabeth had stopped walking at the edge of the meadow to take in the view. She gazed out at the high flat plain, seeing the rise of hills further north. To the south, she could tell that it promised a beautiful view, and her feet, although weary, started taking her that way.

He was pleased to hear such praise of Pemberley. "It is not so much a meadow as it is a plateau. See, if you look towards where you are going, there is a great drop off. Do you remember the cliffs you see from the gardens way off to the northwest?"

"We walked that far up? Goodness, no wonder my legs are tired! I think you intend to test my reputation as a great walker!" Elizabeth laughed to show that she was only teasing, but knew there was an element of truth to it all the same.

"Come see the view from the cliff's edge. It is spectacular, and on a day as hot as this you will appreciate the breeze." The October afternoon could have easily been mistaken for a summer's day; there was no wind and the sun was beating down on them hard. The sky was clear blue and mostly cloudless, with a few dotting the horizon. Elizabeth suspected that the unusually hot weather made it somewhat uncomfortable to be exerting oneself as they did. As they neared the rocky edge, Darcy instinctively took her arm. He would do anything to protect her and ensure her safety. They just stood arm-in-arm for several minutes, gazing out at the view in awe.

Pointing to the south, Darcy said, "Over that hill you would see Lambton. You can barely make out the road to Pemberley, but it is there, winding through those trees. And over there is where my father used to take me shooting, you can see the lake has marshes where all kinds of birds live and migrate to and from each season. We would hunt all autumn and we would talk about everything. He loved most to talk about how he fell in love with my mother. She was already sick at that time, so it made him feel better to recall happier times."

Elizabeth saw a very faraway look in William's eyes. "Tell me about them. How did they fall in love?" She listened as he retold the story that he must have heard many times, so richly embroidered with detail was it. She listened as he told of other ladies who wanted his father, but that his father only had eyes for his mother. She listened as he told of how when they first danced, there was a spark of fire that burned as they touched, and how his father knew that she was the only one he could ever be prevailed upon to marry. He told of their courtship and their first kiss. She listened to his words, but heard what went unspoken between each of them. His words may have been about his parents but he was speaking metaphorically as well. It made her blush to think that he might be talking about her as well. Perhaps all but the first kiss; that hadn't happened yet. This thought made her blush even more, thinking of how much she longed to have him kiss her. *Maybe if I just step closer he will kiss me.* She did so and looked up at his thoughtful eyes.

His body told him before his eyes did that she had stepped closer. She was holding his arm close to herself. He tried to calm his heart but she was so near him that he was certain she would hear its gallop. He could smell her fresh linen and lavender scent, and he allowed himself one good intake of the fragrance before he realized that wasn't such a good idea. He could feel her breath along his neckline which meant she was looking up at him, her face inches away. It was as if she wanted him to kiss her. Could she be ready? Could her heart have changed enough to welcome such a kiss? He knew if he looked down at her, he would capture her beautiful full lips with his own and hold her close, tasting her sweetness. He inhaled deeply through his mouth, breaking the intoxicating spell that bound his body to hers, and then stepped away. "I want to show you the stream." She didn't realize what a dangerous game she was playing. They were very secluded and if he kissed her he might not be able to stop.

Her brow furrowed up and her lips drew together in a faint pout. Serafina's words rung in her head again. "You have to be direct if you want a man to do something." She ran through several schemes in her head, but would any of them work? She had no experience in wooing men. And it seemed to be that this particular man was incredibly talented in self-control. It was as if keeping that promise meant the world to him. He was going to be trustworthy if his life depended on it. *Perhaps a little too trustworthy.*

They reached a small stream that was about a foot deep. Through the clear water, she could see a great deal of moss on the rocky bed beneath. She stepped closer and reached down to touch the water. "Oh, it is so cold!"

"Yes, the hills over there have a natural spring which feeds into this. I have explored the cave several times and seen it myself. You probably will not get cleaner water anywhere in the area." Darcy had just started to regain control over his thoughts when Elizabeth sat down at the water's edge and started unlacing her boots. "What are you doing?" he asked.

"I am going to put my tired feet in the water! What else?" She knew a lady didn't do such things, especially when a man was present, but he was her husband after all. And if he didn't like it then he could look away . . . *And if he does like it maybe I will get my first kiss!* She was reminded of that first night at Darcy House, when she was mortified to have Serafina unlace her boots in front of him. A lot had changed since then. He gave her a surprised look and then sat down next to her.

"Well then, I cannot have a lady be unescorted in such dangerous waters . . ." He laughed, glancing down at the slight current. She would be in very little danger, of course, but he could not resist the temptation. He started removing his boots too.

She let out a laugh, "No sir, a gentleman would never leave a lady in such need!" She tugged at her boots, but her feet were somewhat swollen and she had to work to get them off. He reached over to help just before she finally pulled off the last one. She colored a little to think he was offering to help her take off her boots.

Mr. Darcy had kept himself occupied with removing his own boots, but when she struggled with her own, he had instinctively gone to help. He hadn't meant to offer; he just saw she needed help, and had reached to do so. He caught a glimpse of Elizabeth pulling up her skirts enough to keep them from dragging in the weeds and pebbles. Her delicate feet walked carefully towards the stream. He had to focus on his own task, but it was near-impossible to do so when he thought of how he had never seen her feet or ankles before. He loved the way she crossed them when she sat down and tucked them under her when she was deep into reading a book, or how tempting they were to look at when she tapped them in the library at Netherfield while fully absorbed in her book. He was more than a little mesmerized at his first glimpse of them. She had her back to him so he continued to watch them carefully make each step towards the water. He knew he should play the gentleman and look away but he could not make himself do it. Even her step was lovely, carefully picking her way across the gravel. When she reached the water, she arched her foot, dipping one toe in first.

"Oh!" Elizabeth gratefully sank her whole foot into the water. "That feels so good!" She started walking out towards the middle of the stream. Once she was halfway there, she turned to Mr. Darcy, and, with a mocking smile, added, "Well, are you just going to watch or are you going to help your lady in these turbulent and dangerous waters?" For some reason, his cheeks were flushed pink. He gave her a small, knowing smile before he spoke.

"Halt, woman! Thou shalt not proceed without the proper protection! I come to secure your safety!" He made quick work of removing his last boot. His feet were hardly calloused, and he found the rocks hurt a little as he walked. He stepped into the freezing water. He admitted the coolness was pleasurable, but he found walking on the mossy rocks was a little tricky. He noticed there were several boulders spaced throughout the stream poking their tops out of the water. He made his way out into the middle, navigating around some of the larger boulders, to make his way to where she was. He found it was slightly deeper than expected and bent over to roll his breeches up further.

"Do not tempt me, sir."

He stood back up. He knew how *he* was being tempted, but the humor in her voice tipped him off that *her* brand of temptation was much different from his. "And how is rolling up my pants tempting, madam?"

"Now that you are upright it is no longer a temptation. You are safe from me pushing you over. You may thank me now for withholding my impulses," she said with all false seriousness.

"Indeed? And how would you have accomplished such a feat when I must weigh nearly twice what you do?" he asked teasingly.

"I have learned a few things along the way, and can defend myself quite nicely, or have you forgotten your spill in the chicken coop?"

"Defend yourself? How was I just now threatening you?" He felt his heart start to race when she raised her eyebrow at him.

"You were going to come over and take my arm in yours . . ." She paused dramatically.

He walked the two feet between them. "Like this?" And he reached for her arm. She let go of one side of her skirt.

"Yes." She felt her body react like it always did when he was near.

"I do not see that this is threatening . . ."

Remember, be direct! "And then you were going to put my arms up by your neck . . ." She felt a great deal of nervousness rise up in her at her boldness.

He let a small smile creep across his face, but then schooled his features to continue playing the part. He reached for both her arms and put them up by his neck, causing her to drop the other side of her skirt, "Like this? But I am sure this is not threatening either," he nearly whispered. He could hear his heart pounding in his ears.

She swallowed. "Yes, exactly. Just like that." She stepped closer so that their chests were nearly touching. "And then you were going to . . ." Could she do it? Could she ask him to kiss her?

"What was I going to do, Elizabeth? I must know." His voice was soft and gentle. He tried to step closer to her, but his foot slipped off the mossy rock he was standing on. He tried to catch his balance, but his movement made her slip as well. In one fluid movement her feet went out from under her as he reached for her waist. The weight of her fall knocked him completely off balance, and he fell in her direction. They both tumbled into the water with an enormous splash, and although his arms still held her by the waist, he felt her go limp. He quickly got to his knees and lifted Elizabeth out of the water.

"Elizabeth!" Her eyes were rolled back in her head and her body lay limp in his arms. He realized with growing panic that she must have hit her head. He lifted her up in his arms, trying to cross the stream and reach the safety of the shore. The added weight made the moss even more slippery and he nearly fell twice. He got her to the bank and laid her down gently. She was breathing normally but her eyes were still closed. He inspected her head and didn't find any cuts, but her hair was still in a bun. He took out her pins as carefully as he could to inspect her head. He found a growing lump at the back of her head near her neck. She had hit her head, and she must have hit it hard. She was completely drenched, as was he, and he shook her shoulders a little.

"Dearest Elizabeth! Please wake up!" He put his hand on her face, patting her cheeks. She let out a moan and turned her head to the side, but otherwise did not stir. He stared at her eyes, pleading for them to open. When he shook her shoulders once again, he saw a flicker of movement in her eyelashes. He called out her name over and over again, and then said a prayer out loud.

"Dear God, anyone but her!" It was all he could muster. The sincerity of the prayer was what counted, he told himself, and felt vindicated in his faith when he saw her roll her head from side to side and slowly raise her hand up to her head. He reached for the hand to stop her. "Elizabeth, open your eyes." His heart broke at the sight of her lying there limply. He could not contemplate the possibility that he might lose her in this moment, although an impish voice pointed out that these sorts of injuries could easily prove fatal. The fact that she was moving slightly was encouraging, but it still didn't calm his fears.

Elizabeth opened her eyes, but found that nothing made sense. She could feel and hear William's panicked voice, but her sight was full of blurred colors and light. She blinked a few times and then let out a faint moan. Her head ached sharply, a piercing pain beginning at the base of her neck. If she concentrated, she could make out two persons in front of her, but they seemed to dance from side to side. She could hear William, but who was the other? Elizabeth shut her eyes after a moment. She did not want to see any more of the scene before her. Afterwards, though, she felt overcome by a sudden wave of nausea. She sat up immediately, bracing one hand against the ground, and then she retched, vomiting. Afterwards, she opened her eyes to a world that seemed much, although not entirely, clearer than before.

"Thank goodness," Darcy said fervently. He stroked her brow, holding her hair out of her face. "Are you all right, Elizabeth?" Surely she could not have fainted for more than a few minutes. His stomach twisted. *I cannot even think of losing her!* He watched her carefully, noting her look of confusion and the difficulty her eyes faced in focusing. *Was it my fault she fell in the water? How will I ever forgive myself if she is seriously injured?*

Elizabeth turned her head slowly to face a still-blurred Mr. Darcy, and then gazed around. Hadn't she seen someone else? "Where is the other person who was here?" Her gaze was sharpening with every moment. Once she was able to semi-clearly focus on Mr. Darcy's face, she saw his features tighten with concern.

"It is only I, Elizabeth. No one else is here. How do you feel?" *Please tell me you are well! I cannot bear the idea that I might have injured you!* The fact that she was making complete sentences was reassuring but why was she asking who the other person was?

"Better now, I think," she said slowly. "My head hurts," she added. It was quite an obvious statement, but also one that she could hardly avoid making. She didn't want to worry him too much. She was surely fine; and she could see that he was quite distressed enough without news of her double and blurred vision. It was improving with every moment, and she continued to blink in order to help herself focus. She reached her head back to her hair, tracing the wet and tangled locks. "Where are my pins?"

"I had to inspect your head when you fainted," he explained quickly. "They are right here." He held them out to her, frowning a little as her fingers fumbled in their quest to gather them up. She had not gotten far in pinning up her damp curls before her arms fell slack to her sides. "Do you need help?" he asked.

"No." She closed her eyes for a moment. "I think I will just leave it down. It is so hard to pin while tangled and wet like this." She refrained from adding that raising her arms made her nausea return.

"Is there anything I can do for you? I think there is some wine in the satchel with the bread and cheese." He told himself he needed to do more than watch her movements like a hawk.

"Maybe later. I think now I just want to sit down for a little while before heading home."

In spite of his worry, he smiled at the idea that she could now call Pemberley her home. "It is still early," he assured her. "We have plenty of time before we need to head back." He tried to remember all that he had heard about blows to the head. So far, she did not seem too grievously hurt, but he did not want to see her suddenly decline in front of him.

He helped her move over to a more comfortable spot, but didn't go far. They sat together on the grass for more than an hour, simply talking while Mr. Darcy continued assessing her and her condition. They commented on how unusually warm it was for late October, about Georgiana's state of mind, and about the Autumn Festival. And they even talked about the chicks, but the one thing they did not discuss was what was forefront in their minds. Although he tried to find ways to construe it differently, Mr. Darcy could not help but think that for the first time, she had truly wanted him to kiss her. Her negative opinions of him surely were changing. She was back to being her teasing impertinent self, and she smiled even more often than she ever did at Longbourn. She felt comfortable taking her shoes off in front of him and letting him glimpse her ankles and legs. But most importantly, she seemed to enjoy and sought out his company. *Yes, it is about time I make due on a certain promise and tell her why I married her.* He knew telling her while she was still wet and complaining of a headache wasn't the most romantic time or place to tell her he loved her, but he felt a like a great burden was lifted now that he felt it was appropriate to tell her. He had been patient this long, he could be patient a little longer.

Elizabeth was feeling much better, although she still felt weak and ill when she turned too quickly. She tried to remain as still as possible while continuing to talk. After the first hour she began to feel dry in her mouth. "Is there something besides wine in the satchel? I am quite thirsty." She wanted to rinse her mouth out a little too.

Mr. Darcy was relieved to hear her voice a need that he could help with. He could tell she felt worse than what she let on. He quickly reached over for the satchel. "There is only a wine bottle and the bread and cheese. But if you do not want the wine we could get water out of the stream."

"Maybe wine would be fine and then the water." She was hoping for a little pain relief from the wine, but knew she didn't need anything else altering her vision or equilibrium. At least her nausea was gone. She watched as he opened it and poured her a drink. She took a cautious sip. "That tastes wonderful," she confessed.

"I think you are just thirsty," Mr. Darcy said, looking a little amused in spite of himself. "It is not the finest Pemberley has to offer. You should probably eat something. It has been quite a while since breakfast."

Elizabeth looked at the sky to gauge what time of day it was. The sun was lower in the sky and so it had to be mid-afternoon. She knew it took several hours to get to the stream and knew it would be a slower decent back to Pemberley now that she had a headache. "I will eat a little, but we should be heading back soon."

Mr. Darcy's Promise

She gingerly ate, and was pleased that her stomach seemed to approve. After eating, she had the courage to try standing with support. In spite of some lightheadedness, she found herself able to walk fairly easily, although her head throbbed a great deal.

Darcy reached for her arm to steady her, waiting for her to proceed. Once they started down the mountain, he was careful not to let go of her arm. He kept glancing in her direction to assess how she was doing. Although she sometimes reached a hand to her head, and seemed to blink frequently, she seemed to do well as long as she held on to his arm. The descent down the mountain was indeed slower, and around dusk they finally made it to the gardens of Pemberley. Elizabeth took a deep breath before she spoke.

"William? I feel I need to ask something again and this time I want a direct answer."

He looked to her. He could tell she was quite weary, and he suspected she still had a headache, but she had not complained once in the three hours it took to get home. Her face was serious and his heart began to pound again, this time with a different sort of concern. "I will be as direct as I can be."

"Why did you marry me? You could have said no to my father, and no one would have blamed you. And yet here we are, married." In order to avoid seeing his expression, she gazed ahead at the gardens in front of them. Her forehead creased up at the sight of a groom running through the garden in their direction. "Do you see him running? What could be the problem?" She pointed to the groom who was closing the distance fast.

"David, what in the world is wrong?"

"Sir, there is an emergency and you are needed immediately!" David had caught up to them now.

"Well, what is it man?"

David looked to Mrs. Darcy and back again to Mr. Darcy. "Perhaps I can inform you in your study."

Darcy's brow furrowed and he looked to Elizabeth, "It appears I must leave you sooner than I would like. I will leave you in the care of Mrs. Reynolds." She nodded. They walked the rest of the way to the house. When they got to the door he gave her arm a squeeze and dropped her arm. He then leaned towards her and whispered, "I keep my promises, Elizabeth, and I will tell you soon why I married you. I want nothing more than to tell you why I married you." He told Mrs. Reynolds briefly about the head injury, looking Elizabeth over one last time before he hurriedly walked to his study with David.

Elizabeth watched as her husband left. Without his steady strong arm to hold onto, her head had started to spin again. She declined Mrs. Reynolds' arm but asked that the kitchen begin heating water for a bath, asking that Serafina be sent to her room. She picked her way up the stairs, finally sinking down in front of her vanity, proud of herself for not having fallen in front of the servants. She brushed her fingers down her dress, dislodging the dirt and moss. She did look a fright, she reflected ruefully. She reached back and unbuttoned her dress as best she could before Serafina entered to help.

"Thank you," Elizabeth said once the dress was safely off. "I would appreciate a bath, but first a glass of water?" She settled back down in front of her dressing table, not bothering to remove her chemise and petticoat before the water was brought to her room. She didn't quite have the strength to stand. Serafina nodded and closed the dressing room door behind her.

Elizabeth wondered what kind of emergencies Pemberley would have that would make him leave so suddenly. She hoped it wasn't too serious. She finally let herself think about the "almost kiss." She remembered his eyes being dark— darker than usual, and hearing his gentle encouraging words. *What was I going to do, Elizabeth? I must know.* Both his eyes and words had been full of hope. He had wanted to kiss her. It made her heart beat faster just thinking about it. She found herself feeling embarrassed for being so bold to have almost asked him to kiss her. She heard a knock on the door. *That was quick,* she thought. "Enter," she said, reaching for her brush.

She did not turn at first, but then after hearing nothing from Serafina, she glanced behind her to see William. He stood there with his hand on the door handle, lingering for what seemed like minutes, but in reality it was probably only a second or two.

Mr. Darcy finally averted his eyes after those seconds. Elizabeth's face was suffused with shock and embarrassment. "Pardon me, I just came to tell you . . . never mind, I can see this is not the time. I did not mean to invade your privacy. Forgive me." He closed the door behind him. *Oh dear Lord! I just walked in on Elizabeth undressed! But she had said "enter!* He would never have knowingly intruded on her privacy like that! *But she had said "enter!"*

When he passed Serafina in the hall, he realized she must have meant to admit Serafina rather than him. He hoped this experience would not be a step backwards in their relationship. He had tried very hard to offer her the privacy she had needed over the last month. He had done everything in his power to keep his thoughts and hands to himself even though her beautiful face was near him so often. He had kept his promise and he did not want her to feel she could not trust him. He resolved to apologize after the emergency with the tenant was finished. *You can trust me, Elizabeth! I will not do anything against your will!*

Regardless of his resolve, he allowed himself a smile as he remembered their moment in the stream where it was obvious what her will was at that time. He allowed himself to imagine such a kiss happening and didn't chastise himself in the slightest for doing so. His imagination was quite keen, and perhaps a little repetitive to his delight.

*****

After Mr. Darcy left, Elizabeth turned back around to the mirror to examine herself. Her chemise covered her breasts, but left her shoulders bare. The material was light, but not so thin as to be indecent, and luckily her petticoat covered everything beneath her waist. She realized she had not said one word to him once he entered. She could see the mortification flush his cheeks pink. She laughed embarrassedly at the incident. There was nothing she could do now but see the humor in it. Knowing him, he was probably reproving himself about it, but she could not help but laugh at the memory of his face. They had been husband and wife now for over a month and this was the closest thing to intimacy they had so far. She laughed again.

She heard another knock at the door, "Who is it?" she asked this time.

"Serafina, madam."

Serafina entered, leading in the servants who carried the hot water. Elizabeth sank back into the bath, enjoying the feel of the warm water encircling her as Serafina washed her hair. Afterwards, Elizabeth insisted that she dress for dinner in spite of the early hour. She didn't feel lightheaded any longer, but still wanted to rest for a short time before the meal. Serafina plaited her hair and then secured it in a secure topknot. As she finished, Elizabeth hoped that tonight she and William would have a moment to talk, *and maybe a chance to finish what was started in the stream.* She smiled to herself and laid back against her chaise.

It seemed like her eyes were closed for only a few moments, but after that time she was awoken by Serafina. Elizabeth cautiously sat up.

"It is time for dinner, madam."

She tried to stand, but found that she could not quite overcome her weakness and fatigue, and Serafina helped her rise to her feet. Elizabeth blinked: her head spun a little, her double-vision recurring before she steadied herself.

Serafina clucked tenderly as she examined Elizabeth's hair. "I will need to fix your hair again, I am afraid. Why did you not tell me about hitting your head? I could have been more gentle in washing and fixing your hair! The master told me about your fall and he wants me to keep an eye on you." Serafina's eyes were dark with concern.

"Is he back?"

"No, I am afraid he just came back to change. He said he would probably not return until well after dinner. He also told me to tell you he was sorry. He was quite insistent that I relay his apologies." She brushed slowly and carefully through Elizabeth's hair before she began to plait it again. "I am so sorry, madam, that I did not notice this bump earlier."

Elizabeth could imagine Mr. Darcy giving Serafina the cryptic message apologizing for intruding earlier, but making it sound like he was apologizing for missing dinner. "You know, I got this bump on my head because I was following your advice."

"Which advice were you attempting to follow, madam? Because I doubt I ever told you to fall into a river and break open your head."

Elizabeth laughed, enjoying Serafina's tart response. Speaking with her was beginning to feel increasingly like it did when she talked with Jane. "I was about to ask him to kiss me when our feet slipped on the rocks." She saw Serafina's gaze rise in surprise.

"Truly? And did he kiss you?"

"No, not yet. It did not quite get that far because I blacked out then. I have never been so nervous! It may seem like I have confidence but I do not want him to think me wanton!"

Serafina smiled. "I am sure Mr. Darcy would not think you wanton. His valet, Martin, is sure of it."

Hearing the revelation that Serafina knew what his valet thought reminded her that servants talk amongst themselves. She was not quite sure how she felt about this. "Serafina, I know we have talked about a great deal, but I hope what we say to each other is kept in confidence."

"Do not you worry, my loyalty is to you and you alone. Mr. Darcy knows nothing of what you have disclosed, but if I may be so bold, I think he *should* know how you feel. May I say one other thing?" She twisted the braid up high on Elizabeth's head and pinned it.

"Certainly."

"You deserve him. He is the best of men and he has given his heart to the best of women."

*****

Dinner was a quiet ordeal. Georgiana was still somber and Richard had gone to help with the emergency. Elizabeth's head was still sore, and so she and her sister-in-law made poor company for each other. Afterwards, Georgiana excused herself, leaving Elizabeth alone.

Elizabeth made her way to the front door to speak with the butler. "Mr. Reynolds, have you heard any updates on the emergency that took Mr. Darcy away?"

"No madam, the situation is the same as he told you." Mr. Reynolds said.

Elizabeth didn't quite understand what he meant because William never came and told her what the emergency was. She hadn't seen him again since the scene in her dressing room. Awareness dawned on her. He probably had meant to tell her what was going on, but the state of her dress, or undress, prevented it. She was going to have to extract the information casually if she were to calm her mind. It had been over two hours since he had left and she was beginning to worry. What would keep him out after dark? "I was hoping for some more information."

Reynolds said, "The last update was that the fire was still going strong and threatening the orchard."

Fire? She needed more information. "Which orchard, the orange grove or the apple?" Her heart raced, imagining him fighting a fire.

"Not Pemberley's orchard, madam, a tenant's orchard. The house was engulfed, however, and is a complete loss."

"Thank you. Will you please tell Mr. Darcy I am in the library when he gets in?" Her mind was reeling. William was out fighting a house fire?

"I do not think it will be for some time though. I am instructed to make sure you rest and take care of yourself. Perhaps you should retire and I will have him wake you when he gets in."

Elizabeth shook her head, "No, certainly not. I will just be in the library reading. You will tell him when he comes in?"

"As you wish. Can I send for something? Would you like a blanket or a fire started?"

She nodded. "Please. Thank you, Reynolds." She left to go to her chambers to fetch her book. Her head was spinning, but not because she had hit her head earlier. This time it was imagining his handsome face and warm hands getting burned, or the building collapsing and trapping him inside. Her heart ached at the sudden thought of losing him. *I cannot lose him! He means too much to me!* She felt her worry and pain grow with each step up the stairs. *If only there was something I could do!* She reached her chamber and retrieved her book from the nightstand. *Sense and Sensibility,* by a Lady. It was the book William had picked out for her the day he found her sliding on the ladder. She was only halfway through it, but had enjoyed it so far, and reading it now would be a comfort to her.

By the time she reached the library the maid was nearly finished starting the fire. "Thank you, Ann. Do you think you could bring a bottle of wine as well? My head is still throbbing, and it seemed to help some before." What she really wanted was something for her nerves, not her head, and wine would do the trick. Ann curtsied and left, leaving Elizabeth to the empty library and the small consolation of her book. The cataloging process didn't seem to be making much progress, as there were books everywhere still. Elizabeth shifted over a pile on the chaise and settled there before opening her book to begin to read.

It wasn't long before the maid came in with the wine. She noticed that there were two glasses and she poured herself a glass. Her heart began to pound inside her chest once again. The longing she felt to hold him and know that he was safe was unbearable. He had grown to mean so much to her. She thought of her conversation with Serafina a few days ago about her feelings for him. She had admitted her attraction to him then but didn't know what to call the feelings she felt. Was it love? She took a drink of her wine. She cared deeply for him, respected him, admired him, and trusted him. She appreciated him, was grateful for him, and she was . . . she was attached to him in a way that she could not describe. Her heart had grown so close to his that the thought of losing him tore it apart. Her body ached to be held by him, to smell him, and to finally kiss him. She wanted to spend every moment she could with him, and wanted every conversation she had with him to be permanently etched into her brain.

She relished the time she had with him. Meeting with him had quickly proved to be the highlight of her day, no matter what they did together. They shared moments of companionable silence, and happy moments where she saw the now-familiar smile touch his eyes. They had moments where they flirted with each other. They had moments where all the social rules seemed to fly out the window and they were simply themselves. She realized then where her thoughts were leading her. She felt like herself when she was around him; he was family to her. But he was more than just family. He was her friend, her companion, her husband, and she loved him.

The realization was both comforting and painful. "I love him," she said out loud. She drew in a deep breath and said it again. "I love him!" Why did she have to realize this now when he was out in so much danger! Perhaps it was the idea of losing him that made her confront how dear he was to her. She poured herself more wine. This was going to be a very long night. She curled her feet underneath her and reopened her book. She was determined to stay awake until he came home. She had to see he was safe.

She drank a little more wine. She couldn't tell if this new realization or the wine was relaxing her. It wasn't helping the throbbing in her head much. The warm fire filled the room and soon she found her eyes were growing heavy. She closed her book and placed it on the table with all the other books. *It will not hurt to close my eyes a little. After all, Reynolds promised to send him in.* She allowed herself to stretch out a little on the chaise, and in no time at all, her weary body and mind were fast asleep.

*****

Darcy's body ached from all the exertion of first the walk and now the fire. He shook Richard's hand, "Thank you Richard, you were a real asset tonight." He met his cousin's gaze and smiled ruefully. "I do think you will have to throw away those clothes though, not only are they full of smoke but it looks like you got singed a few times."

They entered the vestibule. He saw Reynolds was in a chair, half-dozing, although he immediately stood, stretching. "Reynolds, what are you doing still awake? It is nearly two in the morning! There was no need for you to wait up for me!"

"Yes sir, there was, Mrs. Darcy is waiting for you in the library. Now that I have told you so, my old body is free to retire."

"Thank you, Reynolds. It will probably be a late morning for the household, so please take the morning off." Then, turning to Richard, he said, "I had best see to my wife. Thank you again."

He took a candle from the hallway sconce and made his way to the library. He opened the door and was greeted with the beauty of his sleeping wife. Her curls had come undone and were draped over the chaise edge, while her delicate feet peeked out from underneath her blanket. He reached carefully over, adjusting the blanket so all of her was covered. He put down the candle and carefully lifted her head and shoulders before he sat down, allowing her to rest against him. He wished he could smell her toilette water, but anything like that was overwhelmed by the thick, sooty scent of the fire. He gazed at the shimmer of her profile, and for the first time really noticed the shape of her ears, which were small and shell-like. He brushed the back of his fingers gently against her face. He traced her brow and her cheekbones, down her jaw and back up to her lips. His hands were still filthy from the smoke and soot, and he told himself he should not touch her until he was completely clean, but could not bring himself to stop caressing her features. He took a deep breath and let it out. *Perhaps I should not have let myself think on the moment in the stream like I did.* He ached to hold her and tell her how much he loved her. His fingers touched her lips again and he groaned. *I definitely should not have allowed my thoughts to get carried away.* He saw her squirm and he removed his hand from her face and placed it on her shoulder.

Elizabeth could smell smoke. She opened her eyes and realized she had slept much longer than she intended to. The room was cold, and the fire had died down, leaving just the faintest gleam of embers.

"I did not mean to wake you, but I was told you wanted to see me?" Darcy said quietly.

Elizabeth sat bolt upright at the sound of his voice. He was here, and blessedly safe! She threw off the blanket, shifting immediately to a kneeling position so she could throw her arms around his neck. She felt his arms reach around her body in return. "William! Oh, William!" When she lost her balance, he caught her waist and held her close. "Are you all right?" she cried.

Now that she was wrapped up in his arms he was more than all right, Darcy reflected. "Perfect, I would say." He smiled.

She pulled away from his neck a few inches and looked intently at his face. His eyes were dark, especially in the dim light, but she could tell from the faint creases that he was smiling. He was extremely handsome when his eyes smiled. She began to feel just how intimate it was to be sitting on his lap, but she couldn't move. It felt right to be in his arms. Her heart skipped a beat as she saw his eyes move down to her lips and back up to her eyes. The moment was golden. She would try to be as direct as possible. She tilted her head to the side, closed her eyes and leaned closer to his face.

Oh, Elizabeth! He met her halfway and touched her lips with his, moving ever so gently. She responded with moving her hands up to his hair and grasping handfuls of it. He kissed her again and again, allowing each kiss to linger a little longer, and to explore her lips with greater fervor until he found himself needing to catch his breath. He had waited for so long for this moment, but it was more than he had dared let himself imagine. A soft moan escaped her mouth, but she did not release her hold on him. Her response to the kiss was invigorating. He let his hands reach around to her back and her neck and caressed her, his embrace pressing her body against his. He could feel the rapidity of her breath, the heat of her body, and pulled her even closer to continue kissing her.

Elizabeth had never known such pleasure. She wanted every part of him, to hold him close and feel him next to her. This new, strange heat that she felt spread throughout her body like wildfire. Their kisses deepened, and she then tasted him on her lips. Her heart beat fiercely. Sooner than she was ready, he slowed the kissing and she felt him release his grip on her. She opened her eyes as he spoke.

"Dearest Elizabeth . . ." He felt her lay her head on his chest, her cheeks pressed against his shirt. He kept his arms wrapped around her and said, "I lied to you a moment ago." He could feel her stiffen slightly.

"What do you mean?"

"I said I was perfect, but now I know what perfect really feels like." She relaxed back into his embrace.

They sat there with her on his lap for a long time. The clock chimed three times, indicating an hour had passed. She had her arms around his neck, her face nestled against it, and he had one hand on her waist. The other moved in mindless circles against her back and shoulders. The silence between them was surely priceless. There was so much to say between them, but for the moment he needed nothing but to hold her, although he knew it could not last. He had just experienced a moment that only begged for more. He wanted only to tilt her head back up and kiss her again and again. But, he reminded himself sternly, a single moment of bliss with her was still not an offer to him to take her to his room. As much as he wanted nothing but to love her further, at some point he would have to part with her for the night. He gathered all the strength he had and said, "Elizabeth, you should probably go to bed."

She sat up and looked at him once again. The moment had been perfect. He was smiling back at her, but his eyes were dark and intense. She gathered that if she stayed it would be quite acceptable to him, but it was late, and she knew it. She might have gotten a chance to sleep, but she knew he had not. She leaned against him and kissed him one more time.

"Goodnight, William. I was so worried about you," she murmured, hoping that her tone would communicate the depth of her newly realized feelings for him. She wanted to stop and confess everything, but was halted by the clock chiming its quarter hour.

"You gave me quite a scare today as well," Mr. Darcy said quietly, but smiled. "I suppose it was now yesterday. How is your head?"

She laughed quietly. Her injury was not what was making her head spin, but rather it was every kiss and embrace they shared that night. "I would say I am quite recovered from that episode, but do not think that a kiss will earn you the forgiveness you need! I believe, Mr. Darcy, that you have not only thrown me in the mud, but in the water as well!" She jumped off his lap and gave him a saucy look. "Good night." Her step was lively as she left the room, leaping from step to step. Things were about to change, she knew, and she could not help but delight entirely in the prospect.

Mr. Darcy's Promise

Chapter 9

M r. Darcy watched Elizabeth saunter out of the library with a flirtatious skip in her step. He let out the biggest sigh. *Good Lord! How will I ever be able to sleep after a moment like that!* His body felt more alive than it had in some time, every bit of him tingling with sensation. Each embrace and each kiss replayed themselves over and over again in his mind. He almost stepped up, wanting to follow her to her room, but forced himself to remain in the doorway before he turned back. Perhaps everything he longed for would come true.

He glanced back towards the door, his fingers tapping impatiently against his thigh. A distraction, that was precisely what he needed. Anything would do. He picked up the book nearest him, hardly caring whether it was a pamphlet on farming or an old encyclopedia. After opening it to a page in the middle, he realized it was Elizabeth's book, *Sense and Sensibility. Perhaps not a romance novel,* he reflected ruefully, as it was hardly something that would help distract him.

Perhaps *A Dictionary of the English Language,* he thought, searching for Samuel Johnson, or even a treatise on biological sciences that he had studied at Cambridge. That was guaranteed to put him to sleep! He tossed Elizabeth's book back into its place, but it bounced off the edge of the table and fell open upon the floor. A letter had fallen out of the book and he reached over to replace it between the pages. He assumed that it was either from Jane or her father, but the familiar dark, slanted handwriting made him pause. Something else caught his eye after a moment. A name, a name he hadn't thought of for some time . . . Wickham!

Without thinking of the intrusion, he unfolding the letter and stood, walking to the candle for better light. What was a letter from Wickham doing in Elizabeth's book? Had they been corresponding? For how long? A wave of nausea came over him, but his hands moved steadily, opening the letter fully before his eyes fixed on the words. He should not be reading this letter, he knew, but he could no sooner stop than he could dismiss any mention of Wickham.

I find myself thinking about our time together not too long ago. Your eyes that last night together told me you think about me too. I must say that your body language that night spoke volumes. You need to know that I do not give up easily. You may be with Darcy now, but eventually I will come claim what should have been mine all along. I am sure you can find a way to stay my hand. If I remember correctly you have an active and creative mind. I look forward to hearing from you and seeing how much your heart can give. For now, you can send any correspondence through Mrs. Forester. She is a favorite of mine, and owes me a great deal. Do not fret too much on the issue; just do what comes naturally in your blood.

Until I hear from you, sincerely,

Your dear Mr. Wickham

Mr. Darcy's hands tightened around the letter before he returned to it, lingering over each word. There could be no other interpretation other than that they had been corresponding. Wickham was obviously referring to their kiss the night of the Netherfield ball! He had long wished to believe that Wickham's advances were unwanted, but had never been able to fully convince himself. This letter proved that Elizabeth was an active participant. Darcy closed his eyes. *Your body language spoke volumes . . .*

How was it possible? After all of her softening towards him, all their gentle flirtations and time spent together— and especially after their kiss— how could she still harbor such feelings for Wickham? He could not for a moment think of any other reason that she would carry such a deeply intimate letter with her. The edges were frayed by constant folding and unfolding, and he could even see the faintest hint of where tears had smudged the ink. Clearly this was a letter she treasured. He pressed his hand to his mouth.

He was disappointed. Hurt, yes, but perhaps disappointed most of all. His heart ached and felt like it had been torn in half. He had done everything in his power to change her opinion of him, and yet her heart was still not his to claim. He had spent every minute possible with her, granting her whatever desire she expressed, asking only for whatever she would give him, and nothing more.

A voice of hope and practicality spoke up. *But she just kissed you of her own will! That has to count for something! You know her feelings for you have changed! Do not dismiss all that has happened because of that blackguard Wickham!* The voice of reason, though, was easily drowned out by the fury and heartache caused by the letter. It was no use. He had done everything to win her, but her heart had never considered coming home to Pemberley— to reside with him.

He saw a bottle of wine and two glasses on the floor. He needed more than a little wine. There was a bottle of brandy he kept in his study for occasions like these. He folded the letter up into a tight, neat square, and then stood up. He would drink himself into oblivion with his brandy this evening. The morning would have to answer for itself.

*****

Elizabeth slept peacefully that night. She experienced all her now-familiar dreams again. William pushed her on the swing under the cedar tree. This time he not only reached around for her swollen abdomen but came around and kissed her protuberant belly. When he did so the baby fluttered inside her, as if saying it loved him too. He then put a hand to her face and pulled it to his own and kissed her lips ever so gently. She had never known such peace. When she woke from the dream, she lay in bed for a few minutes, luxuriating in the feel of it.

The slant of the sunlight through her windows told her that it was later than the hour she normally awoke. She usually was an early riser, and often found William was too. They had shared a walk nearly every day, weather permitting, since they had arrived at Pemberley— sometimes before breakfast, and sometimes afterwards. She blinked the sleep out of her eyes and sat upright. She knew he had a late night and did not want to miss another opportunity to be with William in case he was already awake. She selected one of her morning gowns, a pale rose muslin, and began to dress. She didn't even ring for Serafina although she was eager to tell her that although they didn't verbally express their feelings for each other, their lips had communicated quite nicely last night. Her heart started to beat faster, and she felt her cheeks flush. Those sweet kisses had led to something much more passionate and invigorating. She brushed her fingertips against her lips. Yes, last night had been absolutely lovely, and it was the first time in waking that she had felt some of the peace from her dream linger.

She finished dressing, not bothering to dress her hair beyond a simple braid, and went downstairs. She stopped Martin in the staircase. "Martin, is my husband awake yet?"

"Yes, madam. He breakfasted early and I believe is in his study."

Her forehead creased up at that, but she didn't want to reveal her disappointment. Especially not to William's valet, who seemed to know him so well, and who Elizabeth sensed was protective of his master. Martin seemed to have an interesting relationship with both Mr. Darcy and the other servants. He was one of those people, she decided, who knew more than he let on. She liked him, certainly, but he had to be privy to the secrets of their marriage. It didn't bother her that Serafina knew, and she couldn't quite place her finger on why. Perhaps because she knew the secrets she revealed to Serafina, but she did not know the secrets Mr. Darcy revealed to his valet. He knew things about her husband that she did not. It was jealousy, she supposed. She wanted to know her husband and his secrets better than anyone else, and after last night, more than ever.

She shook the thoughts away. "Thank you, Martin," she said simply, and decided to see him in his study. She felt a tingle of excitement. Perhaps they might share a kiss this morning. For the first time, she felt as if she was truly married. The clock chimed in the hallway, sounding nine times. He must have risen early, then, if he had already dressed, eaten, and was working for the day. She knocked on the door. She probably could have just walked in, but she felt his study was his sanctuary, and she never knew if he had important business he was working on. She waited for a little while, but no answer came. She frowned, raising her hand to knock again, when the door opened. Mr. Darcy was looking at her intensely and it seemed, somewhat impatiently.

When he didn't say anything, she spoke up, "I am sorry to bother you, but I was wondering if you wanted to . . ."

"I am busy right now, Elizabeth."

She was taken aback by the sharpness of his tone and the speed at which he had spoken. He had never been too busy before! She searched his eyes for an explanation, but there was none to be found in their dark depths. "Very well," she said slowly. "Perhaps I will speak with you later." Her words came out more questioningly than a statement, but he gave no indication that he intended to answer her. "I am just going to break my fast now." She hesitated, and then turned. The door shut loudly behind her.

What in the world was that? The reception she just received was nothing like the one she had expected! She hadn't seen such a blank expression on his face since he had first came to Hertfordshire. She stopped in the hallway and leaned back against the wall. He had so completely transformed himself in her view that she scarcely recognized this severe stranger. She had gotten so used to his smiling eyes that she was a little off balance emotionally. Whatever could be wrong with him?

Perhaps the fire last night had something to do with it. Her heart lifted a little at the thought. Yes, he was surely busy handling the aftermath of the fire. How selfish she had been! She had not even inquired after everyone's health and safety. Indeed, she didn't even know which tenant's house had burned down! Who at the estate was in possession of an orchard? Her heart sank at the realization that perhaps men and women had lost their lives in the fire. Her mind started going over the tenants she had visited who had an orchard. She chastised herself for being so self-centered to have not even asked about it. She had barely asked him if he was well! She was beginning to feel very guilty for relishing in the events of last night when there had just been a tragedy! At least realizing that Mr. Darcy's mood more likely stemmed from stress rather than displeasure with her made her feel better.

She ate breakfast alone, lingering over a cup of chocolate, when Georgiana finally joined her downstairs. "Good morning, Georgiana."

Georgiana barely met her gaze. "Good morning, Elizabeth. My maid said the fire was finally extinguished last night. It always worries me when William goes out like that. He gets so involved in those situations that he scares me. Have you seen him this morning? I imagine he got in late and should still be resting, but knowing him he hardly slept. He gets so focused on a problem that he hashes it out over and over again until he finds a solution. I imagine he will be much consumed with this for the next little while."

"He is quite committed to his tenants, is he not?" Elizabeth felt a flash of relief at Georgiana's confirmation that William was simply preoccupied with the disaster.

"You cannot find a more devoted master or brother," Georgiana said, and they shared a smile at the familiar statement. "Nor husband, I imagine."

Colonel Fitzwilliam came in, overhearing the last few comments, "Ah, are we talking about Darcy behind his back? I am all in! If you must know, he was quite the hero last night."

Elizabeth was eager to hear the details of the fire. "What happened?"

Colonel Fitzwilliam settled into his chair, gesticulating wildly as he told the story. "As soon as we arrived, flames were coming out every which way! And you hear this horrible, high-pitched sound coming from the house, but no one knew what it was. Darcy demanded to know where the residents of the house were. It was entirely chaotic, with buckets and helpers going every which way. There was a child outside who would not stop crying, and no one could find his parents. He said nothing besides 'Baxter, Baxter, Baxter!' He could not have been more than five years old.

"Of course, our first impulse was to move the child away from the fire, no matter who Baxter was. But then once he was safely out of harm's way, the child ran straight towards the burning house. Darcy caught him just before he entered, but the child continued to cry for Baxter. He could not speak as to who or where this 'Baxter' was, but Darcy promised to find him if the child would remain safely outside and away from the fire. Now, we had no idea who this Baxter could be. Darcy did not recognize him as any of his tenants. All the same, Darcy picked up a bucket of water, drenched himself with it, and went directly through the door!"

Elizabeth felt her heart hasten its pace, and clutched her fingers together. "What happened next?"

"We wait a few moments, but no sign of Darcy. I was about to risk the flames when I see Darcy signaling to us from the second-floor window! He has a puppy in hand, but by this point the front door is nearly consumed with flames. All the while the little boy is screaming, we are rushing to get him a ladder, and Darcy has to step out onto a ledge. By now, my dear Elizabeth, I am worried that you are going to be made a widow. But the ladder is safely found, and Darcy and the dog both are rescued. He is quite the hero with that lad, I assure you." Colonel Fitzwilliam leaned back in his chair signaling that the story was finished.

The room fell silent for a long moment afterwards. Elizabeth felt herself torn between admiration and anger. Of course, it had been entirely good to risk life and limb for the sake of the child's happiness and the life of the dog. But Darcy had nearly been trapped in the house! *Why does Darcy insist on making all these promises!*

Richard glanced from Elizabeth to Georgiana with a slightly apologetic glance. "Perhaps I should not have told two ladies a story like that. I do apologize; I spoke only in praise of my cousin and in the excitement of the moment. But I pray you not to worry; I do not think Darcy was even singed by the experience." He offered them a quick and warm smile. "Speaking of puppies, why did the puppy refuse to speak to his foot?"

Georgiana, relieved at the change for a lighter topic, smiled, "Do tell us, Richard!"

"Because it is not polite to talk back to your paw!" Richard saw Georgiana laugh and Elizabeth give a half smile. "Ah, come now,

Elizabeth. You must admit that it at least made you smile in spite of your distress."

"You must excuse me. I am still concerned about the events of last night. Did anyone get hurt in the fire? Do you know which tenant's house it was?" She felt ashamed that she had not thought to ask these questions earlier, and a faint blush stained her cheeks at remembering exactly why she had been so distracted.

"Georgiana would know their names, I believe. It is the lady who has two little boys and a girl of, I would say, three or four years old. I believe she was just recently widowed."

Both women gasped. "The Smiths? But we just saw them a few days ago! Is everyone well?" Elizabeth cried.

"Yes, Smith, that was the name! I do not know why I could not remember the name when it is one of the most common ones around. Everyone is fine, my dear ladies. The house is, however, in ruins. I doubt they will be able to salvage anything from it. But at least they have their dog!" He said the last part lightly in an attempt to lift their spirits.

Elizabeth's grim expression did not lighten. "Oh dear, Georgiana, we have to do something! Did your mother keep any of William's or your clothes from when you were younger?"

"Yes, everything! I sometimes go through the things in the attic when I wish to remember her."

Elizabeth rang for the servant with new purpose. At least in this she could be useful. When the servant entered she instructed her to fetch Mrs. Reynolds immediately. The rest of the morning was spent in the attic going through chests of clothes and old blankets with the housekeeper and Georgiana. In the midst of all the chaos, Elizabeth found herself much too busy to reflect on why Darcy hadn't emerged from his study.

*****

Later that afternoon, Richard opened the door to Darcy's study without knocking. He looked at the scene before him with a frown. Darcy had his boots off, while his waistcoat and cravat were thrown on the floor. A near-empty bottle of brandy lay on the desk, while his

Mr. Darcy's Promise

tray from luncheon remained untouched. Richard picked up a piece of dried, uneaten bread, frowning down at the curled cheese that lay beside it. "What the deuces is going on with you all morning? I have never seen you hole yourself up in your study like this. And why could you not come eat luncheon with the rest of us?"

Darcy scowled at his cousin, a look that perhaps he would not have given had the brandy not been exercising a great deal of influence over him.

"My my, I have not seen that look on your face for some time." Richard took a seat across from Darcy. "Is there a reason for your sour mood, or should I guess?"

Darcy knew this game. Richard was merciless when he set his mind to something. It was an ability, he was sure, that was greatly prized by the militia, but not one that was appreciated at this moment. At least not now. Darcy pinched his lips shut.

"I see I must guess. Since I talked to Georgiana and know why she has been in such a mood as she has been, it must not be her that is the cause of your silence."

That piqued Darcy's interest and he sat up straight. "What did she say?"

"He speaks!" Richard was very good at this game.

"Richard, I do not wish to dance with you. Just tell me what has been bothering her." No matter the news, Darcy thought, thinking about something besides Elizabeth and her letter from Wickham would help him a great deal.

"But the music has just begun! Take a twirl with me. There is little reason for Georgiana to be acting so. She adores your new wife, as we all do, and is at the place she most loves in the world. And yet she is deeply troubled." Richard saw Darcy flinch when he mentioned Elizabeth. It was as he thought, then.

"Now, we both know that it is the tendency of the Darcys to keep their problems guarded close, which makes them— and others, I might add— suffer all the more. Like I said, Georgiana told me what has been bothering her; or at least I think she did. I cannot be sure she was being completely forthright, but I was sworn to secrecy. I would not mind revealing the fact that considering the circumstances, she is holding up quite well." *I imagine that, in her place, running into Wickham at Longbourn and being addressed at the ball would have definitely rattled my composure. Yes, Georgiana is holding up quite well.*

"Now you on the other hand," Richard continued, ignoring Darcy's pointed look, "have completely unraveled. You rarely drink and from the looks of your equilibrium, you started early this morning. Do you mind if I join you in your debauchery? It is very impolite not to offer his majesty's Colonel something to drink when you are drinking yourself." Darcy motioned to the cabinet with a vague hand.

After retrieving some claret, Colonel Fitzwilliam sat himself back down in the same space and continued, unruffled. "Which leads me to ask after your dear Elizabeth. How is she? Has she recovered from the fall into the river?" Richard knew, of course, that she was in very good health and was in fact walking up and down the stairs to the attic. But he wanted to see the expression on Darcy's face when he spoke of it. Sure enough, his cousin flinched, taking another heady swallow of brandy before he looked away again.

Darcy felt the burn of the liquid but what was worse was the sting of the guilt. "I only saw her briefly this morning. I did not inquire after her health, but she seemed perfectly well." He should have at least asked after her own recovery. No matter who Elizabeth had been writing, it was no excuse for being uncivilized to his wife. His mind flashed back to the pain and confusion that had mingled in her face this morning. Her eyes had been so bright and hopeful when he first opened the door. He had wanted to take her in his arms and claim her as his and only his, but his heart had never been the inconstant one. He could claim her all he wanted but what he needed was Elizabeth to claim him back. He wanted her to want him and no one else, especially not Wickham!

"So I see this moping is about Elizabeth. Too bad! I thought you two had some real fireworks going on. What did you do this time?" Richard goaded him. Richard was still leading in this dance they were having, Darcy never could keep anything from him, and in spite of his silences, was opening up quite nicely.

Darcy whirled around, "Me? You think I did something?"

"I see, you think Elizabeth is at fault. Well, whatever you think she did wrong, I can assure you that she is quite devoted to you."

Darcy's mind heard the words and yet his heart flat out refused them. As much as he wished to believe otherwise, Elizabeth was secretly corresponding with Wickham. "I do not know what you are talking about. Elizabeth and I are fine," he said, attempting to sound convincing while feeling the deceit in his words.

"Come now," Richard chided. "You will not just stand there with your back to me and flat out lie, would you? You and I feel the same way about deceit of any form." There had always been something odd about his cousin's marriage, but this was a new kind of trouble. Was Darcy now uncertain about Elizabeth's attachment to him? It was clear to Richard that Elizabeth's feelings for Darcy ran deep and true. He had carefully observed them together, and it was clear that Elizabeth had secured his heart. They spent nearly every waking moment together, quietly laughing or in lively conversation. She had even persuaded him to leave the house to feed the chickens. Richard had finally heard the tale of their encounter in the mud. Each of them had tried to be the one to tell it to him the way they each remembered it, and each attempted to condemn the other teasingly, laughing all the while. Their relationship was one that seemed strong and full of fresh vigor.

Darcy turned to look at Richard, "I just need some time to work out a few things. Have you seen her today?" A line was etched deep into his forehead.

Richard held up his hands. "Darcy, I must burden you with some advice. You must not disregard it. Yes, even though I am a bachelor." He looked at Darcy directly. "Speak with her. She will gladly assuage your fears, I assure you. Your Mrs. Darcy is not a woman to trifle with a man." His gaze shifted to the empty bottle of brandy. "And do show yourself at dinner. Perhaps you should refrain from any more brandy until afterwards." He finished his claret with a flourish. The dance was over. At least for now. He rose and left the room.

Darcy glanced over at the cabinet with a rueful look. Richard was right about one thing, at least— he put down the drink. He took out the letter once again and poured over it. What did he mean by *"You may be with Darcy now but eventually I will come claim what should have been mine all along"*? He had to admit it sounded somewhat threatening rather than endearing. And how exactly did he expect to claim her? Where they planning something like running off together? Elizabeth would be a fool to leave a home like Pemberley, which was one thing he was sure of her adoration for. *She may not love me but she loves Pemberley!*

Was it intended as a threat? He had seen Wickham's darker side before. He took a deep breath. All this mental hashing and rehashing of the letter was going to drive him mad! He put it away for the fifth time in the last few hours. His mind was weary. He had attempted to sleep last night but was restless, and when the dawn broke he simply got out of bed. It was useless to lie there when there was so much work to do. But as much as he wanted to free his mind, he could not stop thinking again and again of the letter.

Out of frustration he spread his arms out on the desk and rested his head on his forearms. He started counting to himself. It was a habit that he picked up to handle uncomfortable social situations. He would find himself counting the people, the hats, the canes, and the pictures on the wall, anything to distract him from feeling the awkwardness of the situation. He had found it soothing, and that was something he desperately needed right now. With his eyes closed, he mentally traced over all that was resting on his desk. The estate books . . . there were several of those, at least four. His quill and inkwell, several letters he needed to answer . . . five, six, seven . . . the miniature of his father and mother, the paper weight . . . fourteen, fifteen . . . he moved to the drawers and counted their contents . . . twenty-one, twenty-two . . . Slowly his heart slowed and his mind and body relaxed so much that he fell into a deep sleep.

He dreamed of Elizabeth's laughter and of the chickens. First he dreamed of memories of time already spent with them. Then the dream warped into new and detailed discussions about them. They spoke of everything from their colors and sizes, to what they preferred to eat. She would instruct him and talk metaphorically about them, repeating things she already said, and adding other important pieces of the puzzle. For some reason in his dream he understood what she was saying when she spoke in riddles. He seemed to understand when she discussed their needs or their safety, but knew what she really meant by stating such facts. He finally understood a part of her that had confused him for so long. Then things started getting confusing again and it was like she started speaking another language. He could feel himself waking from the dream and the understanding of the riddles slipping as well. *No! I need to know why those chickens are so important to her!* He opened his eyes. All the understanding was slipping away just like it was some unimportant dream! His eyes opened and he quickly grabbed a paper and pen and started writing down what he remembered her saying in the dream.

The chickens had something to do about Elizabeth. He wrote that down. Nature's timetable was an important piece, but what part did it play? He wrote that down. He closed his eyes trying to focus on the dream. It was slipping away much too fast. The chicks had to get their feathers or . . . or what? What did getting their feathers represent? He let out a groan. He was never going to figure this out. But he wrote how getting the feathers meant something important. He had a flash of the dream come to him of her speaking of the winter storms and he knew that was important too, so he wrote that down. He stared at the paper. It was gibberish. It was a list of facts about chickens but no real interpretation came to him. It frustrated him because moments ago in his dream he understood why they were so important to her! He had listened as she spoke and he had understood! He put the pen down. *What in God's name would a farm animal represent to Elizabeth?*

*****

Elizabeth was pleased to see Mr. Darcy at the table for dinner, but she quickly realized that he was still not himself. Although he had dressed for dinner, his eyes were slightly bloodshot, and it seemed that he was not carrying himself with his usual attention. His eyes, moreover, did not smile back at her when they met hers. In fact, he seemed to be looking everywhere but at her.

"We went and delivered some old clothes to the Smith's after lunch," Elizabeth said in an attempt to enliven the conversation. "I hope you do not mind, but Georgiana and Mrs. Reynolds said that you would not regret parting with some of your old clothes from when you were a boy. Your mother dressed you very nicely. I should give her credit for instilling principles of fabric as a child," Elizabeth said, trying out a quick smile.

"I do not mind."

Elizabeth drew in a deep breath. "Of course, they are going to stay with the Wilkinson's until more permanent plans are arranged."

"Yes, I knew that."

She leaned towards him, speaking softly in an attempt to avoid being heard. "I am just making conversation, William." She moved her hand towards where his rested on the dinner table, and he slid his back, out of reach. Her frown deepened. "You seem out of sorts tonight. Are you well?"

"Yes, I am fine." He continued to eat.

Could she provoke anything more than four clipped words? "Well, we did not get a chance to candle the eggs last night and I did not know if you wanted to do so tonight. It has been three days since we candled them."

"Probably not."

Probably not? His two words stung, and she felt all her old fears and worries rush back. She had all but declared herself last night, and here he was, acting as if the entire business was tiresome. She drew herself up, her chin lifting. Before she could speak again, however, Richard cleared his throat.

"Elizabeth, I hear you play the pianoforte beautifully. What would you say to playing tonight? Georgiana already promised me a piece she has been working on. What say you? Darcy, would you like to hear Elizabeth play?"

She turned her head to her husband, but he was looking at Richard. *Well? Does he want to hear me play?*

"I must admit I did not sleep well last night and I have a headache. Perhaps another night." Darcy avoided looking at Elizabeth, but could see out of the corner of his eyes that she looked away from him. Why would she be disappointed? He studiously attacked his meat and took a large bite. He didn't want to get into a fight at the dinner table but every time he looked at her, Wickham's words would run through his head. *Why have you appeared to enjoy my company these last few weeks? Why would you hold onto a letter from such a vile man? How exactly is he going to come claim what should have been his?* He took another big bite even though he hadn't finished his last one. He glanced up at Elizabeth through his eyelashes. How could he have such angry feelings and still be in awe at how beautiful she was!

Her curls moved as she lowered her head and then offered Georgiana a quick smile. He watched her hands, those elegant small fingers, and then looked up at her soft mouth. Her lips were perfect! He was reminded of their moment in the library where he tasted those lips and felt their warmth and caress, and his body reacted the same as it did then. *This will not do! Either I am in love with her or I am angry with her!* Could it be both? His body ached to hold her once again.

In truth, he wanted any part of her that she would give him. He would take part or all, preferably all, but he must push down the jealousy he felt at finding Wickham's letter. He took a moment extra to fully comprehend what he was deciding to do. Was he deciding his love was stronger than these powerful emotions inside? Was he deciding that she was more important than the pain he felt? Yes, he was.

"On second thought, perhaps some music would be helpful for my headache." Richard's face brightened with a triumphant grin. Darcy shook his head.

"Perfect! Elizabeth, will you play?" Richard asked.

"Only if Mr. Darcy thinks it will help," Elizabeth said, her tone much cooler than before. Earlier today, she had not allowed herself the leisure to devote to his moods, but now it all rushed down upon her. Never in all of their marriage had he refused to do anything with her, but had done so twice today. What had changed? How was the man she had known to be once so warm and engaging now the one who could barely meet her gaze? It was as if he had returned to the "proud Master of Pemberley" she had met at the Meryton Assembly. She struggled with the encroaching sadness and hurt she felt.

Darcy did not miss her change in tone, nor her deliberate use of "Mr. Darcy." He felt a surge of guilt. He had been rude; he could not claim it to be in ignorance, but rather in malice. It takes time, he reminded himself, and his behavior would not help matters. She had come a long way since the uncontrollable tears she had on their wedding day. Last night proved it. *I must be patient. She needs more time.*

*****

After her performance on the pianoforte she knew she needed to slip out and see the chickens. It still hurt that William had declined to join her. If she searched her heart, she knew that she was more hurt than she let on. The chickens had been something special that they shared, and his refusal to join her tonight felt like a twist in the heart. She took a deep breath and decided she had better go before her sadness developed tears of its own. Elizabeth opened the front door, letting the cold air seep into the hall. She could hear the sounds of rain falling heavily against the roof, and then a flash of lightening lit up the sky. A few moments later, a loud crack of thunder sounded. She held the candle and whiskey glass tighter in her hand before turning to see Darcy standing in the hall.

"Where are you going? It is going to storm hard tonight, Elizabeth," Darcy said.

"I told you at dinner that I was going to candle the eggs. Have you changed your mind? Would you like to join me?" she asked hopefully.

Darcy's brows drew together even as she smiled warmly at him. *Why must she be so tempting?* In spite of his resolution, he had not fully come to grips with his anger and jealousy and knew he needed a little space before he could spend any time with her. His heart still ached, and his mind and heart battled over whether or not she cared for him. One minute he knew she cared, cared deeply, and then another he would hear Wickham's words ring in his ears. At the moment, Wickham's words were quite loud.

"No, I do not think so tonight. Perhaps another night." He saw her countenance fall as she turned back towards the door. The last thing he wanted was to hurt her. "Wait!" He watched her spin back around, again with hope in her eyes. He ran into the sitting room and came out with a blanket. He gently wrapped it around her shoulders. "Be careful, and do not be gone too long." Just because he was hurt didn't mean he cared for her any less. She nodded and left for the barn. He watched her walk as far as he could in the darkness and then went inside.

He wanted to go with her, and in fact probably should have gone with her, but he didn't know if he could be civil, much less the attentive husband she deserved. How could she betray what they had built in the last few weeks?

He lingered by the front door, waiting for her to come back. Twenty minutes went by and she still had not returned. He could hear it raining harder outside. Thirty minutes went by and he started to pace. Candling didn't usually take this long. Could she have been hurt along the way? He waited another few minutes before he hastily grabbed his greatcoat and a candle and headed out the door towards the barn. He didn't know quite what he was doing, but it made sense to go looking for her.

He entered the barn to the sounds of faint crying. He wanted nothing more than to wrap her up in his arms. Why could he not have overcome his pride and come with her? He brushed those thoughts aside to make his way in her direction. The blanket was off her shoulders, and she was sitting on a pile of hay by the nest boxes, her shoulders slumped. "Elizabeth? Are you ill?"

"It is so cold tonight!" she cried. He reached for the blanket and tried to place it on her shoulders, but she shook her head. "Thank you though. I did not know if I should have gone back to get you. I could not leave them, not on a night like this."

"Is everything all right? Has something happened to the eggs?" Darcy felt even worse than before.

"No, not really. It is just that they are hatching." She knew her voice was sad rather than excited, and she looked over at Darcy as he sat down beside her. "I know I promised to watch them hatch with you but I could not leave them. Thank you for coming anyway." She squeezed his hand. His arrival meant more to her than she could express at the moment.

"I do not understand. You said it would probably be the day after the Autumn Festival. Are they hatching early?" He had been certain they were not due for several days.

"I had not candled them for three days, so I must have estimated wrongly. I am just glad I came and found them when I did."

The sadness in her voice was unmistakable. Why would she not be relieved to see that they were finally hatching? "Elizabeth, please forgive me, I do not mean to be dense, but I thought you wanted them to hatch. Is this not a good thing? Now they will have more time to get their feathers before the storms begin." Darcy readjusted the blanket and left his arm lightly draped around her shoulders.

Her shoulders shook as she let out a sob. How could she explain her fears to him? A few tears slid down her face before she collected herself enough to speak. "Can you not feel how cold it is tonight? The storms have already hit! The chicks cannot survive their first night in this weather!"

It hadn't seemed all that cold to him, and it certainly wasn't a terrible storm. Some thunder and lighting and rain but nothing serious. He wondered if she was speaking in riddles again. "The nest boxes will be out of the direct rain, Elizabeth. What can we do?"

"I do not know. Maybe once they all hatch we really should bring them inside, at least for the night. It will keep them out of immediate danger. We would have to bring in the hen as well to take care of them."

"Did you not say that was not a good idea because they will not build up their winter resistance?" He truly had been listening and trying to make sense of everything she said about the chickens.

"Sometimes we have to handle the problems day by day and hope that our actions are not harming them."

Now he knew she was speaking in riddles again. In her mind, the storms had already begun and she felt it was especially cold tonight, which it wasn't. She was willing to do something that would help them weather this mild storm but might weaken their chances to weather other more serious storms. *What does it mean that she is so distraught over the storm tonight?* He shook his head. He would have to make sense of it later and add these things to his list he started in his study after his dream.

"May I see them?" She nodded and took off the blanket, stood up, and lifted the nest box door. He peeked in and held the candle up to the nest box. Quiet little chirps sounded, and he could see one chick had already broken out. The other eggs were all cracked, and some even had entire pieces missing. He watched as the eggs rocked back and forth with the movement of the confined chicks. One egg popped a large chunk off, but the chick struggled to pull its wings out. It was all wet, its yellow down plastered to its body. He watched it struggle for what seemed like ten minutes, but it was getting nowhere. The shell did not budge. His heart sank as he realized its wings were trapped inside the shell. Should he help it?

Elizabeth could see he was watching intently. "It takes a while to break out of the shell." She watched as he reached his hand in to help the one struggling chick, and then snatched at his fingers, pulling them away. "No! You cannot help them. Hatching is part of the process. They develop strength with the struggle. If you force them you could kill them."

He looked at her once again. "I did not mean to force anything," he said a little softly. "I was just giving it a little assistance."

"It just takes time, William."

His faint frown grew deeper, and he continued to look at her. Those were words he had used many times in describing Elizabeth. *Time, it just takes time.* He tried to memorize everything she said about the chicks. He had to make sense of this soon or he might lose a very special part of her. He made a mental note that it takes a while to break out of the shell. *Got it.* And you can't force the eggs to hatch. *Got it.* The struggle was part of the process. *Got it.* And it just takes time. *Definitely got that.*

They sat, watching them hatch together. He couldn't help resist resting his arm around her. After a few moments, she let her head drop against his shoulder. Nothing else mattered; Elizabeth was grieving tonight, and he wanted to comfort her.

He had never seen eggs hatch and was struck with the uselessness he felt now that he knew he should not help them. They struggled and fought to get out, all the while their small little chirps seemed to beg him for help. The air between them was thick with their silences. She had talked happily of this moment for weeks, but now that it was happening, she seemed somber and distracted. At one point, she took his hand in hers, but he stiffened slightly and she dropped it immediately. He cursed his own weakness. Why could he not overcome his own doubts? And why could he put his own arm around her but resist her touch?

He wanted nothing more than to see her bright eyes again, to hear her tease and laugh, but even as he craved it, it seemed hollow. He drew in a deep breath and tried to push aside his thoughts of Wickham. It takes time. And the struggles he felt were simply part of the process.

He sat up straighter for a moment, his mind spinning as if he had just emerged from his dream earlier. Something was within his understanding— Elizabeth's words to him earlier. What was it? He focused hard, but the moment slipped away from him.

"Dash it!" He cursed under his breath.

"What is wrong?" she said, drawing away a little, her face tight with alarm.

For a moment, Darcy did not reply as he tried to grasp the furtive understanding, but then he looked at her. Her dark eyes, fringed with those beautiful lashes, distracted him from his quest. He cleared his throat. "It is nothing. I confess my thoughts have been wandering to a dilemma I have been trapped in, and whatever progress I had made was lost. I did not mean to alarm you."

"If you want you can tell me about it, I may be able to help," Elizabeth offered tentatively.

For some reason, Darcy felt that this puzzle was his to work out alone. He wanted to ask her, Lord knew he did, but he also knew intuitively that if he could understand them then it would mean so much more. Instead he changed the subject. "How do you like Pemberley? I do not think I have actually asked you."

Her eyes lit up. "Oh, I like it very much. I have learned to love it even more than Longbourn. You are lucky to have grown up in such a place. It has nearly everything one could want!"

Mr. Darcy caught that she had said "nearly everything." He didn't know what to make of it. "Is there something missing? Would you like something that it does not offer?"

Elizabeth blushed in the candlelight. "I suppose it is just that I have not explored all it has yet. Perhaps I will still find what I am looking for."

What was she looking for? He wanted to give her everything. He wanted to give her his heart and more than anything he wanted her to want his heart. "And what exactly are you looking for?"

Elizabeth swallowed. The question seemed to hang between them for a moment. She gazed back at the chicks to avoid answering for a moment, and then sprang up. The chick that had been struggling with its wings for so long had finally broken out. It was the last one. "Look, William! She got out! Look how strong she is! She struggled so hard against the shell that she has the strength to stand up now! She is not teetering at all!"

Darcy couldn't resist answering Elizabeth's excitement with a broad smile. Watching the chick together seemed to have lessened the distance between them. He opened his mouth to say something about the chick, but instead hesitated. She captivated his every thought. "You are beautiful in the candlelight, Elizabeth."

She beamed down with motherly pride upon the chicks for a moment longer, but turned to William with a warm look in her eyes. "And you are quite handsome when you smile. I wish I would have seen it more often today." She brushed his cheek with her fingers, and he closed his eyes, nearly leaning into her touch. She did not know why he had been so cold and distant earlier, but she could be patient. She loved him, and she would be here no matter the problem. When she had first seen that the eggs were watching, she had been uncertain as to whether or not she should fetch him. His refusal to join her had hurt her deeply.

She had a curious sort of kinship with this hen. They had both entered into such new periods against their own inclination; the hen brooding over her eggs, and Elizabeth sent off to Pemberley to marry a man who she scarcely knew. But they had both survived; and more than that, thrived. Just as the hen was driven to endure, Elizabeth's nature yearned for true companionship. And now they had both been rewarded with what they had worked so hard for. And regardless of whatever William was struggling with, Elizabeth knew that her love was strong enough to guide her through these turbulent waters. Tonight they had made steps in the right direction as he repeatedly wrapped his arm around her. Although progress was made, she still sensed he was holding back.

"Elizabeth, about last night . . ."

She drew in a deep breath. It was the subject she longed to discuss, and yet she wanted to express her patience with him. "We do not have to talk about it if you do not wish to."

He pressed his lips together. Was her response an indication of regret, or in answer to his coldness all day? He remained silent for a moment. Perhaps she regretted their kiss. He let himself luxuriate for a moment in remembering their sweet kisses and the feel of her hands in his hair. *No. She could not regret that.* And, he reminded himself, he would gladly welcome whatever she would give him. He turned his attention back to the chicks. "What should we name them, then?"

She laughed gaily, some part of her relieved that the conversation had turned back to more familiar ground. "Well, there are seven. One yellow, three black with a white spot on their heads, and three brownish-red ones. Do you have any ideas?" She was deeply pleased by how quickly William had taken a liking to the chicks and especially liked that he wanted to name them.

"You can pick the names of all of them but one. That last one, the yellow one, who struggled so hard, I want to name her. Do we know if they are male or female?"

"I have heard of being able to sex them this early but I would not know how. Usually we knew for sure when they started cock-a-doodle-doing around four months old. And as you have waited so patiently for their birth, I cannot claim the honor of naming them all. I insist that you christen at least three of them."

He laughed softly at the improvement in her mood. He would do anything to please her: name chickens, dirty his clothes . . . even if he had to burn Wickham's letter and banish it from his mind. Perhaps that would be best. Could he dismiss all his feelings of jealousy? Yes, perhaps putting it behind his was best. He would take this chance to win her heart. Yes, he would burn the letter.

Elizabeth noticed William's gaze shifted away from her again. What was it that troubled him so? The silence was thick again and she desperately wanted to see him smile. "William? Does Pemberley have a wide tree swing under a cedar tree?"

He was startled out of his thoughts by the question. "No, not under a cedar tree. There is a child's swing under the poplar tree by the maze. Why do you ask?"

She looked thoughtful. "Maybe we could find a good place to put one. Maybe one by the river."

"Consider it done. We shall start looking for the perfect spot tomorrow!" He smiled at her. If a tree swing would make her happy then he would do it. At least he had a task and a mission. And he knew he excelled at accomplishing tasks he set his mind to. "May I enquire why it needs to be a cedar tree?"

Elizabeth wasn't quite ready to tell him she had been dreaming of him and their baby since their wedding day. "I have my reasons, but a lady must not reveal all her secrets," she said loftily, and was rewarded by the sight of his smiling eyes.

"Are there some secrets you would be willing to tell?" he said with a smirk on his face. She was teasing him again, and it felt like balm to his heart.

She let out a laugh. "Perhaps! But you know that you must earn them. I cannot give away all my mystery so early in our marriage."

He laughed as well, and gazed back at the chicks. He owed them a debt of gratitude for drawing them back together. "Well then, I need to inform you that I have my secrets too. I know what I will name the yellow one and I might remind you that you gave me permission to do so. You may not change the name since the right to do so has already been claimed. I may assert my husbandly authority on this matter, Mrs. Darcy." His eyes challenged her to defy his false brevity.

"Is the name, or the reason for the name, the secret?" She eyed him suspiciously.

"Oh, in time you shall know both, but for now I will only tell you why I am naming her the name I chose. That chick is incredibly strong as well as strong-willed. It is beautiful and graceful. It seems to chirp the loudest too. Oh, and it is unique in that it captured my heart the first time I saw it." He smiled, absurdly proud of his own ability to make a riddle about the chickens.

Elizabeth let out a hearty laugh and shook her head at him. "You are not going to name it after me, are you?" She saw the shock in his eyes. "You are?"

He had hoped that his riddle would stump her a little longer than that. He would need to work harder at a game of wits with Elizabeth. "How did you guess?" Her laughter had sealed the tear in his heart. He reached for her hand and placed a gentle kiss on it. "Was it the part where I described her as beautiful?" His voice had grown deeper.

Her heart skipped a beat at hearing his deep, gentle voice. She was quite attracted to him at the moment but she continued to tease him. "Oh no, I caught on from the very beginning when you said it was strong-willed. Do not forget that you called me stubborn right before you threw me in the mud. I am afraid I recall that more than all your pretty compliments, William," she teased, lifting her chin.

"Then I must remind you that it is you who deemed your so-called stubbornness, my dear Elizabeth, and not me!"

"Well then," Elizabeth said, pretending to ignore his assertion. "I must punish you by making your namesake the clumsy brown one. After all, you have twice dropped me. Once in the water, and once in the mud. And although you claim it was an accident, I am afraid that he shall be deemed Fitz."

He didn't care if she named all of them after him. He would gladly accept a flock of Fitzwilliams for one kiss from those impertinent lips. He picked up her hand and kissed the tender flesh of the inside of her wrist. "Lizzy."

She looked up at him. "Yes?" Her breath had caught in her throat. *Is he going to kiss me again?*

"That is the name of the chicken." He smiled at her, and then, at the sight of her rueful grin in return, took her hand to lead her back to the house.

Mr. Darcy's Promise

Chapter 10

What a tease! Elizabeth could not stop her heart from giving a traitorous flutter. If only he knew what such a kiss on her wrist did to her! Would he always affect her so? She inhaled deeply in an attempt to calm her breathing, but it was of no use. He had completely unraveled her self-composure. But what would he say when he asked why she was blushing so? Her entire body ached to hold him, to kiss him again, but he either did not— or would not— notice her unspoken desire.

Good heavens! If she only knew how badly I wanted to take her in my arms! But he could not. Time, he reminded himself again, must be his mantra. Care as she might for him (and he was certain, now, that she did, at least a little), her unwillingness to mention last night's kiss was a sign of the need to wait a little longer. Although his body protested that he had already heavily taxed his resources of patience before they had first kissed. How would he manage to moderate his desires? His lips moved in silent prayer. *Dear God, please grant me all the patience I need for her sake.* He ended the prayer with a soft, rueful laugh, remembering his old governess' adage. *"You should never pray for patience, Fitzwilliam, or you may find yourself in the midst of opportunities to test that very resolve."*

He stepped inside the entryway, glad for the moment that it was too late for the servants to be about. "Are you certain that the chicks will be warm enough outside in the barn?"

Elizabeth's head turned, startled, and she swallowed. Such a question should be simple; indeed, three months ago, she would have laughed at the notion that it would be difficult to answer. But circumstances were so very distracting. Her wrist still tingled, and the heat that had formerly lingered on her lips yesterday now swallowed up all of her torso. "Yes," she said after a long, telling moment. "I think it is warm enough tonight."

He would need to carefully guard his thoughts against their tendency to wander. Such small indulgences like the sound of her laughter or a round of teasing repartee would do nothing but bring him to crave more. He would need to constrain himself to lighter topics. "Tomorrow you and I shall have to discover the best site for your swing," he said. He dared not look at her lest he would take her into his arms. If he saw those perfect lips again tonight or that saucy eyebrow he might just take her and not let her go.

"So long as it is no great trial. But I think it will bring me a great deal of pleasure on days when I cannot go out walking." His familiar scent filled the air, and she could feel her blush deepen. She could not avoid flashes of her recurring dream. For a moment, it almost seemed that she could feel his hands around her waist. "Excuse me," she murmured after a moment. "I should retire. I suddenly feel exhausted." She took a few hasty steps away, moving towards the stairs. Darcy, fortunately, only nodded, and Elizabeth mounted the stairs, feeling an immediate improvement in her composure as she put distance between them.

Darcy watched her step nimbly up the stairs. Her hair fell loosely around her shoulder, the chignon finally working loose after several hours in the barn. A few stray curls tumbled down against her neck, and Elizabeth brushed impatiently at them. How many times had he done the same, and felt the smoothness of her cheek against his hand? He shook his head quickly. He had work that needed to be done, but he had spent more of the day lost in his own turmoil than in his actual tasks. It was too late, he decided. He should go to bed. Fatigue was a friend to neither self-control nor patience, and if he was going to spend the morning with Elizabeth he would need plenty of both.

Martin was waiting patiently in his room, having busied himself with rearranging Darcy's belongings. His books had been neatly stacked near the window, while the suit he had worn earlier was already perfectly brushed without a hint of dust. "Good evening, Martin," Darcy said with a warm smile. Martin raised one eyebrow in surprise.

"Good evening, sir." Martin looked Darcy over: it was a skill that all valets learned, the ability to seize up the master's mood in one quick glance. *Much better.* This morning, Darcy's eyes had not only been bloodshot but the skin surrounding them was tight. And, of course, it was rare and worrisome to see Darcy holed up in his study. It was clear, though, from one look that something in his face had eased. "And how was your day, sir? Better then it started, perhaps?"

"It did get better, thank you." Darcy turned and began to unbutton his waistcoat. He took another deep breath.

Martin took the waistcoat and hung it up before he spoke again. "Sir, the Autumn Festival is in three days. Has Mr. Bingley ever responded to your letter about your missing pocketwatch?"

Darcy frowned as he unfastened his cufflinks. "It seems no one has found it at Netherfield. He is investigating the local shops that buy jewelry and the sort to see if anyone has tried to pawn it. I know nothing more than that." He waved off Martin's expression of concern. "I am not worried. I am certain that it has merely been mislaid." He shrugged out of his shirt. "A greater concern is more immediate. Do you know what dress Mrs. Darcy is planning to wear to the festival?" Martin and Serafina would most likely coordinate their clothing.

"Yes, sir. According to Serafina she will be wearing the green and gold gown."

"Ah." Darcy frowned at the mirror. "I was hoping she would wear her new white ball gown with the red embroidery, although I suppose it is hardly suitable for the festival." There was a ruby bracelet that had been in the Darcy family for several generations, and he had long thought it would perfectly suit Elizabeth's slim wrists.

"Indeed, sir. Would you like me to suggest it anyway?"

"No, no. I just was hoping to give her a piece of jewelry that matched it." He would find another occasion to present it to Elizabeth. "Martin, has Serafina said anything about how Mrs. Darcy has fared in the last day or two?" Beyond Martin's exemplary skills at dressing and maintaining fabric, he also had a talent for extracting and delivering valuable information; unhappiness among the servants, something that needed his attention, that sort of thing. But the thing Mr. Darcy needed most right now was a little help in the area of Elizabeth's heart. Had she confided in Serafina?

Martin had never craved gossip, but there was a certain amount of knowledge that he felt necessary to his job. A valet, Martin had reasoned, should know things his master should know. Consequently, he spent much of his spare time discussing the events and goings on in the household, and excusing it as a job necessity. After all, the Darcy family was his family as well. He had come close— just once— to marrying outside of this life, and had almost left his post here. Although the lady in question had long since married elsewhere, Martin had thought of her often of late. There was a certain warmth and liveliness that she shared with Mrs. Darcy. More than anything, Martin wanted to see Darcy made happy by this marriage. He cleared his throat. "Serafina does prize Mrs. Darcy's privacy, sir, but she does share her concerns. I do know that those spells of dizziness and double vision have stopped altogether."

Darcy's brow furrowed up. Double vision? He knew that he should have insisted on her being examined by a physician after her fall. He felt another pang at the idea that he would have no information from Serafina. It was perhaps unfair, but in these circumstances he wanted to make certain that she was happy. Perhaps, he reasoned, if he spoke personally with Serafina, she would disclose what he needed. More selfishly, he needed to hear if Elizabeth cared for him. He needed to know if her heart raced like his does every time they touch. He needed to hear that the kiss was wanted and enjoyed. He needed to know if she loved him yet like he did her. He needed to know if her opinions of him had changed. He needed to know if he had given her enough time or if she needed more. He needed a lot. He sighed, his body needed to hold her and show her all he felt for her, to tell her how much she meant to him, to tell her how much . . . he needed her, just her. And what he really needed was to hear it from Elizabeth, not her maid. No, his needs were not all that simple.

Martin brought him his dressing gown. "Do you need anything else sir?"

Darcy let out a rueful laugh. "Yes . . . but nothing you can help me with, I am afraid."

The next morning, Elizabeth rang for Serafina. This morning was going to be spent with her husband looking for the perfect spot for a swing: but not just any swing, *their* swing. The swing that she had dreamed about so often since marrying her husband. The swing that at first had alarmed her but now she relished it. The swing that kept getting better each time she dreamed about it.

As she waited for Serafina, she remembered the talk they had shared last night. Elizabeth hadn't had an opportunity to tell her about the kiss since it had happened, and by the evening had been quite anxious to tell her about it.

"It finally happened!" she exclaimed with a wide smile. "And it was so natural, Serafina!"

"And what exactly happened, madam?" Serafina sent her a knowing look. "I have heard of feeding the chickens, walks together, rolling in the mud, falling in streams . . . what exactly has happened now?" Serafina had to suppress a smile. She knew very well what had happened, but wanted to hear all the details from her mistress.

Elizabeth blushed. "He kissed me. Or perhaps I kissed him. I do not know, but it was so gentle!" The color in her cheeks flushed scarlet. "Well, at first it was. After that, I must confess that we both were overcome and shared more than a few gentle kisses."

Serafina's answering look was warm. "I am so glad to hear it." She finished unbuttoning Elizabeth's petticoat and lowered it to allow Elizabeth to step out. She glanced over at the wardrobe where the silk nightdress lay, still unworn. "Perhaps we should wear the new nightdress tonight?" She stepped over, opening the doors and holding up the shimmering length of fabric in front of Elizabeth.

Elizabeth felt her cheeks grow warmer, if such a thing were possible. Would Mr. Darcy come to her tonight? She was not yet prepared to imagine what might happen next, but after experiencing the stirring emotions, she was curious; perhaps even a little hopeful. It would not be long, would it?

And yet . . . she recalled how he had not kissed her in the barn when she thought he would. Why was he holding back? Everything had been perfect: private and warm, intimate and special to the two of them. Something had to be troubling him still. What was it?

"Not tonight," she said in response to Serafina. She set down the garnet cross that she had been holding in her hands. "I do not know why exactly, but I feel certain that Mr. Darcy does not entirely share my feelings. I have been pondering it all day. I do not know if he regrets our kiss, or if he has been consumed with worry over the fire, but he has been cold and distant all day. Tonight, I—" she halted, gazing down at the nightdress. "I convinced myself that he was just busy with the aftermath of the fire. But I saw desire in his eyes again tonight, yet he did not kiss me again. I am afraid that I have married an enigma, Serafina, and I have not yet succeeded in puzzling him out." She laughed briefly to hide her own worry.

Serafina did not laugh at her mistress' wit. Martin had told her privately that the master was very distraught this morning, and indeed, the few maids that saw him reported that he rarely spoke, and ate very little. "When exactly did this kiss happen, madam?"

"Last night. I confess that I behaved shamefully," Elizabeth said, still teasing her. "After he came in from the fire, I threw propriety to the wind and kissed my own husband!"

Serafina's frown deepened. "You mentioned him being cold and distant all day, but yet you are laughing and blushing. Have things improved?"

Elizabeth grew silent for a moment, thinking back to the time they had spent watching the chicks hatch. "I think so," she said slowly. "We spent tonight together in the barn— very romantic, I know," she said in response to Serafina's glance, "but I did feel a connection between us. I had thought, I admit, that he might discard propriety as well and kiss me again, but all he did was kiss my wrist." In truth, she thought, that simple action had unraveled her.

Serafina nodded firmly. "Well then, I know one thing, madam. A man who smells what is for dinner cannot help himself but to eat the food. It will not be long before that nightdress will be needed." She took it back up, folding it neatly back into a square before she replaced it in between the sheets of muslin in the wardrobe.

Elizabeth laughed again at the memory of Serafina's certainty last night. Perhaps, after all, hunger was the best metaphor that any of them could have used. She would never have dreamed that she would have enjoyed being a waiting meal, but now the very idea was thrilling.

Serafina knocked at the door, bringing Elizabeth back to the present morning and Elizabeth stood.

"Come in," she called. Serafina gave her a sweet smile and immediately went to work assisting her.

Serafina was nimbly doing up the buttons on her pale green day dress when she broke into Elizabeth's thoughts with a question. "Madam, I was wondering if you placed the emerald necklace somewhere special. I was going to clean it before the Autumn Festival."

"No, I have not done anything with it." Elizabeth glanced back at Serafina's reflection in the mirror. Her maid's brows furrowed. "Is there something wrong?"

"Then I am afraid that it is missing. I recall distinctly that I placed it in the bottom drawer, madam, but it is not there now." Serafina felt her fingers tremble as she did up the last button. Many servants had been let go for simply misplacing a valuable item. She had heard many stories of carelessness or theft being blamed upon the servants. She brushed the seams on Elizabeth's shoulders. "I am sorry, madam. I only noticed it missing yesterday afternoon, and meant to tell you about it last night, but was distracted by our conversation. I had hoped that you had moved it. I am truly sorry. I will have every servant looking for it."

Elizabeth put her hand up over Serafina's, stilling her fingers. "I am certain that it is not your fault. But Serafina, this is the third thing to go missing. First Mr. Darcy's gold pocketwatch, then it was the silver, and now my necklace. Has Pemberley had problems with theft in the past?"

"No, madam," Serafina protested. "No one is new to the house, either. I suppose . . ." she let out a breath. "I will have to speak to Mr. Darcy about the necklace." She did not want to be the one to tell him; somehow she suspected he would be less understanding, but the necklace had been in her care last. She was responsible.

Elizabeth sat down on the bed, her lips pressed together. "Please speak to Mrs. Reynolds. I think we must comb over the house. I will speak with Mr. Darcy. It will not be pleasant but he needs to know." She felt a pang at the thought. It was a beautiful and valuable necklace, true, but it now carried so many memories. When he gave it to her, it was when he first told her she was tempting. It was when she first allowed herself to hope for something more than companionship. It had once been his mother's, but most importantly, it was from him.

After dressing, she went downstairs for an early breakfast. Mr. Darcy was waiting downstairs, reading a few of his letters over a pot of chocolate. She smiled at him. "Good morning, William."

"And how is my wife this morning? Did you have a restful night?" Darcy said, smiling back at her. He felt considerably and blessedly rested this morning after a few days of exhaustion.

She took a seat across from him, deciding that she would tell him of the necklace after they had dined. She did not want to see his features clouded with worry just yet. "It took a while to fall asleep, but I did sleep well."

"I am glad that we are both refreshed for the new day. I confess that I do not think I can sleep until I take an inventory of the day." He smiled quietly to himself— their late-night kiss had most certainly featured prominently in his inventory. He took another sip of his chocolate and set his letters aside. "I have been considering the fairest prospect for a swing that we can discuss after you eat. There are several natural cedar trees on Pemberley grounds. We have a few my grandfather planted as well that might be the correct size."

Elizabeth had been hungry, but now her anxiety over the necklace twisted her stomach. "I think I will just have tea this morning. How soon can we go?" At her words, the footman disappeared, reentering after a few moments with a copper kettle. Elizabeth waited as he poured the hot water into the teapot, and then sat back, waiting for the leaves to steep, admiring the beautiful Wedgwood tea set that graced her breakfast table each morning.

"Well, there are a few things I need to get in my study and I can show you the map of where we are going too. After that we should be free to leave. Are you sure you do not want to eat anything?"

Elizabeth debated, turning a silver teaspoon over in her hand before speaking. She would need her strength for the walk, but she was not sure she could stomach much food. Perhaps she should tell him now, and risk the opportunity to go out for the perfect cedar tree. She avoided answering him for a moment by pouring herself the tea and slowly mixing the honey and milk in, watching it dissolve in the amber liquid. How was tea always so perfect at Pemberley? It never sat for too long, nor burned her tongue if she sipped it too quickly.

Mr. Darcy waited for her reply. She seemed on the verge of saying something, but did not entirely know how to speak. He broke the silence. "Our namesakes are doing very well. I checked on them this morning and can speak to their health."

Her face lit up. "Truly? I knew that they would do well after the rain stopped, but it was so thoughtful of you to visit them so early."

Darcy was a little embarrassed now that he was being called thoughtful. The truth of it was he wanted desperately to understand the riddles about the chickens and he thought if he thought on them without Elizabeth's distracting presence he might be able to make sense of it. He was still carrying the list that he made with him in his pocket, the added pieces of information from watching them hatch already scratched on it. He had read, pondered, and watched the chicks and the hen, his eyes going from paper to hen to chicks to nest box and back to the paper . . . but he was no closer to understanding them then he was before. "I was enthralled with the whole experience of watching them hatch that I wanted to see that they survived," he said.

"Yes, seeing them hatch gives me a glimpse into what it must be like to become a parent. You anticipate the moment so much that when they finally break out of the shell you are overcome with gratitude and pride. We are very lucky too. All seven hatched and that is not usually the case. That hen was very devoted." Elizabeth was still struck with her own gratitude that William had taken a liking to the chickens. It was a hobby of hers at Longbourn, but they had grown to be much more than a hobby here at Pemberley. It was, strangely enough, what linked her and William together.

Mr. Darcy met her eyes. Would they someday share more than a flock of chicks between them? He held her gaze for a moment before he cut her a slice of cake. "Here, eat a little something."

She took a bite, the knot in her stomach loosening a bit as she did so. She ate briefly making light conversation until her cake was finished. "Well, let us see that map! I have always loved swinging. There is something about it that is invigorating. I used to swing when I was troubled when I was too young to go out walking on my own. I loved the whole experience." She looked at him with a curious little smile. "Pray, Mr. Darcy, have you ever truly contemplated the image of a swing?"

Her eyes were so bright. This was a part of her that he treasured dearly: her sharp wit, her clever observations, and he would do anything to hear her speak. "I am afraid, Mrs. Darcy, that you shall have to enlighten me on such matters. I confess I have never given much thought to a child's plaything before. Do not, however, imagine that my omission makes me any less of a deep thinker."

She saw the mirth in his eyes and began to explain. "Well, it is not so much a parallel as a metaphor. Life has many ups and downs. Sometimes we struggle with trials, or gravity in the swing's case, and feel low and heavy. It even looks like we will hit the rocks below us. That moment where we think we can get no lower is very difficult. We feel the weight of our trials the worst at that moment and we do not have the perspective to see a way out. But the most important part about a swing is after the lows, after the trials and hardships we face, the swing always goes up. Always. Life always gets better. In fact, because we are so faithful and used our strength to pump ourselves during the lowest spot we are rewarded with two very important things.

"The first is perspective. As it swings up we are high enough to see a perspective that we could not get during the low part. We can see everything. I like to swing high enough that the ropes that tie us are not even in my peripheral vision and I feel like am just flying in the air.

"That brings me to the second important reward. As we reach that peak, we are weightless for just a moment. All that irritates, like the ropes or seat of the chair in the swings case, or trials or things that make us anxious in life's case, it all just disappears for a moment and we are free from all that binds us. We feel nothing, not even gravity weighing us down. It is a moment that I relish. To have perspective and be weightless at the same time is indescribable. So yes, life is like being on a swing. We can just sit there at the lowest spot and be miserable or we can fight and struggle and pump ourselves to a position that allows us to see things in a better light. But the most important life lesson you get from a swing is that after every down, the swing always comes back up. Always. Life can be hard but it always gets better." She sat and watched him, his eyes intently focused on hers.

Mr. Darcy was silent for a moment. He had never seen the depth of conviction that she had just demonstrated to him. She was always intelligent and wise in his mind, but to have spent so much time correlating a simple swing to help her understand life's problems was beyond anything he could have come up with on his own. "You are beyond amazing, Elizabeth. And I must admit I lied to you again."

She knew this game now, and smiled at him. "And what might be the truth?"

"You are most definitely a deeper thinker than I am. I must remember that when I try to understand you. I have to admit that a swing has always been just a swing to me." *And a chicken has always been a farm animal, but to her it was more.* He would need to remember her cleverness and powers of observation if he was to make sense of the chickens.

"If you are going to keep lying to me, you might just alter my opinion of you," she teased.

He was most anxious to hear what her opinion of him was. "And what might your opinion of me be that would be so altered?"

"That you are trustworthy." She gave him her best smile.

He had, in his heart of hearts, been hoping for more, but trustworthy? He could live with that opinion. It was better than proud. He had made every attempt to be trustworthy with her, and he was grateful he had gotten that across. He stood up and took her arm and tucked it into his. "Let me show you the map."

She let him lead her into his study, feeling delight at his very presence. His fresh cedar and sage scent was overwhelming, but she closed her eyes for a moment once they were inside, attempting to focus her mind. He spread the map of Pemberley out on his desk and then took some books to place on the four corners of the map. She glanced idly over the objects on his desk: the inkwell, the carefully sharpened quills, the neatly stacked letters. A torn piece of paper caught her eye, and without thinking, she reached for it. It was Georgiana's letter from Wickham. She held it up to him. "How did you come across this?" Had Georgiana given it to him? The last she knew it was still in her book in the library. Had he read it?

Darcy's hands paused in their motion. He should have burned the letter immediately, but he was struck at her reaction. She didn't seem ashamed, but merely curious as to how he had obtained it. Perhaps a little concerned, but nothing greater. What was he to make of this? "I was going to burn it," he said flatly.

"Burn it?" Her eyebrows drew together. "You do not think it important?" Something was wrong. He had always been so protective of Georgiana in the past, and she had expected him to be overwrought with worry and even angry enough to do something. To burn it, though, meant it wasn't worrisome. Did he simply want to sweep the troubles under the rug? She would not have expected such a thing from him. Her mind was very confused. But his next reaction shocked her to the core.

His entire day yesterday was consumed with the severity of his reaction to the letter! How dare she question him, after all that she had done? "Of course I think it is important!" he said sharply, his voice rising. He had not known what to expect: apologies, remorse, but not this moderate concern. "I am your husband! How can you imagine that I might not care?" He shook his head, turning and walking to the window. "Good Lord, Elizabeth! Do you think me totally heartless?"

Elizabeth's face flushed with anger. She put her hands to her hips, her brows drawing together in a glare. How dare he speak to her like that! "What exactly does being my husband have to do with this letter?"

He could not believe his ears! She had not flinched in the slightest. Was she absolutely craven, then? He was getting more angry and his voice bellowed, "Do you know what kind of man you are dealing with, Elizabeth? Do you want me to enlighten you about his prior actions? Or does his kiss still linger on your lips?" He stepped forward, snatching the letter from Elizabeth's hand, ready to tear it up. He watched as her mouth dropped open, and inhaled, standing still. *Patience. Time.* The words ran rapidly through his mind. He would not let Wickham's scheming ruin his marriage. He had gone too far and he knew it. Yesterday he had made the decision to move past the letter, but apparently the decision had not solidified as obviously his emotions leapt to levels he was not prepared to handle. He opened his mouth to apologize when Georgiana tapped on the door and stepped inside.

"Is everything all right? William, why are you raising your voice so?" She came closer and noticed the letter, her letter, in William's hand. She looked at Elizabeth, who had tears in her eyes. "You gave him my letter?" How could Elizabeth betray her like that? Apparently she had taken things into her own hands.

Mr. Darcy looked at the letter in his hand. "Your letter? Georgiana, this is your letter from Wickham?"

"Yes, of course! Elizabeth, how could you give it to him without telling me?"

Darcy unfolded and then refolded the letter, looking between Elizabeth and Georgiana. "This is your letter. . . " He opened it up again and held it out to her.

"Yes, I already told you that, William!"

Darcy looked to the silent Elizabeth as the revelation crashed over him. She wasn't ashamed and didn't feel guilty because she hadn't been writing his enemy after all! She wasn't pining over Wickham! He was so shocked he didn't know what to say. He had been ready to look past the issue, and if fact burn the evidence, and now it seemed it wasn't necessary! Relief overwhelmed him. She hadn't given her heart to that rake! His relief at realizing this piece of information was short-lived. Elizabeth's tears ran freely down her face, and she stood there without moving. He had been a complete beast. "Elizabeth . . ." She snatched her arm away from his reach and walked across the room, gazing at the bookshelves, her hands tightly linked in front of her.

Georgiana did not seem to register the action, turning to Elizabeth. "And if I showed you his other letters would you have promised me you would keep them from William but later just show him anyway? Is that the kind of sister you are? Does your word mean anything?"

"Georgiana," Darcy said hastily, "Elizabeth did not give me the letter. I found it in her book and assumed that it was hers. She has not betrayed your secret." He gazed back at Elizabeth, whose eyes were rimmed with red, her cheeks damp with tears.

He thought it was my letter? He thought Wickham was threatening me? Why was he going to burn it? Did he think the threats meant nothing? She felt a swirl of emotions and the chaos overtook her for a moment. He could not be so trustworthy after all. She had placed her heart at his feet, opened herself to love him, left herself vulnerable, and the moment conflict comes he raised his voice and was cruel. He had shown himself so kind and loving but to see him treat her this way was beyond painful.

If he thought the letter was mine but was going to burn it, what did that mean? What have I done to make him not trust me? Does he doubt the feelings I have for him? She hadn't exactly told him she loved him but they kissed, and that should mean something! She pressed a hand to her mouth to muffle a sob. She almost excused herself to go and weep privately, but then reminded herself there was more than her own concern at stake. She turned to Georgiana and swallowed her tears. Something Georgiana said made her curious. "Other letters? Has he continued to write you these threatening letters?"

Georgiana's eyes were filled with tears as well. "Yes, several of them. I only showed you the first one. I received one more before coming to Pemberley, and two more since coming home. I have done what I could to stop him, but they just keep coming. I do not know what to do!" She bowed her head. She had acted stupidly and her assumptions made her act without thought. "Elizabeth, please forgive my cruelty. You have been both sister and friend to me, and I should have known that you would not go back on your word."

Elizabeth swallowed back another sob. At least Georgiana had the decency to apologize immediately. She brushed the pain aside and reached out to embrace Georgiana. "All this time you have carried this burden by yourself when we could have helped you! You should have told me the letters were still coming!"

Mr. Darcy had listened as they mended the misunderstanding but could not wait long to speak. "Is this why you have been so sullen and withdrawn? I cannot believe you told Richard but not me! I cannot believe Richard did not tell me himself! And how exactly have you tried to stop him? I do not see what you could possibly do to make that man change his ways."

Georgiana looked down and smoothed her skirts, "I did not exactly tell Richard about it. I simply told him I had encountered Wickham at Longbourn. That is all he knows. It is the truth; I did run into him, but it was not the reason for my mood. I am so sorry, William! I wanted to tell you for so long, but I knew you would overreact!"

Overreact? How could he not react to such words? He gazed down at the letter again to read it with fresh eyes. The letter was addressed to no one. He should have caught that before. He reread it, now interpreting the words much differently. *"I am sure you can find a way to stay my hand."* He had ignored it at the time; it hadn't made sense, and it was lost in the face of the overwhelming sense of betrayal. Darcy took the worry out of his voice and quietly asked again, "How exactly have you tried to stop him, Georgiana?"

Georgiana did not want to admit to what she had done. She swallowed back more tears. She hadn't meant to hint that she had tried to stop Wickham. All of it was beneath her, and she deserved to lose any and all of William's trust in her. She walked away and looked out the window. Not seeing his reaction would help her admit to it.

"I mailed some things to him. I only did it a few times but he wanted more. I was going to come to you and tell you because his last letter demanded money." Her voice was barely audible.

Elizabeth gasped as the piece fell neatly into place, "It was you who took William's pocketwatch and the silverware and my necklace?"

Darcy turned a confused look to Elizabeth, and raising his voice again said, "Your necklace? I did not know your necklace was missing! The one I gave you the night of the theatre?"

Elizabeth looked heatedly at Darcy. He had made no attempts to apologize, even now. "Yes," she said stiffly. "The same necklace." She wanted to say more— to tell him how much he had hurt her, but it was clear that Georgiana needed him right now. His duties as a brother could supersede that of a husband. She motioned to Georgiana whose back was turned away, but whose gentle sobs were getting louder. Then she turned to leave. She did not need to be hurt by him any further. She felt worse than she did on her wedding day. At least then she knew he didn't care. At least then she hadn't known he could be kind and gentle. At least then she didn't have hope for a happy marriage. At least then she didn't love him and at least then her heart broke for different reasons. Now she knew he cared for her, which made his assumptions and hateful words hurt even more.

Darcy reached for Elizabeth's arm. "My words just now . . . do not leave. Please . . . just let me handle Georgiana right now. I am sorry . . . Elizabeth . . ." But he watched her pull her arm away, lift her chin, and turn to leave. His heart dropped as he saw her skirts twirl around and her squared shoulders slump as she reached the door. *What have I done?* He realized he had just made a difficult situation worse by his intense reaction. He had just offended; no, he had done worse than that. His actions had been unforgivably cruel to Elizabeth. And here was his dearest sister in tears. He didn't know what to do. Should he follow Elizabeth or comfort Georgiana?

He was slightly embarrassed that Georgiana would do such a thing and his instinct from being her guardian for all these years wanted to discipline her, but her sobbing softened his heart. She was already feeling bad enough. He lowered his voice and walked over to her. "Is it true, Georgiana? Did you send him those things?" Her shoulders shook with her crying and she nodded, bowing her head even further. He reached for her shoulders and turned her towards him and wrapped his arms around her. "Shhh, everything will be all right. He cannot hurt you anymore. I will not allow it." He was struck with memories of telling something similar to Elizabeth the night of the ball after Wickham kissed Elizabeth. Although he was with Georgiana, he ached to apologize to Elizabeth. He prayed he had not ruined it completely. *Please let her forgive me.* He shook his head a little. He could not force her to do anything. All he could do was beg her forgiveness, and beg he would. He turned his thoughts back to Wickham's threatening letters. Something had to be done.

*****

As much as Elizabeth was hurt by his heated words to her when he thought the letter was hers, she knew they had plenty of time to reconcile. This was just a storm, and it too would pass. They would eventually talk about it, he would eventually apologize, and she would eventually forgive him, but right now she needed to see the chicks. They were less than a day old. Ironically, her realization that she loved William was not much older.

She hurried to the only place that always brought her peace when she first came to Pemberley, the barn. Yes, she was hurt, but now a more dire possibility came to her. What would William do now that he knew of the threats? Would he challenge Wickham? She could not bear the idea, even now, that he would injure himself. Fresh tears came to her eyes. *I cannot lose him!*

Mr. Darcy's Promise

Chapter 11

Although apologizing to Elizabeth was at the forefront of his mind, Darcy had a few things to work out before he could go speak with his wife. Less than an hour after Georgiana's revelation in his study, Darcy was deep into conversation with Colonel Fitzwilliam. "These are the rest of the letters that he has sent," he concluded, spreading them out across the desk. "Georgiana promises me that there are no more. It appears that he is demanding money now, and far more than what Georgiana would be able to access. Wickham most certainly knows this," Darcy said heavily.

"And now she must turn to you. You think he wants you involved now," Richard said. Darcy nodded grimly. Richard picked up the most recent letter. "And he thinks you will pay this ten thousand pounds to him? Why? What in the world makes him think you would?"

Darcy gazed out the window at the lawn below. Compounding his guilt over hurting Elizabeth was the knowledge that he was partially responsible for this situation. He knew the seriousness of the situation was worsened by his actions in the past. "There is something I did not ever tell you about Ramsgate and Georgiana. But hear me out before you judge me too harshly. God knows I deserve to be beaten, but I only did what I thought was best."

Colonel Fitzwilliam walked over to Darcy and put his hand on his shoulder. "Cousin, I doubt anything you did concerning Wickham could make me want to beat you; now him, yes, but you, no. What could be so bad that you could not tell me?"

"I never told you I walked in on that scoundrel kissing Georgiana. A habit I seem to be taking up," he added under his breath. Richard's eyes flickered with confusion but Darcy ignored it. "I was so angry that he would dare attempt to compromise Georgiana that I nearly threw him out of the house myself at the very moment. But then he made a vile threat, and it is not one I should have listened to. He said he would tarnish her reputation if I did not pay him to keep quiet. He was going to tell our Aunt Catherine that I was allowing Georgiana to sell herself to the highest bidder, that I encouraged her to act so wantonly. As you know, we had such hopes for her that summer, and the two thousand pounds he demanded seemed a small price to secure her future happiness. In return, I demanded that he leave the area and stay as far from Pemberley and Darcy House as possible. I also instructed him to never contact Georgiana again. Well, it shall not be a surprise to either of us to hear that he cannot keep his promises. He had not come near us, and I thought that was all in the past . . . until he and Georgiana met at Longbourn, just as she told you. When I realized he was in Meryton, and for a justifiable reason, I gave him the benefit of the doubt. I did not think he would pursue her like he has. So you see, this is all my fault."

Richard laughed and shook his head. "So, my dear cousin, you think because you paid him once, you are responsible for every decision that he makes— that you— not him, made the decision to do what he did? Now that is classic Darcy logic."

Darcy sent his cousin an exasperated look. He didn't care to be laughed at and especially about something so serious. "Richard, I am being serious. If I had not caved once to his extortion, then he would not have tried a second time."

"Oh, very well. Play the martyr. It is all your fault that a man would prey upon an innocent young lady twice in one year." Richard reached over for Darcy's decanter, still left out from the other day, and poured himself a glass of brandy. "Let us just drop the subject of who is really at fault because I fear we will not agree. What are you going to do about it? And more importantly, how will I get a chance to be a part of it? He cannot go unpunished after all that he has done."

"I agree," Darcy said emphatically. "I am leaving for Hertfordshire in the next hour. I am going to find him, and once and for all, end this. I need you to stay here with Elizabeth and Georgiana in case they need you."

Richard coughed on a swallow of his brandy. "You are not actually going to duel, are you? It is illegal!"

"No, indeed not. I would and will if necessary. I admit that the idea is tempting, but such behavior is unconscionable from a husband and brother. In fact, I was hoping you might have a better idea." The risk was too great, even if Darcy knew that he was the better swordsman.

Richard's frown deepened, and he sat his brandy glass down with a heavy clink before he reached for the letters. "Do you not realize what you have here? This is proof that he not only was threatening the safety of Georgiana but that he was demanding money to . . . now, how did he put it? Ah yes, to 'stay his hand.' No magistrate will ignore this, Darcy. They do not look kindly on extortion from any man, least of all from those who wear his majesty's uniform."

Darcy picked up one of the letters. It was true that they held power, but could they really solve their problem? "You truly think we could get him convicted with the letters? This is wonderful! All I need do is to ensure that he is brought in to a magistrate." He paused after a moment, feeling his heart sink. "Could it really be that simple?"

Richard frowned. "This is coming from years of serving in the army, Cousin, nothing is as simple as it sounds when you are dealing with thinking, irrational, and conniving enemies."

*****

Elizabeth stepped easily back towards the house, feeling as if a weight had been lifted after visiting the chicks. She paused in front of the house, gazing out at the carriage that was being loaded with suspiciously familiar trunks. "Mr. Reynolds," she called, walking towards him, "whose trunks are those? They look like my husband's."

"Yes, madam, he will be leaving for Hertfordshire in the next half hour."

Elizabeth's brows drew together and her mind went spinning. Why was William going to Hertfordshire? And why so suddenly? She drew in a sharp breath. Why hadn't he told her he was going, or asked her to accompany him? She could not imagine any reason that he would go besides confronting Wickham, and the fear over the scenario nearly took her breath. Suddenly she knew what she needed to do.

"Thank you, Reynolds," she said quickly, turning on her heel to go find Serafina. Luckily, her maid was in the midst of some mending in her room.

"Serafina," Elizabeth said quickly. "I need you to pack my trunks as soon as you can, and get a footman to bring them down. I am going with my husband and we do not have a moment to lose."

"Of course, madam," Serafina said, following as Elizabeth led the way upstairs. She quickly changed into traveling clothes, fastening her bonnet under her chin and gazing back at herself in the mirror, gathered her confidence. She would need all her wits about her to convince William of her plan.

Serafina came up behind her and curtsied. "I believe I have it all packed, unless you want to bring the silk nightdress . . ."

"No. Not yet." Her throat felt stiff as she said it.

"Then I will call for the footman right away." Serafina reached for Elizabeth's hand and pressed it. "Travel safely, madam."

She nodded her thanks and headed downstairs. She passed the study on her way out, noting, thankfully, that the door was still closed. *Perfect. I am not too late.* She slipped outside and into the carriage, bracing both hands against the walls to pull herself inside. The carriage rocked as her own trunk was loaded, and she let out a breath, gazing out the window. Soon she heard William's voice outside and she scooted further back into the carriage, out of sight.

"Is everything secure?" Darcy asked.

"Yes, sir." The footman said.

"Then I shall only be a moment, I need to talk to Mrs. Darcy and then we shall be off." He turned to walk back into the house. *Elizabeth will not be happy.*

"But Mr. Darcy, she is already waiting in the carriage."

Elizabeth braced herself. This was the moment she knew must come. She wished she was looking outside to see his expression at hearing this news; surely he was not happy. She waited for what seemed like several minutes until she finally heard him open the door to the carriage, and raised her gaze to meet his.

Darcy's face was tight with a frown of puzzlement. Sure enough Elizabeth was inside. "Elizabeth? Why are you in the carriage?" he asked, careful to keep his voice quiet enough that the servants could not hear. He didn't like having his servant tell him something he was supposed to already know, like the fact that his wife thought she was coming along. He saw her look blankly back at him. "Elizabeth, this is not a social call. We shall arrange to visit Hertfordshire together at a better time." She did not respond, but looked steadily back at him, her hands clasped tightly in her lap. "Please get out of the carriage," he said firmly. She lifted her chin in response, and he let out a small, exasperated breath. *This is ridiculous!*

He climbed into the carriage and sat next to her. "I have to go, Elizabeth, and we both know that the business I have is not pleasant. Please, get out of the carriage." She looked back at him and squared her shoulders as if readying herself for a battle. He threw up his hands, "Elizabeth, this is not a request! You simply cannot accompany me!" Her lips tightened, and she opened her mouth as if to speak before looking away.

Darcy paused, and then gentled his tone. "You need to be here for the Autumn Festival and to help Georgiana during this difficult time. She needs you." She looked back at him, just once, but it was long enough to see that her face was flushed and her eyes glossy with unshed tears. "Dearest Elizabeth, do not cry. Please, I cannot bear it." He withdrew his handkerchief and held it out to her. She looked at it, her face twisting as if it was filthy and she had no desire to take it from him. He let out an exasperated breath and dropped his hand. "You are so stubborn, Elizabeth!"

She gave him a half smile before resuming her frozen expression. He leaned back against the back of the carriage and sighed. He couldn't physically remove her from the carriage. He couldn't force her against her will. He sighed, "Very well, but we will talk about this. Have you even told anyone else your plans? Or am I the only one surprised?" She mutely shook her head. "No, you have not told anyone? Or no, I am the only one surprised?" Her expression did not alter. "Good grief Elizabeth! I said you could come, can you just communicate with me?"

Elizabeth let out a deep breath of relief. She was not sure how far her conviction would carry her. "I asked Serafina to inform Mrs. Reynolds, but I admit I gave no thought to the Festival. I do not know what to do about that."

In spite of all his concern, Darcy let out a hearty chuckle. Relieved he didn't have to interpret her defensive body language anymore, he said, "I must thank you, Mrs. Darcy," he said, bowing his head to her. "I had begun to worry that the woman I married had long since left Pemberley." She raised her eyebrows quizzically and he smiled back at her. Now that he knew he had her attention, he said, "It is more like you, my dearest Lizzy, to chirp loudly rather than silently." She covered her mouth with a gloved hand, but not until he heard a small laugh escape.

Darcy thought quickly on the matter. "I will speak with Mrs. Reynolds. We will simply postpone the Autumn Festival for a few weeks. The freeze is still at least a month off." She nodded, her gaze attentive. "But other than my permission to have you accompany me— which you have won from me only reluctantly, I might add— may I do you any other service?"

"No. Thank you," she added after a moment. Ideally, she herself would make these arrangements with Mrs. Reynolds, but she would not give him the chance to slip away from Pemberley without her. He gave her a small bow before exiting the carriage, and she gazed out the window at the beautifully tended lawn. In a few short minutes, he returned and settled into the seat across from her. She had assumed that he might care to sit next to her. Darcy tapped on the roof and the carriage started.

The roads from the storm last night were not pleasant to travel on. They rode in silence for a half hour, the carriage rocking them back and forth in spite of all the driver's care, and she finally cleared her throat. The silence was thick and she felt she had to say something. Her emotions were in a jumble over the last few hours.

"You called me stubborn." A small smile crept at the corner of her mouth even though she tried to suppress it.

Darcy looked back at her, relieved just to hear her break the silence, and then broke out into a roaring belly laugh. "You have found me out, Mrs. Darcy. I will confess to all my crimes if only you will reveal why you were so insistent on accompanying me."

Elizabeth was silent for a moment, one finger trailing the seam of her gloves. She owed him an answer. How does one finally open one's heart? How does one explain irrational fears? How does one place one's heart out in the open, exposed for all to see? One doesn't— not yet— not fully. "I was worried about you." She knew it was no closer to expressing her real feelings than what she said after the kiss the night of the fire.

She saw him raise an eyebrow at her. She knew he was asking for a better explanation. "I could not let you leave after all that had occurred, being asked to pray for your health and safety. You did not even tell me you were going, which means you knew I would not approve. And if I did not approve then I was not going to let you do it. And if I let you go by yourself I would have no influence on you. And if I had no influence then I would be powerless." She knew she was rambling. She took a deep, courageous breath, "I cannot lose you William." She bowed her head and looked at her hands. If she had been looking at him she would have seen his eyes smiling and hope shining brightly from them.

He leaned forward and shifted across the carriage to sit by her before he took her chin in his hands, lifting it and studying her face: the beautiful curve of her chin, the delicate rosiness of her lips, her bright and bewitching eyes. "I cannot lose you either, dearest Elizabeth." He brushed his lips across her cheek, and her eyes rose to meet his, locking them together before the carriage interrupted them with another lurch. They both laughed quietly, disengaging and sitting side by side. This time it was Darcy who took a deep, courageous breath. "I thought I had lost you," he murmured, half to himself.

Elizabeth turned her head towards him. "What do you mean?"

"I foolishly thought that Georgiana's letter must be yours, that you were secretly writing Wickham. It was not right, but I acted without pausing. I thought that your heart must have belonged to him all along. I was hurt that after all we had built together that it meant nothing to you." He wanted to say more, to pour out all his anguish and despair, but the look on Elizabeth's face made him pause in shamefaced embarrassment.

Elizabeth's brows knit together. That was hardly a love letter; the threats contained wherein had been quite clear to her. Was William lying to her? But the look on his face said he spoke the truth. He truly believed that she loved Wickham? That she would write without her husband's knowledge or consent? She opened her mouth to speak, but fell silent at the deep rumble of thunder. Outside, she heard the horses grunt in protest. Rain was gathering in dark gray clouds, piled high on the horizon. *Another storm. How will we weather this one?*

"William," she said, "in case I have not been clear enough, let me be so now. I would never be anything but a faithful wife. But duty aside, William, you are the only man who I have willingly kissed. After our time together— which has been so full of meaning and delight to me— I do not understand how you can believe me capable of such a thing."

Her voice showed real pain and confusion and he heard her voice stumble and crack over the last statement, and he was about to kneel at her feet and beg for forgiveness when her phrasing struck him. *You are the only man I have willingly kissed.* Of course. Of course Wickham would have forced himself upon her. He should have realized that Wickham's attempt to compromise her was nothing more than a vile scheme on his part. She was forcibly compromised and he suddenly felt a new sense of empathy for what she must have felt that night of the ball. He could only begin to imagine her mortification and grief. Before he could stop himself, he reached out for her, wrapping her in his embrace. "Please forgive my presumption and cruelty, my love. I should never have assumed your motives were anything but pure. I believe that my detest for Wickham has clouded my judgment, and yet that is no excuse, either. I do not have a better explanation that that. Please forgive me." He pressed a kiss against her dark hair, breathing in the faint scent of lavender.

Elizabeth felt his lips brush against her hair. She knew he was trying to apologize; she could hear his sincerity and humbleness. As she felt herself relax into him, drawing in the comfort she had needed all morning, things started to mend in her heart. She was in his arms again, feeling his fingers draw circles on the back of her hand. Her heart began to race as it always did when he touched her. Would he kiss her? Her head was not far from his. Her face flushed, but she gathered courage from the familiar powerful sensations that came over her, making her more bold than usual. "I shall only forgive you if you promise me something." She lifted her head off his shoulder and looked into his deep brown eyes.

"Anything, dearest Elizabeth. Anything. I feel miserable for not trusting what we have built over our marriage."

She gazed up at him, feeling the warmth from his breath. "Two things. First, do not ever assume my feelings again." She paused.

He waited for the second request, but realized she was waiting for his agreement to the first. "Absolutely. I will ask your feelings next time and every time after that. I will never assume to know what you are feeling again." He waited, all the while looking in her beautiful dark brown eyes, for her to make her second request.

Normally she would have laughed at the excesses of his promise, but right now they were nothing but balm to the sting of earlier wounds. She nodded mutely.

He brushed his fingertips against her cheekbones. He felt so alive around her; so vibrant, every sense piqued by the closeness of her body. He didn't know if it was the rain or his heart making that thudding sound. "And what is the second thing? I promise you, Elizabeth, I shall do whatever you want."

Part of Elizabeth longed to press her chilled hand to her cheek, dulling the furious heat that burned there. "Kiss me," she whispered in spite of the wave of embarrassment at such a request. It was not the sort of thing a lady would ask of a gentleman, but she knew now how safe she was with him. She was placing herself in a very vulnerable situation once again and yet she knew this time he would not hurt her. She felt his hand stop caressing hers, and he gazed at her as if drinking in every tiny detail of her face. Then slowly, ever so slowly, he took his arm from around her shoulders and cupped her face with his hands. He remained here for what seemed like several long minutes when instead of leaning into her, he gently guided her face towards his and pressed a soft kiss against her lips once; and then twice more before he exhaled slowly.

"Elizabeth," he breathed before he kissed her again and again. It was as if a dam had broken between them.

She leaned into him, all her anxiety and worry slipping away with the joyful tears that appeared in her eyes. Each kiss seemed an apology for his cruel words. He was kissing her. It no longer mattered that they had been angry at each other. How strange it was that a simple touch could heal the wounds inflicted by sharp words. She reached for him with her own hands, resting her palms against his chest. The skin beneath his waistcoat and shirt felt warm and firm against his sculpted chest. He continued to place kisses on her lips while she eagerly explored his shoulders and arms. She was literally breathless as she realized his intensity in this kiss was even more than in the last. She pulled away slightly to take a breath but was in no way ready to stop. The carriage jolted hard, and she nearly tumbled away before he grabbed her firmly. Their lips separated with the disruption and she felt him sit up straighter. She was fighting to balance herself and knew she had to let go or she would fall right onto him so she sat up and pulled away.

She was pleased with herself. She had been direct and he had responded; indeed, he had responded exceedingly well. She would have to remember that in the future. She gave him a small smile. It had been a beautiful moment, not just because of the kisses, but because she felt a newness of heart. She felt more for him than she ever had before. More importantly, the pain she felt before was now gone.

Mr. Darcy still had one hand on her face, using the other to stabilize himself, and with his thumb he traced her lower lip. It was still moist from the kisses. He loved her more than anything, and he had hurt her. But even after all he had said and done to her, she had forgiven him. He was in awe at the elect lady he had in front of him. "I promise. I promise to kiss you anytime you desire."

They planned to ride all the way through Hertfordshire in order to make it to London in good time. Darcy explained to her that he needed to work with his solicitor to be certain that he played his cards right and would fully take advantage of the letters to trap Wickham. It was a very long last day of travel: a full eight hours the first day, and ten the next. As they neared Darcy House, Elizabeth reflected on the two-day carriage ride. They both had slept little, but he had remained on her side of the carriage, holding her with his arm around her most of the time. Although she had been sleepy, the closeness of his person kept her from falling asleep. As before, he procured two rooms at the inn last night and, in spite of the fatty mutton served by the inn, they shared a pleasant evening together. Elizabeth couldn't wait to share a real meal from the French chef at Darcy House.

During dinner the night before reaching London, Elizabeth had inquired about Darcy's plans on the trip to Hertfordshire. "You do plan to be safe, don't you?" She couldn't bear the idea of William dueling Wickham. She knew it was still common for gentlemen to have a lack of faith in the court systems. She also had heard that not only did it still happen, but most of the time either one died or was severely wounded, or both. She could not allow that to happen, not to her husband.

Mr. Darcy said, "Richard feels that he will only be drawn out by me, and that I must make it look as if I plan on paying him."

"He really asked for ten thousand pounds? Is that not your yearly income?"

"Not quite by half, but this is not as much about the money as it is in trying to hurt me. If he could threaten those I love then he feels he has won. But to help your fears, I do not plan on dueling him. Although I admit I would like the chance . . ."

Elizabeth gasped. "Do not say things like that!"

Darcy then explained that Richard felt the letters were enough to convict him for life before he added, "But I do not trust him. His last letter demanded money and stated the militia would only be in town for another two weeks. From the date of the letter, that means I will only have about five days after our arrival in Meryton to get him arrested. He is very smart; devious, in fact. I would not put it past him to have a backup plan in place." He sat back. "I am grateful Richard was at Pemberley to care for Georgiana because I do not think I could bear leaving her alone and unprotected. Nor you, that is, if you had not stubbornly insisted on coming." They shared a smile at him calling her stubborn again.

"How long until Richard must return to his regiment?" Elizabeth asked.

"Not for several weeks. So I should have plenty of time to find Wickham and deliver him to the magistrate. Do not worry, Elizabeth, we have the proof that we require. I simply need to lure him into a meeting and have him believe that I want to meet in order to pay him. It is a simple plan. There is nothing to worry about." Darcy didn't feel as confident as he made it sound. Nothing had been simple with Wickham in the past, and he didn't feel like this would be any different.

"I do not trust the man in the slightest. His once-charming ways are dishonest to the core, and he enjoys making people uncomfortable. Whether it is making them blush from flattery or making them feel threatened, he enjoys the game. You must promise me you will be safe." Elizabeth looked at him squarely in the eyes.

Darcy smiled mischievously, "You are asking me to make quite a few promises lately, Elizabeth." He saw her blush, obviously remembering their kiss shared in the carriage the day before. His tone became more somber. "And yes, Elizabeth, I promise I will be safe."

She had then sat back in silence for the remainder of the journey. Their anxiety was palpable. Although neither one wanted to talk about Wickham anymore, there was little else on their mind.

As they neared Darcy house, the carriage slowed and Elizabeth couldn't believe how hungry she was. She placed her hand against her stomach, but was unable to stifle its loud growl. "I am sorry. I fear the mutton was not my favorite and I ate very little." It was still daylight. Would the cook have time to make something delicious?

Darcy smiled. "I did not quite enjoy trying to slide large chunks of fat down my throat either. Ah, now that we are here at Darcy House, the cook will be ecstatic that he will be able to cook for you again. You were so generous in your praise last time that I fear Sparks is not the only servant whose loyalty has turned to you." Darcy exited and handed out Elizabeth from the carriage. He tucked her arm into his as they entered the house.

Elizabeth recalled her feelings of being on the arm of Mr. Darcy on her wedding day and marveled at how they were so different now. This time she didn't want to release his arm. She was anxious to show the household how much their relationship had grown.

Darcy gave instructions to Anderson to take the trunks inside. He then turned to Elizabeth and said, "Shall we?" She nodded and they went up the few steps and entered the house.

Elizabeth was still in awe of the grandness of Darcy House. Pemberley had impressed her even more thoroughly than Darcy House, but it was here that she got her first taste of what her life would be like, and so it held a special place in her heart. She turned her head to see the butler coming up to greet them. "Good evening, Mr. Taylor," Elizabeth said with a warm smile.

"Mrs. Darcy, Mr. Darcy! I was not expecting you, let me take your hat and gloves," Mr. Taylor said.

"It will only be for one night, I am afraid," Darcy explained. "We just have some business before we head back to Hertfordshire. Would you be so kind to notify the chef that we are anxious to see his skills at work. I am afraid the food on the road was difficult to stomach."

"Absolutely, sir. Is there anything else?" Mr. Taylor asked.

Elizabeth spoke up then. "A fire in the library would be nice, and some wine." She looked up to William for approval. He nodded, gazing down at her, and their eyes locked for a moment. Mr. Taylor's words faded away. Elizabeth was sure he hadn't said anything important. She leaned into William further, holding him more tightly than she suspected was appropriate to do in front of a servant. Tomorrow after Darcy met with his solicitor, they would arrive back at Netherfield. She would see her dear Jane again, and her father and mother and sisters too, but tonight it was just the two of them. No morose Georgiana or joking Richard to interrupt them. Since they had not announced their arrival, they didn't anticipate any visitors. She was beginning to wonder if she should have brought her silk nightgown. Perhaps she would finally get the honeymoon a married couple should have. She blushed at such a thought.

*****

To Elizabeth's disappointment, Mr. Darcy ended up being quite the gentleman and made no attempts to kiss her again. Although her thoughts about having a normal honeymoon were fleeting last night, she was quite relieved that it did not happen. She wasn't quite sure why she felt reserved; in fact, there were times when she wished he would be more assertive, take her in his strong arms and whisk her off to his room— but most of the time she feared the unknown. She was unsure about altering the relationship they currently had. What they had built was beyond companionship, beyond friendship, and beyond her hopes. She feared that becoming his wife— in every sense of the word— might alter what she had learned to value so much. Her mind would tell her his kindness would carry over into the bedroom, but her heart would scream at her not to change a thing between them. One moment she would anticipate the change— usually after he touched her and made her body react the way it always did— but the next she worried that he would change once they were together as man and wife.

Most the time she could convince herself her fears were irrational, but this afternoon, as they neared Netherfield, her fears were allowed to run free. Would Jane notice the changes in her relationship with Mr. Darcy? Or worse, would she ask her about what it was like to be married in an attempt to lessen her own jitters? Elizabeth did not know if she could handle admitting to the absence of intimacy. She was ashamed of it for a reason that she could identify. Perhaps it was because she had never heard of a marriage without physical intimacy. Perhaps it was because everyone assumed it was a normal marriage, and she felt like she was deceiving all of those around her.

Elizabeth may have worried that Jane would notice too much, but she quickly realized that a good deal of her anxiety lay in the possibility that Mr. Bingley would notice too little. She doubted Mr. Darcy would have revealed any such thing before they left, and she doubted Jane told Bingley the circumstances surrounding their marriage. She closed her eyes and focused on the fact that Bingley was unaware of the uniquely precarious relationship William and she shared. Her stomach tightened into knots as her fears continued to multiply. Her palms were sweating and she felt short of breath. How could she remedy the problem?

Mr. Darcy had watched Elizabeth grow increasingly anxious over the last two hours. She had shifted her weight, fidgeted unceasingly, wrung her hands, avoided eye contact, and audibly sighed over and over again. The severity of her obvious discomfort only worsened as they entered Hertfordshire. He couldn't imagine what was bothering her. All kinds of thoughts ran through his head. He wanted so much to help her, but he did not know what was wrong. He felt helpless in watching her distress worsen. He reached for her restless hands, but the moment he touched her, she jumped. He withdrew his fingers and put them in his own lap.

Elizabeth cast her eyes down to the ground, embarrassed she had flinched from his touch. "I am sorry. I was just distracted and was not expecting you to reach for my hand. It surprised me; that is all." She reached over and brushed his hand for good measure.

Darcy knew that was not all. He couldn't remember her flinching at his touch in quite some time. "If you do not tell me what is bothering you, I think I might just break a promise I made to you." He watched as her head snapped up, looking quite startled. *I had scared her? Why?* Her anxiety must be severe indeed if she couldn't tell he was teasing her. "I meant it when I said that I would not assume what your feelings and thoughts were, and I promised I would not do that. Please Elizabeth, tell me what is wrong. What did you think I meant?"

Elizabeth did not know what she had thought. Her mind had been so preoccupied thinking about how he had yet to take her to his bed that she hadn't registered the humor in his words. She knew nothing could be humorous in the state she was in. "Forgive me. It appears I did not hear what you said," she lied. She had indeed heard him, and her imagination was sensitive at best.

"Please tell me what is bothering you. Is it seeing your family again? Is it worry about the situation with Wickham? Because, I assure you, I will find him and put a stop to his threats."

Elizabeth gazed out at the familiar countryside. She knew she was only a few miles from Netherfield. She took a deep breath to drink in the smell of the place she once called home. Once. Not now. The thought surprised her. She was with William now, and Pemberley was home. As she looked at him, recognizing the depth of the worry in his eyes, she reminded herself that the relationship she did have with him was fragile. She was just as committed to strengthening it as she had been committed to being a good wife. Her mind offered her an ironic reminder that a good wife did not withhold secrets from her husband. She examined his face. She did not want to hurt him, but she was not ready to change the relationship quite yet. She wanted to feel a more natural progression of affection before they shared a room. "I was just wondering . . ." She stumbled on her words. "I was just wondering what Bingley's plans were for sleeping arrangements." Some part of her was astonished that she had the strength to say it so openly. She turned her head away from his, but not before she saw the awareness in his eyes.

She has been worrying about where she will sleep? He could not believe that the question of where Bingley would put them was one that he hadn't thought about until that moment. Bingley had plenty of spare rooms, but her worry about Bingley's assumptions was not an incorrect one. Of course Bingley would assume they would prefer to share a bed, being newly married as they were. How could this not have occurred to him before now? He had no such problem on the road because the inns always had two rooms. She had never had to express such anxiety before because she did not have anyone but himself making those decisions, and God knew he was fully aware of the precarious relationship. Now Bingley would be making such a decision, and most likely it would be wrongly made. He could see now why she was so distressed.

To admit that they required two guest rooms meant admitting to their unique relationship, and this was something that Darcy did not wish Bingley to know. He hadn't told anyone, not even his valet (although he was sure Martin suspected something) and he was not about to start telling Bingley. He watched Elizabeth's eyes gloss over and saw her blink the tears away. *Dash it! Of all the situations to be confronted with!* If he did not take Bingley aside and explain a few things, then Elizabeth would be pushed into something he promised he would not do. He had promised her that physical intimacy would not happen until she wished for it, and his realization of her anxiety hit him hard in the chest. She was still not ready. He certainly had not expected to share a bed that night, but he had hoped that her feelings had changed. He had even imagined that she would come to him and express her changed feelings. There was no easy way out of the situation. But there was truly only one way to solve the dilemma. He would not go back on his promise to Elizabeth. She needed to know she could trust him. He took a deep breath. "Elizabeth, I will take Bingley aside and make sure he knows we need two rooms."

"Thank you, William, I wish I could explain more . . ." She was relieved that she didn't have to explain more.

He was the one to look away then. His chest hurt like it had been crushed. She still needed more time. How could he have let his imagination run wild last night? His weakness there underscored the hurt he felt at knowing she did not want him that way fully yet. He ached to smother her with kisses and convince her of his love. She had seemed to enjoy those and had responded quite positively to them. She had even asked him to kiss her on the ride from Pemberley. He once again said a silent prayer, asking for more self-control and patience. Then he said another silent prayer that he would have the courage to speak to Bingley. His third silent prayer asked that Elizabeth's feelings would change. At the end of that prayer he added, *soon*. These three prayers were simple and to the point. He opened his heart to the Lord and prayed for that which he needed most. He needed to trust that she would eventually come around. There was more and more evidence of progress being made, but he was not a perfect man. He did not have the emotional or physical strength of ten men. He thought he had been a patient man before he met Elizabeth, but he had been nearly driven to madness at the restraint he had to exercise in her presence. He recommitted himself to be stronger than he had been, kinder than he had been, gentler than he had been, and more chaste in his thoughts than he had been. It was obvious that letting his imagination run free was more dangerous than anything he had done in his life thus far. She needed more from him, and he would just have to find the strength to give it to her.

Soon, he prayed again.

*****

Jane was, of course, invited over for dinner at Netherfield and the men and the ladies were separated as was custom afterwards. It was so good to see Jane and witness the obvious love between her and Bingley. Elizabeth had planned to visit Longbourn tomorrow morning to see all her family while Mr. Darcy did his business with Wickham, but for now she could use the time she had to catch up with Jane. Elizabeth and Jane sat close to each other, discussing Jane's engagement and the two kisses Jane and Bingley had already. Elizabeth laughed inside thinking that she had been married for about five weeks and had only shared two kisses with her husband. Their conversation kept them confined to a corner of the room, talking in hushed tones, nearly forgetting that Miss Bingley was still in the room.

"Where is my brother and Mr. Darcy? It is not like them to be gone so long! I wanted to show Mr. Darcy the new piano piece I have been working on," Miss Bingley said exasperatedly.

Jane turned and spoke up, "They have been gone quite a while now, have they not? Do not worry, my dear Caroline. I am sure that they are just distracted by a billiards game. Ever since Mr. and Mrs. Hurst left he has not had anyone to play with." The sisters had lost track of time as they caught up and hadn't realized how long the men had been gone.

All night, Elizabeth couldn't help but notice Miss Bingley's attentions to her husband. Before the dinner, she kept trying to engage him in conversation while excluding Elizabeth. She even went so far to turn her back to Elizabeth as she spoke to him. The dinner seating arrangements, which she knew Miss Bingley had made, put Miss Bingley between her brother and Mr. Darcy, leaving Elizabeth down the table and across from Jane and Mr. Bingley. Elizabeth had assumed that Miss Bingley's infatuation with winning Mr. Darcy's ten thousand pounds a year would end after his marriage. Apparently she was wrong. She was somewhat perturbed that Miss Bingley would be so open with such attentions, but then she dismissed it because, in the long run, Miss Bingley didn't matter to Elizabeth. She had never desired her good opinion and wouldn't start doing so now. After all, it was still very evident that Mr. Darcy was doing everything besides outright rudeness to dissuade her.

"They simply cannot play billiards that long and leave us waiting for them! It has been nearly an hour and a half! I am going to see what is so distracting." With a huff, Miss Bingley left the room in search of the men.

Jane watched her leave and then whipped her head around to look at Elizabeth, "So? You seem quite happy now. Are you glad he married you? Is it just wonderful to be married? Oh, Lizzy, I cannot wait! Less than a month and I shall be as happy as you two are! I knew you would learn to love him. I can just tell. How did it happen? Was it something he did or said? When did you fall in love?"

Elizabeth laughed. "Jane, Jane, stop! I insist! I cannot even begin to tell you one answer if you ask three more questions before I have a chance to speak!" Jane sighed and put her hands in her lap and just patiently smiled, but Elizabeth knew from experience that her sister would not be content until she had her answers. "If you insist, I shall tell you. It has not been easy; we have had our stormy moments but yes, I think we are in love now. At least I know I love him. I am fairly certain that he returns the feelings, but he still has not actually declared himself. I cannot fix the hour, or the spot, or the look, or the words, which laid the foundation. You asked when I fell in love? Well, I was in the middle before I knew I had begun. One moment I was nervous around him, the next I was nervous without him. There were times that I could see clearly, and others where my mind and heart would battle trying to make sense of what I was feeling. It has seemed so quick, but yet time feels like it is at a standstill as well. I do not know how to describe it, but I love William so much my heart jumps out of my chest every time he smiles."

Jane sighed, clasped her hands at her chest, and leaned back against the chaise. "I still get goosebumps when he puts my arm in his."

Elizabeth teased, "And when has my husband put your arm in his?"

Jane looked alarmed, "Not Mr. Darcy, Mr. Bingley! I was talking about Charles!"

Elizabeth let out a laugh. "I know, Jane! I was only teasing. Have we been apart so long that you have forgotten how I love to tease?" She heard the men enter the room.

"Yes, my wife does know how to tease." Mr. Darcy said as he walked their way. He bumped into a table and hit his knee. Elizabeth was surprised to hear him curse under his breath. "Excuse me, I am afraid I was not quite the gentleman there. My apologies."

Elizabeth studied her husband's gait, realizing after a moment that he had been drinking in their time apart. His feet seemed to shuffle slightly and as he walked, he reached for objects to support him. She stood up and walked over to him. He reached out to her and draped his heavy arm around her shoulders. She could smell the alcohol on his breath. She led him to the couch and helped him sit down before she evaluated Bingley. He seemed to be standing upright and walking normally. So it was just her husband who was well into his cups? They were somewhat by themselves so she asked him quietly, "Are you well? I have never seen you act so."

He leaned into her and slurred his words slightly. "I do not usually drink but I needed a little liquid courage tonight."

Elizabeth wondered what he meant by that. "I do not see why being at Netherfield requires courage."

Darcy looked at her. His words, when he spoke, were biting and sarcastic. "Do you not? I thought it was you who wanted me to talk to Bingley about our . . . how did you put it? Sleeping arrangements . . ." His mouth was dry, and he found that he needed another drink. "Bingley! I left my glass in the library. Fill it up and bring it to me!"

Why was her husband being so rude? He would never order Bingley around like that! Elizabeth saw Bingley's expression shadow with concern as he glanced first at Elizabeth and then back to Mr. Darcy. Bingley dropped Jane's hands and left to go get the requested drink. Elizabeth turned her attention back to Mr. Darcy, "So have you talked to him then? Is it all settled?"

Darcy let out a grunt of a laugh. "I will speak with him. You do not need to fret. I said I would do it and I will. Do you doubt my trustworthiness?" He caught his speech ending with somewhat of a snarl. He hadn't meant to snap at her. His frustrations with himself and his tardiness in broaching the topic yet with Bingley just increased his poor mood. "I am sorry; there is a reason I do not drink," he admitted. "I tend to get is a sour mood when I do," he slurred. He saw Bingley approach with his drink and his thirst worsened. He licked his lips and reached out for it. "Thank you," he said to Bingley. He took a large swallow, downing a third of the glass at once.

*****

Elizabeth reluctantly said goodnight to Jane, and afterwards, encountered a maid who was sent to help her undress and prepare for the night. Elizabeth dismissed her; simply being back in Meryton made her feel less dependent on servants. After all, at Longbourn she had to share one maid with five sisters. Although she missed Serafina's company, she was almost grateful that she would have some private time to reflect on everything. She brushed out her hair methodically, contemplating William's behavior that night. He had not stopped drinking over the next two hours and his words had become more and more slurred. When he rose to bid farewell to Jane, he had stumbled on his own feet and nearly fallen to the ground. Bingley had expressed a desire to retire early, immediately after Elizabeth did, but Darcy insisted that they play another game of billiards. She remembered the look on Bingley's face. It was the same one, she knew, that she had on her own right now. Bingley had to be equally disconcerted by the sight of Darcy intoxicated. And she, of course, knew the real reason Darcy had wanted to have a private moment with Bingley, but Bingley did not. It was then that Elizabeth encouraged them to bet on the game; it was probably the first time in a long time that Bingley could beat Darcy, considering the state her husband was in, but it would also provide them with a place to speak privately and safely. Bingley seemed to get the hint that Elizabeth wanted the two to play even though it was getting late and had conceded. She had tried to make eye contact with William before retiring, but he seemed to be dizzy, as he was holding firmly to the table in the vestibule and was found rubbing his eyes.

She looked at the trunks that lay in the corner of the room. His had not yet been moved, and still remained in the room along with hers. She wrapped her robe around her and tried to tie the top. *I really should have brought a new robe. The broken ribbon on this one is making it very difficult to tie.* She knew as soon as she tried to lay down, a servant would come in to take his trunks to his new room so she took her time getting ready for bed. She rubbed her lavender oils on her neck, she plaited and then re-plaited her hair, took the book she had brought with her, and began to read. She kept waiting for that knock on the door. She even twice thought she heard one, but opened the door to an empty hallway. *What could be taking so long?* She read further but her mind refused to focus on the page. She turned down one side of the bed and propped the pillows up and sat down. It wasn't that she wasn't tired; her eyes were quite heavy, but she didn't want to miss the knock and leave William without his trunks.

She felt chilled, and pulled up the covers to her waist before trying to read again. Plenty of time had elapsed. She estimated that it had been almost two hours, which meant he had probably gone to bed without his trunks. She sighed. She hadn't meant to inconvenience him with her request, but she concluded that he had found another place to sleep. She untied her robe and was about to blow out the candle when she finally heard the sounds of voices outside her door. She quickly tried to retie her robe but when she heard a crash and thud just outside her door, she hurried to open it.

Bingley had been struggling with the weight of Darcy's body on the stairs, and had been grateful to reach the doorway. He realized with a sinking heart that getting him off the floor of the hallway was going to be difficult. He heard their bedroom door open and saw Elizabeth's silhouette looking down at them. He grunted as he pulled Darcy to a sitting position. "Come on, Darcy, we made it this far. Up on your feet." He put Darcy's arm around his shoulders and saw that Elizabeth had come up on the other side to help. The two of them lifted, but when that didn't work, he took his hand behind Darcy's back and grabbed a handful of his breeches. "Elizabeth, on the count of three— just lift with your knees, I do not want you hurting yourself! One, two, three!" They got him to his feet and started progressing towards the open door. Darcy seemed to have woken up slightly and was moving his feet, but his balance was off. He was leaning too far forward to support himself. They had to hurry to keep up with the forward momentum lest they lose him again. Bingley adjusted his grip on Darcy's pants and Darcy seemed to stand up straighter. "Elizabeth, I think I have him. Pull back the covers and I will put him on the bed."

Elizabeth didn't know what to do. Bingley was going to place her nearly unconscious husband on her bed! Darcy had not told him they needed two rooms? She could see they had no other choice at the moment. She would have to figure something out later because Darcy was swaying quite a bit from side to side. She cautiously let go and did as Bingley had told her.

"There now Darcy, turn around and sit down." Bingley nudged Darcy's feet around using his own, and then pulled and guided his buttocks around by the pants he still held tightly. He didn't have to tell him to sit down a second time. Darcy's knees gave out and he buckled backwards. Elizabeth let out a noise of dismay. Bingley pulled on the pants. "Take his legs and lift them up." He was using all his strength to keep him from sliding to the floor. He inhaled and pulled his shoulders up higher. Once they got his buttocks on the bed, the rest would be easy. With one final pull, he yanked hard and was relieved to feel that the weight of Darcy's body was finally on the bed.

Elizabeth numbly reached the sheets and blankets, removing them before lifting her husband's legs. They adjusted him, placing his head where it should be and propping a pillow beneath it. She turned to Bingley. Now was the time to ask for a second room. She opened her mouth to say something, but then hesitated. Her embarrassment far outweighed her courage. She scanned the room to see if there were any other options, but this room didn't have a chaise to sleep on.

Bingley rubbed his hands through his hair and tried to catch his breath. "I have to admit I have never seen him drink as much as he did tonight. It was very peculiar. He kept opening his mouth to talk and then would say something that was— if you'll excuse me— it felt completely random. Like 'did you know lavender grows wild in the hills of Hertfordshire?' He kept doing it all night. I imagined something was bothering him and he was just trying to find the right moment to tell me about it, but then he passed out in the chair. I am sorry, Elizabeth. I would send a servant up but it is late. Just let him sleep in his clothes. It is the natural penalty for drinking like that when he is not used to it."

Elizabeth nodded. "Thank you. I can manage. He hardly drinks, but you know that." She didn't quite know how she was going to manage, but she would figure out something.

"Well, good night. I am sorry I let him fill his glass those last few times. It is not going to be a pretty morning for him after this much brandy. Do take care." Bingley turned to leave and then turned back around. "Elizabeth? He kept mumbling something about chickens and getting their feathers. He brought it up three times, asking me what I thought about them, but I have to admit I could not help him. Does that make any sense to you?"

Elizabeth looked at her sleeping husband. He had been thinking about the chickens! "Yes, but I am afraid it is more complicated than I can explain in one night. Thank you for delivering him safely."

Bingley let out a laugh, "Safely? He landed on the floor in a pile of broken glass from a vase he knocked over! I am lucky we made it, let alone safely!" He then turned and left.

Elizabeth went and closed the door. She looked at the face of her husband and sighed. He looked more like a boy, all those familiar creases smoothed out of his brow. She had never seen him while he was sleeping. She stood transfixed looking at him. She still did not know what she was going to do, but decided to start tugging at his boots. A good wife would ensure that her husband didn't sleep in his boots. She took her time taking them off, trying to come up with an answer to where she would sleep. There were two blankets, but with the chill in the air, one person would probably need two blankets anyway. She could not imagine that sleeping on the cold hard floor was really an option. She pried the first boot off. His leg flopped on the bed, and she heard him moan something that sounded like her name. She removed the other boot, careful this time not to drop the leg. She looked back at his face. His lips were relaxed, and she reached her hand out to touch his face. She took her palm, cupping his strong jaw.

When he moaned and turned his head into her hand, she spoke. "Everything will be well, William, I am here. Just go to sleep." He mumbled something incoherent again. She didn't know what she was doing, but she pulled up the sheets and blankets and tucked them around him. It felt right to care for him while he was in this state. She leaned down and pressed a kiss against his lips. "Good night, William."

He responded with a moan and his words were barely understandable, slurred and mixed, but she heard him say *Elizabeth, do not go.*

His eyes were closed, but his hands reached up for her. She leaned in and let his hands find her waist. He was still very much asleep, but his lips were pursed looking for hers. She giggled at the sight, and then leaned down and kissed him again. She paused just above him. *One more kiss will not hurt,* she thought, and then kissed him a third time. She felt his hands draw her towards him in for one more kiss, his lips now moving frantically with hers. If she didn't know better she would have thought he had woken up. His hands fumbled as he tried to pull her even closer and caressed her back in a clumsy and yet endearing way. *He definitely is still asleep.* She let him kiss her for a moment, and soon he dropped his hands and his lips began to slow. He stopped kissing her and she pulled away. His face wore a gentle smile on it now. She reached for his face one more time. She wanted for the first time that night to stay with him, at least while he was in this sedated state. She wanted to hold him and care for him in any way she could. She sat down on the bed beside him and just watched his chest rise and fall, a habit she had taken up once she had realized how masculine his build was.

He let out a big moan and swung his arm up by his head, flopping it on the pillow. She felt moved with his peaceful state, and for some reason, felt peaceful as well. Her situation should cause her anxiety, but all she felt was a deep love for her husband. She was moved that he would talk about the chickens to Bingley. Some part of her gave as she realized that even in his sedated state he would ask her to stay with him. Even unaware of what he was doing, he wanted to kiss her. She loved him, and she was amazed at the depth of emotions she was feeling. She stood up and walked to the other side of the bed. Without fully examining her behavior, she pulled the covers down and slid in next to him. She wanted nothing more than to spend the night in his arms.

She carefully slid in under the arm that was still on the pillow and placed her head on his chest. He moaned and turned slightly towards her, bringing his arm down around her. She froze for a moment. What he would think of her laying next to him? After a short while, the rhythm of his breathing became regular again. The rise and fall of his chest and the warmth of his body so close to hers made her sleepy. She concluded that since she didn't quite know how he would react to her sliding under his arm, and in bed, no less, that she would rise early and slip out of the position before he noticed. She listened for a while to his steady heartbeat. She would have been shocked at her behavior earlier that day, but at the moment, as her head rose and fell with his breathing, and feeling the comfort she felt in holding him, she didn't want to be anywhere else. She wanted to be in his arms. She wanted to wake up in this position, even if it was before him. With one last moment awake, she whispered, "I love you, William." She then closed her eyes, letting the steady rhythm of his heart put her to sleep.

*****

Mr. Darcy was dreaming he was galloping through a field of lavender. Each thud of the hooves seemed to jar his body and vibrate all the way to his head. Pounding, thudding, jarring. He didn't understand why Calypso was so clumsy this ride. He could hear and feel the wind on his neck coming and going at regular intervals which didn't make sense either. He tried to readjust himself in the saddle, but he could not shake the sensation of feeling heavy and hot. Pounding, thudding, jarring. He focused on the lavender. It was calming and seemed to remind him of something, no, not something . . . someone! *Elizabeth!*

His eyes flung open to an unfamiliar room. Where was he? He was in a bed, but not at Pemberley. Blinking, he looked around the room, but his body told him who was beside him before he actually saw her. Her chocolate hair rested across his chest, and he could smell her familiar lavender scent. She was laying on his chest. *Why is Elizabeth sleeping on me? Where am I? What in the world happened last night?* His mind felt foggy, and his head pounded, his eyes dry and hardly able to scan the room. He made himself do it anyway, and saw his trunks in the corner. Realization hit him like a brick wall. He was at Netherfield, in bed with Elizabeth, when he shouldn't be. He groaned. He drank too much, further explanation for the pounding of his head. He could not remember anything that had taken place after billiards with Bingley right after dinner. He vaguely remembered Miss Bingley interrupting their game but after that he did not know what happened.

Did I take advantage of Elizabeth? He seemed fully dressed; at least he felt like he had breeches on, but the blankets were covering his legs. He lifted his head slightly to evaluate Elizabeth's state of dress, but the movement made him regret it immediately. It seemed like she wore both her nightdress and robe, but he couldn't be certain. All but her shoulders were covered. He closed his eyes and tried to remember what happened. The closeness of her body to his was more distracting than the pounding in his head, and that was saying something. Her chest rose and fell evenly and slowly, her sweet breath blowing on his neck causing goosebumps and chills to run up and down his spine . . . *that explains the wind at regular intervals in my dream.* He kept his eyes closed and evaluated how much of him was actually touching her. That didn't take long to figure out because he was acutely aware of her closeness. Her arm was draped around his chest, her head on his chest with her face angled up towards him, and her leg was on one of his . . . *that explains the heavy feeling in my dream.* He sighed. If she wasn't ready yesterday afternoon to share a room, he did not know how he was going to apologize for not only sharing a room but a bed as well. He concluded that he must not have ever asked Bingley about getting a second room. He groaned again. It was the first time he showed himself untrustworthy and he was beyond reproach.

He wanted to chastise himself, to punish himself in any way possible, but his body was responding intensely to having her so close. His heart thudded faster and his palms were sweaty. He was overwhelmed with her lavender scent that he loved so much. He decided that he would chastise himself later because right now he could barely think straight and it would be a lot easier— and a lot more fun— to simply enjoy the moment. He spent the next ten minutes memorizing every area that was warm from her touch. He even could tell where her foot was on his shin. He could tell where her knee was; that was the bony area on his thigh. He willed himself not to think higher, but she moved slightly and her head tilted down away from his neck. Her breath fell in another direction. That helped. *Thank goodness! I must get myself out of this situation!* He had prayed for patience and self-control and never before had he needed it more than the present moment.

It took all his will power to scoot his hips away, then slide out from under her head and chest. He took both hands and gently placed her head and shoulders on the bed where he had been lying. He slid his leg out from under hers. The movement made her squirm slightly. He froze, watching and waiting to see if she would wake up. Her breathing slowed and became regular again. His body no longer touched hers, and the absence of it was both helpful and painful. He got out of bed and stood up, a task that reminded him of how bad his head hurt. He was relieved to see that he was indeed fully dressed except for his boots. He was not quite sure where they were at the moment. All he knew was he needed some fresh air and a cold glass of water too, if he could find one. A cold bath would help him take control of the moment he was sure. She moaned and rolled over, leaving her face up in plain view of his sore, painful eyes. She was magnificent. He studied her beautiful face for a moment— well, more than a moment— several minutes, in fact. He took a deep breath and reminded himself that basking in her morning beauty would not get him any closer to the door. He slowly turned towards the door. Movement was not pleasant, but leaving her after having been so close to her was even more painful. He stepped out into the hallway in his stockings and carefully turned around to get one more glimpse of her face. He then backed out of the room and closed the door ever so quietly, more to prevent further pain in his throbbing head then in efforts to avoid waking her. He was startled by the sound of footsteps right behind him.

"Why, Mr. Darcy!" Miss Bingley squealed. "I am so glad to see you this morning! But what are you doing in your clothes from last night and why do you not have your boots on?" She looked him up and down. His clothes were terribly wrinkled and she watched as his hand came up to his head.

He closed his eyes, hoping her screeching would be less painful, but it didn't help any. All it did for him was cause her words to echo in his head and remind him of his state of dress. He opened them, taking a good look at her. She was elaborately dressed for the morning, primped and decorated with a feathered hat. Her toilette water smelled of old flowers too. He had to say something because she was staring at him expectantly. He knew if he could just think of something quickly her screeching would not start up again, and it was unbearable at the moment. "I was going to find a servant to fetch some water for a shave. I did not know anyone was awake." He hadn't realized that speaking sent the vibrations from his voice all the way to his head, making him nearly dizzy.

"I will have them send some up right away. They are very quick with those things."

He nodded his thanks and turned to leave but where should he go? He decided that he had better find his boots and find a place to hide until the throbbing stopped. "Then I shall wait in my room." He turned carefully and reopened the door he just exited. He entered slowly, looking at the ground, placing his feet carefully one in front of the other. It seemed to help the head if he was soft footed. He closed the door behind him and leaned against the door with his eyes shut. Keeping the eyes shut helped too.

"Good morning, William. I see you are walking on two legs again. That is an improvement from last night." She watched his eyes fly open and his head whip around to look at her before, in the same moment, his hand flung up and gripped his head. She chuckled, "Have a headache, dear?"

His head was pounding so hard that he struggled to find his words. He had so much he wanted to say, to ask, but he found speaking to be quite painful. He opened his eyes again, this time carefully evaluating her. She was teasing him. Her face wore a small smile, and she had in fact, just laughed. So, he concluded, she wasn't too angry at him, which he didn't quite understand. "I have much to apologize for it seems, but with the state of my head, do you mind if we do so later when it does not hurt as badly? I would really love to know how I ended up in your bed."

"You do not remember sleeping with your wife? I am offended!" She teased. She couldn't help herself. She knew he felt miserable, but the situation was quite funny, considering he was so distraught because he couldn't remember what happened. She saw his eyes show alarm as he took in all that those carefully chosen words she spoke implied. He fidgeted and she heard him groan. She didn't know how long she could punish him like this.

"Elizabeth, please do not play with me. My feelings cannot be trifled with this morning. Did I do anything to you last night?" The words were painful to say: more out of fear for the answer than the actual pounding in his head.

She wasn't done teasing him yet. He deserved to be punished. "Your hands were quite bold last night if I remember it right . . ." She saw him wince.

Oh dear Lord! Please don't tell me my fantasies took over! He looked over at her once again. She had a smirk on her face that she was attempting to cover up with her hand. "I am so sorry; I should never have done so."

"I believe you stole a kiss or two as well." She saw true pain in his eyes and her heart softened. It wasn't fair to tease him when he was hurting so badly. "Come now William, I was only teasing you. Nothing really happened. Nothing that hasn't already happened between us unless you count sleeping in each other's arms. And I suppose that was not so bad considering we *are* married."

He felt no small degree of relief and his knees weakened and he slid his back down the door and sat on the floor. He put his head in his hands and started massaging the temples. He heard her get up and come over to him.

She lifted his head and said, "Come over to the bed and I will rub your head like Serafina does to me when I have a headache."

He did as he was told. Anything to help the pounding would be welcomed, and he had to admit having her hands move throughout his neck and shoulders sounded heavenly. She sat on the bed and he sat on the ground in front of her. Her small hands started at the scalp and started combing her fingers through his hair, pulling the hair outward with gentle pressure. She kneaded his tight scalp and massaged his upper neck. Her hands worked their way to the forehead, and she pressed her fingers in a caressing way, smoothing the tight lines etched into his brow away. Her cool hands felt good on his face. He felt the pounding slowly lessen. Soon she was rubbing firmly at his lower neck and shoulders with her thumbs pushing deep. The sensation gave him chills. He was hyperaware of every movement of her hands and fingers, loving when she pressed and saddened when she lifted them away. He kept thinking she was going to stop every time her hands lifted, but she continued kneading and massaging. He didn't want her to stop, not only because the headache was getting better but because he rather enjoyed having her hands touching him in such a way.

"Is that better?" She finally rested her hands on his shoulders. She may have been in a playful mood earlier, but caring for him in this manner just reminded her of the incredible night's sleep she had. She had never slept so well. Somehow sleeping in his arms was exactly what she needed and she was eager to do it again. She felt relieved that her previous anxieties about how sharing a bed would alter their relationship were gone. If anything, she felt more for him.

Darcy had known that the moment would not last forever. He reached his hands up to his shoulders and took her hands in his. He pulled on them, slightly pulling her to his back. She complied and hugged him from behind, wrapping their clasped hands around his chest. She nestled her face into his neck and kissed the sensitive flesh there. New goosebumps ran up and down his spine, and his heart skipped a beat. She then sat up, pulling away slightly. He turned around and got to his knees facing her. She was so lovely. "I hope you do not mind but I watched you sleep for a little while."

"I admit I rather enjoyed seeing your face while you slept too. I seem to be studying it more often lately," she whispered.

He reached his hands up to her face, "Ah, but your face is one I know better than my own heartbeat." He leaned in and gave her lips a gentle chaste kiss, sending that very heartbeat racing. "Thank you, I feel much better."

Chapter 12

After breakfast, Elizabeth could see Darcy was feeling better, but he still moved cautiously, wincing at loud noises. He was collecting his belongings at the door. "You will promise to be careful, William?"

Darcy looked at her concerned face. He wasn't looking forward to tracking down Wickham, especially given the state he was in. His head was better, but admittedly still throbbed a great deal. He had tried to rehydrate himself with water but couldn't help but drink some of the coffee that smelled so heavenly. Both, at least, had helped to some degree. "Yes, dear, I will be careful. Are you sure you do not want my carriage to take you to Longbourn?"

"No, I want to walk. I am about ready to leave myself. I just have a few things to gather that I wanted to give them. I found a book for my father when we stayed in London and have neglected to send it to him. Now I will have the chance to give it to him in person."

Darcy looked puzzled. "When did you go to a bookstore?"

She blushed a little. "My Aunt Gardiner took me the day I was fitted for the dress I wore to the theatre. I hope you do not mind, but I put the book under your name. The owner knew you well and was sure you would not mind."

He touched her pink cheek. "No, not at all, I am glad you did. What book did you find?" He was pleased she had felt comfortable enough so long ago to get what she wanted without having to ask.

"It is new, on the rise of Napoleon in France. I do not know much about the author, but I admit the topic is what will truly draw his interest." To Elizabeth, it seemed they were talking about everything but what they both knew would happen today. William was going to try to meet with that rake and attempt to turn him over to the magistrate. She was so worried she could hardly turn her eyes from him all morning. She wanted to memorize his face in fear that she would not see it again.

"Sounds interesting," he said as lightly as he could. "I might have to borrow it from him. Well, dearest Elizabeth, I must be off. Have a nice time with your family." He opened the door and walked to the carriage, but realized after a few moments that Elizabeth was still following him. "Was there something else you needed?"

"Not so much needed, but wanted . . ." She leaned up on her toes to kiss him firmly on his lips." He was grinning, his eyes smiling so handsomely. She smiled back at him. "Be careful, and come back as soon as you can. I will probably remain at Longbourn as long as you are gone, so please join me when you can."

*****

As Elizabeth walked the three miles to Longbourn, her mind wandered to the many events that had occurred over the last few weeks. She had gone from feeling forced to marry William, to knowing he was the only one she could have ever been happy with. She had watched the changes in herself as well. She felt stronger and more devoted to her convictions than ever before. She felt loved and wanted, and had grown to love William slowly, but felt it so deeply that she knew she was ready to be with him completely. She wanted to be his wife and to love him in every way.

She trusted him completely; ironically, she had she realized this after the one incident where he had showed himself to be untrustworthy. She laughed. He gave her his word that he would talk to Bingley, and the fact that he didn't was the only reason she now trusted him entirely. If she hadn't seen his peaceful form, she would have never slept in his arms, and finally conquered the fears she once had about becoming intimate.

She had to admit that she understood all too well that any changes to the relationship would be her responsibility. She cringed at the prospect of having to actually admit to such a thing. How does one tell her husband she has been married to for almost six weeks that she is ready to be with him physically? Simply thinking about it made her blush. At one point she had felt grateful for his promise he made in the carriage on their wedding day, but at the moment, the promise was one she loathed. Knowing him, he would be even more trustworthy after he failed with the attempts to speak with Bingley. Although a little vexed with his promise, she loved him all the more. Some promises, Elizabeth had learned, were sometimes made to be broken. Someday she would have to explain it to him.

She opened the door to her old home without alerting any servants. It still creaked when she opened it, something she used to hate when she would sneak out to go walking, but now it brought her comfort. The front hall was empty, but she walked around to see her father's study door was open. She peeked in to see her father pouring over a book. "Good morning, Papa!"

"Lizzy! Come in!" He stood up and embraced her. He took her shoulders in his hands and examined her. "You look well. How is married life treating you? Sit down, have some tea. Hill just brought in a fresh pot."

Elizabeth sat, smiling at her father before she poured the tea, adding sugar to both their cups. Even the typical absence of milk gave her a pang of nostalgia. She waited before he had taken a sip to speak. "Married life is good, Papa. In fact, it has turned out much better than I had even hoped it would."

Mr. Bennet felt relief overcome him. She had written a few times, but it was always more of a travel log then expressing her feelings. He had questioned his decision to insist on her marrying Mr. Darcy many times. His only consolation was that during the engagement Mr. Darcy had shown himself to be a gentleman, and he saw true affection and respect from him. He suspected that Elizabeth resisted the marriage because she hadn't recognized her own feelings for the man. "So, Lizzy, you are happy?"

"Yes, indeed. Much happier than I would have been with Mr. Wickham." She sipped her tea to overcome her wave of revulsion at the name.

"Mr. Wickham? That officer? What does he have to do with it? I saw you danced with him once, but I did not know you had feelings for him." Mr. Bennet had an uneasy sense of being off-balance at the mention of Mr. Wickham. It was like he should know something that he didn't.

Elizabeth looked at her father in confusion. "I am just glad you did not make me marry Mr. Wickham, that is all."

"Why would I do that?" He sat back in bewilderment.

"Because he compromised me at the Netherfield ball! Why else?" Elizabeth had the uncanny sense that she might as well be speaking Ancient Greek.

"It was Mr. Darcy who compromised you, sweetheart. I saw it with my own two eyes, and even though I am advancing in age, I trust that those faculties may still be reliable."

It came on Elizabeth in a flash that her father did not know about Wickham's advances, which meant Darcy had never told him. "My husband never explained what happened?"

"Why should he? I saw it for myself. My darling Lizzy, I am beginning to feel there is something I am missing. Would you care to enlighten me? As you know, I do not like feeling ignorant, especially when you tell me it was someone else that compromised you."

He listened intently to her tale. She spoke first of Wickham's flattery and partiality for her, which he had already seen for himself, and then returned to Georgiana's obvious anxiety around the man. It didn't take Mr. Bennet very long to realize his anonymous letter about Wickham was probably from Mr. Darcy and about Georgiana.

The events of the ball were shown to him in an entirely new light. She told him of them going out to the balcony in all innocence and had been rewarded with Wickham pushing himself on her— his favorite daughter, no less! He felt a knot in the pit of his stomach as he listened to her detail her unsuccessful efforts to resist. He could not believe the man would do such a thing! And it was apparently comfort and protection that Darcy had been offering. "So it was not Darcy who was kissing you? He had rescued you?"

"Yes, Papa. I attempted to explain— I kept trying to tell you all that night and all the next morning, but you would not listen to me. I finally gave up and concluded that Mr. Darcy would explain everything to you. I take it he did not." Elizabeth studied her father's face. Was it all clear to him now? He still looked quite confused.

"Indeed he did not, and I cannot think of a single reason why he would not have done so! What I do not understand is this, Lizzy, why did he agree to marry you then? Why did he let me insist on him honoring your reputation? Why did he feel the need to take you as his wife when a little explanation would have absolved him of guilt?" None of this made any sense.

Elizabeth said, "I have asked him twice, and twice he has promised to tell me. I would sorely like to know myself."

*****

Mr. Darcy had found Colonel Forster easily enough but was not pleased with what he learned. "Wickham is not here? Where did he go?"

"He asked for leave a few days ago and I granted it to him the next day. He was supposed to meet up with us in Brighton. I do not know where he went. And, sir, this question may be impertinent, but may I ask why you are so intent on finding him? I do not mean to offend, but I doubt a gentleman like yourself has need of an officer like Wickham. Unless he has done something? I am afraid that his financial obligations have greatly overcome his income. I have heard quite a few complaints from the other officers about his gambling debts, and as many merchants state he owes them a great deal as well."

Darcy was most displeased with this news. He had hoped that finding him would not be difficult. He had hoped that Wickham being stationed in Meryton ensured that he would be here for the next five days. "It is both personal and business, I am afraid. He contacted me and wished to meet with me." Perhaps if he could lay down the hint that Darcy wished to meet with Wickham, rumors would begin to circulate and get back to Wickham. He then had an idea. "Is there anyone I can speak with who might know where he went? I understand he was close to a Mr. Denny."

Colonel Forster laughed, "Ha, the key word is 'was.' They were as thick as thieves up until the night before Wickham asked for leave.

Word has it that Wickham owes Denny a large sum of money which was promised a few weeks ago. I can see if Denny knows anything."

Darcy knew Wickham better than anyone, and consequently knew where Wickham was most vulnerable. His desperation was clearly communicated through his resorting to threats and extortion for money. Money was the key piece here. Wickham needed it and Darcy had it. If he had learned anything from his father it was that money could not purchase happiness, but it might provide him with opportunities. If he could find this Mr. Denny, pay him what Wickham owed him in exchange for information on Wickham, he might just have a chance at finding him. "I think I would like to speak with Mr. Denny myself. I might have a business proposition for him." He hoped that he made it sound financially promising enough that Colonel Forster would comply. He watched as Colonel Forster rubbed his jaw, obviously contemplating whether or not to hand Denny over to him or not.

"I do not want any trouble. Denny has been a good officer."

"I do not doubt it, Colonel. I intend no trouble to Mr. Denny. I am simply very motivated in finding Wickham." He patted his vest pocket to emphasize his intentions.

"He might be willing to speak with you if it is for the reasons you are implying." He went to the tent door and told the officer waiting outside to get Mr. Denny. He came back and sat down. "I hope you know what you are doing." They waited in silence for quite some time, broken only by Colonel Forster offering him a drink.

Darcy laughed, "No sir, I do not drink anymore, I have had too many bad experiences with the vile stuff. It makes one irresponsible, mean-spirited, and quite clumsy. I have always regretted it when I do imbibe. I think anything that alters one's ability to make one's decisions should be avoided. This lesson I have learned most regretfully."

"Fair enough, the stuff you are used to is probably much better than mine anyway." Colonel Forester poured himself a drink and began sipping it. The early hour was no detriment. He was in the army after all, and like all the other soldiers, had a hollow leg for the stuff.

Mr. Darcy took out his pocketwatch. It was eleven in the morning. His headache had given him a late start. A few more minutes passed before he heard voices outside of the tent. He stood up, turned, and faced the opening. Mr. Denny came in, looked him up and down, and then turned to Colonel Forster.

"What is the meaning of all this?" Mr. Denny asked. He felt cornered by the situation. Why was the man who ruined his chances of ever getting paid by Wickham here in the Colonel's tent? Wickham had promised him double or nothing to retrieve Mr. Bennet, and Denny had done exactly as he was told. He should have gotten paid. It wasn't his fault that someone else found them before they got there. He eyed Mr. Darcy suspiciously. Was he going to be in trouble? He quickly reviewed his actions that night and deemed that nothing he did was illegal. Conniving, perhaps, but not illegal. If he was punished because of Wickham's plan he would personally kill Wickham himself! That cheat wasn't worth it, not in the slightest.

Darcy's head began to pound harder as his heart rate increased. He needed to speak with Denny alone, but he wasn't sure that any associate of Wickham would consent to it. He saw distrust and fear in Denny's eyes; hardly a good start. Mr. Darcy patted his vest pocket where he kept his money and, raising his eyebrows, said, "Would you mind speaking with me for a minute? I might have something you need."

Mr. Denny looked at him. Was he trying to bribe him into speaking with him? When he looked at his fine clothes and saw his gentlemanly manners, he immediately thought of those "gentlemen" who would take advantage of his mother. He didn't trust them, especially those that opened with offers of money. It was one thing to live a free life with the women, like he did, but to profess to be a gentleman and act in the same manner was despicable in his eyes. "I do not think there is anything you can say to me that I desire to hear. And there is definitely nothing I need from you."

Darcy ignored Colonel Forster's presence in the room. "How much? I mean, Mr. Denny, how much did Wickham promise you, because I am prepared to double it." He saw the surprise in Denny's face followed by a twitch of the upper lip. "Just give me a moment of your time. That is all I am asking." He started walking towards the tent door and held open the flap, motioning Denny to go through it. His years of negotiation had taught him to give the other party the appearance of the upper hand without granting them any actual power. Denny slowly walked out of the tent and Darcy followed. Darcy took the lead, another thing he learned from years of business propositions, and led the way to the trees off to the right. One had to make the decisions but make it seem like the choice was still there for the other to agree or disagree, when in reality there was only one option.

"Look here, Mr. Darcy. I do not know what you think you want from me, but it is not worth it. I do not know anything." The fact that Mr. Darcy opened with doubling Wickham's offer only meant Darcy was desperate, and that put Denny in a very good position to negotiate for more.

"Let us start off with some honesty. I know Wickham wanted Mr. Bennet to witness Wickham kissing Elizabeth, and I know you were a key player in making sure that happened. Since it did not happen the way it was supposed to, I am guessing you never got paid. Am I accurate?" Darcy didn't have time to play games. He needed answers.

"I did not do anything illegal if that is what you are getting at. It was Wickham's idea."

"I take that as confirmation that Wickham indeed did not pay you. Let us get to the point. I need Wickham. I have a business proposition for him, and it is one that, if you play your cards right, you might profit in more ways than one." Darcy saw the suspicious look cross Denny's face.

"How so? You think you are going to pay me double what he owes me and then pay him so he can pay me too? That is . . ." *A better plan than I could think of!* He was suddenly very interested in this option. Without realizing it, he licked his lips. He could feel the financial freedom just beyond his reach, tantalizing him. "I confess that is an interesting idea."

"Indeed, you are a great deal cleverer than Wickham gives you credit for." Flattery was always a good tool with negotiations. "Now, we can work out the numbers later but my word is my bond. I will pay you, but you must give me Wickham. He has something of value of mine and I would like it back." Then realizing it sounded like his plan was simply to find Wickham, which it was, instead of paying the man, which it wasn't, he added, "And I am planning to pay the price he dictated in his letter. I am prepared to pay whatever it takes, but I am limited in my business ventures if I do not know where to find the man."

Mr. Denny struggled silently for a moment. Wickham owed him over six months' salary, and he was going to pay him double to retrieve Mr. Bennet. If Mr. Darcy doubled that still . . . that meant nearly three years of salary in his pockets. It did not take him long to realize he really was smarter than Wickham. Mr. Darcy was, if nothing else, at least good for the money. "And if I do not know much? Are you still going to pay me?"

"As long as it is all you know. I am not paying you to withhold secrets from me." Darcy knew he had the man in his grip; he could see him folding right before his eyes. Denny rubbed his chin before he began to pace.

"A couple of nights ago he and I got into a fight. A couple of good punches, that is all. I did not really hurt him much. For weeks he had told me that I would get my money any day. I told him I needed it and I was not about to let his debt of honor go unnoticed any longer."

Darcy resisted the urge to pace. "Can we just get to the point? Where is Wickham now?"

"He said he was heading north for a more 'profitable business' opportunity. He said he knew how to get the money he owed me and that I should be patient. He claimed he would be gone no more than a week. He said it was two days north of here so he would meet me in Brighton after the militia transferred there." Denny watched as Darcy flinched at this news. "He said he grew up there and knew it like the back of his hand and he also said something like 'by now I should be expected to show up on their doorstep.'"

Wickham was going to Pemberley? He felt a little nausea come on. "When exactly did he leave? What day and how was he traveling?"

"I believe it was Tuesday right after lunch. He traveled by post; I know because I lent him the money. Are you going to pay me for that as well?" Denny watched Darcy fall silent, deep in thought for a moment. Had he gone too far and asked for too much?

Today was Friday and it usually took three days of comfortable travel to get from Meryton to Pemberley. Elizabeth and he had traveled uncomfortably long days and made it all the way to London in two. Suddenly the truth hit him; Wickham could already be there! *Georgiana!* Darcy realized that his hasty departure could very well contain the worst timing possible. Even if he left today, and traveled on Sunday, which he didn't normally do, Georgiana would be at risk for at least four days before he returned.

Wickham was dangerous when he felt desperate. Wickham was unpredictable, unstable, and yet very good at his conniving ways. Darcy's nausea worsened and he swallowed the fluids in his mouth before he spoke.

"Was he armed?" He wasn't sure if he wanted to know for sure because there was little he could do about it until at least two and a half days from now.

Denny nodded. "Yes, he was dressed in his uniform and he took his pistol with him. He said he needed a little 'negotiation power.' Look here, Darcy, that is all I know. Truly. I was not all that happy with him and had already succumbed to the realization that I would never see that money again but I took it as a gamble. If I lent him the traveling money, I might actually get back what he owes me. Now can I have my money?"

"Certainly. You were most helpful." He didn't like the news he got from him, but Darcy couldn't deny that it had been helpful. As he wrote out the bank note for the amount Denny claimed, he once again felt the need to vomit. Colonel Fitzwilliam was perfectly capable of protecting Georgiana. He knew that. But at the present moment, Richard was completely ignorant of Wickham's plans. Even as he signed his name to the draft, he began crafting a plan.

He would send an express in the next hour, pay the rider double what he normally would for them to ride hard and fast, and hopefully the horseback rider will get there by tomorrow afternoon. He and

Elizabeth would leave today—hopefully in the next two hours, or they would end up traveling in the dark before they arrived at their country estate north of here. Then tomorrow, Saturday, they would leave for the day and a half ride to Pemberley. But before they left Meryton, he wanted to complete one task remaining to him. That was the jeweler's. He wanted his pocketwatch and Elizabeth's necklace back and knowing Wickham, he pawned them for the much-needed money.

Darcy steeled himself. He felt better with a plan; much less helpless. He handed Mr. Denny the bank note, tipped his hat in the barest attempt at civility, and left in a hurry. He had only the next few hours to complete the tasks he would normally allot to a day.

Mr. Darcy stopped by Netherfield and informed the staff to ready their trunks for immediate departure. He then borrowed Bingley's study to write his express. He sealed it with his crest, silently praying that it would reach Richard in time. He made certain to specifically inform him that Wickham was armed, and that Richard was free to use any of the pistols in the cabinet in his study, should they be needed. He was relieved that Richard would know how to use it if necessary. Once the trunks were ready, he climbed aboard the carriage, and had the driver stop by the jeweler's before heading to Longbourn.

*****

Elizabeth tried to read Mr. Darcy's eyes, but her mother's shrill voice was louder than her own thoughts. Had he found Wickham? Did it go as it was intended to? All she could see was worry and fear. Something was not right.

"Oh, my dear Mr. Darcy! You look so very handsome today! Come in and have some raspberry tarts; they are the last raspberries of the season. You cannot get finer raspberries at Pemberley, and I do not care what how much you refute it!"

Elizabeth continued to watch Mr. Darcy. He wore his old "Master of Pemberley" expression, and, rather than answer, he took out his silver pocketwatch and looked at the time. He wasn't making eye contact either. Something was definitely not right. "Mother, can you give me a moment alone with my husband? I need to discuss something with him."

"Oh yes! *Discuss* away!" Just when Elizabeth thought they would be free of her, her mother returned for one last blow. "Do you know, Lizzy, I cannot wait for little grandchildren to start coming. I should have known you wanted to welcome him properly. What a good wife you are. I knew this was a good match." Mrs. Bennet then departed without seeing— or choosing not to see— the shocked look on Elizabeth's face.

"I am sorry for my mother. I thought she would let up once I was married but apparently now she has her heart set on grandchildren." Even saying it out loud made her blush. Her mother clearly did not know they had not even consummated the marriage yet. Mr. Darcy reached his hand up to her blushing cheek and finally met her eyes with his.

Mr. Darcy wanted to say something like *"I would like to spend many a nights trying to accommodate my mother-in-law's desires."* But he stayed focused. Instead he said, "We have to go. And right away, Elizabeth."

"Is everything well?" He shook his head. "Tell me, William." He was not obviously physically hurt, that she could tell, and she realized with a sinking heart that he had not been gone all that long. Which only meant that he did not find Wickham.

"I can tell you on the way to our second country estate. It is located four hours north of here. If we get on the road early enough we can make it before dark. Say your farewells quickly, I do not want to be traveling in the dark and it is nearly two o'clock now." Darcy squeezed her hand and kissed it. "Quickly, please. You know I would not ask if the situation were not so dire."

Elizabeth took a moment to collect her thoughts. "You have another country estate besides Pemberley?"

"Yes. I rarely stay there, as I prefer to make the trip from Pemberley to London in two long tiring days as we did on the way out rather than break it up into three, but my father thought it would be a useful asset since it is conveniently located on the road to London. It will be perfect for tonight. Tomorrow we can make most of the journey to Pemberley but there will still be fifty miles we will have to make the day after tomorrow, on Monday." He shook his head. "I am sorry, but we must make progress in our travels. Please, Elizabeth, make haste."

Elizabeth nodded, and quickly left to make her excuses and promises to return for Jane's wedding. She took Jane aside and embraced her. She had missed her more than anyone. She picked up her reticule, and when it was heavier than usual, she realized that she never gave her father the book.

"One more minute, I need to give my father his book." She hurried to give it to him. She was back in no time and took her husband's offered arm and he handed her into the carriage. Their urgency of their departure was obvious to any who might look: their trunks were already loaded.

Mr. Darcy did not know how much he should tell Elizabeth, but after some consideration, he decided that telling all of it was appropriate. The more people keeping an eye out for Wickham, the better. He proceeded to tell her what he knew and all he had done so far about it.

"I do not mean to worry you in telling you this news, but I do not feel I should keep that kind of thing secret. I trust you and I have always believed that knowledge always provides power. Ignorance is harmful; secrets worse yet."

"Not to mention that I would simply nag you until you told me." She smiled at him, but his answering smile was vague and distant. She had been hoping to lighten his mood a little, but could see that their three day journey would be a solemn one.

*****

Last night they arrived at the country estate before dark, the sun had set but there was still lingering light enough to make their way through the streets to the estate. The house was smaller than Longbourn, but still beautiful. It had been a quiet ride. Neither one wanted to talk about what they didn't know could be happening at Pemberley. Would the express arrive in time? Would Wickham become violent once he realized Darcy was not there to give him his money? Would Colonel Fitzwilliam be able to keep Georgiana safe?

On the day after their brief stay at the country estate, both fell asleep with worry and lack of sleep from the night before. Elizabeth had fallen asleep first with Darcy's arm around her and he lowered her shoulders and head to his lap, but it wasn't long before Darcy was deeply asleep as well.

He was having dreams again of the chickens, but this time Elizabeth wasn't there. He kept calling out to her, "Elizabeth! Dearest Elizabeth!" But she wouldn't come. He looked for her around the pen and he looked for her in the barn. He looked for her in the hay loft and he looked for her around the back of the barn. She wasn't anywhere. He sat down on the hay bale and felt frustrated. He had looked for her everywhere, had called out "Elizabeth" over and over again but she was nowhere to be found. However, he knew she was here. He could feel her closeness in his body. He went back out to the pen and tried calling her once again. This time he used the nickname she grew up with, "Lizzy! Where are you?" Suddenly the fat yellow mother hen who had sat on the eggs all that time came waddling over to him, its familiar deep brown eyes looking up at him expectantly. Following her were the seven baby chicks who all had their feathers now. The yellow one, the one he named Lizzy, looked exactly like the mother. He just stared at the mother hen. He had called "Lizzy" and the hen came, not the chick he named Lizzy, but the hen. The hen whose eyes were familiar. It dawned on him why they were familiar; its eyes were those of Elizabeth's. He felt like he was beginning to understand something important. Just then Sparks came around with his pitchfork.

"It's about time you see her for what she is. She was very devoted to you and now look what you have to show for it . . . seven little babies, all strong and healthy. That is a lot of love to handle. Are you sure you and the missus can raise them?" Sparks motioned with his hands for Darcy to look at the chicks.

He examined them closely. Babies? They were chicks, just big enough to get through the winter storms, not babies. "You meant chicks, did you not, Sparks?" But Sparks had left him already. He was alone with the chicken that had Elizabeth's eyes. The devoted chicken who had been forced into sitting on eggs at a time of year that wasn't ideal. He knew he was onto something. Elizabeth had once expressed how she felt forced into the marriage. His eyes popped open. The rocking of the carriage reminded him of where he was.

He had to tell her what he just dreamed about! He shook her shoulders gently. "Elizabeth! I figured it out! You are a chicken!" She had her head on his lap and she sat up with the strangest look on her face.

"Are you calling me a coward?" She smirked.

He shook his head violently, "No, no, not a chicken, *the* chicken." His mind felt refreshed and lively. He understood now and he wanted to share it with her. He wanted to show her he loved that part of her that she had kept close to her all these weeks. He wanted to kiss her! He took her by the shoulders and kissed her hard on the lips. "You are the hen!"

Elizabeth wasn't quite sure if her husband was awake or talking in his sleep. She pinched his arm. "There, are you awake now? Because I am beginning to wonder what in the world you were talking about."

He rubbed his arm, but even her teasing wouldn't let him lose the enlightenment he felt. "You love the chickens!"

"William, are you well? Just because I like the chickens does not mean I have grown wings and become one of them . . ." What kind of stress was her husband under to be talking such gibberish? She watched him retrieve a piece of paper from his vest pocket.

Mr. Darcy showed her the list of facts that he had been carrying around with him since the morning he had discovered it was in fact Georgiana's letter from Wickham, not Elizabeth's. He hadn't meant to bring the list along, but when he found it that night he studied it as often as privacy would allow. "I have been trying to figure out why the chickens, the eggs, and the chicks getting their feathers all were so important to you. They are more than some farm animal to you. But I think I know now. You feel like the hen! Or maybe it was *felt* like the hen, I do not know."

The laughing expression in her eyes slowly faded. He knew he was right. "You felt like you had no choice to get married, just as the hen had no choice but to sit on the eggs. Nature decided it for the hen, and your father decided it for you. Have I hit upon the truth?" She nodded slowly. *Yes!* He had finally unraveled this mystery!

"So something besides your free will put you in a situation that you had not wanted . . . Oh! Not simply that, but at a time that you did not want. For the chicken the right time would have been spring, the natural way to raise chicks . . . but for you . . . oh, I do not know . . . for you . . . the right time would have been getting married when you were in love? Am I right?" She nodded. He was thrilled, but continued.

"So you got married before you loved me; no, were forced to marry me before you loved me, but you found a way through it anyway. The hen could not leave or abandon the eggs, it was not in her nature; she was driven to make the best of her situation. That is just like you. You cried so hard on our way to London on our wedding day but then things changed. I saw it in you. It was not right away but you grew to . . . to accept it." He wanted to say she grew to love him but caught himself. She hadn't spoken those words yet. "You found a way to accept your situation and in fact learned to maybe even appreciate the time you had been forced to spend with me?" She nodded. Tears were forming in her eyes. He reached for them and wiped them with his thumbs. He got braver. He dared presume even further in his enlightened state. He lowered his voice and said, "But things changed for you, did they not? You learned to want to be married to me?"

His heart fluttered and it felt like forever before she nodded. He smiled. Her simple nod of the head was more powerful to his body than any kiss or embrace they had shared so far. *She wants to be married to me!* He tried to focus; there was still so much on the paper that he hadn't clarified, like the hatching of the eggs. "And when you said that I could not help the eggs or force them to hatch . . . you were talking about me forcing you to love me." She nodded, and he continued.

"Yes! And the struggle to get out, to hatch, was part of the process! I needed to give you the time and space to fall in love with me on your own time. You said it takes a while to hatch; you said it just takes time. But letting you come to it on your own only makes you stronger. So your love for me was the eggs hatching?" She nodded and fresh tears welled up in her eyes. He leaned in and kissed the tears away, tasting of the salt on his lips. He then felt like he had figured it all out but one thing. If Elizabeth was the hen, forced to sit on the eggs— or get married— and because she endured, her love for him developed, or in other words the chicks hatched . . . but what in the world did getting their feathers mean? If the chicks hatching was a representation of her love then of course she would want them to survive! He let out a big breath. "And getting their feathers before the winter storms? The storms . . . those refer to trials, correct? You want our young love to endure the trials we face?"

Elizabeth had been silent long enough. "You said 'our' love, but you were talking about my love for you. I must stop you before my heart jumps out of my chest."

"I did mean our love. I have loved you for so long, Elizabeth. There was no time I have not. Not since I saw your fine eyes and heard your heart-piercing laughter, or memorized your impertinently raised eyebrow, or saw your kind heart, or tasted of your sweet lips, for there was not a time that I could not admit that I love you. Everything I learn about you only makes me love you more. You are my world now. I cannot think of a time I have been more happy than when I rolled in chicken muck with you! Every moment I have had I simply want to engrave in my mind and remember it always. You may not believe me but it is true . . . and I have been a fool for not telling you the real reason I married you." He drew in a deep breath.

"I see it now in your eyes what has been in my heart since the Meryton Assembly when I first felt my heart strings pull in your direction. I fought it; oh I did, I even said that awful thing about you not being tempting, just so that I would not have to endure the foreign feelings I was having. My heart was gone from the moment I heard you laugh with Miss Lucas at the refreshment table. There is nothing I want to do more than spend my life hearing that laughter. I want only to make you happy and I vow with every fiber of my being that I will! I never want to see that forlorn and hopeless face that I saw on our wedding day. Forgive me for being too careful; no, even cowardly. I should have expressed my love long ago but somehow I knew deep down that you needed time to learn of it yourself."

"I wanted to tell you I loved you when I botched that awful proposal. I wanted to tell you I loved you when you came down to breakfast that morning after our wedding. I wanted to tell you I loved you when I went shopping with you and they measured you for your theatre gown. I wanted to tell you the night of the theatre how much I needed you and could not live without you. I wanted to tell you how you are more valuable to me then all of Pemberley when we got out of the carriage and saw it for the first time together. I wanted to show you I could be everything you needed and wanted. I wanted to tell you I loved you when you called me a beast and then rubbed mud in my hair! I wanted to tell you how I admire your fighting spirit the day you hit your head and still walked three hours to get home. And oh! God knows I wanted to tell you in the library after our first kiss. I wanted to tell you I will always love you no matter what, even when I thought your heart was not mine but rather Wickham's to claim. I wanted to tell you I love you when I woke up and saw your sleeping face on my chest. I wanted to take you in my arms and show you how grateful and lucky I am to have you in my life after you so generously massaged my head when you could have been angry with me instead! I wanted to tell you so many times. But I am telling you now. I love you dearest Elizabeth, I cannot spend another moment without telling you, showing you, and proving to you that I love you."

He then kissed her fervently, finally expressing all the passion he felt inside. He explored her lips like never before, his fingers finding their way into her hair. He could feel her response to the kiss then but she pulled away. He didn't want to stop so early, the other kisses they shared lasted much longer.

Elizabeth put her finger to his lips and said, "Shhh, I would love to continue in such a way but there is a promise you still have not clarified for me. You say you loved me before we were married. Is that the reason you never told my father that it was Wickham who compromised me? Is that why you married me?"

Darcy looked sheepish. "I would have to say I saw the moment as a road of opportunity."

"A road of opportunity? What exactly is that?"

"I have to give the credit to Martin. I was very distressed the morning after the ball and he was trying to help me make my heart and mind cooperate. He said that I should listen to my heart and let my mind find roads of opportunity. I pondered that on my horse ride and realized that being forced to marry you was the best opportunity that was ever placed before me and I was not about to let it slip by. One thing I learned from my father was not to let an opportunity go by that would make me a better man. I am a better man because I married you, Elizabeth. I am not the prideful man I know you once thought I was. I have tried to show you that."

"I have not thought you were prideful since the ball when you comforted me instead of judged me for Wickham's kisses. That opinion started changing even before that when Georgiana showed up unannounced. I saw how kind and loving you were with her and I realized I had judged you prematurely. I still struggled at times but mostly because I too had foreign feelings budding that I did not know what to do with since I could not imagine you loving me like you do now." She leaned in and kissed him, letting her body take over. They kissed on the lips for a moment and then he explored her cheeks and then made his way back up to her eyes and he kissed them as well. Then he pulled away.

"I am truly sorry I did not have the courage to ask Bingley for two rooms. You did not even seem angry at me the next morning. How exactly did we end up in the same bed?"

She laughed, "It was a road of opportunity! It was a way to make my mind and heart cooperate!"

He grinned and pulled her head to his chest to hold her close. When he looked outside, he saw they were slowing and had pulled up to the inn. One more day and they would be back at Pemberley.

"Oh, William?"

"Yes?"

"I love you too. More than I had ever hoped possible."

*****

"What do you mean there are not two rooms?" Darcy bellowed at the innkeeper. Elizabeth put her hand on his arm and he looked at her beautiful face. He took a calming breath. He turned back to the innkeeper, "You must find a way. No one is leaving for the day? No one is traveling tonight? What if I gave you extra money?"

"No sir, it is Sunday. No one travels on Sunday; well, except you, sir, I suppose. But I do not see a problem if it is just you and your wife. It is a large bed and sleeps two quite comfortably." The innkeeper fidgeted. Mr. Darcy was a regular and he always tipped well. He never gave him any problems before now and he didn't know why he was so upset at him.

Elizabeth pulled William aside while addressing the innkeeper, "May I just have a word with my husband?" The innkeeper left the entryway and Elizabeth and Darcy were by themselves. She wasn't quite sure why her husband was so irate. "William, it will be fine. Perhaps there is a chaise. And even if there is not, it is not like we have not slept in the same bed before. Do not get worked up over this. Save your strength for more important things. We are both weary and hungry."

Darcy knew that sharing a bed was in no way possible. What Elizabeth didn't realize was when they did sleep in the same bed together he was passed out and totally unaware of it. There was no way he had enough strength to knowingly, willingly, be in the same bed as Elizabeth and get any sleep at all. The early morning moment he had with her in his arms was still fresh in his mind, and if he relived it, by choice this time, he knew he would not let her go and kiss her all night long. This was not some youthful brother-sister relationship. His feelings were far from platonic. He could not be that near her and keep his promise and although they had expressed their love for each other, he knew she still needed to express her desire to change the relationship in that manner. She had not done that. And he definitely did not want to have their first night be in the Rose and Crown Inn even if she did! There was no way he had the fortitude to sleep next to her. He doubted he could even be in the same room, and a chaise was certainly unacceptable! Tempting as it was, he had to hold his ground.

His voice came out more like a whine, pained and pleading, "I cannot Elizabeth, I proved myself untrustworthy with requesting a room from Bingley. I cannot . . . I just cannot. I promised you that I would not . . . I want you to know I can be trustworthy again."

So it was back to that promise? That wretched promise made weeks ago? Elizabeth was furious! After that deeply moving speech in the carriage, he still was going to hold tight to that stupid promise! What troubled him so about lying next to her? They had done it before and it turned out fine— better than fine! In fact, she had thoroughly enjoyed it! She felt a wave of anger and hurt that he did not want to repeat it. She turned sharply away and under her breath said, "Yes, perhaps a little too trustworthy."

She turned back around, ready to use her newfound stubbornness to her advantage. "William, please, do this for me. I insist. There is no other option. You cannot sleep in the carriage; it has started to rain and is quite chilly. You cannot sleep in the barn with the horses. You cannot stay awake all night in the great room. You cannot buy your way into someone else's bed when your wife insists you accompany her. I insist." She lifted her chin and put her hands on her hips and looked him square in the eye.

Darcy stared at her. He could fight with her but he had no other options. He had no real grounds for saying no— except, of course— those of his own lack of self-control. He had never felt so weak before. She was insisting that he share a room, an option he begged for in his dreams, an opportunity that he simply could not realize tonight. Not until she said so, and she hadn't said so yet. He just stood there looking at her. What should he do? He dug down deep inside and evaluated his strength, but looking deep into her eyes was not helping him gather the fortitude required to do as she was suggesting. He looked away.

Elizabeth saw that stubbornness was not working. She changed her methods. "Please, I beg of you. Stay. I need you. Please William . . ." She heard Darcy groan.

Does she not realize how much I need her at that moment? They had finally expressed their love and it had only made his desires stronger. He had waited this long and she was asking what seemed to him to be the impossible. He turned to the entryway desk and rang the bell. He didn't know how he was going to do it, but he would have to find the strength. The innkeeper returned. "We will take the room but we will require extra blankets and pillows." *Dear Lord! Am I doing the right thing here?*

"Certainly, Mr. Darcy. I will have them bring the trunks up right away. Let me show you to the room."

Darcy couldn't look Elizabeth in her fine eyes. He couldn't offer his arm and escort her. He couldn't hold her hand. He could not watch her chocolate curls bounce as she walked. He couldn't watch her thin waist sway with her legs' movement and he most definitely could not kiss her. These were the ground rules that he would have to obey. He motioned for her to follow the innkeeper, and he followed her, looking right at the ground as he walked up the stairs. He kept a few feet behind trying to remember all the kings in order beginning from King Henry the V. Distraction was helpful. It might even help him get through the night.

"Here it is, Mr. and Mrs. Darcy. Dinner will be ham and potatoes and will be served in half an hour."

Elizabeth looked at her husband who was silently staring at the floor. Was it so terrible to spend the night in the same room? He was obviously preoccupied in his mind so she addressed the innkeeper, "Can you bring dinner to the room?"

"Yes, madam. Would you like tea or wine with dinner?"

"Wine," Elizabeth said.

Darcy's head shot up. "Tea! Definitely tea!" He did not need to have any alcohol in his system tonight, even if it was just wine. He saw Elizabeth's confused face and immediately felt bad for contradicting her in front of the innkeeper. "Bring both," he conceded. He may not want the wine, but Elizabeth did, and that would not affect his self-control. He had to be more careful or he would hurt Elizabeth's feelings. The innkeeper closed the door behind him. He scanned the room, and noted that there was a small chaise with a tall back. Although in normal circumstances it would not look comfortable in the slightest, it appeared heavenly to his eyes.

He had a place to sleep other than her bed. His legs suddenly felt weak.

Elizabeth watched as her husband walked over to the small chaise and sat down and put his face in his hands. She took her reticule and walked to the mirror. She started unpinning her hair and brushing the curls out. It had been a long week. Was it really only a week ago that they kissed for the first time? Was it really only hours longer than that that she realized how much she loved him? She peered at his reflection in the mirror. He still had his head in his hands. She continued to brush her hair before she began to plait it.

Don't, Fitzwilliam. Just don't watch her. He tried to convince himself not to watch her comb her hair, but hearing the brush run through the curls made his own toes curl in desire and his body began to grow warm. His fingers ached to run through them and his mind imagined doing just that. He decided that his imagination was not helpful at the moment and he would probably be better just seeing the simple act. He looked up as she was plaiting her hair. Her hands had pulled all her hair off to the side but he could see the ringlets on the other side of her neck, the ones that would not fit into the braid, the ones that were so charmingly feminine. He looked away. He added not watching her plait her hair as part of the ground rules. He lowered his head again to his hands. It seemed like hours before she was done.

Elizabeth stood up and sat next to him. She took his hand from his face in both of hers and kissed it. "William, please, look at me. I do not want this night to be like this. We love each other. Does it have to be like this? Can we at least enjoy each other's company?"

Darcy sighed. He was hurting her. If he could just have enough self-control to make it through the night! The knock on the door came as a welcome relief. He jumped up and several servants brought in their trunks. As they were leaving, dinner arrived, another welcome relief. A few more of those interruptions and it would be time to go to sleep. Then he groaned. He wasn't exactly looking forward to that anyway. He allowed himself a moment to look at her. Her fine eyes were pleading with him, almost begging him to change his behavior. He did not want to hurt her. He had vowed just an hour ago that he would do anything to hear her laughter. She had given her heart to him and look at what he was doing with it! He was moping around, morose about being in her presence when that was truly all he wanted anyway! He would have to let himself interact with her, look at her, smell her, and not totally ignore her like he had been doing.

"I am sorry, Elizabeth," he apologized, "I am just overwhelmed. So much has happened and I am deeply worried about Wickham. If we get an early start, just after dawn, we should be at Pemberley just around the afternoon luncheon. Do you think we could leave that early?"

She reached for his arm and led him to the small table the food was on. "Absolutely. I am anxious to see that Georgiana is safe as well."

He felt the warmth of her tiny hands on his arm and felt some relief. Why was going against his ground rules helping his anxiety? They talked all through dinner. The mood lightened as he asked what the chicks would look like by now.

"Oh, they will not be the adorable fuzzy things you remember. Their feathers on their wings will be showing and there will be little spikes coming out of their heads. It is not a pretty sight."

"Lizzy will be ugly? I cannot believe such a thing!" he teased her.

Her jaw popped open and she laughed, "I will have you know Fitz will be just as unattractive. Worse, I am afraid, because he is so clumsy."

"But Lizzy likes to roll around in the mud so I am sure she will look worse than the grand Fitz." He knew they were not talking about the chicks. They were teasing each other again, and it helped him relax. This was the woman he loved. This was the laughter that was balm to his heart.

"I am sure Fitz would not know how to find his own food, so he may be helpless and lost," she teased back. His eyes smiled back at her and her heart flipped in her chest. She suddenly got serious. "William? I do not want you to sleep on the chaise. I want to wake up in your arms tomorrow and every morning thereafter." She saw him stiffen but he continued to smile back at her. He reached for her hands and kissed them.

"You do not know what you are asking me to do."

Mr. Darcy's Promise

"I do, William. I know what I am asking."

"I do not want our actual honeymoon to be anywhere but Pemberley, and definitely not because we were forced to share a room. I do not want to push you or make you feel obligated."

"Then let us just sleep in each other's arms tonight. I promise I will be good, you will be good, and we will both sleep comfortably. Please?"

He had already had this conversation with himself. He could not do it. He pulled his hands away.

Be direct. This man needs me to be direct. She took a deep breath and readied herself for her next comment. It took all her courage to do so. "You promised me not until I wished it. I wish it now, William. Please?" She learned that he was bound more by duty than by anything else, and she wasn't about to let the moment to use it to her advantage slip by. She watched him take a deep breath and look at her. She raised her eyebrow in challenge. Would he back out of his promise now after she made her desires known so directly?

He looked in her eyes and he was undone. How could he say no to something both his body and mind were begging for? How could he say no to those beautiful brown eyes? To that impertinent lip and eyebrow? He stood up and leaned over the table to kiss her on the lips. "I did promise you that, and I keep my promises."

She smiled widely at him and reached for his face to attempt to kiss him again, but he pulled away. "But you promised to kiss me anytime I want!"

"One promise at a time, Elizabeth. Do not tempt me beyond what I can handle."

Mr. Darcy's Promise

Chapter 13

M r. Darcy could feel the warmth of the sun on his face. He turned his head away from the glaring light, but his body refused to move, relishing the sensation of Elizabeth still asleep in his arms. It slowly dawned on his sleepy mind that he had successfully made it through the night! He reviewed the events of last night in his mind as his body adjusted to waking. He had given her some time to get ready for bed after dinner; indeed, he had delayed his ascent up the stairs for as long as was possible. He had checked on the horses, informed the driver of their plans to leave at first light, arranged with the inn to have rolls and preserves available first thing in the morning for them and their driver, and taken a moment to draw in some cleansing breaths in the cool night air. The night would be difficult for him, he knew. It was a trial that he most definitely wanted to endure, but he wanted to remain in control as well. As he gazed out at the night, he noted the rain was letting up but still could tell the temperature had dropped. He hoped that Pemberley wasn't this cold so that the chicks would be warm enough. He laughed at himself. Now he cared as much about the chickens as she did!

It was time and he knew it. He headed up the stairs, saying a prayer with each step. His feet propelled him faster than was necessary, as if to show how much he anticipated holding her all night. He pulled at his cravat before he knocked. He heard her sweet voice tell him to come in. When he opened it, he saw that she was already in bed, her hair plaited, wearing her nightdress. He glanced over at the couch to see her dressing gown draped there. His hands continued tugging at the stubborn cravat.

"I can step out if you need to get changed," she offered.

"I think I will just sleep in my shirt and breeches." He needed his clothes on, and all he cared about at the moment was getting this ridiculous knot out of his cravat. He kept working on it without looking up at her, but knew that his frustration was apparent to Elizabeth.

"Come here," he heard her say after a moment. "I will help you."

He did not need her helping him take off his clothes. In fact, that would be the farthest thing from helpful. Just then the knot finally came loose and he pulled on the cravat, the fabric spiraling down into his hand. "I have it, thank you." He slipped out of his frock coat and then his waistcoat, all the while stealing glances in her direction. She was watching him with a barely suppressed smile on her face. He sat down near her and leaned over to remove his boots before he heard her giggle and sat up to face her.

"And why, may I ask are you giggling? No, never mind— I learned my lesson long ago to not ask why you are giggling. But since there is no mud nearby, I will make one request. Would you mind at least not laughing at me? I am sure I appear absurd, but am a little self-conscious at the moment."

She giggled again, but this time attempted to stifle it. "I cannot help finding our situation amusing. Here we are married for almost six weeks and I am just now watching my husband remove his clothes. We have had a strange marriage so far. I do not think I have heard of one like it."

"Nor have I. I do not think I would have exchanged it for any other, though. It has been an enjoyable journey; frustrating at times, but still enjoyable. There were so many times we shared that we could not have had if we were courting. Like that night that we candled the eggs for the first time. I nearly kissed you when the candle went out. I would have never been alone with you at night in a barn if we were courting." He pulled off one boot before starting to work on the next one. Talking helped to soothe his nervousness.

"Or that time I nearly fainted in London and you carried me to my room? I almost died of embarrassment when Serafina started unlacing my boots in front of you. If we were courting we would have never been in a bedroom together and you would have never seen my feet."

He laughed, "Yes, you were determined to keep those feet hidden from me, and Serafina was quite determined to take your shoes off. It was quite a battle of wills. I especially enjoyed watching you get measured right before my eyes; another thing I would never have been party to if we had had a normal courtship."

"Yes, you were enjoying that so much I do not doubt you know my measurements by heart!" He turned around and saw her grinning.

"I do," he teased. Her jaw popped open.

"William! I cannot believe you! Well, I enjoyed the unchaperoned walks and hikes that were like my own private tour of the Pemberley grounds. That is something that I would never be able to convince my sisters to do with me, since none of them are 'great walkers'!"

He laughed easily and took off his remaining boot. "Hmm, I agree. Showing you Pemberley was a highlight of mine as well. I have to admit seeing you each morning and saying goodnight to you each night was something I would not have given up either."

"Like tonight."

He smiled back at her, "Yes, like tonight." He drew his stockings off and pulled back the covers. He moved as if by habit, giving little thought to what he was doing. Having them talk about their marriage had calmed him so much that it had become simply natural to crawl in bed next to her. "What has been your favorite moment so far?" He propped a pillow up behind him and raised his arm so she could lie next to him, resting her head against his chest. She wrapped her arms around his chest and shifted into a comfortable position.

"My favorite moment? Kiss, or experience? What exactly are you asking?"

He listened to the vibration of her voice resonate through his chest. "Tell me your favorite kiss first, then moment."

"Well, my favorite kiss was the second one in the carriage when I asked you to kiss me— no, wait, it was when you kissed the inside of my wrist on the night of the theatre. Oh, I do not know. I have too many favorites. Each one makes me react so intensely that I scarcely know my own body! My favorite moment was most definitely today in the carriage when you told me how you loved me. But that may be because each moment I have with you just continues to get better than the last. Do you think it will always be that way? Will you always affect me so intensely?" She looked up at him and met his gaze.

"I certainly hope so. If it was up to me I never want to lose that racing heart when we touch, or that breathless moment during a kiss, or that tingling and heat I feel when we hold each other."

"Like now," she said, laying her head back on his chest, her arms drawing tightly around him.

He smiled, resting his hand against her neck before he kissed the top of her head. "Yes, like now."

They talked for another half an hour before she began to yawn and speak more quietly. He tucked the blanket around her shoulders then and allowed himself to relax into the pillow. He had never been more comfortable. This was what he had craved for months and it wasn't difficult for him. He remained awake for an hour more, simply listening to her breathe and basking in the moment. He didn't want to miss any movement, any touch, any sensation that he was feeling at the moment. She was his, and he was hers. All that worry about being in control was nearly funny now. He was very much in control of his actions. He was where he wanted to be and the inner turmoil was no longer present. This was enough. Hearing her talk about their unique marriage and laughing about how neither one would change how it worked out was powerful. In fact, never before had he felt more in control of his person while together than at that moment.

He did finally fall asleep and woke to find the sun was just cresting over the mountains and shining through their window. He could tell by her slow and steady breath that she was still deeply asleep. They had wanted to be on the road about now, so he took a moment and kissed her hair. She didn't move. He put his hand on her shoulder and caressed her back. "Elizabeth, it is time to wake up."

She moaned and mumbled, "No." She held on tighter to his chest.

He smiled. He never thought she would be slow to rise or even cross in the morning. The pace of her breathing had quickened, though, telling him that she was now awake. He looked down at her face which had a telltale smile on it. So this was how she wanted to play? "What do I have to do to get you to wake up? Elizabeth?" he jested. He saw her smile widen.

Elizabeth was awake but she had a plan. She started to pretend to snore, and quite dramatically too. She tried not to laugh at herself when he started laughing. He picked up her hand that was draped against his chest and kissed the palm three times. She stopped snoring for a moment, but when he stopped kissing it she began up again.

"Oh, I see, my fair princess must be kissed awake." She let out a large snore followed by a giggle, and then she started snoring again in earnest. Suddenly, in one quick movement William rolled over her and was straddling her, still holding the one hand and trapping it above her head. He quickly found her other hand and pinned it above her head too.

She wanted to open her eyes, but it was taking all her willpower to continue snoring loudly without smiling, of which she knew she was failing miserably at.

Her hair had come loose from the plait and covered part of her face. He placed both her hands in one of his and brushed the curls from her face with the other hand. She was beyond fascinating, beyond beautiful, beyond tempting. He leaned down, and with his lips inches from hers, teased, "Or is it tickling she needs to wake up?" His free hand quickly grabbed her waist and tickled her. She cried out in laughter, but her eyes remained closed. He let up on the tickling and leaned in to whisper in her ear, making sure his lips touched it as he spoke, "Or does she need to hear how much I ardently love and admire her?" He sat up when the snoring stopped, but it was only quiet for a moment. She took a deep breath and let out the loudest snore yet. He laughed. "Well then, there is only one thing left to do." He let go of her hands and placed his own at each side of her head before he leaned down and kissed her.

Elizabeth's plan had worked out very nicely. She kissed him back passionately, wrapping her now-free hands around his back. Their kisses were deep and full of longing, their lips parting briefly before she pulled his chest to hers. Before she had a chance to fully enjoy the moment he was up off the bed with his hands running nervously through his hair. "What is wrong?" she asked.

Darcy had to take a moment to regain composure. He had not thought to set a ground rule about not to roll around on top of Elizabeth kissing her passionately. That, he reflected, should not have needed to be spoken. "I am sorry Elizabeth, I cannot kiss you while you are in bed yet. Certainly not like that. Not when I just want more." He wanted to be completely honest with her. She needed to know he desired her deeply, but he was firm in the matter that their physical relationship would not begin at the Rose and Crown inn.

She sat up, getting out of bed and walking to him, "And if I was not in bed would you kiss me?"

"Please Elizabeth, get dressed. You said you would be good."

"Very well. But I still want a morning kiss. You owe me for the morning of your headache, for a woman does not sleep with a man and not receive a morning kiss for her trouble." She took his hand and pressed a kiss against each finger.

He sighed and kissed her gently once on the lips. "Get dressed," he repeated in a hoarse and strained voice. He snatched up his boots and stockings before he stepped out of the room and closed the door behind him.

*****

After receiving the express last evening around dinner, Richard's first act was to alert all the staff to be looking out for Wickham. He had retrieved Darcy's pistol and loaded it and put it in his belt. He had informed Georgiana of Wickham's plans and when he wasn't personally with her, he placed her in the care of the strongest, tallest groomsman he found while he walked the grounds of Pemberley.

So far there had been no sign of him, nor anything unusual. He continued to pace, eyes and ears alert to anything and everything. He made this his routine for the last eighteen hours, refusing to sleep, his body drawing on all the fortitude he'd gained from his last twelve years of military service. He was methodical in his watch. First he would check on Georgiana, then he would speak with the staff and search Pemberley's interior. Then he would check on Georgiana again, and then he would walk the grounds, asking the outside servants for information. He was readying to perform his rounds inside when he heard a faint splash.

It was high noon, he noted, without a cloud in the sky. He almost stepped back in: it was likely a fish or bird, but something told him to walk further. When he heard it again, his hand went instinctively to his pistol. From his current vantage point, he could see the front of the house, anyone who might approach by road, and down to the barn. He turned his attention to a nearby stream that was shadowed by tall reeds, and frowned. It was small, he knew, and shallow, but fish still swam in it. He waved to a servant down by the barn for assistance. When Sparks acknowledged him, Colonel Fitzwilliam put his finger to his lips, then pointed to the stream where he had heard the sound. The servant picked up a pitchfork and carefully made his way towards Richard and the stream. Richard approached as well, listening intently. The sound of rustling reeds gave him pause. That was definitely not a fish. Sparks crept closer, drawing about ten meters from the stream. Colonel Fitzwilliam waited a minute more, then figured he was close enough to see what made the sound. He lunged towards it, gun in hand, flushing out the man hiding there. Wickham!

Wickham ran towards the house as fast as he could. He looked to the right and saw a servant running with a pitchfork, and he knew Richard was behind him and closing fast. He took the stairs to the house two at a time and was just about to open the door when he felt a hand close around his coat and sharply jerk him away from the entrance. He landed on his back and slid head first down the few stairs at the entryway. He looked up to see a pitchfork inches from his face. He should have known it would Richard who reached him first. "Well, hello Richard! Fancy meeting you here."

"Do not call me Richard. It is Colonel Fitzwilliam to you, *Lieutenant* Wickham."

Wickham grinned. "Are you pulling rank on me, Colonel?"

"I will pull anything I need to, including this trigger. If I were you I would not move an inch."

Wickham realized for the first time that Colonel Fitzwilliam held a pistol in his hand. He had only noticed the pitchfork up to that point. He looked from Richard to the servant before realizing he knew the servant. "Sparks! How good of you to welcome me home. I see you fancy yourself a hero. Tell me, how is that son of yours?" The pitchfork moved down towards his chest, pressing into his ribs.

"Do not be talking about my son. He may not have gone to Cambridge, but he is more gentleman than you will ever be."

Wickham reached up to push away the prongs of the pitchfork. "Do you mind letting me breathe without receiving puncture wounds?" Sparks held his ground and pushed harder into his chest. Wickham flinched. "I guess not." He turned to Colonel Fitzwilliam next. "Are you going to invite me in or what? And where is Darcy, anyway? Did he run off when he was needed most? Too high and mighty to handle his own business ventures? Too proud to rescue his only sister from the likes of me?"

Richard had had enough of Wickham's mouth. He took out his handkerchief and stuffed it in Wickham's mouth, making sure to get it all in. "Just so you know that was a dirty handkerchief and I do not want it back. I would suggest keeping your mouth closed for the time being. Sparks, keep that pitchfork right where you have it. I am going to search him." Richard began by checking Wickham's belt. He found the army-issued pistol and sword and removed them, placing them out of reach on the stairs by the column. He searched his back belt loop, chest pockets, and legs all the way down to his boots without finding anything there. "Got anything else on you, Wickham?" When Wickham rolled his eyes, Richard looked up at Sparks. "Go ahead, Sparks. I would say he is being combative and aggressive do you not think so?" Wickham started making muffled sounds and frantically shaking his head no.

"That is more like it, Wickham. I expect my prisoners of war to be cooperative. Now up on your feet, slowly. And I might add, do not try to run again or you will just die breathless and tired." Wickham huffed and rolled his eyes. Richard knelt down, pressing his hand against Wickham's shoulder.

"What? You do not like my death jokes? Then here is a quote for you. Herodotus, the Egyptian historian, said, 'Death is a delightful hiding place for weary men.' From the looks of your uniform, you have not been sleeping in a bed the last few nights. Are you a little weary? Well, do not expect me to offer you a bed. In fact, nothing is going to be offered to you, not water, not tea, and certainly not money." Richard put away his pistol so he could have two hands again. He pulled Wickham up by his shoulder and grasped Wickham's hands behind his back. He gave him a shove that was less then gentle and Wickham started reluctantly walking back up the steps. Richard still held his hands firmly and said to Sparks, "Go ahead and open the door."

"Yes, sir." He turned to Wickham, "Do not try anything stupid, Wickham, I use a pitchfork three hours out of the day, every day!" He felt bold and lifted his chin high. He opened the door and kept his pitchfork aimed at Wickham's chest as he walked by.

Mr. Reynolds recognized Wickham immediately, but saw the two men were handling him roughly but efficiently. "Colonel? What do you need?"

"I need some rope and I need you to send someone for the magistrate. Keep Georgiana out of Darcy's study for the time being, would you? She does not need to know Wickham is even in the house. Darcy should be here soon. Make sure he knows where to find us."

*****

Elizabeth's hand was beginning to ache. Darcy was holding it very tightly. "William, dear? I know you are worried, but you are hurting my hand." She saw him look at her, startled, before he immediately released her hand.

"I am so sorry. We have made good time, it looks like we will get there quicker than usual." He pulled out his pocketwatch. "We made the five hour journey in four and a half hours. It looks like we will get there just after noon. Elizabeth," he said, his voice changing slightly.

"I have something to confess. I am especially worried about Georgiana because of a prayer I once said." She looked at him quizzically, but he continued without pausing. "When you passed out after you hit your head, you were so very still, and I said a prayer that was something like 'anyone but her.' I am worried that God might take that prayer differently than I meant it. I cannot lose Georgiana or Richard either. I feel like I am being selfish and renegotiating what I promised to God in that prayer. He saved you, just like I meant for him to, but I cannot help worry that something will happen to Georgiana or Richard." He looked out the window. He had made this journey so many times since his youth, and knew he was precisely three miles away from knowing if Wickham had been found and if any of his family had been harmed. The last ten minutes had been harder and slower than the first four hours.

"I do not know what kind of God you believe in, but the God I know does not work like that. He knows the intent of our hearts, even if we do not fully say them aloud for Him to hear." She took his hand back and kissed it gently. "And besides having a little faith in God, you should have a little faith in Richard. If that weasel is found at Pemberley, Richard is a trained soldier who has actual combat experience. Wickham does not."

"I know," Darcy said, and let out a breath. "But Wickham is probably unstable and unpredictable because of how desperate he is. That makes him a foe we should not underestimate." She gave his hand a gentle comforting squeeze and he looked back at her. Her eyes were damp as she gazed longingly at him. He turned around to face her and cupped her face and kissed her. She responded and kissed him back several times. The rest of the journey was spent looking out the window.

When they finally pulled up to the front entrance, no one was there to greet them. "Odd, where are the servants? They should have been expecting us." He stepped out of the carriage and handed Elizabeth out as well. As they stepped up the stairs he paused and put his arm out to stop Elizabeth from walking. On the stairs by the column rested a pistol and a sword. He quickly scanned the landscape. He didn't see anyone, not even a groundskeeper or gardener. "Elizabeth, I think he is here, inside the house," he whispered.

She held his arm tighter. "What should we do?" He dropped her arm and she watched as he picked up the pistol and checked that it was loaded. He gently pushed her behind him.

"Stay close." They took a step forward, but at that exact moment they heard a gun go off in the house. He took the last few steps two at a time and ran into the house. Reynolds and two groomsmen were running down the hall. He quickly turned and followed them. "Where is he, Reynolds?"

"In your study," Reynolds reported.

Darcy's heart was racing, and he suddenly remembered Elizabeth was right behind him. "Stay in the drawing room and do not come out!" he instructed her. He then whipped around and continued down the hall. The door of his study was already open, revealing at least five men standing around in a circle. He caught a glimpse of Richard kneeling down and heard someone ask if they should get a doctor. He couldn't see who they were all gathered around, but it looked like someone was hurt. A great deal of blood had pooled on the floor.

Richard cleared his throat. "Yes, I suppose we should fetch the doctor. Although he does not deserve it. From the looks of the bleeding he will not make it anyway."

Darcy heard a gasp from behind him. He turned around and saw Elizabeth. "Elizabeth! This is not a time or place to be stubborn and not do as you are told! Go to the drawing room!"

Everyone in the room turned towards the door at the sound of Mr. Darcy's voice, and saw that Darcy and Elizabeth had arrived. Reynolds started pulling on Elizabeth's arm, "Come, Mrs. Darcy, this is no place for a lady."

Elizabeth numbly allowed herself to be escorted away from the commotion. Her mind was in a daze. Wickham was shot? By who? How? Her mouth was dry and she gasped a little, struggling to breathe. She needed fresh air and to leave the house. She shook her arm loose from Reynolds' gentle grip before she picked up her skirts and ran out the front door, all the way to the barn. Once there, she collapsed on a hay pile and wept until she could cry no more. Soon after her sobs died, she heard a carriage up at the house and stood to see who had arrived. Was it the doctor? The undertaker? She had never seen or experienced someone dying before. She didn't even know for certain that the figure in the study had been Wickham. But she had seen enough. Richard's hands were bloody, and there was too much blood around him. That was all she knew.

A man she did not recognize exited the carriage. She watched as Darcy came out to greet him. They talked for several minutes at the front door. So it wasn't the doctor. If it was, Darcy would not hold him up like that. She sniffled and used her handkerchief to dry her eyes. A rooster crowed loudly, and she followed the sound outside to the pen. She watched the chickens walk around looking for food. She absently went back into the barn and took out a scoop of corn. Her feet took her back outside and she threw a handful of corn out, too much in shock to call to the first. The hens and roosters immediately gathered to where the corn had landed, and she watched, staring mindlessly until the corn was gone. She threw another handful out and the process began again. When that corn was gone she threw out more.

Soon her eyes were completely dry and her chest no longer felt so tight. At least she knew that Darcy and Richard were safe. She threw out the last of the corn before she rested her arms on the gate, watching them peck and scratch at the last of their treat. After a moment, she realized she hadn't seen the mother hen who had sat on the eggs all that time. She walked past the pen to the barn in search of her. There the mother hen was, and next to her were all her seven chicks who were all busy running around her. She recognized Lizzy right away but she didn't know which brown chick was Fitz. She watched as one of the brown ones flapped its wings and then reached its beak to scratch at its new feathers. In doing so, it lost its balance and fell over. She smiled. Now she knew which one was Fitz. She started to occupy her time with finding names for the other five. After a while she heard her name being called out. She recognized the deep baritone voice and she went out of the pen in search of it.

"There you are, Elizabeth! How are you coping? I am so sorry you had to see that." Mr. Darcy said.

Elizabeth ran all the way to him and threw her arms around his chest, hugging him tightly. He put one hand on her head and one around her waist and kissed the top of her head. Fresh tears formed all too quickly, but they were not tears of fear and shock this time, they were tears of joy. She didn't know how she could have lived without him and just remembering him with a pistol in his hand made her shudder. "What happened? Is Wickham dead?"

"I do not know how much to tell you." He pulled her away from him and looked at her wet eyes. "Yes, he is dead."

She had to know what happened, she had to know! "Please William, tell me what happened."

He looked into her fine brown eyes and took a deep breath. "The weapons at the front door were Wickham's. Richard had checked him and disarmed him at the door. Richard brought Wickham into my study and had called the magistrate. He was proceeding to tie his hands in front of him when Wickham somehow hit Richard in the head, probably with his own head, and then Wickham pulled out a knife from his boot. Wickham lunged, but Richard was faster in pulling the pistol out of his belt, and Richard shot him in the chest. That is the shot we heard. I was right when I said he was volatile and desperate. There were five grown men in the room when Wickham attacked! There is no way he would have made it out alive! After you left he sputtered out a few last words— mostly blaspheming and cursing us all— and then he died. He did not last more than five minutes. The magistrate came and we gave him Georgiana's letters and explained what happened. There were plenty of witnesses who all agree on how Wickham attacked Richard. The magistrate was easily convinced, and we have loaded the body onto our wagon. He is being taken to the undertaker as we speak. It is all over, Elizabeth. We no longer have to worry any more about him and his threats."

Elizabeth let out the breath she hadn't known she was holding. "Truly? It is all over? Do you have to testify or anything? Is Richard distressed knowing he killed a man?"

Darcy took her face in his hands. "Yes, it is over. And Richard, I admit, is more pleased with himself for ending this in a way that was more to his liking than seeing that scoundrel put in jail. Richard is strong and is already trying to tell the story to everyone. I would not put it past him to find some punch line to go along with the story for the future." He hugged her again. He felt her relax into the hug and she wrapped her arms around him in return. "So have you been out here the whole time? How are the chicks?"

"I told you the chickens relax me. Come and see the chicks. I think it is about time that we name the rest of them. I was thinking along the lines of naming them after everyone that has had a part in building our relationship. Like Serafina."

"What has Serafina done?" He was bewildered.

"She was the one who helped me see your love for me before you admitted it to me. She also told me to be direct with you if I wanted you to kiss me." She looked up at him and grinned. "It worked most of the time."

"Most of the time? When did you ask me to kiss you and I did not?" Darcy said, looking down at her, knowing their lips were inches away.

"It happened twice. Once in the stream and once last night at dinner when you finally agreed that we could sleep in each other's arms."

Darcy couldn't help but correct her. After all, he had made a promise to kiss her anytime she asked, and he was not going to be proven untrustworthy again. "Now, if I remember correctly, you never got as far as asking me to kiss you in the stream, and I still kissed you last night, I just kept it in check. But Serafina it is."

"No! It has to be a nickname! See, we named the other two Lizzy, and Fitz, so we have to name it Rafina." Elizabeth said.

"That is a terrible name! How about Sara? It is much more flattering."

"All right," she agreed, "so then the second brown one is Sara, and the last brown one should be named after Jane. She had faith that I would learn to love you. But I cannot think of a way to shorten her name so we will just have to leave it as Jane."

"Very well, but that leaves three black ones. We have to name one after Georgiana because without her surprise visit to Netherfield and pointing out my admiration for you I may not have ever realized how happy I could be with you." He felt thoughtful remembering her tearful face saying *"but if you love her . . ."* He continued, "And I must name one after my horse Calypso, for there were many rides that cleared my thinking enough to do the right thing. It was on her that I finally realized the depth of my love for you."

"Well then, Caly it is. That leaves only one other. It is my turn to pick this time. I would have to say it is a tie between Richard and Sparks. Richard because he makes your eyes smile, and I found I am a sucker for your handsome smiling eyes." She reached up and touched those very smiling eyes. She drew his face down and kissed each corner of the eyes, right where they closed.

He leaned in and kissed her fervently, his lips taking their time exploring hers. "I agree with Richard, but I have my own reasons for that. May I ask why Sparks?"

She leaned in and kissed his lips, something she was becoming quite dependent on, even though it made it hard to think straight. "When I first came to Pemberley he and I would talk about what it was like working for you. He would tell me stories of the things you did for the servants and it made me look at you in a different light. He just respected you so much it was like I could not help but see the generous and kind man that you are. I began to see you differently then." Elizabeth had to admit that Sparks occupied a tender place in her heart.

Darcy grinned. "But since he was going to poke my innards with the pitchfork and feed me to the chickens I would have to say we had better name the last one after Richard. Should it be Rick or Rich?"

"Ricky. So we have a Lizzy, a Fitz, a Sara, a Jane, a Caly, a Ricky, and what should we name the one after Georgiana?"

"I already call Georgiana Georgie, so that would not work. How about Georgette?"

"Yes, Georgette. I suppose that is all of them!" She leaned in and kissed him once again. She felt the warm sun caressing her face while his arms wrapped around her and caressed her back.

Darcy had a surprise for her and it seemed like the right time. "Can I show you something? I think you will truly enjoy it."

Elizabeth didn't want to let go but she did and she looked up at his face. His eyes were smiling back at her. He took her hands from around his chest and kissed the inside of her wrists. It made her heart flutter just like it was the first time. "I should have never told you that was one of my favorite kisses, because now you will do it all the time and I will have to endure its effect on my body. But show me what you wish."

"First let us stop by the house. You never ate luncheon and I need to collect something while you eat. I will meet you by the front door in thirty minutes. Oh, and you might need your pelisse." She looked at him suspiciously.

"It is two o'clock in the afternoon, and plenty warm outside. Will we be gone long?"

"Perhaps, but a gentleman cannot tell all his secrets!" He laughed quite naturally considering all that occurred in the last few hours.

*****

"I believe we have a date, Mr. Darcy." Elizabeth said, tying her pelisse as she met him at the door. He had a satchel draped across his shoulder with a large rectangular object, wrapped in paper, that was sticking out of the bag. The satchel was full of something bulky as well, but she couldn't tell what it was.

"Indeed we do, Mrs. Darcy. Shall we?" He offered his arm and she took it. He led her north, past the gardens towards the river. He continued walking and they talked the whole time, reminiscing about how they met, how they had each changed, and how they had grown over the last few months. "So when were you first physically attracted to me?" he asked.

"I would have to say it was watching your graceful form when we danced at Netherfield. It was the first time I imagined being held by you and the thought shocked me so much I could not trust my feet to make the movements correctly." She smiled to herself as she remembered it.

"You cannot have it both ways, either I am graceful or clumsy . . . which one?" he teased. It bothered him that she thought him clumsy.

"When you are on the dance floor you are quite graceful. It is the same when I see you ride your horse. But in situations where you feel awkward, like feeding the chickens, you become quite inept. Why do you think the chickens still frighten you?" She looked up at him curiously.

"A simple three kilogram farm animal does not scare the master of Pemberley." he said jokingly, but then turned serious. "Only one thing scares me, Elizabeth, and that is losing you." He stopped and she turned towards him. He leaned down and kissed her, pulling her waist close and feeling her warmth against him. His heart was racing and he felt short of breath. He slowly released her and said, "Do you need more convincing of that fact?" She smiled and nodded. He kissed her a few more times, then once more on her forehead before he took her hand to continue walking. They were making good progress and had reached the trees by the river. He motioned with his free arm up above them. "So? What do you think? Do you see one you like?"

Elizabeth looked up and realized they were under an enormous cedar tree canopy. "We are looking for a tree for our swing?" He grinned back at her. She threw her arms around his neck and embraced him. His strong arms lifted her off the ground and he twirled her in circles. "Oh, William! This is exactly what I want to be doing with you after a day like today! Is that what is in the satchel?"

He had never held her so close and his body was on fire. Her excitement and joy was catching. "Yes, but I was hoping you might need a little convincing."

She pulled away and smiled, and then in a very serious voice said, "I do, I must demand you change my mind in any way you can think of."

"You should not have said that." He reached for her hair and started unpinning it. Lock by lock her curls fell around her face and neck. He looked into her beautiful brown eyes and caressed her cheek. Her hair blew into her face and he brushed the tresses away, making sure to let his fingers comb through them all the way to the ends. He repeated this gesture, tucking the shorter curls behind her ear. "I love running my fingers through your hair; I think it is one of my greatest weaknesses; that and your fine eyes." He leaned in and gently pulled her hips towards him, and then captured her lips with his. His hands continued running through her hair as he kissed her. He was overcome with her lavender and clean linen scent. Her sweet lips parted momentarily and he felt complete bliss for a moment. He whispered, quite out of breath, "Are you convinced yet? Are you sure you want to find the perfect place for a swing?" She still had her eyes closed and he kissed them.

Something like an affirmative moan came out of her throat. She opened her eyes and tried to regain her composure. "I might warn you, however, that distracting me might just take longer to find the perfect place for a swing."

"Distracting? I thought I was convincing you!" They both laughed out loud.

Elizabeth slipped out of his arms to begin evaluating the trees. They were big enough, and there was a river nearby, but it wasn't quite right. She closed her eyes and tried to remember her dreams. "The river was on the left."

"Was? What do you mean?"

She blushed, realizing that she let it slip that she had seen the place for the swing before. "I have . . . well, I have dreamed about the swing a few times. Perhaps more than a few times. Ever since our wedding night I have had dreams of you pushing me on the swing under a cedar tree by a river." She blushed deeper than she ever had before, the color reaching all the way to her ears.

Darcy noticed the deep scarlet blush and he closed the distance between them, "You have been dreaming of us since our wedding night? I thought I was the only one afflicted with that disorder." He put his arms around her and kissed the top of her head again. "And were they good dreams?"

"Oh yes, it was basically the same dream over and over again but it just kept getting better. That is all." She wasn't quite ready to tell the details of the dream.

He sensed that she didn't want to tell him about it at the moment but was grateful to know it was more than some silly plaything they were looking for. He was very pleased she had been dreaming of him for so long. He was content to simply gaze at her. "Then there is another spot that might work better, but we will have to cross the river back at the bridge." He took her hand and led her back the way they came. They reached the bridge and crossed it, making their way towards the next grove of cedar trees. They walked hand in hand for about ten minutes when she let out a delighted cry.

"Yes, William! That is it! That big one right there! It is perfect!" She let go of his hands and started twirling as she looked up at the branches.

He took the satchel off his shoulder. He had never imagined seeing her so happy; his heart felt like it would burst with joy to see her so delighted. His voice cracked a little as he said, "Are you sure? I could try to convince you . . ." She had been so free with her kisses and embraces that he was hungry for more. He let his mind wander and evaluate her spinning body as she looked up at the branches. She was tiny, but strong. Her hips were curvy and feminine. Her waist was small enough that he could nearly wrap his hands around it. She was perfectly made for his arms. And tonight, yes tonight, he would know far more than he did.

"William? Are you well?"

His mind snapped back to the voice he loved so much. "What did you say?"

"I asked you how we were going to hang it, but you were just looking at me with a funny look on your face." She walked over to him and rested her hand on his cheek. "Are you well?"

It was his turn to flush a deep red at the realization that he had let his imagination run free again. He would have to wait just a little longer before he could explore her world without restraint. And he would. He would show her everything he felt for her. "I am beyond well. I am as happy as I can be, but I think you might need to convince me of that fact one more time."

Elizabeth grinned, "Well, I am not sure I know how . . . will you show me?" She flirted with the sway of her hips before she tilted her head up and closed her eyes.

"Come here, you minx!" He took her firmly by the waist and wrapped his arms around her before he smothered her face with kisses. His lips finally made it to her lips, and there they stayed for quite some time. He let out a sigh, and brought her head to his chest. If he wasn't careful he might just go exploring right there under the tree for more than a place for a swing.

Elizabeth had never been so happy. The simple act of holding him was invigorating and captivated every sense of her body. When he pulled her closer, it wasn't close enough, when he kissed her gently it wasn't enough. When she held his arms around his back they were eager to feel the shape and tone of his muscles. She wanted to be closer to him than ever before. She took a deep breath and the scent of the cedar trees was overwhelming. He had been thoughtful enough to realize how important the swing was to her, and in spite of all that had happened, had moved quickly to ensure that she had it. She didn't even have to tell him why she wanted a swing. She knew he would give her anything her heart desired, but this simple combination of rope and a piece of wood meant more than any jewels, carriage, or fancy gown.

He loved her enough to value what she valued. He loved her enough that in the middle of all of the Wickham ordeal, he would have his staff make a swing just for her, without knowing why it was so important. Likewise with the chickens; he didn't know why they were so important to her until yesterday, but he was faithful in feeding them and caring for them. He was just as concerned as she was, simply because he knew they were important to her. She had once thought him kind and generous; now she knew he was deeply thoughtful and observant as well. She never had to say that the chickens were important to her. He instinctively knew. She also now knew him to be very passionate, and it was a side of him that he was just starting to show her, a side she was eager to fully see tonight. She now understood that beneath his proud surface, he was tender and emotional, and this knowledge helped her understand all those times his voice would crack and get deep. She now knew him to be sensitive to those around her. She once thought him quiet and reserved but he was playful and jovial with the right group of people— especially with her, and that pleased her. Yes, her Mr. Darcy was everything she needed and wanted in a husband.

"When did you actually have your staff make the swing? We left for Hertfordshire less than two hours after we were going to look for the perfect spot. You were in your study with Richard for most of it."

"I had them start on it the morning before we were going to go looking, before you had even come down for breakfast. I knew it was important to you, so I assigned the task as soon as possible." When Elizabeth looked at him with such adoration, he felt embarrassed. "It is just a board with holes that has been sanded down. It is hardly the most momentous of occasions."

"It is to me and that is what makes it so special. Thank you." She leaned in and kissed him, her lips lingering there a little longer than usual.

"Well then, I suppose I need to climb a tree and make you a swing!" He reluctantly let go of her and opened the satchel. He removed the paper from the seat of the swing before pulling out the ropes. He scanned the branches for the perfect candidate. "Which one would you like it on?"

"That straight one right there— facing the river. That way when I swing I can have the river under me at the peak of the pendulum. But be careful, William."

His hands were full with the rope, but he leaned in and kissed her on the cheek. "I will." He adjusted the rope, throwing it over his shoulder before he headed for the trunk. Luckily, it looked like an easy tree to climb with thick branches that would hold his weight. He climbed it easily and reached the designated branch. He used the branch above him to hold onto as he walked far enough out. He then carefully squatted down and straddled the branch before taking the ropes and draping them across the branch. He measured the height as best he could. "Is that low enough? I will need enough rope to tie to the ends of the board."

"Yes, I think so, they are just now at the ground." She felt a prickle of nervousness at seeing him so high. She watched as he tied each rope to the branch and pulled hard on the knots.

"I think that will do it. I am coming down now." He carefully made his way back towards the trunk and took carefully placed foot and hand holds as he descended. He jumped from the last branch and landed squarely on his feet.

Elizabeth was so grateful he made it down safely that she immediately ran and hugged him tightly. "That was quite graceful. I will have to add that to you list of graceful skills."

"Hmm, I will take that as a compliment. Every successful man needs to be graceful. For when I do business deals and am at a standoff in negotiations, I shall turn their minds towards agreement simply because I am graceful at climbing a tree."

She giggled. "Indeed, it is very important in negotiating business deals."

He lowered his voice and brought his lips to her ear, making sure to brush up against it, "It is good you think I am graceful, for I am very good at negotiating . . ."

Elizabeth felt chills up and down her spine as his deeply sensual voice echoed over and over again in her ear. Somehow she felt like they were not talking about business deals anymore or even climbing trees.

*****

Elizabeth kept stealing glances at her husband over dinner. He would meet her eyes and give a smirk, and then she would smile and look away. A few times when this happened she gave him her most saucy look, daring him to look away first. It never seemed to work; probably because he knew her thoughts and that awareness filled her with embarrassment. He caught her staring at the rise and fall of his cravat a few times as well, causing her to blush and look away, feeling the heat in her face. She was doing just that when her very pleasant thoughts were interrupted.

Richard had seen the silent exchanges between the newlyweds and was feeling a little giddy himself. "So, Elizabeth, do you know how chickens dance?"

Elizabeth colored; Mr. Darcy's smiling face caught her eye briefly as she looked up from his chest. She turned to Richard in an attempt to reclaim her composure. "Even with all my experience with chickens, I must admit I cannot think of anything to say to answer that question, but I have no doubt you will tell me."

"Indeed I will, but I shall apologize beforehand. It is admittedly not my best joke, but I have to say something before the two of you burst into flames." Seeing the discomfort he intended to appear on both their faces, he grinned and continued, "Chickens dance chick to chick! Get it? Cheek to cheek? Chick to chick? Aw, come now! That was not that bad. Darcy, you liked my joke did you not?"

Darcy gave out a chuckle, "Of course, Richard. Your jokes are exemplary. Are we ready to hear Georgiana's Mozart's piece she has been working on?"

They all agreed to listen to Georgiana. Darcy made sure to escort Elizabeth to the chaise away from the piano and away from where Richard had seated himself. Darcy then sat down next to her and put his arm around her. Surprisingly, in front of both Richard and Georgiana, Elizabeth tucked her feet up under her on the chaise and leaned against him, effectively eliminating his ability to appreciate the music as he would have done otherwise. It was quite some time before he realized that Georgiana had finished, and he belatedly applauded her efforts. "Quite wonderful!" he exclaimed.

Richard had had enough of the pair of lovebirds over in the corner. They were nearly entirely preoccupied with each other. "Come, Georgiana, let us go to the library and check on the cataloging process, I hear it is coming along quite nicely. I even hear the books are being replaced on the shelves which may just leave us a place to sit." He turned to Darcy and Elizabeth and winked at them. "We will leave you two to enjoy each other's company."

Elizabeth watched as Richard escorted the confused Georgiana out the door of the music room. She giggled. *Poor Georgiana, she had such an emotional day and first I steal her brother from her for the entire afternoon, and now the evening.* The sympathy only lasted briefly as now the silence between she and her husband was tangible. They sat there for ten minutes with his arm around her, each in their own, but very similar, thoughts. Elizabeth spoke first. "I think I will get ready for bed. I might need my strength if I am going to have to do any *negotiating* in the future." She heard him chuckle as she sauntered off to her room, letting her hips sway a little more than usual.

*****

Elizabeth had rung for Serafina several minutes ago and waited in her bedroom, impatient to begin the evening. When the knock finally came, she opened the door herself, eager to ready herself for the evening that awaited her. "Serafina, thank you for coming. I think I would like to ready myself for bed."

"Yes, madam. Would you like a bath as well?" Serafina had hoped that Mr. Darcy and Mrs. Darcy had finally come together but there was no indication that it was the case. She couldn't help but be disappointed. They both deserved to be happy and she knew that meant giving of oneself fully.

"I think a bath would be pleasant, but we can wash my hair another night." Elizabeth was too preoccupied to notice the disappointment in Serafina's face. Tonight she would fall asleep in William's arms and wake up as a truly married woman. She watched as Serafina took out her old gown and placed it on the bed. She smiled as if hiding a secret. "Serafina, tonight . . . I think I will wear the silk gown."

Relief washed over Serafina, "Well it is about time!" She brought her hand to her mouth in embarrassment. "I am sorry madam, I just think you and the master . . .well it has been so long . . .I simply . . ."

Elizabeth let out a laugh, "It is quite all right. I assure you that I am fully aware of how long it has been." She put her hand on Serafina's arm. "Thank you. Thank you for helping me see what I seemed to be blind to for so long. You truly were invaluable in making sure this night finally come to pass. I have valued your advice, used it often, and I suspect will make use of it tonight as it has shown to be quite helpful— and successful, I might add."

"And which advice will you be following, madam? Because I do not think I have ever given you advice on a wedding night, for I do not know anything about that myself. Indeed, I am certain that I would remember a conversation about that," Serafina said a little archly, a glimmer of teasing laughter appearing in her eyes.

Elizabeth laughed. "I will have to be direct and give him only one thing to think about at a time."

"Do not worry, Mrs. Darcy," Serafina assured her, "in that gown I guarantee he will only be able to think about one thing and it will not matter if you try to distract him with other matters."

For a brief moment Elizabeth's heart fluttered. She had hoped he was just as excited as she was. Would the night would be everything it could be? She watched as Serafina left to fetch the water for the bath, then combed out her hair and twisted it up again. She still had a faint feeling of trepidation, not knowing precisely what to expect, but mostly she was eager to simply be with him. She was eager to kiss him without restraint, without one or the other pulling away.

She stepped into the water and Serafina began washing her back. When she was clean, Elizabeth did not rise, but leaned back against the tub and soaked there for a while. Serafina seemed to know she needed some time to soak and stepped out. Elizabeth simply closed her eyes and thought of his moving speech in the carriage yesterday where he told her he loved her. His words echoed in her mind once again, just as it had numerous times since then. "I love you dearest Elizabeth, I cannot spend another moment without telling you, showing you, and proving to you that I love you." She let her mind wander, imagining all that he would do to show her and prove to her his love. She knew that without a doubt that he would be kind and gentle. She recalled this afternoon's flirtations and numerous stolen kisses that they had shared. Their moment on the swing after he finished it was beautiful and peaceful. It wasn't exactly like the dreams she had— she wasn't with child and he didn't place his hands on her lower abdomen— but he had wrapped his arms around her and kissed the tender part on her neck by her ear. After a while she heard Serafina in the room again and she opened her eyes.

Serafina smiled back at her very peaceful mistress. "Let us not keep the man waiting, for I believe he has waited long enough." Elizabeth nodded. "While you were bathing I pressed the gown. Now it will hang on you like it should for this first time instead of looking like it was in a drawer for almost six weeks."

Elizabeth let her dote on her more than usual, allowing her to apply her lavender oil liberally, and comb out her hair until it shined. Serafina was starting to pull it up into a plaited hairstyle when Elizabeth spoke, "I think Mr. Darcy likes my hair down. At least he said it was one of his weaknesses."

"Then the only thing left for you, madam, is to get dressed into the silk gown."

Elizabeth felt her heart beat a little faster. It was time. She removed her dressing gown before she slipped the nightdress over her head. The fine fabric felt cool, but immediately warmed as it slid smoothly over her skin. Serafina tied it in the front and adjusted the shoulders. Elizabeth looked in the mirror and took a deep breath. She was ready. She did not want any more delays. "Thank you again, Serafina. I think I am ready now."

Serafina eyes widened with tears. "I know I should not cry, but you are beautiful. You are not nervous in the slightest, are you?"

Elizabeth found that she was not, and tried to think of why. "I suppose it is because I know we both have had such a natural progression of our relationship so far and to make this step seems only natural. And when you love someone emotionally so deeply, it feels impossible not to take those physical steps when the time is right because it will only make a marriage stronger."

Serafina wiped her eyes and embraced Elizabeth briefly. "Go now, I do not want to be the cause of making the master wait any longer."

Elizabeth felt like she had just been embraced by her sister Jane. She watched Serafina leave the room and close the door behind her. She looked one last time in the mirror at the flowing fabric and then turned towards the door that connected their rooms. She realized that she had never entered his bedchamber before. She gently knocked. After a brief pause, she heard his masculine deep voice say,

"Coming." So she waited. It was only a moment or two before the door was opened and she saw her husband standing in front of her. He had removed his frock coat, and waistcoat and cravat. The top buttons of his shirt were undone, exposing a very handsome chest with a hint of hair escaping from the opening. She didn't realize how moving seeing his chest would be, and she drew in a deep breath.

She came! She is here! She is really here! He stood there for the longest moment, allowing himself the time to just take in her beauty. He opened his mouth to speak, but only a hoarse whisper came out. "You look magnificent. I am sorry, I think I may just be content just looking at you."

She smiled and raised her eyebrow, "Well, we may have to *negotiate* on that." She blushed slightly, and then she watched as a slow smile crept across his face, finally reaching his handsome brown eyes.

"Indeed, I think we might have to negotiate on that later, but at the moment you take my breath away and I might just agree to anything." He realized after speaking that they were still standing at the door, and he motioned for her to come in. He watched her beautiful form walk across the threshold, the fabric flowing and clinging to her body as she walked. The fire seemed comfortable a moment ago but he felt quite warm all the sudden. She had only taken a few steps into the room when she turned around, her hair cascading over her shoulders, and he could not help himself. He took those few steps with long strides and took her face in his hands and kissed her. He kissed her urgently and thoroughly. He felt her warm lips part against his, and the kiss deepened. His desire soared to new levels but he reminded himself if he did not stop it would not go as he planned. He reluctantly pulled away, but her hands had already found his chest and the movements were quite distracting. He took her hands in his and held them in his to regain his composure. "Wait, Elizabeth, I want to do this right."

Elizabeth's heart had begun to race with those few passionate kisses, and she was confused why he stopped. *This had better not be about some silly promise again, because if he makes me actually ask him to* negotiate *with me I will not hesitate to push him back in the mud!* "Some promises are made to be broken, William," she said sternly.

He took her chin in his hand and kissed her raised impertinent eyebrow that he loved so much. "You might have to explain that to me sometime. Relax, I have something for you. Stay there and close your eyes." He waited until she had done as instructed.

She could hear him walk around her, open a drawer, and then come and stand behind her. His hands took her hair and gathered it to one side, tucking it around her left shoulder. She heard him take a deep breath which formed goosebumps over her entire body. His closeness to her made her heart start fluttering all over again. *Yes, he will always affect me so.* But she found only comfort with this thought. She felt something cold touch her at the top of her gown just above her breasts and soon she felt it come around her neck. She opened her eyes and looked down. It was her emerald and pearl necklace! She gasped. "William! How did you get it back?"

He was having just as difficult a time clasping the necklace as before, perhaps more. He tried to concentrate on the clasp but his hands were shaking and the candle in front of Elizabeth was creating quite the visual distraction as it silhouetted her small body under the silk gown. He cleared his throat. "Wickham pawned it for traveling money and I was lucky enough to find the jewelry store he sold it to in Meryton."

She reached up and touched it, somehow wanting to prove the moment was real. It was the necklace that meant so much to her. She was beginning to, and could have, accepted its loss forever but now that it was back, she felt a wave of emotion come over her. She tried to blink back the tears. "Thank you so much!"

William finally closed the necklace clasp before he leaned down and twisted that beautiful ringlet at the base of her neck, the same one that tempted him for all these months. He put his arms around her from behind and took that final step closer. "You are welcome, again, for it is not often that a man gets to give his wife the same present twice. But I have a confession to make."

Elizabeth leaned into his body, feeling his face warm against hers. "And what is that?"

He leaned down and kissed her neck where the necklace lay and whispered, "I lied to you that night before the theatre when I gave you this necklace the first time." He kissed her neck again and again, working his way down to her shoulder.

Elizabeth knew this game. It was one she rather liked. "And what exactly did you lie about?" The intimacy of his mouth on her neck made it very difficult to focus. He continued placing kisses on her neck all the way up to her ear where he stopped.

Darcy inhaled deeply, smelling her fresh scent he loved, and then whispered, "I said you have never looked so tempting before and that was what I must endure. I must tell you that I lied, for I am tempted far more now than I ever was that night."

Mr. Darcy's Promise

Epilogue

It was every bit just like the dreams she had had five and a half years before. It was spring, the birds were singing their individual melodies, and the sun was warming the cedar trees above them. She felt the wind and momentum of the swing push back the curls on the side of her face. She had been swinging now for half an hour and for the last ten minutes, William had been pushing her. Each time the swing came back he would whisper something sweet in her ear, just quiet enough that their two boys would not hear, and then push her again.

He first whispered to her, "Young William and little Richard and I love you more than life itself." Then next he said, "I want to be with you always." Then, "You mean everything to me." And next, "I want to be everything you need from me; just ask and it shall be done." He continued whispering those verbal affirmations of his love, each time giving her a push so she would go higher. On the last time he took the ropes in hand and slowed the rocking motion, walking her back to stillness. "I think you are even more beautiful when you are with child." He reached his arms around her waist and drew her close, kissing her neck sweetly as his hands caressed her swollen abdomen. And just like in her dreams, she felt the baby move, as if responding to the kisses themselves. He came around in front of her and first took her face in his hands and kissed her gently, "I love you dearest Elizabeth." Then he put his hands on both sides of her protuberant abdomen and said, "And I love you too, little Miss Darcy." And he kissed her belly tenderly.

"William, why do you insist on calling the baby a girl? Our luck so far has given us two boys in a row!" As deeply moved as she was by the realization of her dreams, she couldn't help rekindle the five-year battle between them over the sex of the baby. Ever since she suspected she was pregnant the first time, a mere three months into their marriage, he had insisted that each baby was a girl.

"Perhaps I just want to see a little brown-eyed curly haired little thing bounce around the house, or perhaps I just want to have a reason to name something other than a chicken after you. Perhaps I want more kisses from beautiful girls than you give me!" He said that last part mockingly.

"Well, perhaps you just need to *negotiate* more to get those kisses you say you want." She gave him her most impertinent look. "But I might remind you that, unlike you, I never made a promise to kiss you whenever you want. I know when making a promise is wise and when it is unwise. After all, some promises are made to be broken." Elizabeth felt the baby kick hard. She was due to deliver near the end of May, so she had a few more weeks to go. Somehow, though, she felt differently these last few days, more fatigued.

"Are you ever going to explain why some promises are made to be broken? I think promises are excellent ways to show love and devotion." This was old familiar ground for them, but Darcy enjoyed this conversation. It reminded him of the first time five years ago.

"Yes, but sometimes promises, certain promises, can get in the way of showing love and devotion." Elizabeth felt her belly harden in that familiar way. She put her hand on her belly, glad that she was sitting down on the swing. She tried to breathe deeply because the muscles usually relaxed after a minute or so. The doctor had explained that they were preparatory to real labor pains, but not to worry.

"Are you having the tightening again?" he asked, concern etched in his face. She nodded and he placed his hand on her tight abdomen. She was trying to breathe regularly but he could tell she was hurting. He rubbed her belly in circular motions with one hand and tilted her chin up to look at him with the other. "I am right here, just breathe. It will be over soon, they always go away."

Looking at her dear husband's eyes relaxed her more than anything. It reminded her of that first night they were intimate. She had glimpses of the desire in his eyes before that night but after they made love, he didn't hide it from her. She saw that look often, almost every time he looked at her. He had been so careful with her, gentle and kind, and deeply patient and more passionate than she imagined.

She never slept in her own bed after that. Not once. At night, he would ask her about her day, and she would tell him. They would discuss his business he had worked on and he would inform her of their finances. They shared everything with each other. The more they talked, the more they wanted to be with each other physically. It seemed to be a precursor to each intimate moment. It made the union mean more when they expressed their love in numerous ways.

Elizabeth was breathing normally again and he saw her sit up straighter. William asked, "Better?" She nodded. "That one was harder than the rest have been. Should we head back home? Have I fatigued you too much?"

"We can wait. The boys are so happy with the paper boat you made them. Just let them play a little longer. Now I believe I was explaining why a wise woman does not make promises that she does not see the benefit in making."

"And I am assuming the wise woman you speak of is yourself." He was still kneeling in front of her, looking at her beautiful face. He tried to listen closely because this was closer than she had ever come before to explaining why some promises were meant to be broken.

"Indeed. Promises have a certain power to them. It is like a contract between two people, the one making the promise, and the one it is made to. You are a businessman, what would happen if one of the two wanted out of the contract?" Elizabeth was struck with another episode of tightening and she felt it all the way in her back. She leaned over and tried to regain her relaxed breathing. William started rubbing her abdomen once again, and moved her face to look directly at him. Their eyes locked for the next minute.

Looking in his eyes made her think of Georgiana for some reason; perhaps because they shared their eye color. Georgiana came out into society two years after they were married and found a wonderful man in her first season who cared nothing for her dowry; a welcome change from Wickham. Georgiana's husband was soft-spoken, kind, and very attentive to her. He was everything Georgiana needed in a husband. Georgiana had that love match that Georgiana had once assumed Elizabeth and William had.

Georgiana too was expecting a child— their first— but her confinement was not expected until September. It had taken longer for her to conceive, but so far she had no problems carrying the child. Elizabeth suspected that her dear sister would do very well. Georgiana had insisted on being present for the two boys' deliveries and she found herself quite useful in keeping William's anxiety in check, who had also insisted that he be present for the births. When Elizabeth had begun to labor with her firstborn, William, it was Georgiana who gave the instructions to her older, usually more wise, brother. She gave him little tasks to accomplish, effectively making him feel needed and useful during a very stressful situation. When young Richard was born, Darcy was a little more prepared emotionally to see Elizabeth in such pain and distress but Georgiana again stepped up and told him when he was being helpful or hurtful. Since young Richard's birth, Georgiana had become more and more interested in caring for ladies in that delicate situation. With her husband's support, she extended care and nursing to many of their tenants in their childbed. It was uncommon for a gentleman's daughter to desire to work in any kind of manner but it was what Georgiana enjoyed. Elizabeth remembered asking her about it once. Georgiana had simply smiled and said, "Life has many concertos, I simply want to help the composer create a happy tune. It brings me joy to see their joy fulfilled. It is the one thing that equals mastering a new piano piece for me."

William could tell the abdomen had relaxed. He was beginning to get worried how far they were from home. He tried to pick up the conversation where they left off. "As a businessman, if one wants out of a contract, it must be agreed upon by both parties."

Elizabeth sat up straighter. "Exactly my point. If one of the party does not agree to release the other from the contract, or promise in this metaphor's case, then at least one of the parties is unhappy. If they cannot see eye to eye, then one of them is trapped in a contract that they do not want to be in."

"So you are saying that making promises, even those honorable ones, might make the one of the parties unhappy?"

"Emphasis on 'might.' Not all promises are bad. But even the honorable ones might not be appreciated."

"Elizabeth, will you just tell me which promise you wanted me not to make?"

"It was not that I did not want you to *make* it, I did not want you to *keep* it. There is a difference." Her breath caught in her throat as another round of pain started in her back and wrapped around to the front. This one was powerful and intense. William leaned his head down to gaze directly into her eyes.

"Look at me, Elizabeth. We can do this. Slow, deep breaths." He started rubbing her abdomen in circular motions again with one hand, and with the other, he reached around to her back. He covered her hand with his and pressed gently but firmly against the small of her back. He saw her face wrinkle in pain but she kept eye contact.

His eyes were so serious. She needed to help him relax. They were simply a few preparatory labor pains, nothing to be concerned about. She truly needed Colonel Fitzwilliam's jokes right about now to bring about the smiling eyes of her husband. Thinking of Richard made her want to laugh. He too had found a lady who was exactly who he needed. She was an heiress who had struggled her first few years in society. Although she had all the claims that wealth gave her, she shocked others who expected different things from a gentleman's daughter.

When Richard met her and told his first joke, he was amazed that a woman would laugh so hard and so long in the social setting where refinement was expected and demanded from a lady. From that first joke to the latest, Richard was enamored beyond words. His wife would laugh at every joke, no matter how bad it was, and even beg for more. Richard told Darcy once that he finally didn't want to be funny just so he could appear different and unique. Now that he had found his perfect match, he wanted to be funny simply to hear the joy his jokes brought to others. No, his wife wasn't the refined woman society expected but she had a joyful heart and a great ability to laugh: both of which only brought out the best of Richard.

The tension eased in her back and abdomen. She took another relaxing breath and smiled back at William. "Thank you. It helps to look in your eyes."

Now that the third episode had come and gone he knew it was time to head back home. He stood and gathered the boys who moaned but obediently gathered their belongings. Little William was now four and a half years old and took his role as elder brother very seriously, a trait that he had inherited from his father. Richard, however, was just like his namesake. He was focused when necessary but could be easily distracted the rest of the time. Richard was only two, but Darcy knew that there were definite correlations in personality to the elder Richard. The boys followed closely at the heels of their father who had rejoined Elizabeth by this time. "Come now, let us get you back to the house. You are beginning to worry me with those labor pains." He offered his arm and Elizabeth stood to take it and they began walking.

Elizabeth called out to Little William and Richard. "Boys, run ahead, you know the way. William, take good care of Richard, do not cross the bridge without holding his hand."

"Yes, mamma." Little William said. "Come, Richard, you have to hold my hand."

The proud parents watched their two oldest run ahead hand in hand. Elizabeth turned to William and said, "They are quite close you know. It will be nice to have another boy but a girl would be nice too." She looked at William who smiled back at her.

"I would love to see a little Miss Darcy running around. But I am afraid we will just have to see . . ." Just then she stopped walking and doubled over in obvious pain. "Perhaps we will see sooner rather than later." He knelt down in front of her, touching the creases in her brow with his thumbs. He had seen this before, the baby was coming soon and he was still not in visual distance of Pemberley. "Look at me Elizabeth, do not close your eyes. Breathe. In and out, slowly." He took his hands and supported her shoulders with one and rubbed her back with the other. He stood looking in her fine eyes and knew he needed to get her back quickly. The frequency was one thing, the intensity only added to the concern. He stared in her eyes, the same eyes that captured his heart all those years ago. The same eyes he went to bed with, and the same eyes he begged to see as soon as he woke. She was truly everything to him. She had given herself to him so fully that first night that he very nearly cried with happiness. Her desire for him was equal to his desire for her and it was the perfect union. Their passion had not died down in the slightest over the last five years, for when they couldn't be intimate, like after the babies were born, they would hold each other and let their bodies express themselves in other ways. She truly was more beautiful now than ever before. Her eyes told him when the tension released before she stood up again. He needed to make progress on getting home. He decided distraction was a good idea. He began walking and then picked up the conversation where they left off. "So you are comfortable letting me make promises, but keeping them is not always on your list of acceptable behaviors. Is there a method to your rules of which promises one can make, and which ones can be broken? I am cognizant of the fact that you think some promises are made to be broken, so which ones exactly do you want me to break?"

"William, it really was only one promise that I did not fully appreciate. Well, I did at first, but as the weeks went by I found myself somewhat angry at you for being so trustworthy in keeping that promise." She looked in his confused face and knew she had to be more direct, a lesson she had learned well over the years, thanks to Serafina. "I appreciate now that you did not force me into your bed, but as our relationship grew, you put a lady in very awkward situation where she had to voice her intimate desires in order for you to get it through your thick skull that she desired you."

"'She' meaning you."

"Yes! Who else? Do you have any other ladies who have voiced their intimate desires for you that I should know about? Has Caroline Bingley come to visit once again with Charles and Jane?" Her last words were clipped short as another burst of pain nearly crippled her. She tried to stay erect, but couldn't. She bent over grabbing her abdomen. Between breaths she said, "William, I think I had better return home soon; I think I am in travail."

"I know, but you can do this. I will not leave your side. Look at me, Elizabeth. Focus. Maybe one or two more and we will be home."

She looked deep into his eyes and saw the compassion she now recognized that he showed on their wedding day. She still couldn't believe that she misunderstood the anxiety in his eyes in that carriage ride as evidence that he felt forced to marry her. Her mind tried to focus on anything but that dark day. She thought of Caroline Bingley, who still hadn't married.

Charles had welcomed her into his home permanently, and Jane was, of course, patient and kind with her. Elizabeth had only heard of two times where Jane voiced her frustrations with Caroline. The first was immediately after Jane had her twins, Rebecca and Margaret, and the second after her son, Charles Jr. was born. Apparently Jane's quiet reserve had a limit, and Caroline's flippant— arguably snide— comments about the babies looking like Bennets alone had made the mamma bear come out in Jane. Elizabeth was proud of Jane for standing up to Caroline and asking Caroline to take a "holiday" to Bath both times. Jane was a happy mother, and she and Charles were well-fitted to each other. They now had a permanent home only fifteen miles away from Pemberley and Elizabeth saw her favorite sister frequently.

Her thoughts were interrupted by another wave of pain. Once again his eyes got her through another painful episode. She stood up gingerly and put a little more weight on his arm as they walked.

He held tightly to her, trying to suppress the growing fear for her and the baby. If he was this worried he knew she must be at least a little anxious for herself. He kept the pace of whatever she set, but was grateful that she was able to proceed between episodes. He was determined to keep talking in hopes of distracting her. "So you wanted me to break my promise of letting you decide when to become intimate simply because you were too much of a lady to voice your changed opinions of me?"

"Yes, some promises were made to be broken, and you sir, were a little too trustworthy in keeping that promise." They could see Pemberley now, it was not far, and all downhill from that point on. The baby kicked hard once again and she paused only to feel the fluids start to run down her legs. "Oh no, I think we had better hurry. I just felt my waters break."

She took one look at Darcy's eyes and wondered if she should have told him at all. The panic in his eyes was all too evident. She made it about one hundred meters more before a powerful labor pain knocked her to her knees. She groaned quietly. Her vision blurred slightly as the pain intensified. She was somewhat aware of her husband's voice talking quietly to her, but all she understood was the scared tone in his voice. She gripped tightly to his arm and focused on her breathing. She was feeling too hot and dry in the mouth. It felt like forever until this episode relaxed. She opened her eyes and saw William's face. She could probably only take one more of those before she reached home.

"Help me up, we need to hurry. This baby is coming fast. Neither of the boys' labor pains progressed this quickly." She felt his supporting arm lift her to a standing position. They made quick strides and made it to the gardens when the next one hit.

Darcy looked around wildly and saw Theodore, the gardener, doing some spring trimming. "Theodore! Get help, my wife's time is upon her!" He watched as Theodore ran towards the house. He turned back to Elizabeth. "Look at me dear, do not close your eyes. That is right, this is the last one before we get to the house. Just breathe nice and slow. Open your eyes, Elizabeth. Focus now, only a little while left and we shall see that beautiful baby and you shall hold it in your arms. This is all worth it. Every one of the pains brings us closer to seeing that baby."

Elizabeth struggled with opening her eyes, but she did it. He was such a proud father. He was so diligent in teaching as well as playing with their sons. Through gritted teeth she groaned out loud involuntarily. This one was worse than all the others. She leaned excessively on him but he held strong under her weight. She tried to focus on how much she loved seeing William play with their sons. She looked into his eyes and recalled the effort it took for him to teach Little William about the chickens. He vowed that his sons would know how to feed chickens. Even through all the pain, she grinned remembering her husband try to teach her oldest how to call to the chickens. It was always so funny to see that awkward smile as he yelled in his falsetto voice, "Here chick-chick-chick!" It was even funnier to hear her son try to do it.

"Elizabeth? Are you well? You look like you are trying to smile but it is coming out more like a grimace." She nodded, but then took a deep breath and looked to be concentrating again. "Last one,

Elizabeth, then we will get you inside. You are so strong, it is one of the things I love about you. I love that you could walk three hours after hitting your head. I love that you are doing it now. I love everything about you. You can do this. I am here and I am not leaving you. You are everything to me, Elizabeth." He saw her take another deep breath and her body relaxed once again. It was over for the time being. He gave her a moment to catch her breath. "Let us get moving. Elizabeth, can you go further?"

"Is it negotiable?" she teased with what little energy she had left. She was nearing her ability to stand, let alone walk, but she pressed forward.

"I believe negotiation is what got us in this situation."

She smiled, but leaned on William's arm a little more. She was watching the ground, making sure to take careful but hurried steps. She soon heard Mrs. Reynolds and a few other servants coming. She glanced up and saw Serafina, and felt a sudden wave of relief. She had made it. Serafina took her other arm and gingerly assisted her towards the house. They made it just inside, but going up those few steps at the entrance provoked another labor pain. Her knees buckled under her, but William caught her at her ribs and held her close. She hardly moved with the fall he was so near to her.

Soon she felt a chair under her and she was lowered down but it was too uncomfortable to sit down. "No, help me stand," she mumbled. No sooner had she said it then she was standing again, she focused on putting strength in her own legs. She heard William report how many and how often the pains were coming, but an overwhelming feeling of pressure took her by surprise and she instinctively leaned over and grunted. "It is time . . ." she groaned in the middle of a breath. The pressure finally eased slightly, as well as the pain, and she tried to focus on what was happening. William was saying something about lying down, Mrs. Reynolds was barking orders for linen and water, Serafina was brushing back the damp strands of hair on her face, and one of the maids were escorting two scared little boys who apparently had made it home away from the scene. She heard them discussing carrying her to the guest bedroom down the hall. She could go no further.

As if on cue, another contraction came immediately after the last one let up, "I need to push," she said wildly, "just lower me down to the floor." She fully understood they were in the entryway but she was not in control of her body at the moment because every muscle was contracting. She grunted with it and felt a sense of relief in doing so. She grunted again before she took a breath and then grunted again. She hadn't even noticed that she was now horizontal and laying on the floor until the labor pain eased for a brief moment. She took a deep breath but her respite from the pressure was brief because another round hit her.

She heard the gentle coaxing of her husband next to her and heard something from Mrs. Reynolds about pushing and that was all the incentive she needed. She gave one hard push and felt the baby's head emerge. She took another deep breath and gave one final push, and then groaned again as the rest of the baby came out. She immediately felt relief from the pressure and relaxed back into her husband's arms, panting. She waited. Her eyes were closed and she was trying to catch her breath. She heard all the commotion but was confused. Something wasn't right. She opened her eyes and looked at William. His face was white and wore a foreign look she did not recognize. She followed his gaze down to her feet where her baby was . . .where her baby should be crying . . .where her baby was blue and not moving. "William, what is wrong?" she whispered. William held her head and kissed her forehead. His lips moved to say something, but Elizabeth did not hear it. Everything went black.

*****

She heard William's voice softly calling her name, asking her to open her eyes. Her eyelids felt so heavy! She slowly opened them and tried to focus on his face and her surroundings. She was in bed, and he was sitting next to her. Her vision cleared and a very concerned face was looking back at her. He reached for her face and gently pushed her hair behind her ear.

"Are you finally awake? How do you feel?" He asked.

His tone was so gentle and soft. She evaluated his expression, he was very anxious and had the most concerned look on his face. She quickly recalled all of the moments before she blacked out. Her baby had been born silent and still, with none of the hearty red cheeks she had seen with her sons. She recalled that foreign look on her husband's face. Part of it still lingered in his furrowed brow. She reached up to his brow and tried to smooth it. He leaned into her hand and he reached up and grasped her hand ever so gently and kissed it. The gesture was all she needed; he loved her and needed her during this difficult time. She fought back tears and said, "I guess it is good that we got our feathers before the storm." His concerned look changed to confusion.

"We can make it through anything, Elizabeth, our love is that strong."

She couldn't wait any longer. She had to ask. "Was it a boy or girl?" His expression changed ever so slightly but she didn't know how to explain what she saw.

"A girl." A small smile graced his lips. He leaned down and kissed her on the lips.

Tears started forming in her eyes. He had wanted a girl so badly and now they had lost her. "I think we should still name her."

"Of course we will name her. But since she was so stubborn I know just the name for her, dearest Elizabeth."

She was deeply hurt he would talk so callously about their dead baby. Why was he still smiling? "William, that is not funny. How can you talk about her like that?"

"Oh, you will see, she has quite the fighting spirit too."

"Has? You mean had."

"Oh no, I meant has. She took a full five minutes before she let out the biggest loudest scream I have ever heard from a baby!"

Suddenly she was wide awake and trying to rise from her supine position. "She is alive? But she was not moving and was so blue!" William tried to help her sit up.

"Yes! She is doing wonderfully! Neither of the boys were this loud! I would say she is stronger than either of them were when they were born."

She threw her arms around his neck. "I must see her! Please, help me up!" Her head started spinning. "On second thought, perhaps you should bring her to me." He kissed her and gingerly laid her back down on the pillow.

"You will love her. She is just like I pictured her. I will be right back."

It seemed to take forever for William to return, but when he entered she understood why, He was walking so gently and cradled a squirming bundle in his arms. She heard her then and it was the most beautiful cry her ears had ever heard! Her baby was alive! Tears of joy burst from her eyes as she reached for the bundle. He gently placed the baby in her arms and she saw a bright, energetic, very healthy looking, but crying baby. She couldn't contain her joy any further; her shoulders shook and she sobbed. She could barely see out of her eyes, but after a few minutes she saw that her daughter had dark brown eyes with dark brown hair plastered to her head; hair that was no doubt wavy. She looked up at her husband who was all smiles.

"If you watch her long enough she raises her eyebrow when she cries."

"Stubborn and impertinent? How could we get so lucky?" She teased. She looked to her husband, who had again grown serious.

"Elizabeth, even if she had not survived, *we* would have. No matter what trials come our way, we earned our feathers and we will survive, just like those seven chicks we watched hatch. We would have made it through any storm. Even the death of our child could not break what we have built. I love you more than life itself. You must know that."

"Yes, I know that. But I might need more convincing . . ."

He smiled and leaned in over their beautiful healthy daughter and placed several well deserved kisses on his wife's lips.

The End

Mr. Darcy's Promise